UNDER THE ROSE

Julia O'Faolain

UNDER THE ROSE
Selected Stories

FABER & FABER

First published in 2016
by Faber & Faber Limited
Bloomsbury House
74–77 Great Russell Street
London WC1B 3DA

Typeset by Reality Premedia Services Pvt. Ltd
Printed and bound in the UK by CPI Group (UK) Ltd, Croydon, CRO 4YY

A CIP record for this book
is available from the British Library

ISBN 978-0-571-29490-9

2 4 6 8 10 9 7 5 3 1

Contents

Daughters of Passion

There was a story about her in the *Mail*. A phrase jumped off the page: '. . . the twisted logic of the terrorist mind . . .' Journalists! She'd have spat if she'd had the spittle; but her mouth was dry. 'Violence', someone had said, 'is the only way to gain a hearing for moderation.' That was reckoning without the press.

The argument broke open, porous as cheese. *Cheese* . . . She could smell the reek of it, pinching her nostrils.

Thoughts escaped her. This was the twelfth day of her hunger strike and energy was running low. Half a century ago, in Brixton Gaol, the Lord Mayor of Cork had died after a seventy-four-day fast. A record? Maybe. But how *much* of him could have survived those seventy-four days to die? A sane mind? The ability to choose? Surely not? Surely all that was left in the end would have been something like the twitch in a chicken-carcass, a set of reflexes primed like an abandoned robot's? Her own mind was bent on sabotaging her will. 'Eat,' her organism signalled slyly to itself in divers ways. It slurped and burped the message, registered it by itch, wind-pain, cold, hunger, sophistries. Sum ergo think. But thinking used up energy. Better just to dream: let images flicker the way they used to do years and years ago on the school cinema-screen. Then too it had been a case of energy running low. The generator went on the blink every time films were shown in the barn and that was often, for the hall was constantly being remodelled. The nuns were great builders.

'Come,' they coerced visitors, 'come see our improvements.'

Change thrilled them. The stone might have been part of themselves: a collective shell. Meanwhile, on film nights, rain drummed out the sound track and a draughty screen distorted the smile of Jennifer Jones playing Bernadette. The barn was cold but discomfort was welcomed in the convent. Waiting for the centrally-heated hall put in time while waiting for heaven.

She missed the community feeling.

Her vision shifted. Bricks and mortar from the nuns' hall had turned to butcher's meat. She was choking. Her throat had dried, its sides seeming to clap together. She pictured it like an old boot, drying until the tongue inside it shrivelled. It itched. Food could drive any other consideration from her mind. Images decomposed and went edible, like those trick paintings in which whole landscapes turn out to be made up of fruit or sausages. She could smell sausages. Fat beaded on them. Charred skins burst and the stuffing pushed through slit bangers in a London pub. Three sausages and three half lagers, please. Harp or Heineken. Yes, draught. Could we have the sausages nice and crispy. Make that six. A dab of mustard. Jesus! Eat this in remembrance. Oh, and three rolls of French bread. Thanks. Christ-the-pelican slits his breast to feed the faithful. Dry stuff the communion wafer but question not the gift host in my mouth. Mustn't laugh. Hurts. Where's the water mug? Tea in this one. They'd left it on purpose. The screws were surely hoping she'd eat in a moment of inattention. It hadn't happened though. Relax. Water. What a relief. Made one pee and the effort of getting up was painful but if she didn't drink her throat grew sandpapery. You wanted to vomit and there was nothing to vomit. A body could bring up its guts – could it?

Sitting up made her dizzy. She felt a pain around her heart. Lie back. Her mind though was clear as well water. At least she was too weak to get across the cell to that tray without catching herself. They'd left it there with the food she'd refused this morning or maybe yesterday. Not that she felt fussy. Easier now though that her body was subdued beyond tricking her.

Conviction hardened. It had come with habit. Maggy was here through chance.

'I'm sure I don't know,' the head screw had said, 'where you think this is going to get you. It's up to you, of course, to make your own decision.'

Cool, bored. Managing to convey her sense of all this as childish theatrics and a waste of everyone's time. She knew the system and the system didn't change just because some little Irish terrorist wouldn't eat her dinner. She was fair though, abiding by the Home Secretary's guidelines. Nobody had kicked Maggy or put a bag over her head. This screw looked as though such things were outside her experience which perhaps they were. One lot of prison employees might be unaware of what the other lot were doing. A clever division of labour: those needing clear consciences for television interviews and the like could *have* clear consciences. The best myths had a dose of truth to them.

It might have been easier if they *had* knocked her about: given her more reason to resist.

Dizzy had said, 'The trouble with you, Maggy, is that you're an adapter. I suppose orphans are. They're survivors and survivors adapt.'

She meant that Maggy listened to the other side: a woeful error since it weakened resolve. Look at her now ready to believe in the decency of that screw. 'Sneering Brit,' Dizzy would decide right off. She never called the English anything but 'Brits'.

'Ah come on, Maggy. *Be* Irish for Pete's sake. What did the Brits ever do for you or yours? Listen, it's a class war. Don't you see?'

Dizzy was of Anglo-Irish Protestant stock and had gone native in a programmed way. Her vocabulary was revolutionary.

Her upper-class voice had learned modulation at the Royal Academy of Dramatic Art. This made her enterprises sound feasible, as though they had already been realized, then turned back into fiction for celebrating in, say, the Hampstead Theatre Club or one of those fringe places on the Euston Road.

Rosheen's style was more demotic. She sang in pubs and in the shower of the flat which Maggy had shared with her and Dizzy.

> Another marthyr for auld Oireland
> Another murther for the Crown ...

More exasperating than sheer noise was the spasm in Rosheen's voice. Maggy suspected she got more pleasure from these laments than she did from sex. The two had got connected in Rosheen's life. She had married an unemployed Derryman who took out his frustrations by beating her until Dizzy coerced her into walking out on him. Missing him, Rosheen flowed warm water down her soapy body every morning and belted out verses about tombs, gallowses and losses which would never be forgotten. Defeats, in her ballads, were greater than victory; girls walked endlessly on the sunny side of mountains with sad but pretty names and reflected on the uselessness of the return of spring. Maggy despised herself for the rage Rosheen aroused in her.

'Well, it's all due to history, isn't it?'

The three had watched the Northern Ireland Secretary on the box some weeks before Maggy's arrest. Talking of how a political solution would make the IRA irrelevant – *great* acumen, God bless him! – he had the mild smile of one obliged to shoulder responsibility and take the brickbats.

He got Rosheen's goat. 'He gets my goat,' she said. Maggy winced.

'He gets on my tits,' said Dizzy to show solidarity. But the effect was different since Dizzy could talk any way she felt inclined whereas poor Rosheen was stuck in one register.

Maggy, who had known Rosheen since they were six, had for her the irritable affection one has for relatives. Also envy. They had made their First Communion side by side dressed in veils and identical bridal gowns and Rosheen had made the better communion. Maggy, watching through falsely closed lids, had been stunned to see ecstasy on Rosheen's rather puddingy face. She had been hoping for ecstasy herself and it was only when she saw it come to Rosheen that she gave up and admitted to herself that Jesus had rejected her. It was a close equivalent to being jilted at the altar and in some ways she had never got over it.

'Your First Holy Communion', Mother Theresa had promised, 'will be the most thrilling event in your whole lives.'

'Really?'

'Oh,' the nun conceded, 'there will, I suppose, be other excitements.' It was clear that she could not conceive of them. She had been teaching communion classes for forty years. Photographs of groups dressed in white veils lined her classroom walls. 'Strength will flow into you,' she promised. 'I don't mean', she smiled at Rosheen who had made this mistake earlier, 'the sort of strength Batman has.'

The others gave Rosheen a charitable look. They were practising charity and she was its best recipient. Charity was for those to whom you could not bring yourself to accord esteem or friendship and in those days it had been hard to produce these for Rosheen, whose eyes were pink and from whose nostrils snot worms were always apt to crawl. You had to look away so as to give her a chance to sniff them back up. Even then you could sometimes see her, with the corner of your eye, using the back of her hand.

And then Rosheen had made the best communion.

It was not utterly unaccountable. The nuns had mentioned that the last shall be first. Their behaviour, however, made this seem unlikely. They preferred girls who knew how to use handkerchiefs, scored for the team and generally did them credit.

Maggy recalled quite clearly how, having finally got the wafer down her throat – to bite would have been sacrilegious, so this was slow – and still feeling no ecstasy, she had opened her eyes. All heads were bowed. The priest was wiping the chalice. Could he have made some mistake, she wondered, left out some vital bit of the ceremony so that the miracle had failed to happen? Maybe he would realize and make an announcement: 'Dearly beloved, it is my duty to inform you that transubstantiation has failed to take place. Due to an error, you have all received mere bread and may regard the ceremony up to now as a trial run. Please return to the altar . . .' These words became so real to Maggy that she nudged Rosheen who was kneeling beside her. 'Get up,' she whispered bossily. 'We're to go back . . .' She was arrested by Rosheen's face. It was alight. Colour from a stained-glass window had been carried to it by a sunbeam and blazed madly from her eyes, her nostrils and the lolling tip of her tongue. Rosheen smiled, rotated and then bowed her head. She looked like a drunk or a painted saint: ecstatic then? Could she be pretending? Maggy considered giving her a pinch but instead bowed her own head and concentrated on managing not to cry.

She was crying now. Hunger made you weepy. She'd been warned. It made you cold too, although she was wearing several jerseys and two pairs of leotards.

Rosheen had never been so right again. Probably she should never have left the convent. Someone had told Maggy that she had wanted to enter but the nuns wouldn't have her. Then she'd married Sean. That marriage had certainly not been made in heaven: it was a case of the lame leading the halt.

'A pair of babes in the wood,' was the opinion of Sean's mother, Mairéad.

Mairéad had come to London some months ago to see
Sean and dropped round to Dizzy's flat. Maggy had been the
only one in.

'Tell Rosheen I don't hold it against her that she left him.'
Mairéad was a chain-smoking flagpole of a woman, stuck
about with polyester garments so crackling new that they
must surely have been bought for this trip. 'Half the trouble in the world', she drew on her cigarette then funnelled
smoke from her nostrils with an energy which invited har-
nessing, 'comes', she said, 'from people asking too much of
themselves.' She coughed. 'And of each other. Not that it's
Sean's fault either. I'm not saying that. It's his nerves,' she
told Maggy. 'They're shot to bits. What would you expect?
When that wee boy was growing up he seen things happen to
his family that shouldn't happen to an animal.' She let Maggy
make tea and, drinking it, talked in a practised way about misfortune. 'She's at work then, is she? Well give her my best. I'm
half glad I missed her. I only wanted her to know there were
no hard feelings. Will you tell her that from me? No hard
feelings,' she enunciated carefully as though used to dealing
with drunks or children or maybe men with shot nerves. 'I'd
have no right to ask her to nurse a man in Sean's condition.
I know that. He's not normal any more than the rest of us.'
She had a high laugh which escaped like a hiccup: 'Heheh!
He was never strong. A seven-month baby. I never had the
right food. Then the year he was sixteen it was nothing but
them bustin' in and calling us fucking Fenian gets and threatening to blow our heads off. Every night nearly. That was
the summer of 1971. They wrecked the house; stole things;
ripped up the carpet. Four times they raided us before Sean
left to come here. He's highly strung and his nerves couldn't
stand it. He still has nightmares. Ulcers. Rosheen could tell
you. Sure it has to come out some way. He gets violent. I
know it.' Mairéad stubbed out a cigarette and drained her
tea. 'Have you another drop? Thanks. I'll drink this up. Then

I'd better be going. I've been going on too much. It could be worse. You don't have to tell me. Wasn't my sister's boy shot? Killed outright. He was barely fourteen and the army said they thought he was a sniper. I ask you how could anyone take a fourteen-year-old for a sniper? You're from the south? I suppose all this is strange to you? I'm supposed to be here to get away from it all. You look forward to doing that and then the funny thing is you can't. It's as well I missed Rosheen. No point upsetting her, is there? You'll remember what I said to say, won't you? Thanks for the tea.'

Maggy saw her out and watched her walk away, turning, as she put distance between them, into a typical Irish charwoman such as you saw walking in their domesticated multitudes around the streets of Camden.

Dizzy, who got home before Rosheen, said: 'Don't mention the visit to her.'

'Mightn't she be glad to get the message?'

'Really, Maggy!' Dizzy sounded like a head girl – had *been* head girl when they were at school together, in spite or perhaps because of being the only Protestant. 'You have no sense of people,' she scolded. 'Rosheen has no sense at all.'

Maggy began to laugh at this arrogance and Dizzy – which was the nice thing about her – joined in. 'Seriously though,' she drove home her point. 'Rosheen could easily go back to that ghastly Sean. Just *because* he's so ghastly. She has to be protected from herself! From that Irish death wish. Surely you can see that she's better off with me.'

'With us?'

'With me. Don't be obtuse.'

Dizzy had been bossing Maggy and Rosheen since the day they'd met her. They'd all been about twelve at the time. Maggy knew this because she remembered that she and Rosheen had been on their way back to the convent after winning medals for under thirteens at a Feis Ceol. Maggy's was for verse-speaking and Rosheen's for Irish dance. Suddenly Rosheen let out a screech.

'I've lost me medal. What'll I do? The nuns'll be raging. They all prayed for me to win it and now I haven't got it to show.'

'It's winning that matters,' Maggy tried to soothe her. 'The medal isn't valuable. Come on. We'll miss our bus.'

'I'm not moving from this spot till I make sure I've lost it.'

Rosheen began to frisk herself. They were standing on a traffic island in the middle of O'Connell Street and it wasn't long before her manœuvres began to attract attention. When she unbuttoned her vest to grope inside it, a tripper with an English accent shouted: 'Starting early, aren't you? What are you doing, love? Giving us a bit of a striptease?'

Maggy spat at him. It was an odd, barbaric gesture but, remembering, she could again feel the fury of the convent girl at the man's violation of dignity and knew her rage could not have been vented with less. Give her a knife and she'd have stuck it in him. The man must have seen insanity in her face for he wiped the spittle from his lapel and moved silently away. Rosheen, typically, had failed to notice the incident.

'I've lost it,' she decided, buttoning her blouse. 'I'm going to pray to Saint Anthony to get it back for me.' She knelt on the muddy pavement of the traffic island. 'Kneel down and pray with me,' she invited Maggy.

'Here?' Maggy's voice shot upwards. 'You shouldn't be let out, Rosheen O'Dowd! You should be tied up. People are *looking* at you!' Being looked at was agony to Maggy at that time. 'Rosheen,' she begged. 'Get up. You're destroying your gym-slip. Please, Rosheen. I bet', she invented desperately, 'it's against the law. We're obstructing traffic. *Rosheen!*'

But all Rosheen had to say was: 'You're full of human respect. Shame on you.' And she began blessing herself with gestures designed for distant visibility. Like a swimmer signalling a lifeguard, she was trying for Saint Anthony's attention. He was known to be a popular and busy saint.

'I'm off.' Maggy, unable to bear another second of this, stepped off the traffic island in front of the advancing wheels of a double-decker bus which stopped with a shriek of brakes.

'Are you trying to make a murderer out of me?' The driver jumped out to shake her by the shoulders. 'That's an offence,' he yelled. 'I could have you summonsed. In court. What's your name and address?'

'Magdalen Mary Cashin, Convent of the Daughters of Passion.'

'What's that? A nursery rhyme?' The man was angry. Passengers were hanging out of the bus, staring. 'Tell me your real name,' the man roared, 'or . . .'

Maggy ducked from his grasp, ran and, miraculously missing the rest of the traffic, made it to the opposite footpath.

'What's chasing you?' A girl of about her own age was staring inquisitively at her. 'You're from the Passion Convent, aren't you? I know the uniform. I may be coming next term.'

'You?' Maggy was alert for mockery. 'You're a Protestant.'

'Not really. My parents are, vaguely, I suppose – but how did you know?'

Maggy shrugged. 'It's obvious.'

'How? I'd better find out, hadn't I?' the girl argued. 'If I'm coming to your school?'

'You wouldn't be let come like that.'

'Like what?'

'Look at your skirt.' Maggy spoke reluctantly. She was still unsure that she was not being laughed at. 'And you've no stockings on! Then there's your hair . . .' She gave up. The girl was hardly a girl at all. Protestants almost seemed to belong to another sex. Their skirts were as short as Highlanders' kilts and their legs marbled and blue from exposure. 'Don't you feel the cold?' she asked. Maybe Protestants didn't.

'No. I'm hardy. Do you wear vests and things? I despise vests and woolly knickers!'

The intimacy of this was offensive but Maggy's indignation

had been so used up in the last ten minutes that her responses were unguarded.

'I do too but I'm made to wear them,' she said and felt suddenly bound to the person to whom she had made such a private admission.

'My name's Dizzy,' said Dizzy. 'Is that your friend over there? I think she's signalling.'

'She's odd.' Maggy disassociated herself from the embarrassing Rosheen, who was indeed waving and rising and replunging to her knees. 'Don't mind her,' she begged. 'It's best to pay her no attention.'

'She's praying, isn't she? That's marvellous.'

'What?'

'She doesn't give a damn. Catholicism interests me,' Dizzy confided. 'I think Catholics are more Irish, don't you?'

'More Irish than whom?'

'Us.'

'You?'

'We *are* Irish, you know,' Dizzy argued. 'My family has been here since the time of Elizabeth the First. They're mentioned in heaps of chronicles.'

That, to Maggy's mind, only showed how foreign they were. The chronicles would have been written by the invaders. But she didn't mention this. What interested her about Dizzy was not her likeness to herself but her difference. It was clear that she lacked the layers of doubt and caution which swaddled Maggy's brain as thickly as the unmentionable vests and bloomers did her body.

'I found it!' Rosheen had arrived, all pant and spittle. She waved the medal excitedly. 'Saint Anthony answered my prayer. I knew he would. Isn't he great?' Rosheen always spoke of saints as though they were as close to her as her dormitory mates. 'Do you know where I found it? You'll never believe me: in my shoe.'

'This is Rosheen O'Dowd,' said Maggy formally. 'I'm

Magdalen Mary Cashin and you're . . .?' She was chary of the ridiculous name.

'Dizzy,' said Dizzy. 'Desdemona FitzDesmond actually, but it's a mouthful, isn't it? So, Dizzy.'

'We're orphans,' Maggy thought to say.

'What luck,' said Dizzy. 'Wait till you meet my sow of a mother. She leads poor Daddy a dreadful dance. Drink, lovers, debts,' she boasted. 'Family life isn't all roses, I can tell you.'

The orphans were interested and impressed.

*

'Here's your tea.' The screw had brought a fresh tray. 'You'd be well advised to have it. As well start as you plan to finish and, believe me, they all eat in the end! Chips this evening,' she said.

Maggy smelled and imagined the pith of their insides and the crisply gilded shells. An ideal potato chip, big as a blimp, filled her mind's sky. The door closed; a rattle of keys receded down the corridor. Heels thumped. Teeth in other cells would be sinking through crisp-soft chips. Tongues would be pro-pelling the chewed stuff down throats. If the din of metal were to let up she would surely hear soft munching. Her own saliva tasted salty. Or was it sweat? Did they count the chips put in her tray? Wouldn't put it past them. Tell us is she weakening. Keep count. They'd never. Wouldn't they just? Besides, to eat even one would surely make her feel worse.

There was no political status in England. No political prisoners at all. So why insist on treatment you couldn't get? They had made this point laboriously to her, then given up trying to talk sense to someone who wouldn't listen. People had died recently from forced feeding so they were chary of starting that. They followed the Home Secretary's Guidelines and what happened next was no skin off their noses. The country had enough troubles without worrying about the bloody Irish. Always whining and drinking, or else refusing to eat and blaming the poor old UK for all their woes. They had their own country now but did that stop them? Not on your nelly, it didn't. They were still over here in their droves taking work when a lot of English people couldn't find it. Rowdy, noisy. Oh forget it. When you saw all the black and brown faces, you almost came to like the Paddies if only they'd stop making a nuisance of themselves.

A man had come to see her, a small man with a glass eye whom she'd seen twice in Dizzy's flat. He was from the IRA. He winked his real eye while the glass one stared at her. He had claimed to be a relative, managing somehow to get visiting privileges. She must play along with his story, winked the eye. Was she demanding political status? Good.

'They'll deny it but we have to keep asking. It's the principle of the thing.'

There had been a confusion about him as though he didn't know whom to distrust most: her, himself, or the screws. His dead eye kept vigil and it occurred to her that one half of his face mistrusted the other.

Impossible to get comfortable. Her body felt as if enclosed in an orthopaedic cast. She had a sense of plaster oozing up her nose and felt tears on her cheeks but didn't know why she was crying, unless from frustration at the way she had boxed herself in like a beetle in a matchbox. She was boxed in by her ballady story. It didn't fit her, was inaccurate but couldn't be adjusted, making its point with the simple speed of a traffic light or the informative symbol on a lavatory door. She was in a prison within a prison: the cast. Slogans were scrawled on it: graffiti. She was a public convenience promenading promises to blow, suck, bomb the Brits, logos, addresses of abortion clinics, racial taunts. 'Wipe out all Paddies and nignogs now!' shrieked one slogan cut deep into her plaster cast inside which she wasn't sure she was. Maybe she'd wiped herself out?

She had committed a murder. Performed an execution. Saved a man's life.

Depending on how you looked at it. Who had? Maggy the merciful murderess.

Her story was this: she had been an orphan, her mother probably a whore. Brought up by nuns, she had lost her faith, found another, fought for it and been imprisoned. This was inexact but serviceable. If they made a ballad about it, Rosheen could sing it in a Camden pub.

When she was very small the nuns told Maggy that she had forty mothers: their forty selves. An aunt, visiting from Liverpool, was indignant.

'Frustrated old biddies!' These, she asserted, were mock mothers. 'You have your own,' she said. 'What are they trying to do? Kill her off? What do they know of the world?' she asked. 'Cheek.'

'What world?' Maggy wondered. She was maybe four.

'Now don't *you* be cheeky,' said the aunt.

On what must have been a later visit the aunt reported the mother to be dead. Maggy remembered eating an egg which must have been provided for consolation.

'I'll bet they'll say it's for the best,' raged the aunt and began painting her face in a small portable mirror. 'You didn't love her at all, did you?' she interrogated, moistening her eyelash brush with spit. 'I told her not to send you here. She'd have kept you by her if she could. Children', the aunt said, 'have no hearts.'

The aunt too must have died for she didn't come back – and indeed maybe 'aunt' and 'mother' were one and the same? Maggy, when she grew older, guessed herself to be illegitimate, as there had never been any mention of a father. And so it proved when eventually she came to London and applied for a birth certificate to Somerset House.

'You don't know your luck. No beastly heritage to shuck off!'

Dizzy had come to the nuns' school to spite her mother

who favoured agnosticism, raw fruit, fresh air and idleness
for girls.

'Not that it matters where she goes to school!' The mother
was mollified by the smallness of the nuns' fee. 'Nobody of
my blood ever worked,' she said. 'Dizzy will marry young.'
She spoke without force for she was to die of diabetes when
Dizzy was fourteen. After that Dizzy's father became very
vague and did not protest when she became a Catholic. Thus
fortified, she was allowed by the nuns to invite Maggy home
for weekends.

They spent these talking about what they took to be sex
and dressing up in colonial gear which they found in the attic.
Much of it was mildewed and so stiff that it seemed it must
have been hewn rather than tailored. There were pith helmets
and old-fashioned jodhpurs shaped like hearts. Dizzy's father
had served in Africa, although she herself had been born after
his return to Ireland when her mother was forty-four.

'I'm a child of the Change,' she relished the phrase. 'I'm
not like them.'

Who she wanted to be like was the bulk of the local population, and, on Poppy Day, she hauled down the Union
Jack which her father had raised. He was apologetic but this
only annoyed her the more for she felt that he ought to have
known his own mind. Dizzy was eager for order and when
she became a Catholic fussed unfashionably about hats in
church and fish on Fridays.

On leaving school, Maggy won a scholarship to an
American university. Coming back, after eight years there, she
met Dizzy again in London. This was a Dizzy who seemed to
have lost much of her nerve for she blushed when Maggy
asked: 'Did you know I was in love with you when we were
in our teens?'

This was a requiem for someone no longer discernible in
Dizzy, whom Maggy recalled as pale and volatile as the fizz
on soda water. Dizzy had had fly-away hair worn in a halo

as delicate as a dandelion clock. Her skin might have been blanched in the dusk of her secretive house. Agile and seeming boyish to Maggy who knew no boys, she swung up trees like a monkey so that one could see all the way up her skirt. She was Maggy's anti-self. Once, in a spirit of scientific inquiry, they showed each other their private parts. Later, Dizzy discovered this to be a sin or at least the occasion of one.

'You knew,' she accused. 'You should have told me.'

Maggy was disappointed to find freedom so fragile and each felt let down.

Now Dizzy's skin was opaque, thickish. She had lost her charm, but Maggy, although she might not have liked her if they'd just met for the first time, was responsive to memory. She felt linked by a bond she could not gauge to this woman who had first alerted her to the possibility of frankness. Dizzy had provided a model of mannish virtue at a time when Maggy knew no men and now Maggy, who had lost and left a man in America, found herself eager for support. Dizzy could still act with vigour. Look at the way she had rescued Rosheen.

The two – Maggy had heard the story from each separately – had not met for years when one night, a little over a year ago, they sat opposite each other on the North London underground. Rosheen's eyes were red; she had just run out of the house after being kicked in the stomach by Sean. For want of anywhere to go, she was heading for a late-night cinema.

'Leave him,' said Dizzy, 'you can stay in my flat.'

'I love him,' Rosheen told her. 'He needs me. He can't cope by himself. Poor Sean! He's gentle most of the time and when he's not, it's not his fault. He's sick, you see. His mother warned me: Mairéad. It's his nerves. Ulcers. Anyway we're married.'

'All the more reason', Dizzy told her, 'to get out while you can. Are you going to have kids with a chap like that? You should call the police,' she lectured.

'I couldn't.' Rosheen was an underdog to the marrow.

'I could.' Dizzy had Anglo-Irish assurance. 'Just let him

come looking for you.' She herded Rosheen home to her flat and the husband, when he presented himself, was duly given the bum's rush. He took to ambushing Rosheen, who went back to him twice but had to slink back to Dizzy after some days with black eyes and other more secret ailments.

'You're like a cat that goes out on the tiles,' Dizzy told her. 'You need an interest. You should come to political rallies with me.'

When Maggy arrived in London and agreed to move in with the two, Rosheen was working as an usherette in a theatre where Dizzy was stage manager. The plays put on by the group were revolutionary and much of Dizzy's conversation echoed their scripts.

'You have a slave mind,' she said without malice to Maggy, who claimed she was too busy finishing a thesis to have time for politics. Dizzy did not ask the subject of the thesis – it was semiology – nor show any interest in the years Maggy had spent in America. Having gathered that there had been some sort of man trouble, she preferred to know no more. To Rosheen, who showed more curiosity, Maggy remarked that her situation was much like Rosheen's own.

'Convalescing?'

'Yes.'

'This is a good place to do it,' said Rosheen. 'Though I sometimes think I won't be able to stand it. Sean keeps ringing me up. Crying. And I'm in dread that I'll break down and go back to him. I miss him at night something awful.'

'So why . . .'

'Ah sure it'd never be any good.'

'Is that what Dizzy tells you?'

'Yes. But sure I know myself that when a relationship has gone bad there's no mending it.'

'Relationship' would be Dizzy's word. But Maggy wasn't going to interfere. Rosheen she remembered from their childhood as unmodulated and unskinned: an emotional bomb liable to go off unpredictably. Better let Dizzy handle her. She herself was trying to finish her thesis before her money ran out. She spent her days at the British Museum, coming home as late as 9 p.m. Often a gust of talk would roar into the hallway as she pushed open the door. 'Bourgeois crapology,' she'd hear, or: 'It's bloody *not* within the competence of the minister. Listen, I know the 1937 constitution by heart. D'ya want to bet?' The voices would be Irish, fierce and drunk. Maggy would slip into the kitchen, get herself food as noiselessly as she could manage and withdraw into her room. Towards the evening's end, Rosheen's voice invariably reached her, singing some wailing song and Maggy would have wagered any money that the grief throbbing through it had not a thing to do with politics.

Sometimes, the phone in the hall would ring and Rosheen would have it off the hook before the third peal. It was outside Maggy's bedroom door and she could hear Rosheen whisper to it, her furtive voice muffled by the coats which hung next to it and under which she seemed to plunge her head to hide perhaps from Dizzy.

'You're drunk,' she'd start. 'You are. Sean, you're not to ring here, I told you. I suppose they've just shut the pub . . . it's not that, no . . . even if you were cold stone sober I'd say the same . . . Listen, why don't you go to bed and sleep it off? Have you eaten anything? What about your ulcer? Listen, go and get a glass of milk somewhere . . . you can . . . I can't . . . it's not that. I do. I do know my own mind but . . . She's not a dyke, Sean . . . You know as well as I do it'd never work . . . If only you'd take the cure . . . Well it's a vicious circle then, isn't it? . . . Please, Sean, ah don't be that way, Sean . . . I do but . . . ah Sean . . .'

Sooner or later there would be the click of the phone. Rosheen would stand for a while among the coats, then open the door to go into the front room. Later, she would be singing again, this time something subdued like one of the hymns which they had sung together in school. This tended to put a damper on the party and the guests would clatter out shortly afterwards.

Next day smells of stale beer and ash pervaded the flat, and Rosheen's voice, raised in the shower, pierced through the slap of water to reach a half-sleeping Maggy.

> Mo-o-other of Christ,
> Sta-a-ar of the sea,
> Pra-a-ay for the wanderer,
> Pray for me.

'You missed a good evening,' Dizzy reproached. 'I don't know why you can't be sociable. Mix. There were interesting, committed people there. One was a fellow who escaped from Long Kesh.'

'I have reading to do.'

'Piffle! Do you good to get away from your books. Live. Open yourself to new experiences.'

The man Maggy had lived with in San Francisco had made similar reproaches. Books, he said, made Maggy egocentric. Squirrelling away ideas, she was trying to cream the world's mind. His was a sentient generation, he told her, but she reminded him of the joke about the guy caught committing necrophilia whose defence was that he'd taken the corpse to be a live Englishwoman.

'Irish.'

Irish, English – what was the difference? It was her coldness which had challenged him. He was a man who relished difficulty. Beneath her cold crust he'd counted on finding lava and instead what he'd found inside was colder still: like eating baked Alaska. Maggy, feeling that she was in violation of some emotional equivalent of the Trade Descriptions Act, blamed everything on her First Communion. She'd been rejected by her maker, she explained, thrown on the reject heap and inhibited since. This mollified her lover and they took an affectionate leave of each other. Now, in wintry London, where men like him were as rare as humming birds, she groaned with afterclaps of lust.

Well, if her thaw was untimely, the fault was her own.

What was really too bad was that Rosheen, who had passed the First Communion test with flying colours, should be unable to consummate her punctual passions. She was slurping out feeling now, steaming and singing in the shower while the other two ate breakfast.

'*Mother of Chri-i-ist . . .*'

'How was your First Communion?' Maggy asked Dizzy. 'Did you experience ecstasy?'

'I don't think anyone mentioned the word. I thought of it more as a way of joining the club. As a convert, you know.'

'*Sta-a-a-r of the .. .* Fuck!' Rosheen had dropped the shampoo. Now they would all get glass splinters in their feet.

'Didn't you notice the prayers?' Maggy wondered. '*May thy wounds be to me food and drink by which I may be nourished, inebriated and overjoyed!* Surely you remember that? And: *Thou alone will ever be my hope, my riches, my delight, my pleasure, my joy . . . My fragrance, my sweet savour?* It goes on.'

'Do you think bloody Rosheen's cut herself? It's a responsibility having her around. I didn't think you were pious, Maggy. More toast?'

'I saw it all', said Maggy, 'as a promise of what I'd find outside the convent: men like Christs who'd provide all that.'

'I do think semiology is the wrong thing for you, Maggy. You should put your energies into something practical.'

'Dizzy, you're a treat! You've been trying to de-Anglicize yourself since the day we met, but your officer-class genes are too much for you.'

This was going too far. Dizzy, hurt, had to be sweetened by a gift of liqueur jam for which Maggy had to go all the way to Harrods. The trip made her late and when she got back to the flat Dizzy had left for the local pub. Maggy, joining her there, found her chatting to a man who sometimes dropped in after work. He was a sandy-haired chap who probably worked in an insurance office. Dizzy imagined him as starved for life and in search of anecdotes. 'I drop into an Irish pub in Camden,' he would tell his wife who would be wearing an apron covered with Campari ads. Dizzy, nourishing this imagined saga, had tried to get Rosheen to sing while he was in the pub, though it was always too early and the ambience wasn't right. 'It *is* an IRA pub, you know,' she had told him, slipping in and out of Irishness as though it were stage make-up.

'I believe less and less in democracy,' she was saying when Maggy arrived. 'Hullo, Maggy. What're you having? Don't you agree that democracy is a con? Do you know who said "the people have no right to do wrong"? Also "there are rights which a minority may justly uphold in arms against a majority"? Bet you don't.'

The man in the belted mac and sandy hair had nothing to say to this. Dizzy, however, could carry on two ends of a conversation.

'You might say,' she supplied, 'that the people have a right to decide for themselves. But "the people" are people like that gutless wonder, Sean. *They* never initiate change, so . . .'

Maggy left for the loo. Through its window she saw Sean and Rosheen embracing in the damp and empty garden of the pub. Both seemed to be crying. It might, however, be rain on their cheeks. She went back to the lounge.

'Saw it in Malaya,' the macintoshed man was saying. 'Bulk of the people were loyal. Just a few agitators. You've got to string 'em up right at the start. Cut off the gangrened limb. Else you'll have chaos.'

'But I', said Dizzy, 'was speaking *on behalf* of the agitators, the leaven, the heroes!'

'Oh,' the man moved his glass away from hers. 'I could hardly go along with that.'

Rosheen stood at the door of the lounge and beckoned Maggy behind Dizzy's back. She put a finger on her lips.

'I'm going.' Maggy got up.

*

Rosheen rushed Maggy down a corridor. 'Let's get out of here. That man's in the Special Branch. A detective. He's looking for Sean.'

'Why . . . but then Dizzy . . .?'

'Dizzy's an eejit, doesn't know whether she's coming or going.'

'You think Dizzy's an eejit?' Maggy couldn't have been more astonished if a worm had stood erect on its tail and spoken.

'You know she is, Maggy! She's in way over her head. Wait till I tell you.' Rosheen's eyes were red, but she spoke lucidly. 'It's Sean they're after. They want him to turn informer and if he doesn't, they'll spread the word that he *has*. Then the IRA will get him. And you know what *they* do to informers.'

'Are you sure?' Maggy asked, but it was likely enough. She remembered Mairéad's description of the nerve-shot Sean. He was the very stuff of which the police could hope to make an informer. His family had a record. Had he one himself? 'Is he political?' she asked.

'No, but they could nail him. They can nail anyone.'

'But what does he *know*? I mean what information has he?'

'That's the trouble,' Rosheen told her. 'He doesn't know much at all. But in self-defence he'll have to shop someone and the only one he can think of is Dizzy.'

'Dizzy?'

'You see she's not real IRA: only on the fringe, expendable. Sean thinks they mightn't mind about her. The IRA, I mean. And naturally *he* hates her.' Rosheen blushed and added quickly, 'This is killing him. He's passing blood again. Both sides have their eye on him now. He's been seen talking to that detective, so if anything at all happens in the next few weeks, it'll be blemt on Sean. I think he's a dead man.' Rosheen spoke numbly. 'If one lot doesn't get him, the others will.'

'And what *is* Dizzy up to? I mean what could he tell them?'

Rosheen turned stunned eyes on Maggy, who saw that there was no turning *her* into an Emerald Pimpernel. Dizzy, having stumbled onto territory which Rosheen knew better, might be revealed as an eejit and a play-actress but Rosheen herself, helpless as a heifer who has somehow strayed onto the centre divider of a highway, could only wait and wonder whether the traffic of events might be miraculously diverted before it mowed her down. 'What do they get expendable people like her to do?' she asked. 'Plant bombs.'

*

Dizzy, when faced with the question, reacted violently: 'Maggy, are you working for the Special Branch? Shit, I should have known! All that pretence at being apathetic – or', her eyes narrowed, 'is it Rosheen who's been talking? I always thought Sean had the stuff of a stool pigeon.' She went on like this until Maggy cut her short with the news that who *was* in the Special Branch was Dizzy's drinking companion whose phone number Maggy – thanks to Rosheen – was in a position to let her have.

'It's a Scotland Yard number. Check if you like,' she said, astounded at the way Dizzy's authority had crumbled. It was like the emperor's clothes: an illusion, nothing but RADA vowels, that officer-class demeanour, thought Maggy, who now felt powerful and practical herself. Rosheen, like one of those creatures in folk tales who hand the heroine some magic tool, had made Maggy potent.

In return, the helper must herself be helped. Maggy remembered Rosheen's telephone colloquies with Sean seeping, regularly as bedtime stories, under her own bedroom door and that Rosheen's renunciatory voice had quavered like a captive bird's as she hid among the heavy coats in Dizzy's front hall. Now she must be allowed to unleash her precarious passion in peace.

'*You're* a security risk, you must see that,' said Maggy to Dizzy, making short work of her protests. 'So you'd better let me pick up your bomb. Never mind why I want to. That's my concern. Motives', she told her, 'are irrelevant to history. If I do this for the IRA, I shall be IRA. Wasn't that your own calculation?'

This bit of rhetoric proved truer than foreseen, for a number of squat, tough-faced, under-nourished-looking people turned up at her trial and had to be cleared from the public gallery where they created a disturbance and gave clenched-fist salutes. They seemed to have co-opted her act, and her lawyer brought along copies of excitable weekly papers which described it in terms she could not follow because their references were rancorous and obscure. One was called *An Phoblacht*, another *The Starry Plough* and there was a sad daily from Belfast full of ads for money-lenders, in memoriam columns and, for her, a bleak fraternity. Dizzy did not come and neither did Rosheen.

Who did attend the trial and visit her afterwards was the glass-eyed man. 'All Ireland is with you,' he said, 'all true Irish Socialist Republicans.' Was this a joke? Did the eye gleam with irony? Or had he meant that her act was public property, whether she liked this or not, and despite the fact that her victim had not been Dizzy's target at all? *That* was to have been a building and there was to have been a telephone warning to avoid loss of life. Maggy thought this ridiculous. A war was a war and everyone knew how those warnings went wrong. The police delayed acting so as to rouse public feeling against the bombers – for how much anger could be generated if explosions hurt nobody, going off with the mild

bang of a firework display? Property owners would be indignant, but the police needed wider support than theirs. Yes,
the police were undoubtedly the culprits. They bent rules.
Detective Inspector Coffee had been bending rules when he
told the nerve-shot Sean that he'd put the word about in Irish
pubs that Sean was an informer unless he became one. An old
police trick! It had landed men in a ditch with a bullet in the
neck before now. How many had Detective Inspector Coffee
nudged that way? How many more would he? None, because
Maggy had got him with Dizzy's bomb.

'For personal reasons,' she told Glass Eye.

'It's *what* you did that counts.'

What she had done astounded her. She had been like one
of those mothers who find the sudden strength to lift lorries
and liberate their child. Unthinkingly, almost in a trance, she
had phoned the number given her by Rosheen and asked for
an appointment. She had information of interest, she promised, and evidence to back it up. Could she bring it round at
once? Where she'd got the number? Oh, please, she didn't
want to say this on the phone. '*They* may be listening, watching. Maybe I'm paranoid but I've got caught up in something
terrifying. By chance.'

Her genuinely shaky voice convinced him and he proved
more guileless than she could have believed for she had gone
to the meeting fearful of being frisked by attendant heavies.
But no. There were no preliminaries. She got straight to the
man himself.

'Detective Inspector Coffee?'

He was the sandy-haired chap all right. Perhaps he had
recognized her voice on the phone? She handed him a bag.
There were documents on top of the device which was primed
to go off when touched.

'I brought you papers. You'll see what they are. I'm afraid
I'm a bit rattled. Nausea. Could I find a loo?'

He showed her the way, then walked back into his room. She

was two flights down the stairs, when she heard the explosion. Oddly – she had expected her fake nausea to become real – she felt nothing but elation. There were shattering noises, shouts, a bell. She thought: that's put an end to his smile, his assurance, his smug, salary-drawing, legal murder. The word registered then and, seeing him in her mind's eye blown apart, she began to sweat. The smell was pungent when she reached the outer door where a policeman stopped her.

'You'll demand political status?' asked the glass-eyed man. 'Go on hunger strike until they grant it.'

'Political?'

He was impatient, the visit nearly over. A group in another wing of the prison were all set to strike. He was planning publicity which would have more impact if she joined in. 'Listen, love,' he said, 'you're political or what are you?'

Political? The notion exhilarated. Old songs. Solidarity. We shall overcome. In gaol, as in church, that sort of language seemed to work. On a snap decision, she agreed and, in after-image, the gleam of his eye pinned her to the definition. As she grew weaker, her weathercock mind froze at North-North-East. The strike gave purpose to her days and, like the falling sparrow's, her pain became a usable statistic. 'Get involved,' commanded an ad in the *Irish News* which the glass-eyed man brought on a subsequent visit. '*They* did.' A list of hunger-strikers included Maggy's name.

Her mind was flickering. Sharp-edged scenes faltered and she wondered whether thin people like herself had less stamina than others. It was too soon, surely, to be so weak? She had a fantasy – some of the time it was a conviction – that her lover from San Francisco had come and that they had done together all the things she – no: he – had always wanted to do. Like a drowning person's flash vision of a lifetime, a whole erotic frieze unrolled with convincing brilliance in her mind. Sensory deprivation was supposed to make you hallucinate, she remembered, but confused this false prison visitor with real ones. His eyes gleamed like glass. 'Sentient,' he had said of himself and 'cold' of her, but her memory of him was bright like ice and cold. She *was* cold. It was part of her condition. And her mouth was dry. In her fantasy – or reality? – he offered her an icicle to suck.

'Don't talk,' said someone, 'save your saliva.'

Now her lover was lying naked and wounded beside her and offered her his wounds to moisten her lips, but they too were dry and not as food and drink to her at all.

Vitamins and hormones were being used up.

This was the prison doctor talking now. He had checked her blood and urine and felt it his duty to warn her that irreversible effects could occur.

'Jaundice,' warned the doctor.

'Golden, gilded skin,' said her lover. 'Here,' he presented her with a golden potato chip. 'Eat this for me.'

'Eat,' said the screw.

'Do yourself a favour,' said the doctor.

Maggy put the chip in her mouth. It was dry. She couldn't swallow it. It revived her nausea.

Diego

Diego? He hasn't been in touch? Well, but that's his way, isn't it? He can just drop out of sight, then come back later, bubbling with good humour and gifts. He's so good-natured one has to forgive him. Of course he trades on that. I did see him recently, as it happens. Mmm. About two weeks ago and a funny thing happened then – funny things do when one is with him, don't you find? Or maybe it's he who makes them seem funny because he enjoys a laugh so much. He was giving me a lift home to have dinner with his wife and Mercedes, the little girl. Yes, she's ten now and bright as a button, a bit spoilt I'm afraid. Well, you'd expect Diego to spoil a daughter, wouldn't you? Of course he's in love with her and I must say she is a lovely creature. What was I going to tell you? Oh, about the supermarket. Well, Marie had asked him to stop and pick up some mangoes – you've never met *her*, have you? Am I putting my foot in it? Sorry. I know you're much older friends of Diego's than I am – but that's just the trouble, isn't it? You belong to the days when he was with Michèle and he has never felt able to present friends from those years to Marie. It's his delicacy. Another husband wouldn't give a damn. Hard on old friends. But you know what he says: 'How can I tell my wife "Here are my friends, X and Y, whom I've known for ten years but never brought home until now"?' In a way you can see his point. He neglected Marie awfully during all that time. Excluded her from his social life. You'd be a reminder of his bad behaviour. It would be different if they'd gone through with the divorce. His good nature prevented that. He couldn't bring himself to leave her and now he can't bring himself to leave Michèle, and so someone's always getting the short end of the stick.

I was telling you about the mangoes. Well, we went into the market to get them and it was one of those places in the *banlieue* where they weren't used to selling exotic fruit. Nobody knew the price and a girl was sent off with the ones Diego had picked to try and find the manager. Then she got waylaid or went to the phone and didn't come back. The woman at the check-out shouted on the intercom, *'Où sont les mangues de Monsieur?'* At this, Diego began to fall about laughing and then everyone in the shop began to see the thing as a gag. They began shouting at each other: 'His what?' – 'His mangoes!' – 'Lost his mangoes, has he? Oh that must be painful!' – 'What? Mangoes? Oh, unmentionable!' And so forth. It was pretty mindless and any other customer might have been annoyed, but not Diego. He was delighted. 'They come from my country,' he told the girl and when he did I noticed that he *looks* like a mango: reddish and yellowish and a touch wizened. 'I'm half Red Indian,' he told her and it was obvious that if his mangoes hadn't turned up just then in a great burst of hilarity, he would have started getting off with her. He has a great way with him and he knows how to take the French. He keeps just that little touch of foreignness while speaking very racy Parisian and knowing everything there is to know about life here. They love that. He loves their ways and that makes them able to feel they can love his.

When we got back into the car, he started telling me of how once, years ago, when he first met Michèle, he was walking through the old Halles market, with her on one arm and Marie on the other, on their way to dine at an oyster bar, and one of those hefty lorry-drivers who used to bring in loads of produce began pointing at tiny Diego walking between these two splendid, *plantureuses* women – they looked like assemblages of melons, according to Diego – and, pretending to wipe his brow, raised his cap and roared: 'What a constitution!' *Quelle santé!* It was like the mango joke. Diego attracts such comments. When he told me the story, I got the idea that *that* could have been what started off his affaire with Michèle.

Because dear old Diego *is* a bit of a *macho*, isn't he, in the nicest possible way? '*Moi, j'aime la femme,*' he says. Awfully Latin! It sounds impossible in English. I mean you can't say it really: 'I love woman' sounds absurd. And if you say 'women' in the plural it sounds cheap. But what he means is the essence of woman, something he sees in every woman, even in his mother and, of course, especially in little Mercedes, right from the moment she was born. 'She was a woman,' he'll tell you – well, he probably *has* told you. He talks about her all the time. 'From the moment she was born she was a woman, a coquette, a flirt.'

As I was saying, he has spoilt her a bit – I tell a lie, he has spoilt her a great deal. In fact something happened later that evening which pointed up the dangers of this and was really quite upsetting. I don't know whether Diego will draw the lesson from it.

You haven't met Mercedes either, have you? You'd really have to see her to understand. You see, in a way, Diego is right. She *is* remarkably bright and perfectly bilingual because of his having always spoken Spanish to her. She *is* like a coquettish little princess stepped out of a canvas by Goya or Velázquez. This is partly because of her clothes which come from boutiques on the Faubourg Saint Honoré. Ridiculous clothes: hand-tucked muslin, silk, embroidered suede. I don't know who they were intended for, but Diego buys them. He buys her exactly the same sort of thing as he used to buy Michèle, and there is Marie in her denims with a daughter wearing a mink jacket at the age of ten. I don't know whether she approves or not. Their relationship is odd. Well, most marriages seem that way to me. What do I know of yours, for instance? Married people always strike me as treating each other a bit like bonsai trees. They nip and clip and train each other into odd, accommodating shapes, then sometimes complain about the result. Or one partner can go to endless lengths of patience with the other and then be obdurate about some trifling thing. It's a mystery. I watch with interest. I think you're all a dying species but fun to watch – like some product of a very ancient, constricting, complex civilization. Perhaps that's why I'm a gossip? As a feminist, I am in the same position as the Jesuits who watched and noted down the ways of the old Amerindians while planning to destroy them.

Diego claims sometimes to be part Amerindian. Maybe he is. Some of them used to cut out their victims' hearts with stone knives, used they not? I'm not sure whether *he* may not have blood on his hands. Metaphorical blood. After all, he's a member of the oligarchy of that repressive regime. It's true that he has been twenty-five years in Paris, reads the left-wing press and has picked up a radical vocabulary – but where does his money come from? Well, one doesn't probe but one can't help wondering. Another complexity. The troubling thing about sexists and members of old, blood-sodden castes is that they can be so delicate in their sensibilities and this does throw one. I keep meeting people like that here in Paris. It seems to draw them as honey draws wasps. Am I being the Protestant spinster now? Forthright and angular and killing the thing I love as I lean over it with my frosty breath? In delighted disapproval? In disapproving delight. I mustn't kill this little story which I'm working my way round to telling you. It's about Mercedes and Michèle's dog. Yes, but first, have you got the background clear in your minds? Diego is so jokey and jolly and often – to be frank – drunk, that you mightn't. *Your* dealings with him were always social, weren't they? You'd meet in some smart night club or restaurant and, I suppose, dance till dawn with money no object and champagne flowing. That's how I imagine it – how Diego's led me to imagine it. Am I wrong? No? Good. Well, but, you see, that's only one side of Diego: the Don Diego swaggering side. There's also the plainer homebody. Did you know that Diego is simply the Spanish for James? I didn't either. Think of him as 'Jim' or 'Jacques' coming home in the dishwater-dawn light from those evenings to the suburban house where he'd parked Marie and the child.

Marie's *my* friend, by the way. I knew her before I did him. She had gone back to university to study law and we met in a feminist student group. Well, what would you have her do all those years while he used the house as a launching pad for his flights of jollification? He brought home the minimum cash – just like any working-class male taking half the budget for his pleasures. She could have left. She didn't. *There's* an area of motives which one cannot hope to map. *He* could have left and didn't. There's one I *can* map for you. He met Michèle through Marie. In those days she had prettier friends. I do occasionally wonder whether *I* was chosen as being unthreatening? No, no need to protest. I'm trying for accuracy. I like to take hold of as many elements in a situation as I can and I've admitted that Diego/Jim fascinates me. He is the Male Chauvinist Pig or Phallocrat seen close up, as I rarely get a chance to see the beast, and I do see his charm. It is his weapon and, when I say I see it, I really mean that I feel him seeing the woman in me. Men don't, very often. That's what I mean about Diego's *amour pour la femme* being non-sexist or sexist in such an all-embracing way that it gets close to universal love. He loves half humanity, half the human race, regardless of age, looks or health. Of course he is *also* a sex-snob and wants to be seen with a girl who does him credit – Michèle. That's the social side of him. But he responds to femininity wherever he finds it: in his mother, an old beggar woman, me. He's inescapably kind.

Why didn't he divorce, you ask? Kindness again. Really. He had fallen in love with Michèle: a tempestuous passion, I gather. They were swept off by it simultaneously, like a pair of flint stones knocking sparks off each other, like two salamanders sizzling in unison – he tells me about it when Marie's in the kitchen. He has to tell someone. It was his big experience and he made a mess of it and is still shocked at himself, yet can't see how he could have done other than he did. What he did was this: he proposed marriage to Michèle, was accepted and, brimful of bliss, looked at poor, blissless Marie and thought how lonely she must be and that he must do something for her. Now here is the part that touches me. He didn't think in terms of money, as most men would have. He thought in terms of love. He wanted her to have someone to love when he had gone off with Michèle and decided that *he* had better be the one to provide her with a love-object. Can you guess the next move? He made her pregnant. The noble sexist wanted to leave her with a child. Imagine Michèle's fury. She thought that he had got cold feet about marrying *her* and had cooked up this pretext for backing out. He assured her that he did very much want to marry her but that now he must stay with Marie until the baby was born so that it should be legitimate.

The baby, of course, was Mercedes and he fell in love with *her* at first sight, at first sound, at first touch. He was totally potty about her, obsessed and *at the same time* he was painfully in love with an estranged and furious Michèle on whom he showered guilty, cajoling gifts, spoiling and courting her and putting up with every caprice in an effort to earn back the total love which he had forfeited – she kept telling him – by his sexual treachery.

Those were the years when you knew him – the champagne and dancing years. He and Michèle had not got married and so their relationship became one long, festive courtship and she, from what he says, responded as someone who's fussed over for years might well be tempted to respond: she became a bit of a bitch. She brought boys home to the flat where he kept her like a queen, stood him up, tormented him and then, between lovers, just often enough to keep him hot for her, became as loving and playful as they had been in the early days. She was his *princesse lointaine*, radiant with the gleam of loss and old hope and he was romantic about her and probably happier than he admits with the arrangement which kept his loins on fire and fixed his wandering attention on her in whom he was able to find all women: the wife she should have become, the fickle tormentor she had become, his wronged great love and familiar old friend, his Donna Elvira and his spendthrift, nightclub succubus. She was all women except one and that one, to be sure, was Mercedes, the little girl who was growing up in an empty, half-furnished suburban house with a mother who was busy getting her law degree and a father who swept in from time to time with presents from Hamleys and Fouquets and organdie dresses and teddy bears twice her size which made her cry. Every penny he had went on Michèle and Mercedes. I remember that house when it hadn't a lamp or a table because Marie was damned if she'd spend *her* money on it and he was so rarely there that he never noticed what it did or didn't have apart from the Aladdin's Cave nursery in which Mercedes was happy while she was small. Later, at the ages of six and seven and eight, as she began to invite in her friends, she began to colonize the rest of the house and, as she did, he began to furnish it for her. Michèle's share of his budget shrank as Mercedes's grew. Shares in his time fluctuated too. He spent more of it at home; friends like you began to see less of him and Michèle had to start finding herself new escorts, not from bitchery but from need. But he would never abandon her completely. He had wasted her marriageable years and now he felt towards her the guilt he had once felt towards Marie. But what can he do? He's not Christ. He cannot divide up and distribute his body and blood.

He was telling me all this that night on the drive out from Paris and he got so upset that at one stage he stopped the car and walked into a hotel where we had a drink. This made us late for dinner, but Marie, of course, never complains. Who did complain was Mercedes. It was past her bed-time and she was irritable and sleepy when we arrived. She had waited up because she wanted to have a mango and, besides, Diego had promised her some small present. Right away she started being whingey and angry with me whom she blamed for keeping her Daddy late. Diego was amused, as he is by all Mercedes's caprices, and kept saying, 'She's jealous, you know!' As though that were something to be proud of! 'She's very possessive.'

There was a dog in the house, Michèle's silver poodle – perhaps you know it? – Rinaldino, a rather highly-strung creature which Marie and Mercedes had been told was mine. Michèle had asked Diego to keep it for her because she was going on a cruise and it pines if left in a kennel. Diego can never say 'no' to Michèle, and so a story was concocted about my flat being painted and how I had had to move to a hotel where I couldn't take my new dog. All this because of Diego's not wanting his wife to know that she was being asked to house his mistress's dog. Surprisingly, the plan had worked up to now and Rinaldino had been three weeks at Diego's. Mercedes was mad about him and everyone had been pleased about that. This evening, however, she suddenly announced that from now on the dog was hers. She wasn't giving him back. She just wasn't. So there. The dog loved her, she claimed and, besides, she had told her friends it was hers and didn't want to be made to look a liar. She said all this in her grown-up way: half playful, half testing and I couldn't help having the old-fashioned notion that what she really wanted, deep down, was to be told 'no'. That used to be said, remember, when *we* were children. It was thought that children needed to know the limits of their possibilities.

Anyway, she kept on and Diego wouldn't contradict her and neither did Marie. I kept my mouth shut. It's not my business if Diego spoils his daughter as he spoils his mistress so, even though the dog was supposed to be mine, I didn't react when Mercedes started clamouring for a promise that Dino, as she had rechristened Rinaldino, should never leave. She would not go to bed till she got it, she said. It was obvious that she was trying to provoke me, but I pretended not to notice. Poor child, it's not her fault if she is the way she is.

'Dino likes me better than he likes you,' she told me.

'Why wouldn't he like you?' I asked. 'You're a good girl, aren't you?'

'He likes me whether I'm good or not. He likes me even when I hurt him.'

I can't remember what I said to that and doubt if it mattered. She had taken against me and the next thing she did was to start twisting the dog's ears.

'See,' she said. 'Even when I do this, he likes me. He likes me because he's mine. I'm his Mummy.'

Then she began to cuddle the animal in that way that children do if they're not stopped. She tied a napkin under its chin, half choking it, and held it as if it were a baby, bending its spine and pretending to rock it to sleep.

'Mine, mine, mine,' she crooned.

I had an odd sensation as I watched. What struck me was that in a way the dog was *Michèle's* baby, her substitute for the family she might have had if Mercedes had not been born. And now, here was Mercedes trying to steal even that from her. I found myself wondering whether some instinct was making her do it. An intuition? The thought was absurd but I let myself play with it to keep my mind off what the brat was doing to little Rinaldino. The French *are* insensitive about animals and Marie seemed indifferent. She often goes into a sort of passive trance when Diego is around and he, of course, has no feeling for creatures at all. Maybe I was showing my discomfort in spite of myself? I can't be sure. Anyway, the little beast – I'm talking about Mercedes – began to pull Rinaldino's whiskers and it was all I could do to keep myself from slapping her. I was on the point of warning her that she might get bitten when she gave a shriek and threw the dog violently across the room. For a moment I thought she might have broken its back, but no, it got up and scuttled under the sofa. That, it turned out, was good canine thinking.

It had bitten her cheek. Not deeply, but it had drawn blood.

Well, the scene after that was beyond description, unbelievable. It literally took my breath away: hysteria, screams, foot-stamping, hand-wringing – all the things you think real people never do, they did. And no initiative at all. *I* had to take charge and clean the child's cheek and put disinfectant on it. You'd think I'd cut off her head from the way she carried on. Diego was crying. Marie was tight-lipped and kept clenching her fists as though she was about to explode.

'Look,' I told them, 'it's a scratch. It's nothing. She'd have got worse from a bramble bush. Just *look*,' I kept insisting.

But they wouldn't. Not really. They kept exclaiming and averting their faces and clapping their hands over their eyes. They wanted their drama and were working each other up, so that when Mercedes shouted, 'I want the dog killed. Right now. It doesn't like me. It doesn't love me. It must be killed!' I realized that the adults were half ready to go along with the idea. Diego was completely out of his mind.

'Supposing it has rabies?' he whispered to me.

'It's been inoculated,' I told him.

'Are you sure?'

'Of course I am. It's on its name tag. Look. With the date.'

'I want it killed now! Here. Now. It doesn't love me. It's a bad dog,' screamed Mercedes.

'It's my dog,' I told her. 'You can't kill my dog.'

She began to kick me then. Hard. I still have bruised shins. She carried on as if she had rabies herself and her mother had to pull her off me and take her to bed.

'I want it killed!' She was screaming and scratching and biting as they went through the door. Later, I heard her still at it in her bedroom.

Diego looked distraught. He said he had heard of dogs which were rabid in spite of having been inoculated. Was I *sure* it had been inoculated? What did a name tag prove after all? It struck me then that he had either forgotten that the dog was not mine or was trying to persuade himself that it was. We were alone together now but he avoided mentioning Michèle's name. Maybe he felt that some sin of his was coming to the fore and demanding a blood sacrifice? He kept pouring whiskey and drinking it down fast. At one point he went into the kitchen and looked at the rack of knives.

Well, you can never tell how much that sort of thing is theatre, can you? I mean that theatre can spill into life if people work themselves up enough. Maybe he was seeing himself as an Amerindian priest? I don't mind telling you that I began to get scared. The thing was taking on odd dimensions as he got drunker and guiltier and the screams ebbed and started up again in the bedroom. Rinaldino, very sensibly, stayed right where he was under the sofa and that affected me more than anything. After all, dogs do pick up bad vibrations, don't they? Anyway, the outcome was that when Diego went into the lavatory I phoned a taxi, took the dog and left. I was convinced that by now he wasn't seeing the dog as a dog at all and that if I hadn't got it out of the house he would have ended up killing it – or worse.

Marie wouldn't have interfered. Even if she'd been standing beside him she wouldn't. I'm sure of that. They're extraordinary that way. I keep thinking of them now. Each is so intelligent and kind and – I want to say 'ordinary', when they're on their own. Normal? But let a scene start and you'd think you were dealing with members of the House of Atreus. Marie's passivity has started to seem sinister to me. I've started dreaming of that evening and it's become deformed in my memory. Sometimes it seems to me that she was the silent puppet-mistress pulling the strings and that even I was one of the puppets. Even the dog. Well, certainly the dog.

Maybe it's self-referential to bring myself in? But I've started worrying whether Marie as well as Mercedes see me as an intrusive female. 'She's jealous,' Diego told me that evening and laughed. He could have meant his wife. Could he? I'm only his confidante but Marie might dislike that, mightn't she? It's very unhealthy on my part to dwell on the thing and it would be absurd for me to have a crush on a man like Diego and I hope nobody thinks this is the case. In my more sober moments I know that any bad feeling that came my way that evening was really directed through me at Michèle. I was her stand-in. After all, I'd pretended to own her dog. But somehow, emotion sticks. I feel a little as though mud had been thrown at me and that I can't quite clean it off.

Dies Irae

'. . . your hair?'

'By myself.' A fib. But to say 'at Fulvio's' would draw sneers from Leftish friends ('Ha! Consorting with Black Florence, is that it?') and a governessy nosiness from Black Florentines themselves: 'So you've found your way there? Isn't Fulvio a pet? And . . . have you discovered yet where to buy the best chocolate in all Florence? My dear, *let* me. . . . My grand-aunt's cook whom she brought from Vienna when. . . .' And off one would be in danger of being led to some den where there would be time, while each sweet was hand-wrapped, to ruminate on how these were probably going to be less good than the obvious commercial brand. 'The best chocolate in all Florence . . . !' Another myth. Black Florentines live by myth. It gives matter to their conversation and a breathless impulse. 'What!' the next B(lack) F(lorentine) would cry, 'you *didn't* let Bibi take you to that dreadful little confectioner where the cat sleeps on the chocolates! The poor thing is quite doddery! Bibi feels obliged to help her out with a small income, so any sale he can promote is to *his* good. *D'ailleurs c'est un mytho-mane! Surtout,* never buy any of Bibi's wine. *Not classico!* Can't blame him, poor chap. He's a dear really. Just crackers!' B–F–s speak as little Italian as possible. They were occupied for long periods by an army of English nannies.

Sneers at their taste are well grounded. Though not about Fulvio. I've forgotten who recommended him to me. I must have been a student at the time for I remember my terror lest I be unable to pay his bill. Yet I never went to another hairdresser in Florence afterwards and, as the *carovita* sends prices spiralling, his have remained steady. (At least for me. Cocking an ear to those he charges tourists, I suspect him of making new customers pay for the old.) He is a good hairdresser, though it is less this that draws me back to him than the pleasurable femininity one puts on with his lavender pinafores. Anonymous in one of these, I agree to be an odalisque. His voice, mirrors and tuberoses are peremptory and, while hands and feet lie at anchor in the grip of his manicurists, I find my will receding; my mind drowses; Fulvio has taken over. Above our heads, heavy vaulting weaves vaguely – the stone roots of his old palazzo – burying us in a reckless vacancy. Delicate-featured apprentices hover and my blood, slowing to the indolent pace of the cosseted old Florentines around me, purrs and contentedly restores itself. All my defences are down. Which is why this morning's incident was so upsetting.

Maria was brushing my hair. She is the prettiest and palest of the apprentices, weak-chinned, long-nosed, sweet and brittle-looking with a heron's legs. Today she brushed longer than necessary. Fulvio came up. 'Is Maria busy?' he asked. 'Yes,' said one of the master hairdressers, 'yes, I have a job for her.' 'Because', Fulvio said, 'the *principessa* is coming.' Maria tore at my hair. 'The *principessa* makes Maria vomit,' said a manicurist. 'She makes her sick for the rest of the day.' Maria tore on and Fulvio said nothing to this. Instead, he fingered the gold chain which descends from his left lapel to the right back trouser pocket, where he keeps a pair of gold scissors inscribed with his name and the date of some aestheticians' banquet held in the '30s. He smiled at me. 'It is more pleasant to work on the signora,' he said. 'The signora is beautiful no matter what one does to her. She doesn't really need us at all. But I don't', he turned his smile on Maria, 'pay you to do only what you like.' 'Do you pay her for getting sick?' the manicurist asked. Fulvio moved off to work on a customer in the jabbing manner which suggests he is building up a picture lock by lock. 'I can hardly turn the *principessa* away,' he called, still smiling. 'Can I now? I run a shop, not a club.' 'You *could*,' threw back one of the cherubic male hairdressers. 'What's so unfair', said an apprentice, 'is that she always wants Maria. Every time. . . .'

Maria had begun giving me a friction and I could hear no more. I could see, however, that she was not taking part in this discussion at all. Her face in the mirror floated calmly above my own, and she might have seemed impassive but for the harsh knuckles she was grinding into my skull. When Beppe came to set my hair he kept Maria on to pass him the rollers. She was still with us when an odd pantomime figure strode into the looking glass and began to twirl within its fanciful stucco frame. 'Good morning, *principessa*. Make yourself comfortable,' invited Fulvio. 'Maria will be with you presently.' But the figure continued to plunge about in its tall felt boots, over-long greatcoat and soiled pink turban. '*Io sono puntua-a-ale!*' piped the *principessa* since this was she. 'I am on ti-i-ime!' She intoned the words to a nursery-rhyme rhythm, half mocking, half whining. Maria kept her face resolutely focused on the basket of coloured rollers. 'Two red,' demanded Beppe, 'one green. Old witch,' he whispered to Maria. 'I'd refuse if I were you. The sight of her is enough. A maid servant wouldn't do it, why should you?' He jerked his head towards Fulvio. 'Snobby old sod,' he whispered out of the corner of his mouth, 'let him look after her himself if it means that much to him to have her here. A blue one for the bottom please.'

I strained to catch a glimpse of the *principessa*'s face, astonished at the licence her presence unleashed in this formal establishment. But she had twirled off again. She had, I had noticed, a foreign accent. Could that be the matter? Could she have lice perhaps? Surely not! I found myself shuddering, caught in the general excited distaste. Her costume was like something out of Delacroix – an Eastern merchant's redolent of unwholesome travels. 'I am being kept wai-i-iting!' carolled the *principessa* coyly, 'although I telephoned!' Beppe put me under the dryer and I heard no more.

Minutes later, I felt curious enough to squirm out again on the pretext that I had to make a phone call. The *principessa* had taken off the turban. She was near bald. Wisps of cobweb hair clung like spiders to her pink scalp. Her face was ancient and livid. A manicurist held one outstretched foot: a yellowish grey appendage, like those of dead saints miraculously preserved and exposed in crypts. Maria was sulkily stirring something which she showed to the old woman as I passed. It must have been unsatisfactory for she was still tinkering with it when I returned, and it was another ten minutes before I saw her start to massage her customer's pate. The old woman's mouth kept going all the time but of course I could hear nothing. The staff were by now in stitches of laughter which they concealed by turning their heads or grinning on one side of their faces like glove puppets. By the time I came out from under my dryer their mood had changed. The princess was under the steamer, and now they talked with open anger, insisting that Maria had done enough for one day and that someone else should finish the old woman off. 'But she always asks for Maria,' objected the manicurist. 'Maria,' called the *principessa* at that moment from under her steamer, 'Maria!' 'What do you want?' asked an apprentice irritably. 'I want Maria.' 'Maria is busy.' 'Which Maria do you want?' another girl asked cunningly, 'we have three Marias you know!' The old woman subsided.

Beppe came to comb me out. 'Who is she?' I asked. 'A White Russian,' he said, 'filthy rich and mean as an ant. She never pays.' 'You mean she never tips?' He laughed, *'Macchè!* She never pays! Not a lira. It's not just for Maria's sake that we're angry, though that's unfair enough. Why should we have her here? Is she pretty? Does she pay? Is she poor? There's no reason,' he concluded harshly. 'Signor Fulvio *è grullo!* He's a fool! Your hair came out well,' he ended professionally, 'those uncombed styles suit you.'

'Everything suits the signora,' smiled Fulvio coming up. 'She has good bones,' he flattered, 'fine skin. That's beauty. You have to admit it when you see beauty! When we see a painting,' he went on in a louder voice, haranguing the *salon*, 'we admire it, so why not a beautiful woman who is a gift of nature and', he bowed at Beppe, 'of art?' Beneath him, as he bowed, the gold scissors chain bellied with the pendulous delicacy of an udder. When he straightened, it subsided. He was a trim little man.

'Beauty!' I recognized the old woman's accent although what she had released was less a word than a sob. 'Beauty!' she repeated. She had come out from the steamer and was standing behind us. On her scalp, the sparse few hairs, now dampened, stood out like feelers on some pale primitive fish. 'I was never beautiful,' she said in a haggard voice, 'but now I sometimes stare in the mirror' – she moved over beside me to the glass – 'like this!' Her eyes fixed their image and she went on in a voice which the departure of its earlier querulous and mocking note had left disturbingly intimate, 'And I say: can *this*, this be Nadia?' She stared at us, then back at her own image. 'It's horrible,' she muttered, 'appalling!' She paused for a moment, her widening orbs fastened to their own reflection. The girls held their breath.

Fulvio tried a little laugh. '*Principessa!* It comes to us all!'

'Yes,' she said eagerly. 'I wasn't beautiful, but I was not like *this*! I wish I had a photograph, Fulvio, to show you. Just to. . . .' She trailed off.

'All of us,' said Fulvio consolingly.

'*No!*' She wouldn't have such. 'You, Fulvio, may be in your sixties.' (*Could* he? Perhaps.) '*I* am eighty-six, *eighty*-six. . . . These young things come to you, Fulvio, and you work on them but I . . .' She seemed to try to collect herself, giving him the fossil of a worldly smile from teeth whose newness was bleak among the marshes of her flesh. 'I. . . .' Again she foundered. Closed, her receding mouth was gentle, blindly soft as perhaps a fish muzzle. 'I can't bear a wig now. The itch. . . . Fulvio. . . . Oh, what an old wreck!' She was crying. The deepened wrinkles drew stars and goose's footprints across the lost face.

'We'll try something else.'

She was not listening. 'Older,' she murmured, 'every day! Fulvio! And when you know what it means. . . .'

'It doesn't matter. . . .'

'*OOhh!*'

'But *principessa*,' Fulvio spoke with ardour. 'It comes to us *all!* Truly,' he pleaded, 'princess!' The word was magic to him. He would have performed feats to restore the poor hag to the image that went with it, to energize her blue and sluggish blood.

'Ahh!' She was unconsoled.

'Every mother's son of us,' he assured her. 'Earlier than we think! We're in the same boat. From the beginning. From adolescence. Cells in our brains – I was reading only the other day – begin to decay, to die. You envy the signora!' (He was preparing to sacrifice me. Let him. Poor woman, I thought, poor wretch, do what you can for her, say what you like. I tried to signal my complaisance but Fulvio was staring at me as though at some creature in a pet shop which he had decided not to buy.) 'Her beauty', he said, 'is fading already. Not obviously perhaps but I can see. The expert detects what will be plain to all in a year or so. Look at the dry parts of her face.' He bent towards my reflection in the mirror. 'See,' he invited. He pointed to the corners of my eyes and I could feel them cringe, crinkling into the folds he wished to find. 'Crows' feet,' he cried. I tried to smile through this but what appeared was not unlike the old woman's nervous simper of some minutes before. Old hag, I thought suddenly, just because she's some sort of a princess! 'There's a pout line,' shouted Fulvio, 'by her mouth. Laughter, pleasure – it takes its toll!'

'Signor Fulvio!' Beppe giggled in embarrassment.

'Oh,' the *principessa's* groan was gentler now. 'The signora has time before her.'

'Phuitt!' Fulvio dismissed it. (I'll get up, I thought. I'll leave now. But they were standing around me. It would look like pique.) 'Her bones', he reneged on his earlier compliment, 'won't save her. Do we admire skeletons? Thin women wear worse. All this talk of carbohydrates now. It used to be calories. Pupupuh! I say to them. Our generation, princess' – gallantly – 'had more sense!'

I stood up. 'I'm going, Fulvio.'

He stepped aside. 'Eh? Ah, you're finished? Well, your hair looks very nice, signora. An excellent job, successful! You're not . . . no hard feelings, eh?'

I walked out to the hall. Blushing and shrugging, Beppe followed me. He helped me off with the lavender pinafore and accepted his tip. 'You know,' he said, 'Signor Fulvio is a bit, well . . . he has Russian blood himself, like the *principessa*. It. . . . Oh, one must make allowances and . . . he's getting old. . . .' Realizing that this was the wrong tack, Beppe rushed me to the outer door where he sprayed my hair with a lacquer smelling faintly of incense. Visible even here in the mirrors, Fulvio's image seemed to be still castigating his own pomps and artifices. The mournful gorgon beside him did not appear consoled. There was a retch from the cloakroom. Maria? From the street I saw them again through the plate-glass window. Fulvio's hands were upturned, his mouth agape in the traditional gestures of impotence. In the polished marble slab on which gold lettering spelled FULVIO, *coiffeur, friseur, parrucchière*, I could see the fashionable outline of my lacquered hair.

Her Trademark

The captain – fastidious, with a complexion like raspberry fool – had a smile of great sweetness. From teeth that seemed to have been overlaid with a film of honey. A blond patina – nicotine lichen – clung to his fingers. Hair and moustache were ginger still. A golden lad. He brought scope and a festive dash to the management of local affairs, adoring to organize auctions of garden produce or a charity fête with bunting on his lawns. He treated women with gallantry, called them 'the gentle sex', and showed for his own a preference to which scandal did not attach. Neighbours, meeting him with his mother on daily walks, noted that, of the two, she – once toasted at the hunt balls of half Leinster – had now the more military demeanour. Her voice wielded authority, her grip vigour, and she was rarely without an instrument for beheading ragweed blossoms, poking pennyleaves from walls or earthing up wasps' nests.

He retired early to join her on their small estate which he currycombed with fervour. In shining gumboots, shears in hand, he waded through sway-tipped meadows with two handymen at his beck. Like himself, these fellows liked to build pigeon coops, lay stepping-stones or adjust sundials. Between five and six he went in to drink tea – Indian and China – with his mother. Sometimes they tuned to the news, vaguely sipping the aromas of lost empire. Their own concerns absorbed them and it was a shock to find these also threatened. Prices crept up while pensions lagged. The handymen left one day for factory work in Dublin, and professional gardeners, who seemed to be all one could get now, demanded an alarming wage.

Eggs, fruit, tomato plants and dung were offered on a hoarding placed at the lodge gate and sold from the front door as he and his mother, with the ingenuity of their kind, staved off decision. Yet, in the end, like a cosily entrenched weed, he had to tear himself up. He ran an ad in the *Irish Times:* 'Retired Brit. Officer (Dunkirk, Tripoli), RC, some French, seeks congenial post. Anything considered.'

The solution that turned up was just the ticket. A devout Catholic with an old soldier's savvy and organizing ability was *the* man to guide pilgrimages to Lourdes. The salary was small but the job, being seasonal, allowed him to spend half the year at home with his mother. Then, as he remarked waggishly to her, it would bring him the stir and opportunity for mild military bullying that had been lacking since his retirement.

His parties did not include charity cases or invalids – the nursing Orders saw to them – but paying pilgrims who visited the shrine from piety or to ask for some Intention and were usually of the better type. Less better than the captain himself, they enjoyed and looked up to him. For his part, he took an interest in them and grew good at guessing the rub or worry that lay behind each trip. Some were offering it up for the conversion of a free-thinking relative or an alcoholic. Others were barren wives. Most frequent were the modest but hopeful women civil servants, female bank clerks or school mistresses who were going to ask the Virgin for the husband it was so hard to find in the rural regions to which they were posted. These were toughish, thirty-fivish, die-hard Dianas and, although the captain was in the position of a fox watching preparations for bloodsports, he had to admire their grit. Through living without men they had become mannish, played poker, drank gin together and talked – deplorably – in an endless and anguished gush, as though each were at pains to reconcile the waiting maiden in herself with the harpy she had been obliged to develop in order to protect her. With awe – recalling how often his mother had been photographed

just as she was for *Country Life* or *The Irish Tatler and Sketch* –
he assisted at their efforts at femininity. Chiffon squares from
the Galeries Lafayette wavered on the gaunt masts of their tai-
lor-mades; Rouge Baiser caked off inexpert lips, and the straw
hats they bought at the beachwear counter and deposited on
their heads for church visiting filled him with such distress
that he could have wept for them. He had a flair for clothes
himself, having often done wonders with a table-runner and
an old topee at houseparty charades, where his impersona-
tions of well known female actresses were certs to bring down
the house. Yet, from diffidence, he refrained from advising. A
full-scale Pygmalion operation could hardly have been con-
ducted within the scope of their ten-day tour. Anything less,
he saw, would merely make matters worse. He would have
liked to help these lame dogs find and cross their stile, for he
had always been a man of quick sympathy, and was touched
by the dual glow of hope with which they greeted France:
country of the Virgin and of Aphrodite.

'Our Lady doesn't want us to approach her with long faces,'
he would say in their defence if an older woman made a cutting comment. 'We can worship through joy.'

After his first season's guiding, he became as much at home
with the pious lingo of his parties as he had once been with
military jargon. He took to distributing blessed rosaries and
pastilles of dehydrated Lourdes water among veteran friends,
pulling them out of his waistcoat pocket at dinners with a
feeling that this was akin to showing the flag. He had become
convinced of the need for propagating the faith by the irre-
ligion he saw in France. 'Things look bad on the Continent,'
he told his mother and her neighbours, returning from his
pilgrimages with little bulletins as he had once done from
the Front. 'Churches empty!' One day, as his touring bus was
held up by a demonstration on the boulevard Antoine in Paris,
he surveyed the crowd through his window. 'Bally Reds!' he
told his pilgrims. 'Put on a pretty poor show! Listen: they're

singing two different anthems! Still,' he peered ardently about, 'I see a lot of fine looking young chaps out there! Poor Marianne!' He was glad to get back to Lourdes whose clock-work ceremonies consoled him as did the scale on which it was run. A more efficient army. Still, in the older, 'native' part of the town, he could not help noticing a couple of hammers and sickles chalked impertinently on walls. 'We need counter publicity,' he told his flock. 'If we could point to a couple of A1 miracles, it would take those Commies down a peg!'

Two more guiding seasons rattled by with the brisk monot-onous rhythm of the touring buses which told on his ankles and, although his spirit did not waver, his breath grew faintly sour. His health suffered from the food in cheap pensions which he was obliged to substitute regularly for the hotels booked by the agency. This was standard practice. Guides were underpaid and the game without perks would simply not have been worth the candle. He disliked such manœu-vres. They, and the expenditure of sympathy required by his interchangeable charges, slowly bled him, so that off-seasons became convalescence periods.

Then his mother began to fail. She withdrew herself so slowly that her death, at the end of his third season, was sim-ply confirmation of a forefelt loss. The house, empty now and more of a problem than ever – since he had only one pension to count on – tormented and distracted him from his mourning so that, feeling guilty, he suffered even more. Yet he could not bear to sell it, although the drains were bad, rewiring urgent, the roof sagged and moss, soft as old silk, was creeping, loop after loop, like a crocheted shawl, over the hump of the gable. He could not afford a caretaker but friends discovered a handsome, deficient young man who, in return for board and lodging, would look after the place. Suddenly shy of his own house, the captain got a job in the next off-season taking skiing parties to Switzerland and for eighteen months was hardly home at all. Now and then it occurred to him that, with the young man's help, he could run a chicken farm or take paying guests, save his house and give up the guiding. But each time he thought of it, the young man's mild, beautiful, mad eyes flashed in front of his vision and he rejected the idea.

The last group on the last pilgrimage of his eighteen-month stint was a small one and the captain got to know them better than usual. Three sisters were the core of the party: the Miss Laceys from Sligo with whom he played bridge and pretended to flirt. He could tell that this was as much masculine attention as they had ever commanded, and they had not reached Lourdes at all before he had sensed, loneliness having quickened his apprehension of such things, that they were going to pray for husbands.

'Daddy', Miss Kitty Lacey told him, 'died last year.'

Frisky as gun dogs at the season's start, they were emerging from a year's mourning.

They lived in deep country, he found, in unrelieved idleness: a bickering family which had carried childhood games into pre-middle age. (They still, they admitted, liked to make toffee and had a Christmas tree with secret presents.) They played tennis and croquet and clock golf on the lawn. Dance? They loved to and had given 'hops' in the front room, rolling back the carpet and inviting Daddy and a few of his younger friends – until last year. All three belonged to the local tennis and mountaineering clubs and *all three* took continental holidays together. They even played bridge, as now with the captain, sitting at the same table. What man would have the courage to drive a wedge between them? That none had might be guessed from the unwavering hockey-field voices. They were friendly and crossed muscular legs with nonchalance. Maisie was forty, Kitty thirty-five and Jenny, the baby, thirty-two. It was on their passports. Unabused but a trifle neglected like that of nuns, their skin had the firm, unaromatic texture of linen long preserved in drawers. The captain, who would be free in ten days – after this tour he would have six months in which to tend his estate and decide about his future – watched them with understanding and an occasional stab of horror. (The same sensuous fascination froze him when the post-mistress at home larded his letters with her gummy spittle, rummaging with lubricated finger for the envelope on which a little extra postage must be paid.) The sisters were not identical. The eldest, either more intelligent or merely more resigned, had, visibly, set herself to cultivate inner resources. She had learned French, tutored by an Irish priest who had studied in Belgium, and all through the trip was to be seen, in lounges after dinner, fingering her way down the columns of *France Soir*. The captain, remembering country aunts who had died in maidenly loneliness akin to madness, pitied the Miss Laceys. Kitty and Jenny's noisy laughter – empty vessels – had a desperate note and he had seen them sidle with provocative demureness around French railway officials who responded with icy courtesy.

'Wouldn't you think that trio would have the sense to divide up?' Mrs O'Keefe, an elderly widow who had been three times to Lourdes – it was the nicest way she knew of taking a holiday – was interested in the Miss Laceys' predicament.

The captain said something about the Miss Laceys being nice girls.

'Isn't that the shame of it!' she agreed with him. She sighed: 'Mind you, three at one go is a tall order even for Our Lady of Lourdes! It'd have to be a real miracle!'

*

On the return journey, a lightning plane strike stranded the party in Paris. A couple of the older ladies dreaded the crossing by boat and as nobody, it turned out, was pressed for time or money, the group voted to spend a few days at the Hôtel de la Gare.

'Captain! Captain! Maybe we'll have our miracle now!'
Mrs O'Keefe hissed exultantly up the well of the stairs as
he descended for dinner. An expert pilgrim, she got dressed
faster than anyone and posted herself on the route to the
dining-room, ready to pounce on him. 'Look! Look!' She
nodded at the bar.

The captain saw the three Miss Laceys sitting on high
stools, laughing over gin fizzes with two men. He raised his
eyebrows. '*Well!* How did that happen?' The men looked nice
chaps, and the sisters were chattering nineteen to the dozen.
Miss Kitty Lacey's laugh ricocheted across the lounge. 'Ca,
ca, ca, ca!' High and repetitious like the cry of an anxious
crow. Maisie, as if to emphasize a lack of hope, was sitting on
the edge and turned half away from the others.

Mrs O'Keefe had overheard all. She lowered her voice.
'They met them', she muttered, 'at the tennis tournament
at Mount Merrion two years ago. Kitty and Jenny partnered
them in the mixed semi-finals. One's an architect. The other
works in a bank. They're staying in the hotel. English!'

The captain's mind raced in unison with hers: 'Catholics?'
he whispered.

Mrs O'Keefe drew back in annoyance. '*Captain!* I'm
surprised at you! After the present pope's encouragement
of mixed marriages! Anyway, they could turn.' She leaned
forward to his ear. 'The drawback is', she whispered, 'that
there's only *two*!' Again she withdrew herself, this time to
give him one of her fixed-eyed, pursed-lipped, slow and pon-
derous nods.

'Ah!' agreed the captain.

'We', she prompted, 'can invite *one* of them to make up a
party after dinner. I'll get Miss Taylor to play so we'll only
need one to make a fourth. *Maisie*,' she judged. 'Then the
men can invite the other two out on the tiles.' She laughed
with the innocent vulgarity to which the captain was becoming used in pious women.

The plan worked. Maisie's sisters took a boisterous, shame-faced leave of her and had not come back with their beaux by the time the bridge party went to bed. It had been a strained little session, for Mrs O'Keefe, frustrated by Maisie's presence from discussing her sisters' prospects, was too fidgety to concentrate on cards; Maisie played badly too so that by the end of the evening the pair, who were partners, had lost quite a bit.

'Poor me,' Maisie lamented as she paid up.

'Ah well! Unlucky in cards you know!' said Miss Taylor abstractedly and was kicked by Mrs O'Keefe.

The captain's sympathies, repelled by Maisie's play, returned to her on the boomerang of pity. 'Well, this has been an agreeable evening indeed!' He drained his glass. 'One of the pleasantest on the trip. But all good things and all that. Remember, tomorrow we have to rise early for our tour of the City of Light.'

The ladies lumbered upstairs, slowed by drink and confidences. Walking behind them – he had paused to say something to the concierge – the captain saw Maisie's box-shaped form tilt towards that of Mrs O'Keefe. 'Oh super! A regular charmer!' Mrs O'Keefe's hiss floated down the stairs to him. 'Isn't it funny, now, he never got married!' He went into his room and locked the door. He polished his shoes, inserted the wooden trees and carefully tied the laces over them. He had a shower, gave himself a friction with eau-de-Cologne and remembered that the golden rule was to keep things from getting personal. Be *nice* as pie but – off parade, off parade. A bit sticky sometimes. He climbed into bed to read a war memoir in which the human element was considered from a safe, abstracting distance.

Next morning the blue-pennanted busload visited the Sacré Cœur, the Sainte Chapelle, Saint Sulpice and Notre Dame. The pilgrims, weary of churches, gabbled prayers, collected the available indulgences and settled back in their seats with a profane zest when the captain proposed a drive into the country. He took them towards Rambouillet, along roads where mistletoe hung hairy smudges on the limbs of poplars, and sounds were spasms in the air. Returning, they decided to stretch their legs in the Bois de Boulogne and gaped at crisp-figured riders on distant bridle paths. The lake was diamond bright.

'Golly!' Jenny Lacey squeezed old Miss Taylor's arm. 'Doesn't it *thrill* you to be here? Doesn't it make your blood run faster?' Heels puncturing the clay, she took off to sniff the passionate humours of the wood.

Kitty Lacey flung out her arms. 'I want to hug you, captain,' she threatened and did so with a buoyant gesture.

'Oho!' Mrs O'Keefe whispered. ''Tis easy seen a gay old time was had last night!' A conniving elbow stabbed the captain's waistcoat. As they got back into the bus, he noted that Maisie was wearing sensible flat shoes.

*

The next two days the captain left the group to their own devices until dinner time. He slipped off each morning, avoiding Mrs O'Keefe who was lurking at loose ends in the lounge, and did not return before seven. He spent one morning looking at pistols in an antique shop, another reading *The Times* in a bar where he partook of a liver paste sandwich and some Beaujolais by the glass, then meandered through grimy streets in the bleak vicinity of the Santé prison, coming in time to the Jardin de l'Observatoire where he sat by the lake and felt lonely for Stephen's Green. At dinner, Mrs O'Keefe twitted him on his 'mysterious double life', remarking that things moved faster when one was abroad, didn't he think?

The two younger Miss Laceys had meanwhile had their hair done. ('Paris, ha, ha,' said Miss Taylor, 'has gone to their heads!') A sculptural cut, removing the fuzz that had shadowed their faces, revealed hitherto disguised rapacities.

On those two nights the captain played bridge again with Maisie and the two elder women while Jenny and Kitty went dancing with their Englishmen.

'Toodloo!' screamed Kitty, waving an arm bright with a dozen plastic bangles.

'Keep your eye on sis, captain! She'll clean you out!'

'Still waters run deep! She's a cardsharper!'

'And a cannibal man-eater!' They screamed with laughter. Their sister winced. They were gone.

'Whew!' The captain caught Maisie's embarrassed eye. She laughed back at him and he was pleased that she seemed in better form. Probably decided those young chaps weren't worth being jealous over! He couldn't have agreed more. Anyone who would put up with those screeching termagants. . . . Well, Mrs O'Keefe had shown judgement in isolating Maisie from the quartet. She was clearly several cuts above them. . . . Maisie and Mrs O'Keefe won back their losses that night.

The next day was to be the pilgrims' last. The strike had been settled and seats were available on a plane the following morning. In the afternoon the hotel was taken over by a provincial wedding party which sang songs that reminded the Irish group of some of their own and struck up a gaiety in which they soon became involved. They were in the thick of it when the captain returned from his stroll. Someone was playing the accordion and a pair of highly liquored Frenchmen – rural types in stiff suits – had threaded arms through the armpits of Maisie and Mrs O'Keefe and were stamping about to the tune.

'Captain! Come on! Where have you been all day!'

The barman handed him a glass of something and Maisie's partner surrendered her. She was an excellent dancer. Lightfooted.

'I've always said', the captain told her, 'the best dancers come from down the country. Where are the other two?'

'They've been out with their fellows since morning,' she said. 'They're letting the last day be the longest.'

'Well so can we,' he comforted her and whirled her off again, for the accordionist had started up a waltz. The captain had won prizes for waltzing with his mother and told Maisie about this. 'My father was killed when I was twelve. I used to take her to dances from the time I left school, but I never got a look in after the first dance or so. She was so popular.'

'And she never remarried?'

'No.'

'You must miss her.'

'Yes.'

The hotel service had been disrupted by the wedding, so guests had to be content with a supper of cold sandwiches, mostly left-overs. They ate them in the pauses between dancing.

'It's mad,' Maisie said. 'Like an Irish country hotel.'

'It's fun,' said the captain.

At 2 a.m. he sponged his forehead with a damp handker-chief. 'Been overdoing it,' he apologized. 'If you'll excuse me, I'd better retire. Ladies,' he turned towards Maisie who was resting on a couch. He sketched his usual departing bow and toppled into her lap.

There was a snigger from one of the dancing French, too far gone themselves to interpret the situation correctly.

'Captain! Oh! Captain!'

Maisie had been thrown backwards by his impact and now he lay prostrated across her breast. Male smells breathed into her gasping mouth. She tried to lift him but he seemed to have gone rigid and her fingers merely managed to peel his jacket up his back. She probed the intimacy of flesh sweating through his shirt.

'Someone . . .' she begged. 'Please . . . Mrs O'Keefe!' She pulled the flaps of his coat down again. Hugging him vio-lently to her, hands braced beneath his armpits, she got him into a half sitting, half reclining position beside her on the couch. People gathered round at last.

'Captain! Captain!'

'Monsieur le Capitaine! Mais qu'est-ce qu'il a? Il est soûl?'

'No, no, he must be ill!'

'There's a medicine chest in our room! Please, Monsieur, veuillez bien porter le capitaine. . . . Do you mind carrying the captain. . . .'

The accordionist and a friend lugged him up the stairs and along a corridor. His eyes opened, glared. 'Just a touch!' he kept gasping out. 'Nothing to worry about . . . passes over . . . malaria. . . .' O'Keefe and Maisie clucked along behind him. 'Mind his head now!' 'No, no!' he heard Maisie squawking. 'Not here. This is *my* room!' Like one of the three bears. 'Mais alors?' the accordionist complained. The captain, the captain thought he understood him to say, was no feather-weight. If she didn't want him here, why didn't she speak up sooner? *He* wasn't a paid stretcher bearer. ('Elles en font des manières, ces gonzesses!') A door closed. 'Put him on the bed,' O'Keefe's voice cut in. 'Have sense! The man's ill!' 'Yes, yes,' the captain tried to shout. 'Ill! It'll pass. Only cover me up!' His body was shaking with the cold. He hadn't had a bout like this in years. His teeth, his very bones, were clattering with the cold. 'More blankets,' he commanded. 'Hold my hand. Tightly. More tightly. More blankets. More. It'll pass. It'll pass.' He clutched a hand, closed his eyes and heaved like an agonizing fish: his whole body leaping in spasms from the bed. 'Just a few minutes. Never takes more,' he heard himself say. 'Half an hour at most. Hold me, Mummy! Mummy, hold me. Hold me tight. Lie beside me. Keep me warm.'

When he awoke from the nightmares that always came with his bouts, he felt her beside him, turned absurdly the other way so that their bottoms bumped and the arm he was clinging to held her pinioned like a clamp. When she felt him stir, she unclenched his fingers and sat up.

'Would you like a cup of tea, captain?' she asked, brushing down her skirt, tidying her blouse. 'I have a spirit lamp and tea and sugar.' (Wise virgins, they carried plastic-wrapped props against every incursion of the unforeseen.)

'What? What?' the captain groaned, his head throbbing less than he would have liked. There was something to be faced he could already tell. A trifle . . . what? Unorthodox? He could smell scenty stuff. An animal smell not his. He closed his eyes hopefully. Sleeping dogs. Let lie! The malaria dreams rushed at him.

'Tea!' said Maisie with assurance. 'Wake *up*, captain. It will do you good.'

He sat up. 'Where . . . your sisters?' The three had shared a room.

'With Mrs O'Keefe.' She was laying out plastic cups. 'Feel better? I can see you do!'

'Yes.'

'Good!' She plumped his pillow efficiently.

'You gave me some stuff?'

'Quinine.'

He laughed. 'By golly you're a good nurse. I should marry you!'

She laughed, 'crisply', enjoying the role.

'And get me cheap? Have you a drop of Scots blood, captain?'

Mild whiff of scent from her.

'You called me "Mummy",' she told him.

He blushed and decided to expire again.

A minute later Mrs O'Keefe bounced in in a satin kimono to know 'how's the patient?'

Maisie told her he was in the best of form. 'Been proposing to me,' she said. 'I think that's a good sign, don't you?'

Mrs O'Keefe's gargling intake of breath was like the last exodus of water from a bath. 'We-ell! Of *all* the miracles!' (He opened an eye, saw her fling her arms around Maisie's neck, and closed it quickly.) '*This* is what I've been praying for!' gabbled she. '*Wait* till I tell the others! I can't think of nicer news! I declare I'm happier than yourselves! My heartiest congratulations! I'll say a prayer this minute to Saint Bernadette!'

'Mrs O'Keefe! We were joking!' He heard Maisie's squawk.

'*Joke!* After spending the night together! Sure the whole hotel has its eye on the pair of ye!'

The captain trembled.

'We . . . I . . .' Maisie strangled.

'You're excited! Shy! *I* understand! Bridal nerves! I'll keep the others away!' The door closed.

The captain opened his eyes again to see Maisie rush to it, lock it, unlock it and sit miserably in an armchair. 'I *hate* that woman!' she hissed.

'A monster,' the captain agreed timidly.

'We'll straighten things out,' she told him. 'It's ridiculous! Maybe one day it'll seem funny! Old cat!' She began to cry. 'This is nervous! I'm sorry. It's . . . just that *I'm* never going to hear the end of this! Never! Oh!' She buried her face in a cushion.

'Maybe I should go after her,' she said into her cushion. 'At once. But they'd all be at me! I couldn't face them this minute. In the morning,' she promised. 'We'll straighten it out!' She wept.

The captain stared unhappily about him. Charity towards one's neighbour began by leaving them alone. Don't rush in. Give her time to pick up the shreds. Poor girl! Tough furrow! Sisters like harpies! Hyenas! Think of them sucking the marrow from each others' bones for years while he'd been in Egypt, Burma. . . . Locked up together like inmates of some female reformatory! He could just see their house in Sligo! Grey – Connemara stone – with a bumpy tennis-court – no man to roll it – wind-bent trees, fringes of nettle and dock. His eye skidded off the bidet where stockings had been stretched, rose to observe flies and lees of dust in the ceiling lamp. He felt depressed. Squashed somehow. Normal enough after an attack. Drains one. But why the attack? Old age? Ha! No such thing! The wardrobe looked like a pair of upright coffins with claw feet. All the better to trail you with. He would be glad to get out of here.

'I have always tried to be d-d-dignified!' From behind the cushion.

Poor child! 'Now, now!' He comforted. 'This could happen to a bishop. Go on,' he advised. 'Cry! It'll do you good.' But as she did he added: 'What would you say to a walk?'

'Now?' She looked at her watch. 'It's 4 a.m.'

'Why not? We won't sleep after the tea. Fresh air! Clean the cobwebs out of our heads. This is Paris. All sorts of things go on! Let's do a little reconnoitring.'

'And your head?'

'Best thing in the world for it. If you're game we'll slip out on the QT.'

They found a taxi rank and the captain, remembering something he had been told about being able to get a meal at any hour at Les Halles, asked the driver to take them there. 'Some modest place,' he directed. 'We didn't get much of a meal last night,' he told Maisie restively. 'We can go for a stroll afterwards and see the dawn maybe over Paris.'

The restaurant was shiny and noisy. Nobody looked at Maisie's red eyes. Over white wine and oysters she grew febrile.

'God!' she groaned. 'In this city one could be *alone* or choose one's company.' She watched a well-dressed woman who was eating a large meal alone with a book. A bottle of wine in front of her was three-quarters full. 'People don't stare and tattle and pity each other's failures. . . . Oh, what do I know about it? Maybe they do!' She lowered her eyes and ate.

'Couldn't you take a job?' the captain asked. 'Break out as it were? Go to Dublin or London. . . .' Shocked at his own indiscretion, he let his voice trail vaguely away. 'Lots of women are secretaries, aren't they?' he murmured.

'I'm forty,' said Maisie. 'And I have had no experience.'

At the baldness of that he quivered. The unusual hour, the place, the wine after quinine perhaps, above all her frankness stirred him. The captain had rarely probed beneath the patina of conversational formula. What Maisie had shown of her private self troubled him.

'My dear,' he laid down knife and fork, wiped his lips and leaned towards her, 'you could come and live with me! Why not? We can work out a *modus vivendi*. That is, if you would not greatly object. I would respect your privacy. . . . You could depend on that!'

She looked up. 'You mean . . .?'

'Yes, yes!' He smiled in triumph at his own initiative, in assent to the warmth of solidarity, the possibilities that fanned out like fireworks once one removed the lid – the lid of what? The wine danced like a centipede in his throat.

'Marry you?'

'Why not? Why not? Absolutely. . . . That is to say. . . .' He put down his glass. 'In a sense.'

'Because of Mrs O'Keefe? The fuss?'

'Why not,' he insisted bravely. 'We would be marrying to protect each other. From the others.'

'Oh you are *kind*! You want to save my face. . . . We *could* simply let them go on assuming what they do. For a while.'

'No, no, I want you to take the idea seriously! Now that we have it. Unless it strikes you as ludicrous! I think we are compatible!' Over that hurdle, he smiled with his old charm.

'Oh!' she cried. 'No! I mean not at all, but, really, I don't know what to think!' Her colour was as high suddenly as the rouge of women at other tables.

He looked at his watch. 'We have three hours,' he told her shyly, 'until we face them.'

'Three hours. . . .'

'And we needn't tell *them* the truth even then!'

They laughed, astounded at themselves, and he filled up their glasses. They ate their next course in silence. An old man with a heavily painted face sat weeping in one corner over a plate of choucroute. Their glances shied away from him, back to each other, down to their plates. Workers from the market came in on a gust of cold air smelling of mushrooms and wet dungarees, straw, sooty brick, the night. At the cheese Maisie asked: 'Why would you let yourself be rushed into marrying me?' There was coquetry in her tone now. Her eyes were bright. The captain felt he had restored her nerve.

His own wavered forthwith. He patted her hand and an aviary of doubts were flushed up to be shot down like clay pigeons in his head. Pim, pam, poum! They soared again like phoenixes. A wife? Him with a . . . ? But she was discreet. If any woman was. If, if. The gentle particle furred his inner ear. She was making up now, powdering, toning down her triumphant flush, reddening her lips. She smiled at a flower seller passing their table. He bought her a gardenia and she pinned it on. Bending to smell it with the movement of a cat about to lick its own chest, she said:

'My second gardenia! The first was – oh a long time ago – from a young . . .'

'Maisie, don't!' The captain stopped her. 'Don't tell me now!'

He was astonished by his own agitation. Felt like cavalry surprised in the Russian steppe, congealed in mid-stream by sudden ice. He *must* break out of this!

'My dear,' he began. He had cards to be put on the table which he had chested all his life. 'Shall we have a liqueur?' As she smiled he guessed she was remembering that recalcitrant Irish swains drink to give themselves courage to make love to their women. Her bosom was swelling; the mounds on either side of the cleft nuzzled the edges of her dress. Had his offer done all this? Turned her into a Juno? He felt himself shrivel. His limbs folded with the dry movement of a scissors. Yet. . . . She would be a splendid businesswoman. They could run a

chicken farm together – battery system – they would give up
the pilgrimages. . . . Tossing down his drink, he began, 'Maisie,
do you know my name? Being called "captain" unnerves me
and I have something to tell you.'

She laughed a full-throated peal. 'Can *I* unnerve you –
Edwin?'

This time the coquetry was open. He felt the stiffening in
his bones. What did she expect? He glanced at her big moving chest, her voracious mouth.

'You sound ominous!' she teased, her eyes rolling above the
rim of her brandy glass. Self-sufficient now as planets; like
searchlights, like drills they bored into him. Her lips sipped
the fiery liquid. Multimouthed animalities stirred beneath
her skin. Perspiration glittered around her nose.

'Maisie, I. . . .' He eluded her grin.

She stretched out her hand. 'You *are* jumpy!' she exclaimed.
'Are you worried?' Gently: 'You are no more bound than
before you know!'

He grasped the hand. 'Please try to understand', he gabbled,
'that I *have* to tell you this at once. Now! To avoid . . . ambi-
guities. Out of consideration for both of us. I am fifty-four. I
have lived too long alone to fancy myself able to contract for
more. Maisie,' he held her hand in both of his, 'I am suggest-
ing a . . . a union of souls, of affection, not. . . . The Church
has provision for such limited marriages. In special circum-
stances.' He could feel her hand go limp between his. He did
not dare lift his glance to her face. 'I think we could make
a go of it – if you were to agree. There is so much left. So
much of life apart from that side of things. Companionship,'
he begged, 'mutual respect, affection. We would collaborate
on the farm. You would be mistress in your own house. It's a
nice place, Maisie. You would be your own woman. . . . I think
we could help each other. . . .' He stole a glance at her, fell
silent, let go her hand.

She was looking through the windows to where artichoke

crates had been piled high as the door and at the sky where daylight was unemphatically seeping through, like milk soaking a black cloth. Having delivered himself, he began to feel for her. He guessed her to be reviewing – perhaps closing a final lid on – a vivid hope chest, resigning herself perhaps to the soundness – and damn it, he guaranteed *that* – the safety of second best. He stretched out a hand. She did not see it. Poor girl! Was she mortified by the eagerness she had displayed?

'Maisie,' he whispered, 'you needn't say anything now. Let me know later. If . . . we don't have to meet again. I *had*', he pleaded, 'to tell you while I could. . . .'

Or had she understood at all?

She did not look at him again until she had finished her brandy. Her features had contracted. 'Perhaps we'd better be getting back,' she said.

They walked. Buildings were emerging from the night. Tramps slept on gratings along the pavement, kept alive by a minimal flutter of warmth or the memory of warmth on air unconsidered and exhaled by surrounding houses.

'How do they survive? They must be perished!'

'Would you like my coat?'

'Who's the invalid?'

In the middle of the Pont Neuf, she stopped. 'I am going to give you my answer now,' she began. 'I know you to be considerate, kind. . . .'

'Oh,' he cried sadly. 'This means I've been . . . that you're going to say "no"!'

'No! It's "yes"! Yes, Edwin!'

He took her hands. He was touched and would have liked to say something festive, even tender to her. But he did not dare. Instead, he seized her by the waist and rushed her across the bridge in a kind of dance, an access of exuberance that always accompanied (and saved him from dealing with) feelings of a powerful or uncertain nature. 'I'm so glad, Maisie,' he told her breathlessly as they paused on the other side. 'Old

Mrs O'Keefe is right you know! This – for me – *is* a miracle!
A gift. Loneliness you know. . . .'

She gave him her little smile. 'The Virgin left her trademark on her gift, didn't she?' she observed. Then, quickly,
putting her hand on his sleeve. 'But I'm glad too,' she said.
'Truly.'

He seized the hand. 'That's right!' he cried. 'The Virgin!
You've hit the nail on the head! Oh you understand things!
I'm sure we shall get on like a house on fire! You'll see!'

They quickened their pace. It was late and she had to finish
their packing.

In a Small Circus

For moments tight smiles hovered on the solicitor's lips, then expanded thinly as though on the wires of an abacus. 'Desmond Lynch,' the solicitor introduced himself, and thrust a hand across his desk. Jittery! Sean was not surprised. The late Father Tim Cronin had been Lynch's cousin.

'And you are Sean Dunne. Sean, how are you? A sad occasion.'

'Yes.' Guardedly.

'Sit down. Sit down.'

Leaning back and away from each other, the two made reticent probes. Hadn't they, each wondered, met before? Neither could quite say when. Maybe when Sean, then still in short pants, had earned tips by carrying fishing tackle to and from the landing stage? Above on the lake? Fifteen years ago, could it be?

'I'm afraid it could.'

'Back in the slow old days,' said Lynch.

'Yes.'

In Sean's memory a rowboat scored the lake's shine with a wake like a kite's tail. Bottles of lemonade, towed through those waters, stayed cool even on the hottest days, for the lake was fed by mountain streams. Churning past peat and stones, these jinked from silver to amber, leaving a gauze of froth on reeds and sedge. For years Father Tim had been the parish priest in the valley, and Lynch had spent almost all his weekends in a lakeside cottage now rented to Germans.

'Tim Cronin and I were close,' said Lynch. 'Poor Tim! He was a good man!' As though startled by what he'd said, he began to talk about the will and about how, lest unforeseen claims be made against the estate, the bulk of the money could not be paid out just yet. This, he explained, was normal practice. No need for concern! He shook his head, and this time his smile lingered. Did he think Sean still needed reassurance? Sean did. He felt numb: the news gagged him. This legacy, he told himself with shamed eagerness, could change his life. Money! His mind reeled, then raced, working out that there'd be more than enough to get a phone hooked up, employ a boy full time and put his market garden on a sustainable footing! Maybe buy a refrigerated van?

'Sustainable' had been the bank manager's word, last year, when refusing Sean's request for a loan. 'I'd like to be more positive,' the man had said, 'but it's out of my hands.' A business, he had explained, must look sustainable before he could advise the bank to invest. Sean's didn't.

'My bosses like to allow no margin for error.'

'Hard men!' Sean had tried to make a joke of it, but the manager didn't return his grin.

Now though . . . In a way, Sean was just as glad there were drawbacks. They made his luck look less odd – the way silver linings weren't odd when there were clouds. Well, there were plenty of those! Scads! Poor Father Tim had had a bad time at the end. It was what had given him his stroke. Massive and sudden, this had cut him down from one day to the next! A man who had never been ill! Though wasn't it queer that he'd had time . . . queer – the word tripped Sean, but he swept it aside, marvelling instead at the surprise legacy: his big chance. Manna! Come to think of it, wasn't there a lot more money coming than he'd just mentally disposed of? There was! Yes! Jesus! What would he do with the surplus? And so what if people said it was tainted and that there was a stigma attached! He didn't care. Or rather, yes, he cared greatly about poor Father Tim, but not . . . Confusion, spreading, like ink in water, darkened his mind. It could become chronic, he told himself. It could recur like one of those freak pains that are put down to wind or allergy, signals of some hidden trouble that needs to be addressed.

As if pinpointing this, his suit, unworn in years, was painfully tight. The bus-ride into town had left it wrinkled; the waistband was cutting into his stomach, and his feelings were haywire. Sorrow for his dead – should he call him benefactor? – was snagged in awkwardness. He hadn't attended the funeral, so wearing the penitential, dark suit today was his tribute.

He wished now that he *had* gone to the funeral. Paid his respects. Who had, he wondered? Mr Lynch must surely have, but probably nobody else from around here. It was held in Dublin. Father Cronin had been retired from parish work some time ago and put to teaching in a Dublin school. Just as well, people had murmured later, when rumours began to leak.

Sean was anxious about publicity. Would there be more, he asked, hoping the question didn't sound ungrateful, then saw that it did. Hot as metal, a flush burned his cheeks.

'Have some decency!' he told himself. 'Keep your gob shut!' Aloud he attempted to withdraw the query but heard his voice blab out of control, making things worse. 'I . . . it's not the publicity itself, but . . .' He had no idea how to ask for the enlightenment he craved.

'Well that's not my province. However . . .' The solicitor glanced out the window, then back at Sean and paused. The will, he said at last, would have to be published in the newspaper. There was no getting around that. It was the law. When Sean asked how the case would be if he said no to the legacy, Mr Lynch noted that a refusal would not make the matter less public.

'It might make it more so!'

Mr Lynch's spectacles shone, and when he dipped his head to stare over them, his gaze doubled. 'Four eyes', thought Sean idly. A refusal, said the lawyer, would excite comment. Busying himself with papers, he imposed another pause.

This one had a suppressed hum. It was sly: the sort you

got in towns like this, in out-of-season pubs while drinkers stared into the black of their pints and dreamed up slanders. Jokes. Hurtful gossip about – never mind about what! With luck, Lynch was thinking less of slanders than of how to fend them off. That surely must be a lawyer's job, and he looked just the man to do it. Judging by this office – the glass! The pale wood! The space! – he'd got his hands on some of the money now pouring into the county thanks to the tourist boom and grants to big farmers. Sean had seen none of it. But once he got going with his market garden – an idea of Father Cronin's – he could sell with profit to those who had. Not all of Cronin's enthusiasms had been in step with the times, but this one was shrewd. Almost four years ago, while here on a flying visit, he had dropped off a stack of seed catalogues along with samples and advice that had proven spot-on.

'Your farm's too small for livestock,' he'd told Sean. 'That's why your Dad could never make a go of it. But have you thought of draining the lower field and putting up polythene tunnels? There are markets now for fresh vegetables.'

How had he known that? He wasn't even living here any more! He was alert. That was how! Concerned. Interested! A lovely, lively man! And look what thanks he got. Poor Father Tim! He'd put himself out for people – and come a cropper. But he'd been right about the markets. Customers *were* ready to fork out and pay fancy prices for novelties: lamb's lettuce and wild rocket. Chicory, artichokes, mangetout and fennel. Endive and radicchio. Baby marrows. Anything out of the ordinary. The plants thrived in the raised beds of rich mud which Sean had reclaimed from the lake, and already he was sending deliveries to three towns. By bus. With a van he'd be able to go further afield. Posh restaurants were springing up like mushrooms.

Poor Father Tim, who was always ready to rejoice in other people's luck, would have been pleased.

Was there a risk though, Sean worried, that spiteful talk

could hurt sales? How stop it, he wondered? By sending out solicitors' letters? To whom? Best ask Lynch. Paper was plainly *his* weapon. Wedged into box-files, it manned the shelves behind him while, smoothed out on the desk, thumb-worn documents, soft with creases, looked ready to split along the folds. Some, no doubt, held the sort of secrets to which lawyers were as privy as priests. The thought wound back to Cronin and to the stacks, not of paper but of crisply porous pancakes seasoned with jam and whiskey which he had loved to cook for Sean and his mother when he came to their cottage for supper.

'Wouldn't His Reverence make someone a grand wife!' The tart joke had signalled Sean's mother's resistance. The priest, as a friend of her late husband's, had wanted Sean to go to boarding school.

'He's got the grey matter. We could get him a scholarship. Would you not think about it, Maire?'

But the widow thought only of her loneliness. Few, she argued, who left came back! Look what had happened her poor husband, Bat.

What had happened was that Bat, being desperate for cash to stock their small, rundown farm, went to work for a North-London builder, fell off a roof and died. Hopes of compensation died too when witnesses blamed the fall on Bat's having drunk too many pints on his lunch-break in a pub called *The Good Mixer*.

'Poor Bat! Why wouldn't he drink and he far from home?'

Once tears started, talk of boarding school had to be set aside and the widow comforted with more pancakes and hot whiskey.

'*Crêpes*,' the priest called the light concoctions which he tossed with a flourish of his frying pan – he always brought his own – turning them out as thin as doylies and as lacey with air-bubbles as fizzy lemonade. 'Gluttony', he'd say, patting his troublesome paunch, 'is a safe sin and unlikely to lead to worse.' He kept the paunch more or less in order by rowing round the lake or hiking over mountain bogs to shoot snipe.

Another hobby was writing children's books which, to his amazement, made money. He was a lively man whose popularity was heightened by rumours that he had been exiled to this parish after falling foul of Rome. Cronin was a local name, so he was liked for that too; but what gave him glamour was the whisper that he had been groomed to be a high-flier, then grounded. Connoisseurs of sad balladry, the locals commiserated. The false dawn of the 1960s had misled Father Tim who, having joined the Church in its moment of exuberant reform, felt he'd been sold a pup when ex-classmates were punitively dispersed and their mentor, a liberal theologian, kicked upstairs to Rome where the Polish ecclesiastical mafia could keep tabs on him. Cronin himself ended up in what some wag dubbed 'this Irish Siberia'.

'Remember what they say about ill winds? They've blown our own man back to us! We should be grateful!'

'We should be thanking our stars!'

Sean couldn't remember who'd said that. It could have been almost anyone softened by pity and the pleasure of hearing Father Tim sing. For he had that talent too. Both in the gloom of the hotel bar – brown but glinty with glass cases displaying stuffed fish – and out on the lake he would always oblige with a song. And he sang well. Though no one wondered at first whether he felt drawn to riskier pleasures, the question, later, grew hard to dodge.

*

'The Church', Mr Lynch assured Sean, 'has no claim on the money coming to you. It's from his children's books. Did your father read them to you? When my kids were small they loved me to read them aloud.'

Sean, who had thought the books silly, didn't say so. They

were about some animal, and his father's copies had been lent or given away. Sean had been ten when his father fell from the roof, and what he remembered was the priest saying he'd try to take his place, 'until we're all together again'. Cronin had put his arms around Sean and soothed and rocked him until it felt as if his father really were in some way present. After that the priest sang a great, deep, glum but somehow comforting hymn which made Sean cry. Father Cronin had had a thrilling bass voice. Calling him 'father' was embarrassing though, so Sean wouldn't.

'Nor "Daddy"! I can't call you that!' Half laughing, he'd licked smeared tears from his fingers.

'Call me Tim so.'

'I'm too young. People here wouldn't like it. '

'Why wouldn't they?'

'Because you're a priest.'

Father Cronin blew out an angry breath. 'Do they think I should be on the job full time? Wearing the aul' collar?'

'Collar?'

'The Roman one. It's like being on a leash. Like having a sign that says "the wearer of this may at no time be teased, shown affection or otherwise distracted from his function".'

Sean must have looked puzzled, for Cronin squeezed his shoulder and began to sing a song about a cowboy who was 'wrapped in white linen and going to die'. It had an Irish tune and he said that what it was really about was syphilis.

'Don't be shocked,' he told Sean. 'Stories about the pain in everyday lives hold more for us than ones about shootouts and bent sheriffs.'

But Cronin wouldn't have mentioned syphilis to a ten-year-old, so that must have been said years later – maybe when the priest was being obliged to leave the valley and was once again singing his sad songs. Both times he advised Sean to forget the story about his father's drinking in *The Good Mixer* and any notions he might be harbouring of going to

73

London to sort out the treacherous witnesses. 'That's cowboy stuff,' he warned. 'Dangerous! Indeed most dreams of justice and improvement do more harm than good.'

'Was he unhappy?' Sean asked Lynch, who said Tim might have been better off in some foreign slum or shanty town where he'd have felt needed.

'His parish here was getting depopulated, so what was there for him to do? Fish? Chat with me on the 'phone? Take a trip to Cork or Dublin? Mostly, there he'd be, stuck in that grim presbytery with sly young curates whom he daren't trust. Having to mind what he said. A brilliant man who'd loved company and adored children. The stories he wrote for them tell a lot! You'll remember, maybe, that they were about a seal which played so restlessly in the water that a great foam ruff formed around its neck, and people cried, "That seal should be in a circus!" But this was the creature's downfall for it grew ambitious. Of course,' Lynch shook his head, 'it was a secret parable. The seal was Cronin himself: black with a white collar, too clever for his own good, stuck in the wrong element and yearning to be on a bigger stage. That private joke gave the stories edge.'

'It passed me by,' Sean admitted.

'It did?' Lynch looked disappointed. 'That's because you hadn't known him when he was young. I suppose you won't remember the talk of priests marrying either? Tim firmly believed for years that that reform was in the pipeline. Wishful thinking, to be sure! He'd wanted kids of his own, you see. He envied me my three and desperately needed something more than he had in his life. He'd gone to Rome very young as secretary to one of the more go-ahead theologians working on the Council and found it hard, later, to simmer down. I used to tell him that the fiery haloes the old painters drew around saints' heads showed that their brains were boiling like his, and that their purgatory was going on inside them. He'd laugh and say I should have been a theologian. When I read his stories, I told him that his seal's foam ruff was a fallen halo. Ash! '

'Rome was the circus?'

'Oh the Circus Maximus! What else?' Lynch's tone was lightly scornful. 'I suppose you read the stories *about* him too? Later. In the press? Flimsy speculation amplified by gossip! To my mind they'd not have stood up in court. Remember what was said?'

Sean nodded. How forget? It was a year now since Sergeant Breen had delivered his tip-off. The day had been clear and cool. A breeze, ruffling the lake, made it shiver like foil, and the dazzle in Sean's eye lingered long after he'd stepped, squinting, into the shade.

Broom in hand and clad in a cast-off cassock, he was busy cleaning the lake-side chapel for the May devotions when a shadow alerted him. The policeman stood in the arched doorway, blocking the light. The arch was narrow, and Breen was a burly man. The chapel, a Victorian-Gothic folly, stayed locked all winter, and Sean kept the key.

'Mister Dunne!'

'What can I do for you?' Sean's mock-formality matched the sergeant's. He had been to school with Breen's sons, Seamus and J.J., so being addressed as 'Mister' was either a joke or it meant something was up.

'Let's talk in my car.' As Breen's silhouette backed towards the light, the nap on his uniform glowed like filament.

Sean followed him out, then, once in the garda car, wished he had stopped to remove the niffy, soiled cassock. It was only good now for use as an overall when clearing out the mould and mouse-droppings which collected in the chapel every winter. One year he had found bats.

'You've been a sort of volunteer sexton, have you?' Breen put the car into gear. 'Since Father Cronin's day?'

There was something about his tone.

'You know I have.' Sean tried to get the cassock off, but

75

lacked space for manœuvre, and the cloth tore. Rotten! At one time he had enjoyed wearing the old garment. It had carried prestige, set off his waist, and swung pleasingly when he strode. A label with a coat of arms was sewn into one seam. The young Father Cronin had had it made by a Roman tailor, and in its day it had had style. Now, well . . . Sean started to undo the buttons.

'Good thinking,' said Breen. 'Between myself and yourself, Father Mac doesn't like you wearing that. '

'Oh?'

'I thought you should know.'

'Did he ask you to tell me?' That would be like the new PP. Father MacDermot, Cronin's successor, was leery of local resentments and fond of delegating.

'In a way.' Breen drew up in a rough slot hacked out between tall rhododendrons. Once prized, these were now growing too vigorously, and foresters had turned against them. Blossoms, filtering the sunlight, threw purple patches on the grass. 'Have a read.' Breen handed Sean a folder of newspaper clippings. 'It's background. Father Mac wants you briefed before we meet the men from Dublin. They're trying to mount a case against Cronin.'

'Against Father Tim? What kind of a case? Who?'

The sergeant nodded at the folder. 'That'll help understand.'

Sean ran his eye over headlines which someone had haloed with a yellow marker. '*Roman Catholic monks*', he read, '*to attend sex-offenders' programme. Church in disarray. Former headmaster denies assaulting boys in dormitories. Priests to resume duties after police find no basis for allegations of abuse. Teacher at St Fiachra's suspended pending . . .*' St Fiachra's was the school where Father Cronin had been teaching.

Sean handed back the file. 'What's this about?' he asked. 'I'm a gom and an innocent. Make it clear to me.'

'Buggery,' said Breen simply. 'Child-abuse.' A charge, he explained, had been made by a past pupil of Father Cronin's, and was being investigated. There was no corroborative evidence, so detectives planned to look into the priest's record in this parish. 'Two are coming down this afternoon. We got a message to say they'll want statements from men who were close to Cronin when they were boys. Such as . . .' Breen's voice wobbled, 'yourself. Mind you,' steadying, the voice soothed, 'it may all fizzle out. '

*

'You can't prove a negative.' Mr Lynch gave Sean a shrewd look. 'So if rumours bother you, you'd best up sticks and move. Go to Dublin. City people have no time to waste on the past. Here . . .'

'My mother . . .'

'Ah, I forgot. Bedridden, isn't she? With arthritis? So you can't leave.'

'No. '

*

There was probably nothing to it, concluded Breen. Cases of this sort were often either fanciful or touched off by mental trouble. But even those stirred up a stink, and no way did Father Mac or the superintendent of the local gardai want fall-out reaching this parish. 'I suppose that cassock was Cronin's? Best give it to me.' Getting out of the car, Breen took a plastic bin-liner from the boot, folded the cassock into it and stowed the package away. Returning to his seat, he said he hoped he'd made it clear that Father Mac and the super wanted us all to mind what we said to outsiders. That included Dublin detectives.

'Discretion is in everyone's interests. Tell them as little as you can.' The big danger, Breen warned, was the press. Sensational newspaper stories could force the hands of the gardai and maybe lead to cases for damages. Later. Down the road! 'Then who do you think would be left with the bill? Not Dublin! Us.' Breen's tone was weary. His message whorled like the design on a finger print.

*

'You weren't serious,' Lynch hoped, 'just now about maybe saying "no" to the legacy.'

Sean blushed. 'No.'

'That's all right so. Because if you did, people would see it as a guilty verdict. That, coming from you, would be damaging.'

*

'There's nothing *to* tell,' Sean told Sergeant Breen. 'Father Cronin was always an innocent.'

'Good man. Stick to that.'

'It's true. He's . . .' Sean, who had been about to say 'a lovely man', didn't, because just now the words did not sound innocent at all. Neither did 'idealist', which, he knew from Cronin himself, could be code for 'disloyal'. 'What are people saying?' he thought to ask.

'What *aren't* they saying?' Tipping his cap back on his poll, the sergeant threw up his eyes. 'Mostly,' he told the car ceiling, 'they're telling jokes about priests!' Taking a last, red drag from his cigarette, he dropped it through the window, then opened the car door to stamp out the butt. As if ungagged, he began to talk angrily about priest-baiting. 'It's the new sport! People are taking revenge for the way they used to lick clerical boots. That's how it goes! The wind changes and flocks attack their pastors. Killer sheep! Anti-clerical mice! They'll turn on poor Cronin because they used to bow and scrape to him! They'll have it in for you too because they used to envy your friendship with him. Nowadays if they saw you in a cassock, they'd say you were in drag. Cassocks are out! Coats have been turned. Don't look at me like that. I'm too old to turn mine, which is why I'm giving you the benefit of what I know. Steer clear of the lickspittle who gets a chance to spit! My granda told me it was the same when the English left.'

Breen raised his big, soft policeman's palm. Wait, it signalled. 'I know we all wore clerical gear when we were kids serving mass. I did and so did Seamus and JJ. But you kept it up.'

'Jesus, Sergeant Breen!'

'Sean, I'm trying to help. I know you don't go much to pubs because of your father and all. So you mayn't know what people are like now.' The sergeant shook his head. 'They're rabid. Did you hear about the two altar boys in a parish I won't name who tried to blackmail the priest? Threatened to accuse him of abuse if he didn't pay them a hundred pounds apiece, so he denounced them from the pulpit. Guess what happened.'

'The parish wanted to lynch them?'

'Wrong! It wanted to lynch *him*.' Breen's fist thumped his palm. 'What one parishioner told the gardai was that most priests – note the "most"! – only became priests so as to mess with boys. Girls were a risk, but boys were as safe as goats, and access went with the job. "There they used to be", says this fellow, "rows of them with bare thighs and short pants. Choir boys, altar boys and the confirmation class. A sight more convenient than a trip to Thailand."'

Breen's snort of laughter could have been pure shock. The rhododendrons threw a purple splotch onto his already vivid face.

Sean had trouble taking all this in. 'What harm did Father Cronin do anyone?'

'Probably none.' Breen's mood had changed. Adjusting the peak of his cap, he started the engine. 'We'll do our best for him anyway. No need to tell the Dubliners that you and I talked. They asked who here had been close to him, so your name came up. You *were* close, weren't you? What's this that Vincentian used to call you? The one who came every May for the fishing? When you and our J.J. were teenagers. Cronin's "fidus Achates", was it? What did that mean?'

'How would I know?' Sean remembered the Vincentian. Cheerful Father Jones, a demon at the dart board. He'd been one of a succession of holiday priests whose mass Sean had served in the island chapel. 'Fidus?' Sean guessed must be like the dog's name 'Fido'. Faithful?

*

'Remember the talk of false memory syndrome?' Lynch asked.

'Of course. It showed the charges were lies.'

'Not quite. It stopped them going to court. But stories are like viruses. They mutate.'

*

Driving past the lake's sparkle where sharp waves tongued the shore, they reached the small cemetery whose roughly cut tombstones reflected the sparkle. 'What's that tag about not speaking ill of the dead,' asked Breen. 'De mort . . . what? You used to be a great one for the Latin tags.'

'I forget.'

'It's a dumb message,' said the policeman. 'It's the living we shouldn't speak ill of. What harm can slanders do the dead?'

Sean, only half listening, burned to think how he'd gloried in being called Cronin's 'fidus Achates'. He hadn't studied Latin, and the visiting priests must have thought him a parrot. No, it seemed likely now that they'd thought something worse! And Cronin let them. Hot with humiliation, Sean thought 'bastard', then told himself that no, the priest had been moved by – what? High spirits? Carelessness? Loneliness? Affection? Poor bastard! Poor Father Tim.

'De mortuis', he told Breen, 'nil nisi bonum.'

'That's it,' said the sergeant. 'Nil nisi bonum! A pity we can't manage that for the living? Here you are home. Someone will come for you when the Dubliners get in. In the morning, maybe around ten. Will that be all right?'

Sean said it would. Getting out of the car, he started up his own pathway.

'Oh, I'll forget my head yet,' the Sergeant called after him. 'I meant to tell you two other things.' He lowered his voice. 'One is that the fellow accusing Father Cronin isn't suing him personally. Oh no! He's suing the diocese for negligence. That's what they do now. Go where the money is. That's what all these buckos are after! Thousands they want in compensation. Millions if you add it all up. No wonder Father Mac is worried. The other thing is this. One of St Fiachra's School yearbooks has a photo of the bloke when he was fourteen, which is when the abuse allegedly took place. He was the image of yourself at the same age.'

'Of me?' Sean stared. 'What am I to make of that?'

'No idea,' Breen told him. 'Not the foggiest. I just thought it best if you heard it from me and not one of the nosyparkers from Dublin. It might unsettle you coming from them.'

*

Sean's mother was in bed. Her arthritis had flared up, so he brought her tea and listened to complaints about her medication's side effects and general inadequacy. She didn't ask where he had spent the morning. Then, very gingerly he removed the tray. Touching her painfully stretched skin and distorted bones was like handling a bag of eggs.

Taking a plateful of dinner with him – it was warmed-over stew – he went outside and, when he'd eaten it, used his licked fork to prick out a tray of rocket seedlings. The tines were just the right size for disentangling the fine, white, thready roots.

Next, using his fingers, he pressed the sooty compost around each stem. As always, he relished feeling the grain of it ooze soothingly under his nails. He had read somewhere that humans shared genes with plants, and was reminded of a picture Father Tim had had on his wall showing a naked girl turning into a tree. Already her fingers were leaves; the whole of her was as pale and frail as seedling roots, and Father Tim had told a story explaining what had made this happen. Sean couldn't remember it. Some spell no doubt. Some enchantment.

As though the memory had caught him off guard, restraint peeled away and he began to shake. He had, he saw now, been holding himself in and down since the sergeant's shadow fell on him this morning. He hadn't allowed himself to think, even less to feel and now that he did, tears started to flow and he cried as he hadn't done since he'd cried for his dead father. That, of course, was when Cronin had taken him in his arms. Was that what those bastards meant by 'abuse'? Or was fear of the word – or of some addictive reality? – the reason why Cronin had only kissed and cuddled Sean that one time? He had soothed and stroked and held him tenderly – then stopped. Why had he stopped? And never done it again? Why? Was it Sean's fault? Sean had wondered about that, but hadn't liked to ask. How could he ask? He couldn't. His life and Cronin's were hedged in, blocked and braked like – like an arthritic's. By now tears were pouring down his cheeks. They were running into his mouth and ears.

'I think I'm jealous', he said aloud, 'of the abuse-victim. I am! I'm jealous of the bastard!' Hearing his words, he laughed in shock and covered his face with his hands. It was true though. That was the real shock.

*

Lynch stood up and came round his desk. It was time for Sean to leave.

'He told me', said Lynch, 'that you wrote him a great letter. When he was going through the dark night. Sensitive. Private. A bit mad, but comforting. Naturally I never saw it. But did you know that it was after he got it that he changed his will? He wanted to open things up for you, make *your* life a bit easier. Ah, I'm sorry. I didn't mean to make you cry.'

It's a Long Way to Tipperary

For years our garden was full of memorials of Captain
Cuddahy and his weekend visits. A bird-house, our swing,
successive rustic arbours as well as an abortive millrace and
wheel were devised and knocked together on days when he
fled to us from the sulks and furies of his wife. They are fallen
memorials now, for even while he was hammering them in,
the damp Irish air began to corrode the nails, spoiling his
most skilful creations. Not that he cared. 'Play the game for
the game's sake,' was one of his many mottoes. 'Play for your
side and not for yourself,' he would go on if he got started
at all, for he talked for talk's sake too. 'No loitering! Hand
me the mallet. All hands on the job. A bit of elbow-grease to
the fore. Fire away, chaps. When is a door not a door? When
it's ajar! Full marks! Go to the top of the class.' There was
no reason to stop. He was an unharnessed dynamo, eagerly
offering his energy.

I don't know whether he bullied my father into the garden
carpentry or whether it was a dodge of my father's – like his
way of using us as buffers – for keeping the Captain at arm's
length. After an hour or so of sawing, my father would usually
sneak off to write letters or perhaps just to lie down, while
my brother and I engaged the Captain in croquet or clock-
golf. In between shots Cuddahy shadow-boxed, conjured his
handkerchief out of our ears, harangued us with the relent-
lessness of an ack-ack gun. 'Brian, you chump! Golly what a
clot! Your sister can lick you with one hand tied behind her!
Yoicks, a dirty swipe, Jenny! Eye on the ball, Brian! Don't
bend your knee. That's right! Keep the step! Now you have

it and don't forget! Wizard shot! A1.' The Captain was the
only person we knew who actually used the English slang we
read in our comic books and to us it had a Martian glamour. We never tried it with our school friends but preserved
it for him, marshalling our ritual stock of cries whenever
my mother told us he was expected. 'Cooee!' Brian would
scream, 'the Captain's coming. I *say*! How ripping!' He was by
far our favourite person. ''Ands up!' the Captain would greet
Brian and leap over my mother's sofa cocking a bright new
water-pistol or some other unsuitable present. 'Yer ducats or
yer life, yer sweetheart or yer wife!' His stage accents were
always either Cockney or Tipperary. His natural delivery was
a more refined blend of the two. He had known my father
when my father was a boy and he a young man in 'Tip' and
his assumption of the old accent was no doubt a plucking at
the common chord of memory, a reminder of the link which
must have seemed at times rather thin.

When I first remember him, the Captain had just
returned from twenty years abroad with the British army.
He had been in Flanders and India, fighting Germans and
guarding the Empire at a time when my father's generation of Irishmen was promoting a revolution against it. The
Captain, who had joined the British army in 1914 when it
was the only army *to* join and been loyal all these years to a
cherished memory of 'home', was confused to find 'home'
hostile. He must have met countrymen who regarded him
as a renegade, one who, in the words of the song, 'took the
Saxon shilling/And left poor Ireland in her hour of sorest
need'. This sort of language upset the Captain. It was the
sort he liked to use himself. He clung to those people who,
like my father, had known him in his youth and must see
him as the true and honourable Irishman he was. It wasn't
much of a basis for friendship. Hence, I suppose, his unease,
his air of always being in a hurry. 'Must get cracking, must
get cracking,' he would say the minute lunch was over, and

rush off to dig a lazy-bed or mend the seesaw.

If it was any comfort to him, my brother's and my admiration was unlimited. I can remember him with a clarity I cannot achieve for anyone else, not even for my school crushes of that time. He was in civvies then but only recently and unresignedly so. Tailored, perky, small – though *this* only became clear when we grew up – tanned, wrinkled, jerky, chattery, given to making faces, he promoted us during mealtimes, addressing asides to us in the middle of adult conversations and making us feel involved. I can't decide whether he liked children or whether this different and additional audience, permitting him to keep up a second spate of talk, simply satisfied a need to disburse noise.

Adoring him we assumed he adored *us* and never wondered why the father of several children living quite close should spend so much time away from them. Three or four times though, on returning from some errand, I remember coming on him as alone with my mother he paced the laurel walk or drooped with uncharacteristic abandon in an armchair. Unanimated, the wrinkles of his face shocked me. Into my mother's ear he was pouring monologues. Always about his wife. 'Emily,' I heard him sigh at her, soughing and echoing the syllables like a monotonous, single-cry bird. 'What Emily would like. . . . How I failed Emily. . . .' After a first pause of distress I remember rushing in, seized with some of his own nervousness, to interrupt all this. 'Captain Cuddahy, Mummy, guess *what!*' Twitched into action, he turned towards me the face of the familiar merry marionette.

In the years when we met the Captain oftenest, we met his family least, so I suppose relations between him and Emily must have been at their nether point. An Englishwoman he had met on the way to India, Emily had pretensions – 'notions' said my mother – and Cuddahy, hoping to make the money she wanted, had taken his pension in a lump sum and invested it in some small business in the Irish Free State. This effort to graft himself financially on to his old roots failed and he and Emily lived by expedients until the Second World War mercifully broke out and he could join up again. Whenever a glimpse *was* caught of her, Emily tended to be draped in a cashmere shawl and feeling slightly unwell. Her children were notorious cissies – the boys had long curls – and we were not surprised that the Captain preferred to play with us. Clearly, he was permitted no influence over them.

It was at this time that Emily made two or three efforts to run away. She took the children with her and disappeared to stay with English relatives. Once she did this at Christmas and the Captain spent the entire vacation with us. The frenzy with which he helped stir the pudding, folded napkins into hats, and newspapers into boats, birds or bishops' mitres must have driven my father and mother half mad. Even we were getting to know his stories by heart. They were worked-out tales, good for any audience and judged sufficiently well turned to be repeated for the benefit of any guests who might drop in. I suppose the Captain regarded this as singing for his supper.

There was nothing exotic about his memories. He clearly had not often looked out of the mess-room window or beyond the clubs and cafés where his cronies yarned. He was however – and why should he conceal this from *us*? – a bit of an outsider himself. Much of the British soldier's morale and mores did jibe with his Catholicism, but much did not, and many anecdotes hung on a difficult reconciliation of loyalties. A Tipperary tailor's son who had left home to join the army, he had found home waiting for him again among the thousands of Irish recruits and volunteers. These were underdogs; and he too, although in the Second World War he was to become a brigadier, must have known that he was never regarded as a gentleman. This prevented his conforming utterly. More intelligent than he might have been without his underdog's itch, he was progressive, as he saw it, in the treatment of his men. 'Fine, plucky fellows! A gallant bunch! I talk to them as man to man. "If there's anything you don't like, Murphy, you come to *me*," I tell them.'

We had heard this an endless number of times before Brian chose to make his remark. I don't think he meant anything by it. He said afterwards that he was just being argumentative and at fourteen he was certainly a contrary enough chatter-box for this to be true. ' "Come to me," ' the Captain was quoting himself on the start of a long breath when Brian piped up. 'Like Christ,' he cut in. ' "Come unto me all ye that suffer and ye shall be comforted!" A fat lot of good that would do any private soldier', he remarked, 'if the sergeant was down on him!' Cuddahy's face congealed. His open mouth might have just launched a soap bubble. My mother grew upset and there was one of those family rows in which the adults' embarrassment drives them to exaggerate and the children feel the presence of first-degree crime. I have forgotten what punishment Brian got but it overshadowed the holidays. Blasphemy and disloyalty were invoked. Brian wept and explained desperately, 'I didn't *mean* that!' His lean big boy's face grew blotchy and swollen and distressed me because I felt he was too old to cry. (This would have been the Captain's teaching. Only funks and namby-pambies wept.) Mother told us that Cuddahy was very hurt and that it had been dreadful of us not to be kinder on a Christmas when he couldn't see his own children. 'You're a mean pair,' she said. 'Look at the presents he brought you. Don't you know he's poor?' The Captain came up to Brian's room to make peace. He was shy but very manly, cracking jokes, calling Brian 'old chap', 'brick', and giving him a staunch, open, straightforward hand to grasp. Brian wept again, and I who was a year and a half younger than Brian but prouder and more cynical began to turn against the Captain and his code.

*

He was no longer poor when he came to see us next, but we were. The war had begun, hitting my father's business and bringing promotion to Cuddahy who had joined up and was now a major. He could not wear his uniform in the Irish Free State but showed us photographs of himself in battle dress. The presents he brought for my parents had an air of largesse: a case of whiskey, white flour, and tea which was short in Ireland. He seemed to have forgotten Brian's blunder and talked happily about the Irish boys who had volunteered 'to fight the Jerries'. 'All the Irish need is discipline. They've got natural pluck and gallantry. It's interesting too how their religion keeps them up to the mark. Gives them standards of honour you can't expect in recruits from English factory towns, what!' From the pimply, country boys who were pouring across the Channel to enlist for want of the training to do anything else he was constructing a myth, a comforting myth.

He still had troubles, and the private sessions with my mother were resumed. Emily had come back. Her smart relatives had snubbed her when she arrived on their doorstep a few days before Christmas. She was dissatisfied with the rooms they gave her and with the quality of their sympathy. Moneyless, incapable of looking after herself, she returned after a few weeks to Cuddahy. But the humiliation had soured her. She had always refused to send the children to school, insisting that they were delicate and she would teach them herself. To this Cuddahy had acquiesced. Now, however, the eldest boy was thirteen, boisterously healthy, and ignorant as a squirrel. He *must*, the Major insisted, go to school. Very well, said Emily, a *Protestant* school. Never! Certainly! No! They fought every day of the Major's leave until in the end he packed the boy's bags himself, took him off in the train with him and parked him in a monastic boarding school, leaving instructions that he was not to be allowed to see his mother or any Protestant relatives. Emily screamed, sulked, scratched, bit and wept. The boy wept too and refused at the end to shake his father's hand or say good-bye. He was clearly going to be miserable and Cuddahy could see that he would be unmercifully teased by the other boys, for he had had no time to buy him the correct uniform or even take him to a barber. The boy's averted face on the school steps was shadowed by the girlish curls in which Emily took such pride. Cuddahy turned his straight back to the school and set off for the railway station, half throttled with remorse. 'I had a lump', he told us, 'in my throat.'

'Emily . . .' he whispered to my mother as they walked the tennis court which he and my father had begun and which thanks to the war they would never get round to finishing. 'Emily hates me!' He loved her. Strongly. Wretchedly. It was months since she had let him touch her. 'No!' said my mother, '*no!*' 'She hates my religion,' said the Major. 'She hates the Church because for three years it kept me from marrying her. In the end, I married her in spite of it, but she still hates it.' The words came briskly. Clearly these were notions he had gone over and over in his head. 'She wants to be revenged on it.' He sighed. 'Maybe I made her suffer more than I knew. How can I blame her?' Later in the evening he sang 'By Jingo' and 'Your Old Kit Bag' for Brian and talked animatedly about the Jerries and Ities. We were growing older, however, and resentful at not being in the war, so his gusto only left us feeling depressed. He took the night mail-boat for Holyhead and his regiment. We talked of him for several days and my mother told me all she knew about Emily.

*

Cuddahy had met her on a boat bound for India when he was twenty-five and still a lieutenant. She was pale, not pretty, said my mother, but appealing with immense eyes and a good bust. Very feminine. A kitten. Cuddahy had been through the Great War, but a serious view of schoolboy honour and

Catholicism must, my mother guessed, have left little leeway for experience with women. He walked the deck with Emily. They confided. He probably wrapped her frequently in those shawls she still wore when I knew her. He would have taken care not to touch her skin for he was a man of honour and she was married. Being only an imitation English gentleman, Cuddahy was simpler than his models and had nothing of the cad in him. She told him she was unhappy. She had been home to England to have a baby but had miscarried. Now she was returning to her husband who beat her. She played with the fringes of her shawl and turned sad eyes on the Lieutenant. 'There doesn't seem to be any reason to go back to him,' she sighed. Cuddahy looked sternly over the water, reflecting that as a Catholic he was not free to marry her. 'Go back to your husband, woman!' he said. Or so he told my mother later. The boat was a long time getting to India. Afterwards they wrote. Cuddahy began going to confession with unusual frequency. Wherever his regiment was sent he would seek out the English-speaking priests and try them one by one. 'Father, I am in love with a married woman whose husband maltreats her. . . .' 'My son,' he was told, 'do not trifle with the sixth commandment.' Catholicism was at loggerheads with Chivalry, and to Cuddahy, already suffering on the horns of bisected patriotism, the clash was agonizing. Emily wrote imploring letters and he wrote painfully back. For three years he exhorted her to mind her conjugal duties and forsake the mad notions she had dangled before him. Priests whom he continued to consult, offered no comfort, but his confessions kept her image fresh. The shudderings of her shoulders above the Indian Ocean vibrated plaintively on the nerve of memory. At last he formally begged her to leave her husband. She came and they were married outside the Church. Cuddahy – good, plain, loyal and limited Cuddahy – was now a renegade Catholic as well as a renegade Irishman.

I suppose they were happy for a while. Cuddahy's faith

in Emily was unmeasured. She was his idea of an English officer's lady and he was humble before her. She was the real thing and he – well, he must make up by delicacy and honour what he lacked in quarterings. Her tantrums, her inefficiency, her coldness and discontent only reinforced this notion of her. So did her disappointment at having to live in Ireland. The Major understood nostalgia. Experience with her first husband had turned her against colonials, and Cuddahy's scruples made Catholicism odious to her. She made no friends among the Anglo-Irish, who weren't Cuddahy's sort anyhow. It may have been from shyness that she snubbed his Catholic friends. Having met such obduracy in her husband, what might she expect from them?

When the children were born he baptized them secretly with the connivance of the nurse. 'Protestants often find us dishonourable,' he told my mother when confessing this. 'Maybe we are. I've been a rotter with Emily.' Yet not to baptize the children was to deny them salvation. So what choice had he? With each birth a fresh betrayal increased his wife's moral ascendancy over himself and the rift between her and has Catholic neighbours.

'I won't have him brought up to call his mother a concubine,' she screamed when Cuddahy talked of sending the elder child to catechism class. There was no way of regularizing the marriage. Cuddahy remained a stickler and suffered. He never achieved the suppleness of a full-time gentleman or Catholic.

Meanwhile, Emily, who throve on courtship, again found herself restless in marriage. She confided with melancholy flirtatiousness in all the men she met that Cuddahy maltreated her, beat her – the same stories which had hardened *him* against her first husband. They may have been true. Emily invited beating. Who knows what dreams she had dreamed during the years Cuddahy had kept her waiting? There was apparently some solid distinction in her own background and she took badly to the thin times when they were living on debts and the residue of his unfortunately invested pension. Denying their poverty, they rented larger and more pretentious houses than she could keep up or he afford. From visits to play with their children I remember neglected tennis courts, mildewed orchards, hairy shrubberies. Slatternly, unsupervised maids fed us remnants of *foie gras* or cornflakes and water when I stayed to tea. Emily was usually resting behind closed shutters in a part of the house we were not permitted to approach. Her relatives, angry at her second marriage, neglected her and, after that Christmas flight, she did not try to contact them again. She sketched, taught herself Italian, played the lute. Cuddahy admired everything she did. Her framed sketches hung all over their rented houses. He presented one to my mother with some ceremony. She was, he considered, a genius with the lute, and he once attempted to patent some invention of hers, the precise nature of which I have forgotten. With unhappy tenderness he lapped her in shawls and brushed her long hair, losing his temper only when she declared Catholicism a 'religion for servants'.

The war, coinciding with his victory over the children's education, put an end to strife. Within months Cuddahy had a second promotion. As a lieutenant-colonel he was able to rent a Jacobean mansion for her in Tipperary. It had an ornamental lake and some impressive furniture. The drains, we heard, were bad but Emily would not notice a thing like that. She, like Cuddahy, lived largely in her fancy. It was what they had in common although checked in him by considerable competence in his own field. Emily in her mansion, at last satisfied with the setting of her life, felt equipped to meet people on her own terms. Unfortunately, there was no longer anyone to meet. It was too late for her to start in with the Irish, and English people were prevented from coming over by the war. She had no friends.

My mother called on her once when bicycling in Tipperary. Coming in from the pale, fizzing out-of-doors, the mansion seemed mildewed to her, shadowy and full of old paintings, woodworm and rats: 'You could hear them pounding in the attics.' The children were away at school and Emily so uncommunicative that, after drinking the tea slopped out for her by a skivvy, my mother fled.

Cuddahy stopped in with us occasionally at the end of a leave. 'How's Emily?' we asked. 'Grand, grand,' he told us. 'In tip-top form. She enjoys the country. She's a woman of great inner resource.' They were getting on better. Cuddahy's affluent noisy visits must have provided all the company Emily needed. She was cold – 'spiritual', Cuddahy called it, when confiding in my mother. 'My wife's spirituality is hard on a man of my temperament.' After the birth of their youngest child he had said: 'Emily has grown more spiritual. I suppose it's natural in women? It makes me feel a brute.' He was *such* a compact little dynamo! The conversion of his unharnessed energies into desire might have daunted someone hardier than she. Seeing him less, she liked him better. One day he came to us boiling with pleasure: 'Emily's becoming a Catholic.' A padre attached to his regiment was instructing her by correspondence. 'I wouldn't let her consult one of those Tipperary bumpkins,' Cuddahy told us. 'I didn't want some bally overbearing Mohawk threatening her with hell-fire and brimstone and frightening her off. . . . Emily's a spiritual woman. It will have to be handled with delicacy.' Cuddahy wept a little. 'I've prayed for this', he told my mother, 'for twenty years.' We congratulated him warmly. 'You're on the homestretch now,' my mother told him, a little tearful herself. 'Your troubles are behind you.' Cuddahy gripped her hands in his and thanked her for 'her loyalty and friendship in good times and bad'. We drank toasts to him and to Emily and by the time he left were a little squiffy with emotion.

But what, we wondered, about the marriage? Would Emily be expected to return to her first husband to whom she must still be married in the eyes of God? My mother asked her

confessor. He lost her in technicalities. 'Depending on cir-
cumstances', he summed up, 'and the opinion of the priest
involved, I would say he'd advise your friend to live hence-
forth in chastity with his wife like brother and sister. . . .'

*

Cuddahy, who had had a good war, was shortly to become a
brigadier and with the signing of the armistice was offered
a coveted post with the allied command in Germany. He
refused. Emily could not have joined him at once and he
felt she needed him now. Leaving the army he retired to
Tipperary and, hearing no more of him for eighteen months,
we imagined him happy in his obsolete, briar-ridden estate,
instructing Emily in the mysteries of religion and perhaps
making an occasional foray out to renew acquaintance with
the country of his boyhood. We told each other that when we
saw him next he would have absorbed some languor from that
lush country of shadowy fields and greasy rivers. Cuddahy
put out to pasture, like animals released from their function
or driving animus, should have grown torpid, amiable and fat.
We were wrong, of course.

The letter asking my mother to put him up for a few nights
did not tell us much but as soon as we saw him we saw how
wrong we had been. Either Cuddahy's aching nerve had been
imperfectly removed or else the ghost of an ache persisted to
torment him still.

He had come to town on Legion business. He was in
charge of the Tipperary section of the British Legion. Didn't
we know? 'That's the trouble,' he sighed and fumed. 'People
don't *know*! We're forgotten! We need a publicity campaign.
The indifference in this country is worse than the hate! They
don't care about the Irish veterans. Let 'em starve. Let 'em die!
Who cares?' He began to instruct us, pulling papers out of a
Gladstone bag, explaining this activity which perpetuated his

love of the army and loyalty to 'my men', the one-time Irish volunteers, now veterans of an alien army living on small pittances in 'Tip'. Returned like himself to their birthplace, they were outsiders still. Their army memories, even their voices subtly altered by exile, seemed treacherous to the solid shopkeepers whose teenage sons stoned the Legion hall yearly, trampling the red cloth flowers that are sold to raise funds for disabled men on Poppy Day. Above all, claimed Cuddahy, they were forgotten and discriminated against by London headquarters in the allocation of Legion funds. He was coming to Dublin to enlist the support of regional authority in a campaign to help the Irish veterans. 'Where would the British army have been without them at the Somme and El Alamein? The most gallant fighting men. . . .' The Brigadier steamed with all his old enthusiasm.

And Emily, we asked? How was Emily? Emily was happy, happier than she had ever been. 'I reproach myself,' he told my mother. 'I insisted too much in the old days. I tried to ram Catholicism down her throat. If I hadn't she might have converted long ago. She has found serenity and fulfilment in her religion,' he told us. 'It has brought her peace of spirit.'

'Still reproaching himself!' said my mother when Cuddahy had gone out on his Legion business. 'Well, at least it's brought *him* peace,' she said. 'It's a wonder she never did turn before,' said Brian. 'I should have thought she had just the sensibility that makes for the more gooey sort of convert. I'll bet she has a devotion to the nine Fridays and the child saint of Lisieux.' My mother disapproved of this sort of talk. 'I can see', she conceded, 'that all those years alone would turn her in on herself. Well, the ways of the Lord', she hastened to add, 'are many. And *I* am glad for both their sakes.'

Cuddahy returned from lunching with a British Legion man in a considerably shaken condition. His humanitarian arguments and proposals had been scarcely considered before being dismissed by the official. 'A little tinpot bureaucrat,' gasped Cuddahy, 'without the imagination to see beyond the tip of his nose.' The reception was unlooked for, unbelievable. Cuddahy was overcome. 'I'm not a bally nobody, a bally ass. Forgive me, I'm a bit upset.' He shuffled the pages he had not been allowed to show. 'I have experience,' he pleaded. 'I know the situation. I know the men. Helped some of them out of my own pocket. And then that little *clerk*, that bumph-eater – excuse me, excuse me – that self-important, snivelling little paper pundit who's probably never seen any active service at all – oh *I* know the type! – tells me it's impossible. "Why, sir?" I ask him. "Why?" And do you know all he could say! "Figures!"' Cuddahy spat the word out like an obscenity. '"Figures, Cuddahy," says he. "These are the figures! We can't trifle with figures!" "Yessir!" I told him. "Yessir, three bags full, sir, those are your *figures*, but tell me"', Cuddahy grasped Brian's arm above the elbow, staring into his eyes as though they belonged to the tinpot bureaucrat himself. Brian craned backwards from the Brigadier's mad gaze. Cuddahy's zeal was excessive: where it should have persuaded, it repelled. '"Tell me, sir,"' said Cuddahy, and his body, a taut arc, capped Brian's retreating chest in a curiously amorous pose, '"tell me, sir, do you know what a man, a *man*, sir, with appetites, not a cipher, can buy today with such *figures*? You are starving men to a mean and dwindling death who faced a gallant one in two wars! Do you know what your pension is worth, sir, to these men? It's worth blankety-blank-blank! Excuse me, sir, but that's what it's worth!" He released Brian. '"Cuddahy," he told me, "Cuddahy, we simply administrate!" Administrate; pfah! A shivering little rotter!'

The Brigadier stared vacantly at the floor. He began putting his papers away. There was not much to say to him. My parents were worried by his excitement, for although he was only forty-seven he could sometimes look livid and terrifyingly old. Yet to ask him to take things easy would have been to question his indispensability to his men. He left that evening for Tipperary. At Westland Row Station, the old-fashioned Gladstone bag, too big for a brief-case, too small for regular luggage, gave him an odd wanderer's air.

He must have handled the Legion authorities more roughly even than he had admitted, for some days after returning to Tipperary he rang my father up in great agitation. He had been suspended from his functions as head of the Tipperary section. Could my father do something about it? Pull a string of some sort, calm the chap down? 'It's not for my sake,' Cuddahy explained simply, 'it's for the men. They need me.'

My father invited the Legion official to lunch. He was a calm, pipe-sucking, mild-and-bitter Englishman who agreed to reinstate Cuddahy on the strength of a sob-story and incautious promises of good behaviour. 'He gets rather carried away, doesn't he?' he remarked of Cuddahy. 'Hasn't any sense of limits at all really.' He gave my father to understand that he had had to deal with a lot of crackpots in the Legion. 'Idealism and authority are hard habits to lose,' he remarked. 'Bad in civilian life.' Cuddahy, he told my father, had overspent his Legion kitty for the next three years. 'On a lot of deserving cases, of course, but we can't work the miracle of the loaves and the fishes, you know. Figures are tougher even than a brigadier, what!' After brandy and the usual Irish discovery of common friendships, he relaxed further, saying of the retired officers with whom he worked: 'In their heyday none of the old buggers would have tolerated half the nonsense from subordinates that I get from *them*! They're all full of cock-eyed schemes and all would have you know, sir, that they're practical men. . . .' The official grinned. 'They probably were, too, in their delimited sphere – we hope. Let them out and they're dangerous. *Your* friend, for instance, has no sense of the possible. . . .'

*

A year went by without Cuddahy or his wife again emerging from their remote late entrancement. Beyond the dank vistas of Tipperary they pursued their purpose with passion, embattled and in concord at the last. It was a common friend from Cashel who told us of Emily's quarrels with the local clergy and of how she was ardently seconded in them by the Brigadier. Our gossip aroused curiosity by hints and denials before skirling off into a series of what seemed unlikely tales. The parish priest had preached against Emily. Emily had been to see the Bishop. She accused the parish priest of heresy and had written to monsignori she knew in Rome. But what did she want? Probable details stood out, islands among the fantasy. Emily, it seemed, had given a dance in her great mansion to raise funds for the insolvent Legion and the parish priest had forbidden people to attend. *That* we could believe. 'Then that's why she went to complain to the Bishop?' Our gossip shook his head. 'There's more to it than that. She's a dangerous woman,' he said. 'I'd go so far as to say that they're a dangerous pair!' Poor Cuddahy, we thought with amusement. There was no quiet port for him. My father wrote him a jocular postcard about treading delicately in the provinces. A curious letter arrived in reply. What surprised us was the S.A.G. – Saint Anthony Guard – dear to schoolchildren and to servant maids, written on the flap. My mother claimed the printing wasn't Cuddahy's but must have been done by Emily. 'Probably the postmistress,' said my father. 'Forward all available information on Matt Talbot,' directed the letter; 'am doing monograph for *Tipperary Courier.*' *That* was normal enough. Matt Talbot is or was Ireland's most recent candidate for canonization. A blackleg worker who wore chains around his middle even when on the job, he would appeal neither to unions nor to efficiency experts and perhaps, accordingly, has never been seriously pushed as a worker saint. From time to time, however, his cause is taken up. We sent a Catholic Truth Society pamphlet to Cuddahy. Two months later the tragedy happened. We, particularly of course my mother, were deeply involved and upset, and there has been so much talk by now that it is hard to reconstruct what actually did happen. I shall give only the facts that seem reliable.

Emily apparently had a devotion to Matt Talbot even before her reception into the Church. She wrote and put to music little prayers to him and began a biography. So far so good. It kept her busy. She noticed that Talbot had performed no first-class miracles and that therefore one of the essential conditions for canonization was lacking. She started hoping for a miracle to attribute to him. There is great discordance about the rest of the story but everyone agrees that she had a quarrel with the wife of a veteran afflicted with an incurable disease whom she attempted to heal by the imposition of a relic. The man got better, then abruptly worse and died. The widow accused Emily of frightening him to death. Emily claimed that her cure would have worked if not interrupted, while the priest, already offended at Emily's receiving religious instruction from an army chaplain rather than himself, supported the widow and blamed Emily publicly in his Sunday sermon. From here things degenerated quickly. Cuddahy tried to rouse his veterans to boycott the priest's men's club. Emily began to commune directly with the spirit of Talbot, and the priest advised several mutual acquaintances who hastened to refer the opinion back to the Brigadier that Emily was suffering from religious mania and was a danger to herself and to the parish. 'Neither one of them', said the priest of the Cuddahys, 'has a pick of sense.' It threw him off stroke to have the Big House inhabited by Catholics. 'Busybodies,' he said. The Protestant gentry had kept to themselves.

Cuddahy would naturally not accept criticism of Emily, yet he too must have seen that she was growing odd. The village had witnessed several manifestations of her eccentricity and he may have seen others more alarming, for the two of them began to live in strict confinement, emerging only on Sundays to drive to mass in the next parish. It was rumoured that he kept her under sedation. She was, the servants said, more often in bed than out of it. 'She's daft,' the villagers guessed, 'and he's afraid of what she might do next!'

*

On an afternoon when Cuddahy had been morosely considering his insolvent account books, he looked out of the window to see the long snout of the county ambulance drive up his briar-clad avenue and the priest get out of it. Inside the vehicle the Brigadier saw the heads of two other men. The priest, having accepted a lift from the local hospital where he had been attending a sick parishioner, was calling to discuss the matter of the men's club. His own car had broken down the day before and the ambulance happened to have business in the Brigadier's neighbourhood. None of this was known to Cuddahy and, at the sight of the ambulance and his enemy, he assumed that they had come to certify Emily; his dear suffering Emily who had joined the Church because of him was being persecuted and might even now be taken away from him. He was already overwrought. The skivvy declared later that he had been up all night soothing and fussing with his wife. He had only just got her to sleep.

Grabbing hold of an old shotgun and rushing to one of the front windows of the house, he began to yell at two of his veterans who were employed weeding the orchard to come to his aid. The men moved rather cautiously towards the house and meanwhile the priest, seeing this wild figure at the window, shouted what he claimed later was a greeting but which the Brigadier took for a threat. Cuddahy pulled the trigger. The gun was luckily not very dangerous at that distance and the priest only suffered superficial skin wounds.

Cuddahy fired again, this time on one of his own veterans whom in his excitement he failed to recognize and who, as he was nearer, was more seriously wounded. The Brigadier was quite unaware of what he had done and it was the other veteran who rushed into the house and succeeded in disarming him. 'Murphy, what are you doing here? Go and see to the mistress,' Cuddahy yelled as the man took his weapon from him. 'OK,' he agreed. 'Take that and fire if you have to. They're closing in on us.'

The ambulance took away the wounded veteran and a little time later a van from the asylum came with two attendants to pick up the Brigadier. Murphy was busy getting a doctor for the priest and no one seems to have wasted much thought on Emily. Whether she observed the incident or not was never established, but it is probable that she did because that night after closing time drinkers returning from the pub saw her wandering along the road very unsuitably dressed for the time of year – it was November. She had on one of the Indian shawls she always wore when resting and under it a thin nightgown and slippers. She was carrying and clanking a set of bicycle chains which had, she thought, belonged to Matt Talbot. She was quite calm and when the doctor and his wife came to pick her up and bring her home she accepted their offer of hot chocolate with amiable politeness. 'My husband has just joined up again,' she told them. 'He left for his regiment this afternoon.' It was her only reference to him.

*

They are both in the asylum now although I doubt if they meet. Emily is totally estranged from reality but poor Cuddahy has sane intervals which must be painful. It appears that the saner periods are the very ones when he is subject to attacks of violence. My father asked the asylum authorities if we, as his closest friends, might have him over for a visit.

(The children have all gone out to Rhodesia to join Emily's relatives who have settled there.) The authorities agreed, insisting, however, on first administering electric shock treatment which calms him down but also badly impairs the memory. He arrived with an attendant and sat sleepily fingering his teacup – we had been told to hide all decanters and bottles, which made us feel rather horrible, as if we were involved in punishing him. He kept smiling vaguely. Did he remember us at all?

'Sugar?' asked my mother. 'He takes three,' the attendant told her. My mother was vexed. She remembered that herself, had wanted Cuddahy to speak. My father waved out of the window. 'Well, we never finished that tennis court, Cuddahy,' he remarked. Cuddahy blinked, said nothing. 'We were interrupted', said my father, 'by the war. You joined up . . . you went back to the army.' Cuddahy drank some tea and wiped his lips. The attendant watched like a governess. 'Yes,' Cuddahy told him, 'the army. I'm an army man myself. An army man.' There was a pause. 'You, sir, I gather, are not?' he questioned. My father ignored that. He asked Cuddahy instead if he ever went for walks these days around the Tipperary countryside – his attendant had told us that he did. Cuddahy put down his cup carefully. 'Where, sir?' 'Tipperary,' said my father. The Brigadier screwed up his eyes. 'Tipperary,' he said uncertainly, groping in his well of muddied memory, 'it's a long way, sir, a long way to Tipperary.' He smiled contented at having fished up something of consistence. 'A long way to go!' He laughed and wiped his lips.

Legend for a Painting

A knight rode to a place where a lady was living with a dragon. She was a gently bred creature with a high forehead, and her dress – allowing for her surroundings – was neat. While the dragon slept, the knight had a chance to present himself.

'I have come', he told the lady, 'to set you free.' He pointed at a stout chain linking her to her monstrous companion. It had a greenish tinge, due the knight supposed to some canker oozing from the creature's flesh.

Green was the dragon's colour. Its tail was green; so were its wings, with the exception of the pale pink eyes which were embedded in them and which glowed like water-lilies and expanded when the dragon flew, as eyes do on the spread tails of peacocks. Greenest of all was the dragon's under-belly which swelled like sod on a fresh grave. It was heaving just now and emitting gurgles. The knight shuddered.

'What,' the lady wondered, 'do you mean by "free"?'

The knight spelled it: 'F-R-E-E', although he was unsure whether or not she might be literate. 'To go!' he gasped for he was grappling with distress.

'But where?' the lady insisted. 'I like it here, you know. Draggie and I' – the knight feared her grin might be mischievous or even mad – 'have a perfect symbiotic relationship!'

The knight guessed at obscenities.

'I clean his scales,' she said, 'and he prepares my food. We have no cutlery so he chews it while it cooks in the fire from his throat: a labour-saving device. He can do rabbit stew, braised wood pigeon, even liver Venetian style when we can get a liver.'

'God's blood!' the knight managed to swear. His breath had been taken away.

'I don't know that recipe. Is it good? I can see', the lady wisely soothed, 'you don't approve. But remember that fire scours. His mouth is germ free. Cleaner than mine or your own, which, if I may say so with respect, has been breathing too close. Have you perhaps been chewing wild garlic?'

The knight crossed himself. 'You', he told the lady, 'must be losing your wits as a result of living with this carnal beast!' He sprinkled her with a little sacred dust from a pouch that he carried about his person. He had gathered it on the grave of Saint George the Dragon Killer and trusted in its curative properties. 'God grant', he prayed, 'you don't lose your soul as well. Haven't you heard that if a single drop of dragon's blood falls on the mildest man or maid, they grow as carnal as the beast itself? Concupiscent!' he hissed persuasively. 'Bloody! Fierce!'

The lady sighed. 'Blood does obsess you!' she remarked. 'Draggie never bleeds. You needn't worry. His skin's prime quality. Very resistant and I care for him well. He may be "carnal" as you say. We're certainly both carnivores. I take it you're a vegetarian?'

The knight glanced at the cankered chain and groaned. 'You're mad!' he ground his teeth. 'Your sense of values has been perverted. The fact that you can't see it proves it!'

'A tautology, I think?' The lady grinned. 'Why don't you have a talk with old Draggie when he wakes up? You'll see how gentle he can be. That might dispel your prejudices.'

But the knight had heard enough. He neither liked long words nor thought them proper in a woman's mouth. *Deeds not words* was the motto emblazoned on his shield, for he liked words that condemned words and this, as the lady could have told him, revealed inner contradictions likely to lead to trouble in the long run.

'Enough!' he yelled and, lifting his lance, plunged it several times between the dragon's scales. He had no difficulty in doing this, for the dragon was a slow-witted, somnolent beast at best and just now deep in a private dragon-dream. Its eyes, when they opened, were iridescent and flamed in the sunlight, turning, when the creature wept, into great, concentric, rainbow wheels of fire. 'Take that!' the knight was howling gleefully, 'and that and that!'

Blood spurted, gushed, and spattered until his face, his polished armour and the white coat of his charger were veined and flecked like porphyry. The dragon was soon dead but the knight's rage seemed unstoppable. For minutes, as though battening on its own release, it continued to discharge as he hacked at the unresisting carcass. Butchering, his sword swirled and slammed. His teeth gnashed. Saliva flowed in stringy beardlets from his chin and the lady stared at him with horror. She had been pale before but now her cheeks seemed to have gathered sour, greenish reflections into their brimming hollows.

Abruptly, she dropped the chain. Its clank, as it hit a stone, interrupted the knight's frenzy. As though just awakened, he turned dull eyes to her. Questioning.

'Then', slowly grasping what this meant, 'you were never his prisoner, after all?'

The lady pointed at a gold collar encircling the dragon's neck. It had been concealed by an overlap of scales but had slipped into view during the fight. One end of the chain was fastened to it.

'He was mine,' she said. 'But as I told you he was gentle and more a pet than a prisoner.'

The knight wiped his eyelids which were fringed with red. He looked at his hands.

'Blood!' he shrieked. 'Dragon's blood!'

'Yes,' she said in a cold, taut voice, 'you're bloody. Concupiscent, no doubt? Fierce, certainly! Carnal?' She kicked the chain, which had broken when she threw it down and, bending, picked up a link that had become detached. 'I'll wear this,' she said bitterly, 'in token of my servitude. I'm your prisoner now.' She slipped the gold, green-tinged metal ring on to the third finger of her left hand. It too was stained with blood.

Man of Aran

Dear Rose,

You ask for details. Well, Paul turned up here in a stew after Phil and her Greens left Paris without telling him. They were sick of his wanting to protect her from what he considered 'bad' company, when some would say it was the company – Paul included – which needed protecting! Phil, in another age, could have been a great, bossy, troublemaking saint. Or whore. Did you ever come across those porny woodcuts labelled 'Phyllis riding Aristotle'? They show a whore straddling a frail old man who is down on all fours. Cruel? Well, better to laugh than cry! Paul must be seventy!

Anyway Phil and Co. were protesting at the pollution of the Gulf Stream and had got together some small boats and hemmed in an oil tanker somewhere near the Aran Islands. There was a stand-off and a few newspapers took notice. Nothing major. The protesters hoped the oil company would lose its cool, while the oilmen were counting on storms to disperse the boats.

Enter Paul.

He borrowed a yacht from his rich cousins and reached Aran at the same time as the forecast storm. He then had a row with his cousin's skipper, insisted on taking the helm – in his youth, it seems, he sailed a bit – and set forth, in bad visibility, to find and persuade Phil to give up her mad enterprise. This was just as the tanker was attempting a getaway which the little boats meant to stop. Phil's boat was in the lead and Paul sailed right up to her across the bows of the tanker which, having no time to slow, had to swerve so as not to run him down, and hit a submerged rock which tore a hole in it. This led to the spill.

He has, as you'll have seen, been vilified and will almost certainly be sued. His old record was mentioned. There is unpleasant coverage on the enclosed video. Whoever introduced him to Phil did a bad day's work. Write to him. He needs support.

Love,
Dympna

Rose thinks: how sharp Dympna has become! *She* wouldn't make rash introductions as Rose did last Easter in Paris. Not that Rose meant to either. As she remembers it, the thing happened almost by itself.

*

The occasion was ill-judged. The city had shut down, but shops in the old ghetto were open and Rose, racing to lunch, was relieved to see that she could get some sort of groceries here later: a stroke of luck since she had none laid in. Tins, though labelled in unreadable scripts, showed pictures of recognizable food and she could buy that flat Arab bread, since the bakers seemed to be closed. No baguettes sprouted from under shoppers' arms, and the restaurant where she was lunching had only matzoes. Squeezing between tables, she saw a basketful on each.

Paul, rising to kiss her, exclaimed: '*Ma chérie, ma chérie*, you don't look a day older! After – how long has it been?'

One reproach? Two? He didn't let her answer. Afraid he'd be toppled from some high-wire topic! Today it was global calamity. Warily she listened while he hectored her with shy, expectant eyes. Expecting what? In that lean-bean coat he looked like an old-time pedagogue.

'It is good of you to come! But then,' he coaxed, '*you* are good! *Tu es bonne, ma chérie!*'

Unfolding her napkin, she shook her head at this. *No!* Not good! 'I remember', she said, to illustrate this, 'when this street was sooty and smelled like a bazaar. I came here once with a friend who hoped to sell a violin . . .'

'So the universe, darling . . .' Not listening.

She was a touch *distraite* herself. Vintage memories brimmed, starting with the violin on which her lover had played courtly music which mocked their lives. It was curvaceous and reddish and she too had been like that and had needed money for an abortion.

'Which was illegal!' She laid claim to recklessness: 'Not to say scandalous!' And remembered Sephardic women stepping through bead curtains in dim shops to lift the violin from its cradling velvet. Marvelling at its owner's willingness to sell, they warned him in lowered voices against women who could cost him dear. '*Muncho*,' they'd said in their queer Spanish. A non-Jewish woman cost *muncho!*

'Keep your violin, *hijito*,' they'd advised, recognizing him as one of their own. 'A violin will stand to you! Women . . .' They shook monitory heads, not caring that she might understand.

There were women like that here today. Glossy and noisy, they were savouring a taste for North African cooking. *Pieds-noirs*. Or had that word passed from use? Prosperity had reached the ghetto and this restaurant was too dear for Paul.

It was her fault he had chosen it. He had rung to say, 'I heard you were back. People avoid me now,' and she, in her fluster, proposed meeting straightaway, forgetting about Easter and that restaurants might be closed. Poor Paul! He must have tried ten places before finding a free table.

'I'm not coming,' had been her husband's ultimatum. 'And I don't want you making rash promises on my behalf. I bet you made some when you thought he'd die in gaol!'

'Yves! You must! If you don't he'll pay. He'll insist.'

'Sorry.' Yves could be ruthless. 'You'll have to work that one out.'

How? What would the clever Sephardic women have done? Slipped off to arrange things with the cashier? No, that would hurt Paul's pride. Claim to be dieting so as to save him money? Oh dear! How sticky this lunch was going to be! As Yves had known. His knowingness could be maddening. 'He', she had once written in a letter to Paul, who seized on the notion, 'has betrayed us spiritually.' A silly remark! It was touched off by Yves' taking a job with the political party which had pressed to have Paul's appeal quashed. A naive reaction, as Yves had made her see. He worked for the state and that party had come to power. Were its opponents therefore to strike or starve until the next election? No? Well then?

Across the room, a pale face floated among the dark ones. Red curls reminded Rose of, might even belong to – could they? – Philomena Fogarty.

'Aren't you appalled, *ma chérie*?'

Paul wanted a response to some moan about – what? She teased: 'You bring jeremiads to the ghetto, Paul. That's coals to Newcastle.' Had someone said that Phil had become a Green?

'Newcastle?'

'Just a way of speaking.'

Could he be unaware of the pessimism which he sprayed like a tomcat appropriating territory? Or might he – his fingers had questingly clasped hers – be *too* optimistic? This was her first real meeting with him since his release, though there had been a welcome-out party. Right afterwards, she and Yves had gone abroad for some months. She had, though, continued to write to Paul. How drop him?

While he ordered wine, she took back her hand and slid a glance at those red curls. From the age of four, Phil Fogarty had been the star of Miss Moon's dancing class in South County Dublin. At parties she would toss the ringlets which

Rose envied, fluff her skirts, point a toe and sing. Adults adored her. She must be forty now and the hair-colour out of a bottle. Did Greens dye?

'. . . garbled, as I . . .'

She – Phil – was also said to be some sort of healer. With crystals, was it? Or kinesiology?

'. . . no rigour in their . . .'

Like a peg-bag on a shaky clothesline, Paul's bones jigged. He spoke of chaos theory and randomness. A shoulder jabbed the air. Rose sighed. For years Paul had owned an influential magazine and seen no need to please anyone. Now, like a pet creature released in the wild, he misread signals and reacted to trouble with a martyred spite. The world, he noted, was getting its comeuppance. The Soviet collapse had unbalanced it. And what was worse, thought was dead. A Dark Age of the Mind was upon us.

'*Je t'assure, ma chérie!*' He was balding, transparent, furious and frail. When the waiter came to say there's no more sturgeon, Paul gleamed. Pollution! exulted the gleam. Dying seas! *Après moi le déluge!*

'They can only live in one near-saltless sea in Russia.'

'No,' Rose argued foolishly. 'In the US they raise them in pools. I've seen them.'

He pretended not to hear. The waiter said there was sturgeon for one.

'The lady will have it.'

'No, I'm on a diet!'

His disappointment reproached her. But why had he chosen a place where the guest's menu showed no prices so that, for all she knew, the slimmer's salad was the dearest dish? Meals with him had been jinxed since, in his wealthy days, his cook gave her fish-poisoning. Rose had guessed the food was off but Paul, his mind on some cosmic threat, could not be alerted and, from sheer frustration, she'd found herself nibbling the fish. After that she swore not to see him again and would not have but for the blow which fell, freakishly, out of a clear – no, out of a murky sky.

What had happened was that towards the fag-end of the Cold War some secret-service people, enraged by Paul's even-handed editorials, cooked up a charge that he was a dis-informer paid by the KGB, and to back this up got a double agent at the old Soviet embassy to offer royalties for articles of his which had appeared in Russia. The money was handed over in a plain envelope in a public place, the transaction filmed and Paul stitched up.

In retrospect, this justified his contempt for Western par-anoia!

'Westerners', he used to scoff, 'think the Russians engage in industrial espionage, but why would they? The Japanese do it for them! Do you know how many of *them* work in Western labs? They sell what they learn to the Soviets.'

Mocking! Knowing! Like some slick cartoon-figure – Speedy Gonzalez or the Roadrunner – he got so far ahead of himself that, smashing – SPLAT! – into a trap even an innocent could detect, he ended in gaol. Yet Rose knew that his puncturings of pedestrian thinking were performed not for the KGB but for private demons of his own.

Hearing him now expound the notion of randomness, she wondered if he saw it as an absolution. 'On the micro-scale . . .' he said, 'patterns, darling, do not exist!'

So how could Roadrunners foresee a trap?

Or was it the macro-scale? No, Paul did see patterns there. Big. Macro! Those he watched – not the small. Her mind slid back to when she was pregnant by the poor-but-promising violinist who had hoped to keep her, the baby and the violin. A folly. They would – as she had told him, citing Swift – have been reduced to eating the baby. An abortion – legal even then in Switzerland – was the sensible move.

'All right,' he said at last, 'ask your friend Paul for the money. It's peanuts to him.' So she had both men to dinner in her tiny flat. But Paul talked all evening about some macro matter and neither she nor her lover could get through to him about the micro fish inside her which they needed to abort. Selectively deaf, he left early.

'That violinist, What's-his-name,' he told her years later, 'was all wrong for you.'

'I know. We both did. We told you we wanted to separate but couldn't because . . .'

His eye mottled as if reflecting clouds.

'All wrong.'

'We needed money to . . .'

'Such things are never a matter of money.'

She wondered if he thought that still, now that his lawyers had cleaned him out.

'Please see him,' a mutual friend had begged Rose. 'He's convinced people avoid him. The publicity was devastating.'

Remorsefully, she took his hand. It was the colour of the sturgeon.

*

They had first met when Rose was twenty in Southern California, at the sort of party where distinctions blur. Incense stunned taste-buds; orchids were tumid and guests' names a puzzle until she guessed that they belonged to second-generation Hollywood: sons of movie moguls who had made their mark in Europe in the thirties, then fled here from the war. Some Slavic surnames slithered like centipedes. Others were haunted by lopped syllables.

Paul told her, 'I don't belong here.'

Indeed he seemed to lack a skin – unless it was the others who had an extra one? Gleaming, as if through clingwrap, they smiled past her.

'They're not interested in us,' he told her.

Perhaps she had been invited for him? To put him at ease?

In Paris, where it turned out that they both lived, this was often her role. She worked in fashion and was in L.A. to show a collection. Paul had come to wind up a legacy.

'It's my first visit,' he told her, 'since I was six. Forty years ago!' Later he said, 'These people write memoirs about the parents they loathed. It helps pay their shrinks.'

'What about you?'

His reproving kiss set the tone for a friendship which, in Paris, would flourish in a jokey way. He became her Pygmalion, correcting her French and grooming her mind – when they met, which wasn't often. Her relations with the violinist had grown difficult and she preferred not to talk about them. Besides, Paul was nobody's idea of a confidant. He was a man for whom a kiss would present itself as a metaphor or semiotic bleep. A gag, joke or echo. Or so it seemed to her.

She was impressed by him though. He was an eccentric mandarin, boiling with revolutionary ire which was stimulating at a time when it was widely held that intelligence, like the heart, was on the Left. Subversion was the fashion and Paul was generous, hospitable and rich, read four languages and had a court of clever young men, one of whom would eventually marry Rose.

This led to awkwardness when Paul said he had been in love with her all along, but had refrained, through delicacy, from pressing his suit.

In fact he had pressed it, but she had taken it for a joke. He called her his 'wild Irish Rose' and she, playing along, had, he now claimed, raised his hopes.

Hopes? How? Surely, she asked, he remembered her lover the violinist? The dinner in her flat? But Paul had interpreted what he saw in ways to suit himself.

'I thought you were living with him like a sister. To save on rent. I knew you were both admirable and poor!'

And the abortion they'd needed? Their request for a loan?

He didn't remember any of that. 'I thought you were shy and Irish. I thought you were a virgin.'

It turned out that, when he was small, his Irish nanny, shocked by his parents' morals, had consoled him with tales of pure colleens. 'When you're big we'll find you one', she'd promised.

Nanny Brady had had a 'boy' back in Ireland who was waiting for her to put together a dowry and come home and marry him.

'He waited years. And both, she somehow made clear to me, were keeping themselves pure. Why would I think this odder than the rest of what went on in our canyon off Sunset Boulevard?'

'When you were six?'

'Earlier. I was ejected at six. Sent to my grandparents in Paris. Cast out.'

'From Eden?'

'A celluloid Eden.'

It was a sad little tale. Paul's father whose movies charmed millions also charmed his son who, at four and five, lived for the few, short minutes each morning when he was allowed in with the breakfast trolley to snuggle up to a dazzling Dad who would then disappear for the rest of the day. Naturally, this radiant absence ignited the child's fancy more than the humdrum presence of his mother and Nanny Brady.

One day, when both were out, he made for his father's room where he hid in the closet. There, amid vacant suits, tie-racks and leathery smells, his father seemed already half present and Paul waited happily to surprise him. The wait was a long one. Paul drowsed off and some time later was awoken in pitch darkness by frightening noises. Failing to find the closet light, he stumbled out and into the bedroom where he beheld his naked father doing something dreadful to a groaning lady. Paul got hysterics. Secretaries rushed in. Scandal sheets got wind of the thing and his parents' marriage came to an acrimonious end.

'And they blamed you?'

'My mother did. I don't know whether he cared. I never saw him again.'

His father had other wives, but no more sons, so Paul remained his heir. Maybe then, suggested Rose, he should be reconciled with his memory?

'Ah, *ma chérie!*' Squeezing her arm. 'You have a good heart. Good! Generous! Just like Nanny Brady!'

This nanny, despite an alarmed disapproval of films – 'trash' – once took him to see one. It featured Irish peasants whose strengths were the opposite of those animating his father's jaunty movies and equally jaunty life. At this time nanny herself hadn't seen Ireland for years. As the man and woman on screen struggled over barnacled rocks to get seaweed to fertilize their little fields, her tears began to flow and, to hide them, she took Paul in her arms. He had never felt so needed. The feeling quickened his understanding and there and then, he told Rose, he became a man.

'Don't cry, nanny,' he whispered while she sniffled in shame: 'I'm not really, Paul. It's just . . . Oh, I'm sorry; pay me no mind!' Then she hugged him until he too began to cry, while the pair on screen laboured to fill their creels, and sea spray spun rainbows which could have come from his and nanny's tears.

'She was seeing the life she had exchanged', Paul explained, 'for a life among our fake Louis XV furniture. Louis XV was all the rage just then because of one of my father's studio's successes: a smash hit whizzing with sword-play. Thinking back,' he said, 'I see that she must have been quite young – younger than you are now, *chérie*. I lost track of her when *he* gave us both our walking papers.' Paul's morose smile conferred a connection with all this on Rose. A bond and obligation.

His was a name one could see in lights just about anywhere. Like Fox, Pathé, Rank, Warner, Gaumont,

Metro-Goldwyn-Mayer or Disney, its syllables pulsed glamour: bright dustings which the silver screen had been trickling into a drab world for the better part of a century. Once, high in the Andes, Rose saw the name glint in an Indian mud village.

'I'll bet your nanny had just decided *not* to go back to her boy in Ireland after all. That's why she was crying.'

For Paul, this, if true, was one more reason to blame his father's industry's false values. Its pampering dreams.

'*Man of Aran* was the film!' Rose realized. 'Was that the bit of Ireland you saw? Aran? No wonder she didn't want to go home.'

*

'Paul', Yves liked to explain, 'can't forgive himself for accepting his Dad's dosh – *le pognon de papa*. It explains everything about him. His politics. The lot!'

He would then point out how, like Zeus descending, the father had created a seminal scatter. And how the son, as though dreams were dynamite, had laboured to disable them. Just as the Nobel family had funded their Peace Prize with money from explosives, so Paul put his into a magazine dedicated to defusing the soft illusions of our time.

A fanatic! Just look, Yves invited, at Paul's face furled in the ruff of his coat collar! See those white lashes and black-bullet eyes! Black and white as a bag of gobstoppers! 'He wears pinstripe suits as though wrapping himself in writing paper. Or news sheets! Why? Because his Dad was a king of the silent cinema! Paul went back to the medium which his old man's medium displaced! Symbolic parricide!'

Yves should know. Paul, a father-figure to the men who had worked on his magazine, still hoped to revive it. Coming out of gaol with his ideas of eight years ago intact, he could not accept that the political scene had changed as much as Yves said it had. The magazine, Yves had had to insist, *even if* Paul could fund it, had no place in the new order. Its staff had dispersed. 'And,' Yves broke it to him, 'we've all taken new jobs.' Symbolic parricide!

'Remember the riddle,' asked Yves cruelly, 'that asks "what's black and white and red all over"? Answer: "our old mag". Who's going to read it today?' Sometimes, Yves could overstate his case. Uncomfortably. Like a man with a bad conscience.

Paul, fighting back by fax and phone call, would not take no for an answer. He was this way with women too, as Rose knew, for she was one of several whom he courted doggedly. For years he had been urging her to leave Yves for him who was a worthier man. She must, he was confident, see this if she would weigh the facts.

'Do you', she had marvelled once, 'think women are weathercocks?'

'No, no, my dear. I admire women. And your loyalty does you credit. But Yves is not the right man for you, whereas I . . .' And he proceeded, without shame or pride, to lay out his arguments: his superior understanding of her, his age – Yves was 'a mere boy'– equable temperament, income – until he lost it – idealism and knowledge of the world . . . 'I'm speaking', he said, 'for your sake.' He was perfectly coherent, believing as he did in the revolt of reason, the end of cant and the coming of a Golden Age.

Amused, she had once copied out the old quote about the heart having reasons which reason cannot comprehend and sent it to him: a mistake, for he took it to mean that her reasons were weak.

'I'll make a bargain with you,' she'd offered then. 'I'll help you find the sweet colleen that your nanny promised.'

She tried, though Yves made fun of her efforts to procure a Mademoiselle O'Morphy for Paul – who seemed oddly ready to play Louis XV. So perhaps his Dad's taste for bandy-legged furniture had affected him after all? And perhaps some similar lure had dazzled Rose? The shine of Paul's high-mindedness? Of his having perhaps really been an agent loyal to a fading dream of the Left.

'You romanticize each other!' Yves accused.

*

In the end, though the women she found *liked* Paul, they didn't like him enough – while he, susceptible to them all, kept breaking his heart, an organ she thought of as perennially in splints.

What did he lack? One could only guess that turning his back on the cinema – his father's creation – had disabled him. The rest of us speeded our pulse to its rhythms; it was our lingua franca, a thesaurus of codes and humours which Paul refused to learn. Ironies passed him by. Refusing to use its spyhole, he had no idea how people lived and got things wrong – with Shiobhan, for instance, who shared a tiny flat, every bit of which could be metamorphosed into something else. Part of the kitchen became a shower. Beds slid into walls. Bicycles hung from the ceiling.

Into this one day a florist's delivery boy, acting at Paul's behest – 'Send her flowers,' Rose had coached – attempted to deliver a flower arrangement with an eagle's wingspan: a bouquet such as might be delivered to a prima donna on a first night. Had there *been* a first night? If so, its commemoration was tropical. There were lilies with spotted tongues, reported Shiobhan, bird-of-paradise flowers, 'and some willowy thing which caught in the banisters'.

With difficulty this was manœuvred up her staircase – she lived on the sixth floor. Through her door, however, it would not go. Nor was there room to leave it on the landing, so she – in whose budget this made a sizeable dent – had to tip the boy for bringing the thing up, then tip him again to take it away.

'Too wide for my aperture!' she told Rose with ribald wrath and put an end to the courtship. She was trying to stretch a grant for mature students and her life had no space for complications.

'He's too old-fashioned,' was her verdict on Paul. 'A nineteenth-century man!'

*

Add to that his stubbornness – over, for instance, paying for today's lunch.

'I wish you'd let me!'

Sad-eyed headshake. 'Darling, you repay me by your mere presence.'

'But I want to pay. Give *me* pleasure. Please?'

'No, no.' His martyred look.

Rose was starving. The 'slimmers' salad' had turned out to consist of rocket leaves plus one sculpted radish. If let pay she could, even now, order a substantial sweet. A Tarte Tatin or – a man nearby was guzzling one – a Grand Marnier soufflé. Its fumes tantalized her. Hypoglaecemic hunger blurred her mind. She felt a migraine coming on. There was a queue waiting for a free table.

'Perhaps we should go then? As neither of us seems to be eating much? I think the waiters . . .'

'Oh never mind them!' He lit a cigarette. His smoking, which gave her nausea, had got out of hand in prison, so how complain? 'I reserved this table,' he stated firmly. 'It's ours.'

If she could get away from him she could buy something in the street to stave off the migraine. Some quick, sugary fix. Nougat. Baclava. But – she glanced covertly at her watch – he was staring at her with a reflection of her own need. He was an old, needy friend who had requests to make. Stoical, she batted away smoke.

She reproached herself. Hunger, the threatening migraine,

and their joint obstinacy over the bill were pretexts for refusing him; yet he was a man without self, a last, gallant, monkish struggler for Liberal hopes born here in France and now almost universally dashed. All he asked was support. Friendship. Yes, but how did he define that?

He laughed abruptly, 'Remember the poem: "Just for a handful of silver he left us . . ." and what you wrote to me in gaol? You wrote that Yves had betrayed us spiritually. What's the next line? "Just for a riband to stick in his coat."'

*

Her head swam. Had her thoughts leaked? She mustn't get into this argument.

'Spiritual,' Paul gloated. 'That nailed him. You know he's refusing to restart the magazine . . .'

The maître d'hôtel was definitely eyeing their table.

'If we're not leaving we'll have to order something. I', she resolved 'will have a coffee.' That couldn't cost much, could it? Wolfishly, she chewed the sugar lumps which came with it and, energized, found herself marvelling yet again at Paul's persistence. He seemed to brim with expectancy and she could tell that not only he but she was about to be presented with a bill – an emotional one. 'Irishwomen', he repeated, 'are good.'

To sidestep this, she told him, laughing, that for her the word had drab associations. Her school nuns had reserved it for girls of whom nothing else could be said: dim or daft girls who were made to sit on a special bench.

'With me,' said Paul humbly. 'You Irish were goodness itself!'

This was true. She and the others – Eithne, Dympna and Shiobhan – had revived the serviceable old quality, as you might take out your grandmother's furs during a cold snap, once he went to gaol. Arranging rotas for prison-visits, they acknowledged relief as relations with him took on frankly charitable status. 'Poor Paul!' they exclaimed with safe affection. Briskly. Like four nannies.

Rose chewed two more sugar lumps and defied the smile which this evoked. Illogical female, signalled the smile. Chooses the slimmer's salad, then stuffs herself with sugar!

*

Escaping to the loo – let him simmer down a bit! – she was confronted by the gaudy curls of Philomena Fogarty bouncing in three mirrors and sparking in the bristles of her brush. 'Rose!' yelled Phil boisterously. 'It *is* Rose Molloy?' So Rose said 'Not Molloy' and gave her married name. They embraced.

'I thought it was you across the room. Is that your husband?'

No, said Rose. Then the two, who had a lot to catch up with, began to tell about themselves, while freshening their make-up. They agreed that now they'd met they mustn't lose touch. Phil's luncheon companion had had to rush off, so why didn't Rose come and see her flat which was close by? Well, it wasn't hers, but . . . Rose, not listening, tried to remember why she had lost track of Phil and whether there hadn't been some hushed-up story back in Dublin years ago. Gossip, scandal? Yes. That reminded her that she'd better warn Phil about Paul, so she told some of *his* story fast.

'He'll fall for you!' she warned. 'An Irish redhead! He can't resist them.'

Phil said she kept her hair tinted because fire colours were propitious. She had studied colours. Studied them? Yes. Colours had an influence . . . But Rose didn't take this in for they were now heading back to the table where Paul looked less disappointed than Rose had feared at having their private talk curtailed. Have a brandy, he offered recklessly, but Phil said, no, they must come to her flat for some Colomba

di Pasqua which Italian friends had dropped off. 'We'll partake', she said, 'of the dove of peace! Don't you think that's a
noble ceremony?' Then, to Rose's shock, she sat down, leaned
towards Paul and said, 'You mustn't feel bad about having
been in gaol. *I* was for two years!'

Rose blushed at this betrayal of her confidence and was
sure that the usual restaurant noises had stopped punitively
so that everyone could hear. But this was an illusion. And anyway Phil was speaking in a soft Irish voice. A lullaby voice.
She murmured: 'People care less than you think. I was inside
for shoplifting. I was twenty-one at the time and had a record.
I wanted to be caught.'

They left the restaurant and stepped, in single-file, along
a narrow pavement. Phil led the way, followed by Paul and
a dizzy Rose whose headache had begun. She thought of
leaving, but felt she must monitor what Phil would say next.
Besides, the Italian cake drew her. She craved sweetness as
her temples drummed.

The flat had a nursery look. Posters in primary colours
showed smiles and rainbows. A mirror was crisscrossed with
stickers saying 'Refuse to buy ivory!' and 'Elephants are social
animals which live in herds led by elder females!'

When Phil went into her kitchen Rose caught Paul's eye,
but he wouldn't return her grin. Phil brought back a dove-
shaped brioche covered with almonds and smelling of vanilla,
and Rose gagged herself with greedy mouthfuls. Phil, she
remembered now, had been described to her as 'a nutgreen
maid' and dangerous to know. 'Bonkers, a way-out activist,'
the man in the embassy had said. 'She's no end of trouble.'

She had an idea that Phil's troubles had begun about a
dozen years after Rose and she had stopped seeing each other.
This came about when Rose was asked to leave Miss Moon's
Irish dancing class after the boys refused to be partnered with
her, saying she was clumsy and tripped them up. Her mother
was indignant but Rose herself was relieved. At the age of

seven she hated having to wear green kilts and falling over her feet. She would not, however, go on being friends with someone who had witnessed her disgrace.

'Death in the eyes and the devil in the heels,' encouraged Miss Moon and tiptapped a jig with her metal-toed shoes so fast that Rose's eyes were dazzled by her devilishness. Phil was the only one who could keep up with her, but it was hard to see the sprightly seven-year-old in the thick-waisted woman who was now perched on a barstool, wearing odd – propitious? – colours. She returned to her confidences. Prison, she told Paul and Rose, had been a refuge at a time when she could neither stay at home nor go anywhere else. She had planned to be a nun, then, at her farewell dance, an uncle had done some-thing – 'Well, you could call it attempted rape' – which made her feel sullied and unworthy to enter the convent. But she didn't want to stay home either. Thence the shoplifting.

Rose began to argue that Phil should not have blamed herself, but Paul said, no, *no* she had been quite right. Compromises were no good. He'd seen that. 'We in the Left thought we were being practical by accepting them, but in the end we whittled away our principles. An erosion takes place. Hindsight shows that the naive Silone was right and the subtle Togliatti wrong.'

Phil who, Rose was sure, had no idea who Silone or Togliatti were, nodded vehemently at this and nodded again when Paul said his own life had been a mistake. Rose was horrified and tried to argue but couldn't. It was partly her headache. But also the other two seemed to have entered some dense element where they were at ease and she wasn't. A gravity had descended on them and they kept murmuring 'yes, *yes*!' and approving of each other's most outlandish notions. Phil said she was a healer and Paul said she should cure Rose's headache. But there was some impediment to this – Rose's disbelief perhaps? – so, instead, they put her into a taxi and sent her home. Just before she left, she heard Paul agree to

help Phil start up a magazine on Spiritual Ecology, a movement designed to encourage people to think more deeply
about the planet.

*

The video which Dympna sent Rose has news footage of the
oilspill which must have appeared on TV. An RTE anchor
man talks. Oil-spattered seabirds and indignant locals are
featured and then there are shots of a white-faced Paul wearing oilskins and apparently in shock. He doesn't speak. His
mouth forms a small O as if he were about to release an air
bubble. Phil, sitting in a studio, denies that he was a member
of her group or that violence had ever been part of its plan.

*

He would understand that, thinks Rose. Strategy. Sacrificing
the one to the many. Wouldn't he?

She and Yves have returned from a trip abroad to find
Dympna's letter and video waiting. The last time they saw
Paul was some months ago when they invited him and Phil to
dinner to celebrate the first issue of Phil's magazine. It was a
convivial, if odd, occasion when Paul formally thanked Yves
for advising him not to revive their old journal, then thanked
Rose for introducing him to Phil. He seemed dazed with
admiration for *her* and wore a suit of dingy 'green' cotton
which had not been treated with chemicals likely to cause
environmental damage.

Phil spoke of plans for the magazine, some of which seemed
unobjectionable and others demented. She neither discriminated nor made allowance for surprise, and Rose and Yves
found themselves being backed into a polite bafflement which
grew ticklish when Paul asked Yves to help her get a subsidy.

'Governments have a responsibility,' said Phil. 'We have

abused the planet so badly that it may not recover. Some of the abuse was spiritual. This country in particular has poisoned its air with evil. The guillotining of Louis XVI, the crimes committed during the Commune need to be exorcized . . .'

Paul's smile did not waver. Was his pliancy due to senility or love? What damage, Rose wondered, had she wrought by introducing him to this mad woman? Yet now Phil was talking sensibly about pollution. You could neither dismiss nor trust her. Her mind was a gallimaufry, a promiscuous jumble. Maybe for Paul all untrained minds were? Did he think that of Rose's? He had said that with the collapse of Marxism a Dark Age of the Mind was on us. Perhaps he was merely adapting to a new norm?

Rose, in distress, took comfort from knowing that Yves was as upset as she. Gratefully, she reached for his hand and, over the next hours, felt reassured each time they caught each other marvelling with the wistful pity of adults at the simplicity of the ancient young. Phil, who had given up Catholicism, seemed to believe in every other transcendental promise, and Paul applauded her with meek, nodding beatitude. As they left, she insisted on taking a hair from Yves' head to cure a pain he had complained of in his back.

'I need something with your DNA in it,' she explained.

'An odd couple,' said Rose afterwards.

'You're jealous,' Yves accused jealously. 'You loved it when Paul was romanticizing you. Now it's Phil's turn. Irish women appeal to him because they come from a country inured to bondage. He yearns to rescue a needy Irishwoman, an Irish Andromeda.'

'What about asking you for a subsidy? A bit of a nerve, no?'

'Oh *he*'d never mind sacrificing social considerations. He'd sacrifice himself.'

*

The RTE video has cruder things to say about Paul: Cold-War insults from the coverage of his earlier trouble to which she does not intend to listen. She turns off the sound and watches his blanched face. It has achieved the simplicity of archetype: hero or villain. No nuance. And it strikes her that he has come into his true reality. And that this is the reality of his father's hated old medium: the black-and-white newsreel. Now, however, the image shifts, and the boat on which he inexpertly crossed the tanker's path appears, all sails bellying, proud as a racer, yawing and canting to one side as the wind tugs it forward in a great white cloud of obliterating spray.

*

At their dinner some months ago he described a trip he and Phil had just taken to the West of Ireland and how Phil, who had to be with her Greens or her family, left him alone in a hotel for a day or two. It was the off-season. The hotel was empty but for him, and the proprietor and his family had to go to a funeral. 'Will you be okay alone?' they asked Paul and gave him the keys. 'There's food in the kitchen and drink in the bar. Just note whatever you drink on the slate.' This easy-going trust enchanted him and he kept repeating the story with astonishment. 'Just put it on the slate,' he quoted again and again as if he thought of the words as a formula initiating him into a tribe.

Man in the Cellar

Signora,

Yes: 'Signora'!

You will see why we must become more formal. I have a message for you. Take it seriously. IT IS NOT A JOKE.

Carlo (yours and mine) is at this moment chained to a bedstead in the lower cellar of our house. He can only move about a yard or so. His shouts cannot be heard outside the house and nobody can get into it. The doors and shutters are locked. The keys are in a bucket at the bottom of the backyard well. All you have to do when you get there is turn the crank and pull it up. Inside, on a key-ring, are the keys to the front and cellar doors and a smaller one for the padlocks which fasten Carlo's chains.

Relax, Signora. His discomfort is minor. Think of Bangladesh.

He has food and water for several days. He has air, electric light, warmth and a slop bucket within reach. Unless a fire breaks out – and why should it? – he is safe. It is up to you to release him. You can give him life a second time.

I can't.

It was I who chained him up – to his astonishment and, I may fairly say, frenzy. If I let him loose now, there is a real danger that he might kill me before he comes to his senses. You know what his temper is like. You never taught him to control it. This dilemma has been growing more acute over the last few weeks – I have held him prisoner for a month – and the only solution I can see is for me to send you this letter and leave. Obviously, I do not expect to return and shall tell neither you nor Carlo where I am going.

The following points should be clarified at once:

1. Carlo's employers and colleagues think he has resigned from his job. I sent them a letter to that effect a month ago. I forged his signature.

2. I have given it out locally that he is in England where my stepfather has offered him a job and where I expect to join him shortly.

3. *For Carlo's sake*, try not to blab the truth about at once. Give him a chance to think up some cover story to save his face. Also: don't bring anyone else with you when you go to release him. Do you want him to be a laughing-stock?

4. I regret the mess in which our marriage is ending, and I shall do everything I can to make it easy for Carlo to get an annulment. A divorce would be good enough for me but I know it wouldn't suit you and may not Carlo. His experience with me may send him quailing back to the ways of Holy Mother Church: Mum's religion. He may want a Mum-picked, virginal bride next time and girls like that want a church wedding. I have written a page of a longer letter which I intend to leave addressed to you in my bedroom-desk – stating that I never intended our marriage to be permanent, that I entered on it in bad faith and never intended having children by Carlo. I should think any canon lawyer would find all he needed here to invalidate the bond – especially the way they're handing out annulments these days. You see: I didn't entirely waste my time at those churchy dinner-parties of yours where your eminent friend, Count C., used to hold forth so interminably. I recall, by the way, with some joyless amusement, the occasion when I asked him wouldn't it be easy to fake the conditions required for an annulment and *you* cut in with: 'But, Una dear, what would be the point? One cannot lie to God.' I do not say that my page x is all lies but *if it were* would you object to my lying to God on Carlo's behalf? Or might you not feel that the lie of a lapsed Protestant was

justified by its end? Luckily, you don't have to reply!

5. I shall stay on with Carlo for twelve hours after posting this. Posts between Volterra and Florence being what they are, I daren't stay longer. This means that, at best, he will have been alone only an hour or so when this reaches you and, at worst, a day. It shouldn't take you more than two hours to drive here.

By the way: did you notice anything odd about the letters you got from Carlo while you were in Austria? I wrote them.

Never mind, Signora, I'm on my way.

I hope you are too. Get into your car or taxi. Yes: take a taxi. You are distraught and we can't afford an accident at this point – which is why I'm registering this. It tells you all you need to know for now. You will find a fuller explanation of what happened in the letter in my bedroom-desk drawer. That took me some days to write. It is an apologetic [sic], not as formal as I would, in retrospect, have liked, but I have no time to rewrite it. Now that I am finally leaving, I regret the bitterness – the insolence – of its tone. But what do I not regret? And what use is regret? Embittered relationships pollute lives. Better dissolve them and recycle the elements. I am recycling myself. I'm orbiting off. Good-bye, Signora Crispi,

[signature] Una

The following pages, sealed in a large foolscap-size envelope addressed to Signora Francesca Crispi did not, as the narrative will show, ever reach her.

When I think of the satisfaction this letter will give you, I have to stop myself tearing it up. You, I have to remind myself, are a minor figure in all this and your reactions do not matter one way or the other. Besides, I *want* to write everything out once, sequentially – then I will probably never think of it again. I will manage to muffle as much of it as possible in that private blanket of oblivion that I can feel, almost *see* in my brain sometimes. I pull it down like a soft, hairy, comforting screen. It is brown, woolly (maybe a memory of a pram-rug in my infancy?), and I summon it when I want to blot out some nasty memory. It always works. One can only use it when one intends getting right away from reminders or witnesses to the event to be blotted out: which is what I am doing. I've done it before. It is surprisingly easy to do when you live in big cities. I can see your disapproval, poor provincial lady! You twitch and tut-tut and nod and shake your head and start in on your repertoire of gesture – like an animal. Half the words you use are meaningless. I used to count them at meals sometimes, the number of meaningless words you used: baby-talk, grunt-words, expletives. Even *I* speak better Italian than you do most of the time, Signora! If you were forbidden to say *uffa, tsts, bah, beh, ma, macchè, magari, thth* (tongue wetly parting company with pre-dental palate), *toh, totò, caca, pipi, poppò, moh, già, eh, oh, ah, eeh* and a few more, you would be at a total loss. You might even lose your reason, like animals whose familiar environment has been abruptly changed for some scientific experiment. I used to imagine I was the scientist doing it to you. It was one of my favourite fantasies: blot *uffa, tsts, bah,* etc. out of Signora Crispi's mind and observe results. Subject shows signs of incipient paranoia. Begins to cluck. Prevent clucking. Subject whimpers. Prevent whimpering. Subject reveals withdrawal symptoms, reverts to animal posture, crawls on all fours, barking. Memo: prevent this. Subject stupefied in trance or fit or otherwise. I played this scenario in my head through many a lunch. Tell me where is fancy bred? In frustration, rage or sheer bloody boredom.

Maybe I should have had some sisterly pity *for your* frustrations? Even proverbs know that '*chi dice "ma," core contento non ha!*' But I was too unhappy myself to worry about you.

Sudden doubt: could it be that you truly *are* paranoiac – I've wondered on occasion – that you might not release poor Carlo but keep him tied by the legs, the way you had him as a baby? That I've given him back to you just as you always wanted him: dependent. You can clean up his *caca*, give him *totò*, be *la mammina* again to your somewhat oversize *pezzetino, donnino, piccino-picciò*? God, how I hate baby-talk. I take this seriously. It is not inconceivable. I think I'd better send a telegram from Milan to the local police chief, warning him to check on you. I owe it to Carlo. Three days after my first letter reaches you, the telegram will be sent. And another to the family doctor. So watch it, lady.

Facts: I want to tell you the facts. In sequence. I despair of explaining *why* I did what I did – though, oddly, I feel you may understand. Power-games are well known to you, Signora Crispi. *How* I did it will be more easily narrated.

First: my need for equipment, i.e. weapons. Carlo, as you know, is a big man for an Italian and in good shape. When we fight, he wins: history of the sex-war. I wonder did you ever fight his father? Physically, I mean? *Macchè!* I see you sniff, purse your lips, half shrug, turn away. *Tsts!* A woman has her own weapons. A true woman uses tact, charm, humour, patience. Translate: guile, pussy and a readiness to let herself be humiliated. Right? Right. I've used them all. I've enjoyed them. Some sick pleasures can be touched off by nausea. In Carlo too. Your son, Signora, is not quite the clean-cut Mamma's boy you sometimes like to think.

The last few sentences may not mean much to you. That's just too bad. I have no time to bridge the culture divide *and* the generation gap. It would take more than Caesar and his minions to build a bridge like that. I was coming to the question of equipment, tools, weapons in the most simple sense – metaphor will get us nowhere. To spell it out: Carlo used to knock me about.

Try to understand this: I had never known people hit each other until Carlo did it to me. My parents never hit me, much less each other. It would not have occurred to them to do so. It was not part of my experience. It was something one saw happen in films or read about. It happened, one knew, in the more old-fashioned boys' schools: a purely masculine, father retrograde practice which should, and soon would, be abolished like hanging and the birch. If Carlo had threatened me with a chastity belt or infibulation, I could have hardly been more outraged and determined to resist, whatever the risks – and there were risks.

You've seen me with a black eye. It wasn't the only one I got. I had to go to a doctor with a dislocated neck, and again with my nose. The inside is all twisted up even though the line of my profile is unchanged – which is lucky since I intend to peddle my wares on new markets. (Am I annoying you?) Anyway, these rows didn't always end in bed. Sometimes, as the front door banged, I was left alone and seething with the bitterness of the impotent. Oh yes, I have hated Carlo. Remember we had practically no money. That miserable job your cousin got him with the safe pension at the end was – but I must keep to the point. We were going through a bad time, fighting maybe once a day and although I was terrified of being disfigured, I put my pride in never backing down. Verbally, I am a champion. I can humiliate, ridicule, provoke, dose my effects, deviate things towards a little sado/masochistic romp or escalate to what sounds like a final rupture – would *be* a final rupture if we weren't living in Volterra and, as often as not, without the fare to Florence in our communal kitty. I suppose I half enjoyed those rows. I had nothing else to do. Volterra is not a jumping place. The cinemas seemed to show a sequence of slapstick films by Ciccio and Ingrassia – a *purely* Italian taste, may I say – or else those panoramic wet-dreamers' fantasies designed for Near-Eastern markets. They bored me. I was bored. I had intended doing some designs for shirt fabrics and sending them back to London where an old art-school mate was to try and flog them for me, but somehow I did very few during our year in Volterra and what I did didn't get sold.

I blamed Carlo. The letters from London were kind but I

could tell my old friend thought my stuff lousy and that it was living in Italy and being spoilt and lazy that was the trouble. This bothered me. You see I *had* been good. I had been one of the few people who actually got work while still at art school. Nobody doubted but that I would make out. The scholarship to Rome – won in the teeth of several talented men – was supposed to have set me on the high road to success. It turned out to be a high road to Carlo and an existence just a shade more stimulating than a battery hen's.

Oh, you tried to help! You used to invite me to Florence and 'occupy' me with visits to dressmakers and hen parties. God, the grotesquerie of those! The quintessential vacancy of the talk! Its sediment is stuck in my brain: kernels of dehydrated, interchangeable chat. Just mix and stir: 'Darling/ super/oh/ genuine/real/pure Austrian loden/English tweed/ morals/mohair /porn. . . . My little-woman-who-knits. . . . My little antique dealer. . . .' (You had nothing but dwarves at your service!) 'Have another cup of. . . . What a lovely cup. . . . Yes, from Capodimonte. My aunt left me a set of cups, but when the charwoman broke a cup and I tried to replace it, they said, "Signora, that cup." . . .' Uuugh! Eeeegh!

I used to imagine someone had done a lobotomy on me. It was a nightmare I kept getting: my brain had been furtively removed. When I woke up I was never really reassured. I'd hear myself sounding like *you*. When I was still trying to perfect my Italian I used to copy your intonations and later began to feel I'd sucked in your mental patterns as well. '*Sì, diamine,*' I'd hear me say, 'I always wear pure silk next to my skin: so much cooler and a natural fabric. . . .' Actually, when you got intellectual, you were worse. It could be so embarrassing when you sounded off on ecology that sometimes I'd interrupt to ask how to make a 'true' lentil *purée* and get you back to what you understood. You never minded. Lentil *purée* was closer to your real interests. '*Pian, pianino,*' you'd recommend, 'that's the whole of it. Never let them boil up.

Pian, pianino. Slow but sure! *Chi va piano va sano e va lontano!* Remember that, Una!' Once I dreamed I was making lentil *purée.* All night, endlessly, repetitively, I kept stirring the brown, manure-like slop, the smooth, cosy *caca. Pian, pianino!* Stir, stir. When I woke up I had a crying fit.

'I've lost my mind,' I told Carlo. 'I'm turning into a cow like your mother!'

'Must you be rude about my mother?'

'I'm not rude. *She* thinks women are cows. She's quite happy to be a cow!' I said. 'She's always saying it. "Pick women and oxen from your native district," is her number one favourite saw. *Donne e buoi dai paesi tuoi.* Do you think', I screamed, 'that that's polite to *me?*'

'She's very patient,' said Carlo. 'She's a saint. You do everything you can to embarrass her with her friends. What would it cost you to conform a bit?'

'A saint? Shit!'

'Words like that . . .'

'Shit, shit, shit!' I roared so the neighbours would hear.

Carlo went to have his breakfast alone in a café.

That was the day I bought the shackles from the old-iron man, the *ferraiuolo* who used to pass by once a month with an old cart drawn by a mule.

I wonder can I make you understand? Am I mad to try? How could you see my reality with my eyes? But I want you to. I want to make you. Once. Even if only while you read this. Then you will reject it, feel contaminated and try desperately to wash off the memory and flush it out with talk, exclaiming and wringing your hands.

The *ferraiuolo* is a dry old man whom I like. He goes down our street at regular intervals, shouting his cry, buying and selling old iron – buying mostly or even cadging. He scarcely expects to *sell* any in our middle-class district. Sometimes, though, he has a few hooks for hanging flowerpots from balconies or some other appurtenance of bourgeois living: an old lantern, some piece of wrought iron he hopes might please our knowing eye. I often give him coffee. This is not the done thing. You disapprove. You've told me so. The neighbours find it odd. Oh all your forebodings are being confirmed! I can see your smug, martyred look as you read this.

I had been fantasizing a lot over the previous months: day-dreaming. My scenarios were banal. In one, a design of mine won a prize and led to my getting a job in London which was so well paid that Carlo threw his up and followed me. This made me the breadwinner and very soon he began to feel diminished. This was the climax of the dream which would then taper off in a *largo maestoso* with *me* comforting *him*. A more satisfying scenario dealt with our fights but reversed their pattern. In the dream I won. Usually, I turned out to have been taking secret karate lessons and one day when he was being especially odious I would suddenly throw him over my shoulder. It was an orgasmic dream and had to be used sparingly. I only indulged in it when I was feeling particu-larly humiliated. It was a great pick-me-up. After a few good dream kicks or karate throws, I felt sorry for Carlo and rather tender towards him. When the real Carlo came home, he was astonished to find me changed from a resentful termagant into quite and amiable wife. I think he concluded that I was responding to firm treatment. He was wrong. What was hap-pening was that I was beginning to believe in my dream.

It was one of those slapstick Ciccio and Ingrassia films which gave me my next idea, which was this: I would creep up behind Carlo and hit him judiciously on the head. The blow must not be fatal but must be hard enough to knock him out cold. While he was out cold I would tie him up. Next I would drag him down to the cellar where I would keep him a prisoner on bread and water making him do my will.

Puerile, Signora? But remember where Carlo is now.

I didn't for a moment think I would do it. My fantasies were – I thought – purely therapeutic. They kept me from breaking up a marriage which I wanted to keep going. They helped me through what I thought of as a bad patch. Because something was sure to turn up soon. Carlo would get a transfer to some proper city where I would find work and where we would have friends and more money. It was just a matter of hanging on.

As the dream grew too familiar, I had to keep escalating it. Like a drug, I had to up the dose, and like ink in water it began slowly to spread until it was thinly colouring my waking life. The first actual move I made was to buy some pieces of old lead piping from the *ferraiuolo*. They were quite short, about a foot long. I told him I was going to do an assembly of metal scraps as a sort of garden sculpture. That sort of thing was popular enough and he was not surprised. Instead, I wrapped each separate piece of piping in a number of old socks and hid it. Piece number one was in our bedroom below my underwear. Piece two was in the kitchen behind the pressure-cooker. A third was in a drawing-room vase. And so on. The idea was that next time Carlo and I began to fight I would put my cellar plan into effect.

It must start with a row. I must have provocation. This was riskier than just creeping up on Carlo when he was reading the paper or eating breakfast, but the game, I felt, had rules. *He* must hit me first.

Oddly – or perhaps understandably? – our rows slackened off after I bought the lead piping. When we were sitting in, say, the dining-room a tiff would begin to simmer and danger, unknown to Carlo, would loom. There was, for instance, the time he complained about the pasta and asked how long did it take an intelligent woman to learn to time it? His sister had known how to cook pasta since she was eight and he had no doubt I thought myself cleverer than she. Behind his back, in the cutlery drawer of the walnut sideboard, wrapped innocuously in a damask napkin, lay piece of lead piping number four. All I had to do – but I don't have to tell you. I gloated – and conciliated.

'Well,' he heckled, 'deny it. Deny that you think Giovanna is a dumb little thing.'

'I do deny it.'

'Can't you sound more convincing?' His fork was embedded in glutinous spaghetti. He tried to extricate and wind a few tubes. They broke. 'Glue!' he spat. 'Giovanna . . .'

'I *like* Giovanna.'

'You'd like to influence her. I must say I admire your gall. You're only two years older than she. You don't understand this country.' (Another poke at the congealing mess.) 'Yet you take it upon yourself to lecture her.'

'You weren't supposed to be listening.'

'Well I was.'

'Anyway *she* was lecturing *me*.'

Giovanna of course is *your* spy, Signora! Your victim, doll, mouthpiece and punching-ball. Poor Giovanna. She's waiting to be married before settling down to being one person. Meanwhile there's no trusting her. She and I – though she may deny that now – got on quite well. Alone together, we both let ourselves say a little too much. I liked drawing her. She has that frail blonde Florentine beauty and it bothered me to think how some sexy brute like Carlo will one day squash her flat. *I* enjoyed Carlo's juicy gaminess, but I'm tough, whereas you brought poor Giovanna up to be subservient. Oh yes, you did. Can you deny that when we stayed with you, you always got her to iron Carlo's shirts? Over my protests, of course.

'Oh,' you said, laughing, 'it's good practice for when she'll be married.'

Putting *me* in my place.

'Una', you said, 'is an artist. She designs shirts. We can't expect her to iron them.'

The galled jade winced.

'You're an artist,' said Giovanna the day Carlo – as it turned out – was eavesdropping. 'So it's different for you. Besides, you're not a Catholic. Nobody has to be a Catholic. It's a free choice. If you make it, you live by it.'

We were talking about birth-control.

'Tell me,' I asked, 'when were *you* offered a choice? To be a Catholic or, for that matter, a woman?'

'Or', threw back Giovanna, 'to be alive at all. But I *am* alive and if I live I ought to do it coherently. If I try to change the rules, I'll make a fool of myself. I have no power. The best *I* can do is conform elegantly. That's the civilized way.'

'You have power over your own body.'

'Uncontrolled appetites', Giovanna stated, 'are obscene. One must practise restraint. What would you think of a glutton who pierced a hole in his belly, evacuating the masticated food through a pipe – let me finish! Through a pipe into, say, a disposable plastic bag so that he could go on ingurgitating more unnecessary edibles? The idea disgusts you, doesn't it? Well *I* feel the same disgust at the idea of a man evacuating all that risk-free sperm into a disposable plastic container!' (Had she got the hideous image, do you suppose, Signora, from some preacher at that convent school you sent her to? Or was it some lewd local confessor who fanned her scruples with his prurient, garlicky breath?)

'But, Giovanna,' I answered, 'if your husband doesn't do it with you he'll do it elsewhere. *You've* been brought up to control yourself but the male half of the population has not. Assuming that you *can* control yourself once you get married – which is highly questionable – no Italian male is going to accept the same restraints for himself.'

We argued it back and forth and it ended up with Giovanna having a crying fit.

'I'm asking you', said Carlo next day, 'to leave Giovanna alone. She must wonder about *me* after the way you talked. She must think I'm a sex maniac.'

'Come off it, Carlo, the only thing wrong with Giovanna is

that she's a virgin, twenty-two years old, idle and living with her mother. She's bursting with repressed sex. Put a match to her and she'd explode. All she needs is a few months on her own in Paris or London.'

'If ever I leave you', said Carlo, 'you should try your hand as a pimp. It's a good refuge for sex-obsessed women in their decline.'

When he is as nasty as that I know I have him. He has lost his cool and I can toast him on the spit of his contradictions. For Carlo – did you know? – is an uncomfortable hybrid. He's two-thirds cool cat, a third residual Latin. The cool cat carries the Latin like a caudal growth: something disagreeable and reversionary whose removal would require painful surgery. It makes him easy to torment. But I forbore. Piece of piping number four restrained me. I savoured the responsibilities of power.

I was going to tell you about the shackles.

That purchase was a consequence of my earlier one. The *ferraiuolo* decided I was obviously a good market and took to showing me his most unpromising junk. I suspect he sold my name – there is a trade in such tips – to other pedlars as a likely gull, for all sorts of beggars, tripe-vendors, rag-and-bone men, gipsies and tramps began to call. None of them had anything I wanted until one day, about three months after I bought the lead piping, the *ferraiuolo* himself turned up with an object which he assured me would figure marvellously in an artistic assemblage. It was a set of fetters. Or perhaps two sets. I'm not sure, since I could never decide whether they were intended for shackling one four-footed or two two-footed animals or perhaps merely the rear hooves of two four-footed ones. Anyway there were two separate units involved. Each consisted of a pair of U-shaped pieces of iron with holes through which an iron bar was threaded. The iron bar itself was about five feet long and pierced at its extremities with holes through which stout chains were passed. These chains could be fastened by a padlock. Since each U-shaped fetter contained six holes in all, the bar could be threaded through at varying levels so as to diminish or enlarge its size. At their largest, the fetters would fit a man's ankles, at their smallest, a child's wrists.

'What were they for?' I asked the *ferraiuolo*.

He shrugged. 'Maybe they were used in a slaughter-house? Or a stud? Maybe they were an instrument of torture? They're very well made anyway. Lovely handiwork! You won't get a finish like that nowadays. An odd object anyway. It'll intrigue people. Nobody will have seen another. They could even be part of some old historical object.' The *ferraiuolo* waved his hand imaginatively. 'Like, ah, I don't know, maybe a set of stocks, why not? *Un ceppo, si.* Maybe I should try and sell them to an antique dealer, if you don't want them. I'm giving you first refusal because you're a customer, that's fair, isn't it? A night club might use them. They're suggestive.'

'Mmm.'

'Listen,' the *ferraiuolo* tried humour. 'If your husband has an eye for the women, you could use it to tie him by the leg, haha! I'm only joking; you understand, Signora. It's just my way. No offence meant.'

'OK,' I said. 'I'll take them.'

*

In fairness to myself, I think I should describe one of our rows – started, as it happens, by you. It was last December and you had driven over with your guilty Christmas gifts and gossip. An American friend of mine, you reported, had walked out on her Sicilian husband. *He* had retaliated by kidnapping their six-month baby and fleeing to Messina. An English girl who works at the British Institute had taken her in and, together with some left-wing lawyer friends, they were about to take legal action to recover the baby.

'Of course she hasn't a hope,' you said. 'A mother who leaves her husband has no rights at all.'

'But surely *you*', I asked, 'are on her side.' In view of your regard for motherhood, I thought you might at least be on the fence.

'Me? No. Why? If she made a bad wife, she'd make a bad mother.'

'How do you know she was a bad wife? Because she is an American?'

You dodged that one. Though you mayn't care for foreigners, you probably rate Sicilians a bit below them.

'A woman', you said, 'who can't make a success of her marriage will never make one of child-rearing. A woman's first obligation is to her family. No matter what her husband does, *she* must work to keep it together. Your American friend made rather a mess of that, didn't she?' You shrugged.

The argument dwindled off. I forget the rest but have a strong image of you with your freshly highlit hair, bolt upright on our couch: a stiff old mummy decked in the pride of matriarchy and certitude. When you left, Carlo said I had been disagreeable. I denied this.

'She knows Mary-Lou is a friend of mine. She needn't have sounded so pleased.'

'It's a matter of principle with her.'

'Well I', I told him, 'have principles, too. I think I was forbearing.'

I went into the kitchen. I'm not domestic. I've gone through that phase. However, this year, I had made an effort and cooked a number of plum-puddings. Plum-pudding is one of the few English dishes foreigners like and I was going to serve one at Christmas, one at New Year and a third at Twelfth Night. The rest were for giving away. For the honour of old England I had gone to a lot of trouble, taking no short-cuts and making everything as traditional and genuine as possible. There were eight altogether ranged on the shelf in their cloth-covered bowls and I was looking at them now, realizing that I'd forgotten to give you yours to take with you. Suddenly, Carlo came charging into the kitchen. He had obviously been smouldering blackly for some minutes. The Mary-Lou case is the sort that can upset him badly. In a calm moment he would be totally on Mary-Lou's side and indignant at the anomalies of Italian justice. But let a for-eigner – me – express that indignation first and Carlo can do an about-face in no time at all. Seeing me absorbed in admiration of my plum-puddings, he put up his fist and swept all eight of them from the shelf. Two broke. The cloth cover came off another so that it spilled its contents. Five were intact. He began kicking at these.

'Stop! Carlo!' I caught his shirt, pulling him away from my last puddings. He pulled backwards and the shirt tore. I clawed at it some more. It was silk, especially made for him in London and he was proud of it.

He began banging my head against the wall. I reached for his balls but he caught my elbows. . . .

No need to give you a blow-by-blow account. As usual, I was left, when he finally stormed out of the door, with bruises, a headache, a torn dress, no plum-puddings and a strong sense of injustice. He came back in a couple of hours and apologized, wept, accused himself – *and you* – said . . . What does it matter what he said? My nose was swollen and stayed that way for a week. My eyes had begun to have a permanent puff. Sooner or later he might disfig-ure me and what I resented and could not forgive was the permanent disparity between us, the superior muscle which he could use even when he was wrong and knew it. But – I didn't want to leave. There was my recurrent dilemma and we both had bad tempers.

I suspect – I *know* – that your favourite image of Carlo is as Mamma's little-boy in his First Communion photograph: about three feet high, squared shoulders, milk-toothy smile,

'English-tailored' suit and great white rosette. No matter what I tell you, about the Carlo of today, you will close your eyes, shrink him back to manageable proportions and present him with that satin rosette for innocence. If innocence means ignorance of other people's needs, then Carlo certainly gets that rosette. If it means – as my dictionary would have it – 'guileless or not injurious', he doesn't. Carlo's guilelessness is a self-deceiving act: guile camouflaging itself.

Shall I tell you more about our rows? They always started for no reason but the root-reason: resentment-left-from-the-row-before and ended with Carlo sitting on my chest weeping over the damage done to me and proclaiming his innocence.

'Una, *you know* I can't control myself when I get started. Why do you provoke me?'

'What's provocation?'

'Look at the state your face is in! Your looks are being ruined. Una, don't try to tangle with me! I beg you. Look, I *try* to hold myself in. I *do* hold myself back. You *know* that! Christ, if I were to let myself go I'd have killed you ten times over. *I'm stronger than you*, you silly bitch. *Madonna Santa!* You'll have to hide in the house for a week now or people will think I'm an animal! *Che figura!* Una, look at your neck! And your eye! Do you realize I could blind you? Why do you do this to us? Una? Why?'

Carlo wept a bit, caressed me a bit, blew his nose and began to talk again.

'Your trouble', said Carlo, 'is that you're not sure of yourself as a woman. You're afraid to *let* yourself be womanly. But womanliness is a wonderful thing! Una, Una,' his fingers promenaded my neck, 'why do you look so ironic? Irony is the weapon of the timid, do you know that? Of the people who are afraid of the great – the simple things in life!' He had an erection. 'Close your eyes,' he whispered.

I did for a minute; then I opened them. Carlo had closed his. He was lying on his back, his head a piece of forgotten jetsam, his hips working, his teeth bared, laughing only in the sense that we sometimes say an animal 'laughs'. A line of verse swam into my head: 'Those great sea-horses bare their teeth and laugh at the foam.'

'Ha!' Carlo crowed. 'You're liking it! Aren't you? Aren't you? You can't help yourself, can you? *Donna, sei troppo donna!* Ha-aaagh!'

After making love – not right after but in, say, three-quarters of an hour – Carlo tended to become testy, even truculent. He may have felt he needn't be pleasant any longer since he wouldn't need me again that day or he may have held some sort of grudge against me: a sense perhaps of loss. He usually began by taking back his earlier apologies.

'The truth of it is you're a masochist. You *like* me to hit you. What's more you know it gives you an advantage by making me feel bad. My mother always said . . .'

'Your mother . . .'

'Don't say a word against la Mamma! She sees through you all right. It takes one woman to see through another!'

'If only she would keep out of our affairs! If only she would shut . . .'

'If *you* shut up we wouldn't have any problems. Women aren't *meant* to argue with men. Look, Una, in the natural world every animal has its weapon. Some are passive. Take the skunk or the hedgehog or the snail . . .'

'Pleasant company. Come on, you stupid bastard. Get up off my chest and get me a drink.'

We'd probably laugh then and make up, but peace was precarious. Carlo was alert to the distinction between humouring and submission. He hated to be laughed at. He would try to laugh back but usually the laugh persisted until it became a bellow.

'Sense of humour,' he would begin in an amused voice. 'The great British invention: weapon of the inarticulate. When in doubt, laugh. It covers a multitude, doesn't it? Especially it covers snobbery, because one always laughs *down*, *vero*? One laughs at the inferior, the mildly grotesque! No *proof* of one's own superiority is needed. The laugh does it all: Haha, haha, ha!' He rushed at me suddenly. 'Haha!' he howled.

'You're hurting me again!'

'Laugh while I'm hurting you. Let's see the sense of humour working while I hurt you! Mmm? Not so easy? Why don't you laugh!'

'I'm waiting for you to cry.'

'Me? Cry?'

'Didn't you know you always do? It's your gimmick. I laugh. You cry. Tears,' I would howl, for by now he would be twisting my arm or pulling out handfuls of my hair, 'tears prove, ha, sensibility. Stoppit, you bastard! You're a repentance addict,' I yelled, 'you got hooked at the time of your First Communion when they gave you that nice white rosette. Stop, you're breaking my arm.'

And so on. Only the venue changed. Once we fought in the bathroom of a party in Florence where Carlo thought I had been flirting with a bearded hippy and I got so messed up that Carlo had to bribe the hired help to smuggle us out at the back. Another time when we were fighting in one of the backstreets of Volterra – cowboy-style we had left a trattoria to finish things outside – a policeman challenged us. Carlo explained that he was my husband and merely arranging his domestic troubles in the only way that seemed to work. The policeman was welcome to see our identity cards if he wished. The policeman did. He may have thought I was a whore or Carlo a molester of women. However, when he saw the cards, he agreed with some embarrassment – Southern gallantry may have been a touch uncomfortable – that, yes, a husband did, in effect, have certain rights, though not exaggerated ones nowadays – '*Siamo un popolo civile*' – such matters *were* better settled within the family domicile, but the law was chary of . . . well, yes . . . Good evening Signor Dottore, Signora . . . He retreated.

*

Carlo lies dead.

I hit him too hard. I finally hit him and, in spite of being wrapped in three of his own old socks, the piece of lead piping smashed his skull. Maybe his skull was one of those freak ones: paper-thin. Some English literary figure, I forget which, fell backwards off his chair and cracked his skull and died. The autopsy revealed that the bone had been so thin that the slightest tap could have killed him at any point in his life. Maybe Carlo's too was paper-thin? But will the Italian police find this out? Will they consider it an attenuating circumstance?

'*Commissario*' – should I say *brigadiere*? What *are* they called? What? *Maresciallo* perhaps? – 'I swear I never meant to kill him.'

The *Commissario* has heard that one before.

Carlo lies limp, blood oozing thickishly through the roots of his hair. The neighbours crowd in: all women at this hour. They wear housecoats or else carry string-bags full of greengroceries and udder-shaped flasks for oil. They stare at the unnatural foreign woman who has killed such a fine man, such a decent, good-looking stud lost now forever to their timid lusts.

'*Gesummaria!*'

'*Che strage!*'

I could say it was passion. Passion-crimes are respected in Italy, leniently punished. Jealousy? Say he was sleeping with one of the neighbours. Which? They all look ready for it: tumid, womanly women. It might even be true. They'd deny it, though, band together, make a liar of me. And then: are Englishwomen *allowed* passion? Madness more likely: *pazza inglese*, mad Englishwoman. The photographers are being let in. Flash. Shall I look mad? Throw myself on the corpse? Cry, scream? No. Close my eyes. It *was* passion. It *was*. Not their sort, perhaps, but passion, yes. I could have left if I had not been so possessive: just said, 'Good-bye, Carlo, sorry it didn't work out better. I shall remember you fondly.' He'd have found someone else. The shit! *Stronzo!* This way he's mine – for all he's worth. Cut off his head, shall I, and plant it in a pot of basil? A bit disgusting really. There's no death penalty in Italy but they have *mediaeval* prison conditions. I've read about them: scandalous. How shall I get out of this? The policeman is writing his *verbale*. Words from the crime columns of the evening papers agglomerate like flies on jam: black flies attracted by the jammy blood of Carlo. *L'imputata*, that's me: the accused. But I have accused myself. I rang the police. Will that count in my favour? I should have a lawyer. Don't say another word until I get one. The moment I put down the phone I started bashing myself up, trying to leave convincing bruises. I threw myself against furniture, beat myself black and blue with a belt – beautiful variegated welts. I wanted to have a black eye but I hadn't the nerve. (Try punching *yourself* in the eye!)

'We were having a fight, *Signor Commissario*. I reached for something, I didn't know what, to hit him with. I was mad, blinded with pain, not thinking, *Signor Commissario!* He was much stronger than I!' Look at my bruises, my torn hair, my dress in ribbons – pity about that eye! 'It turned out to be the meat mallet!' (As you might imagine I'd got rid of the bits of lead piping. Down the well.) 'Poor Carlo, I never thought . . . I bought that mallet only a month ago. It's made of boxwood. I got it to flatten veal so as to make thin, thin veal scallops for him, cooked with sage the way he liked them. In oil. . . .' Distraught wife! 'How could I imagine. I didn't even aim, *Signor Commissario!* He was twisting my other arm. Look at the bruises! And then . . . it happened before I knew it. How *could* I . . . Poor, poor Carlo went down like a sack of potatoes!' Not a good simile. Stop. Cry a bit.

Clever Una did remember to smarm a little of Carlo's

bloody hair on the mallet. Oh, we have all read the crime col-umns. *La cronaca nera*. But do they tell all? I'm manic. Maybe they *will* find me mad? I regret Carlo's death but less – con-siderably less – than the loss of Carlo alive. The crime of passion is the meanest of all: ungenerous, grasping, crime of the weak and the unloved. It should be doubly punished, not less. My blood fizzles in my veins. Murder exhilarates. Power thrills. Meanwhile I am afraid. And sorry. All at once. I have an urge to talk. Mustn't talk, might incriminate myself. Beware. Everything I say may be written down and used as evidence. Twenty years I might get for this. *L'ergastolo*. And the one I really want to tell about it all is Carlo, Carlo, Carlo. . . .

'Una, wake up! You're shouting!'

Carlo is shaking me, laughing at me.

'What's the matter with you, Una? You're completely bonk-ers! Shouting in your sleep! Do you know what you shouted: *"Pazza inglese!"* Honestly!' He laughs witlessly. The light bulb hangs nakedly over our double bed. For a year I have been promising to make a Victorian-type ruffled lace shade for it and never did. Naturally. Because I never *do* anything, do I? I only dream of doing. Carlo is still shaking me even though I am awake. He thinks it very funny that I should talk in my sleep. He has a smug, placid look.

'You were talking about yourself, weren't you? Calling yourself the mad Englishwoman? *Pazza inglese!*' He laughs. 'Poor Una, *poverina, va!*' He has a superior look. His superi-ority sticks in my craw.

I pull away from him, leap up, clutch the flex by which the bulb hangs, yank it out of the ceiling and smash the hot bulb down on Carlo's head. There is a satisfying smashing sound and we are in the dark. Have I killed him? What if his skull . . . ? But no, he has leaped on me, all sweaty thirteen stone of him, he's squeezing my throat and rolling me on a sheet covered with smashed glass. My eyes dazzle from the after-glare of the bulb. I try to scream but he's strangling me.

'You mad bloody bitch! Mad is right. I could kill you. DO YOU REALIZE THAT?'

He lets go. I am choking. My body is scratched all over by the glass and there is no light. I crawl into the bathroom and vomit, then sit, shivering on the lavatory. Mindless.

I look at the mirror. There are bruises on my throat. Fresh bruises. They will get more dramatic. My back and thighs are streaked with blood from the glass. Now would be the time to show myself. *Signor Commissario.* . . . Ah no! No more fantasy. There *does* lie the way to madness. The weak fantasize and resign themselves.

Coldly, deliberately and with no sense of release, I take out the piece of lead piping that I keep in the lavatory cistern, dry it in a towel and use it to smash the bathroom mirror in which I have just been contemplating myself. It is six feet square and less than a year old. Smash! The blow is not on a level with murder but is at least a real act. I leave the piping in the washbasin and go to sleep in the spare room.

*

You see, Signora, I was obsessed. I had him, as the French say, in my skin. Like a burr. His image was stuck in the folds of my brain.

You can't live on sex and the memory and expectation of it but, once we came to Volterra, there was little else for me to do. Mine was worse than a harem-life. Harems have other women in them.

Men used to follow me in the streets. I had that free, foreign look. They had that furtive Italian disease of desire. Their pockets bulged as they fingered their genitalia – Americans call this 'playing pocket-pool' – and their trousers were always too tight. Thin gabardine suits covered but outlined their flesh.

'Do you like Italy?' they hissed. 'Do you like Italian men?'

'No.'

I did not like Italian or any other category of men. I was riveted by a resentful passion to one man. I resented his violence, also his having filled my mind with trivia, interrupted my independent life and drawn me into the game of playing house. I had enjoyed this while it was novel, never seeing the drudgery in it. During my first months with Carlo – in Rome before we got married – I willingly spent hours making salads which were edible mosaics and got up at seven to go marketing. Every act was pleasurable. It was as if some bolt had been adjusted in my body heightening all my senses. I could not tell whether the agency was sex with Carlo or swimming at Fregene or listening to a baroque concert in some old courtyard. Or even the food? I was seduced by basil smells and the gibbous gleam on an egg-plant. That summer went by in a welter of animal gratification. I don't think I read a book. I certainly never bought a newspaper. My mind slept and while it did I contracted for a life which left it little scope.

As an Italian, you can never experience that first stultifying impact of Italy and its pleasures. You know them too well: their techniques, how to dose them and how to make them tick. You are amused by the speed with which we succumb. *L'arte della vita*, that self-congratulatory phrase, celebrates your adroitness at dealing with the body. '*Vi piace l'Italia?*' you ask. 'Do you like our country?' The question is pure rhetoric. You know we do, and our liking is often so gluttonous that you manage to feel spiritually superior as well. Our later dissatisfactions escape you or you put them down to a dyspeptic inability to live. To Puritanism. OK. The word is as good as another. Its residue in me is a need for balance: a need to think as well as feel, to structure my life. I will *not* spend it plotting the best ways to serve the senses and making endless trips to little knitting women and trimming women and little men in the hills who can sell me demijohns of unadulterated olive oil or wine or rounds of *pecorino*. I know all this is necessary if food and clothes are to be exquisite. But the price is too high. I choose against *l'arte della vita*. From now on I shall buy my dresses ready-made and nobody in England will notice that the quarter-inch dip of my left shoulder has not been countered by an especially constructed pad. I shall forget the distinction between good and less good oil. I renounce a repetition of that summer with Carlo: sensual ecstasy, the incandescent pinnacle of what Italy has to give. I tear myself away from him while I still want him – and I don't see Carlo as a hook on which to hang sensations. I love *him*. Himself. His every tic and inch of flesh is photographed on my retina. Possessively. Tenderly. With lust. But he can't be separated from the life here – he wouldn't come with me and, if he did, it wouldn't work. My feeling for him has turned poisonous. I have to go and let him go.

At the time I was telling you about I hadn't come round to accepting this.

I had the shackles. I put them on my own legs: sourly modelling them. They cut my shins. If ever they were to be used they must be padded. I cut up a red velvet cushion – cardinal-red, rather pretty; I had made it during my playing-house phase. Now I used it to swathe and upholster the shackles. I thought of other things while I sewed. Then I hid them.

The *ferraiuolo* meanwhile sold me an iron bedstead with a wrought-iron back and base: one of those period extravaganzas in which twining vines and fronds fan out from an enamelled picture – this one is of the Madonna – in a network more appropriate for a gate or balustrade than for a bed back. They are usually brass. This one is iron. As you know they are fashionable again and fairly expensive. However, I happened to have received a cheque from my mother a little time before. Her second family absorbs most of her attention but when she does think of me she is quite generous.

I got the *ferraiuolo* to help me down to the cellar with it, telling him that I was keeping it as a surprise for my husband's birthday. He assembled it and I put a mattress on it and laid the shackles on the mattress. Then – as though I had paid my fantasy sufficient tribute – I managed to put it out of my mind.

Next came a goodish period. Carlo and I went to Milan for a fortnight and were quite close. When we came back I found I'd skipped a period. I didn't tell him. Here, Signora, is the page I promised you in my note:

Carlo, as you know, insisted on our having a church wedding. I agreed easily. I was in love with him and with Italy and a church wedding seemed the appropriate ceremony to celebrate both loves. Its binding nature did not bother me since, as a non-Catholic, I could disregard its purely spiritual bonds the day the marriage proved unworkable. I could get an English divorce. I fully expected that this might happen. My mother and father are divorced and quite happily remarried, so divorce has always seemed normal to me. First marriages – my mother calls them 'trial marriages' – especially between foreigners are often impermanent. The words of the marriage ceremony are to me pure ritual: nicely put but rescindable. It follows that I had no intention of getting pregnant by Carlo. Unknown to him, I had been on the pill from the time we started living together. Unfortunately, I did not always take it regularly – no subconscious conflict here, just plain sloppiness. So when my period didn't come I was worried. Having no friends in Volterra, I had no way of finding an abortionist there and no money to pay one if I did. It looked as though I might have to go to England for an abortion and, as getting the money and setting up a cover-story for my trip were likely to take time, I had plenty of reasons for anxiety. You may imagine my mood. By the way – I have letters to and from my mother written when I was contemplating marriage to Carlo. They prove that my attitude at the time really was the one I have just described.

OK? Do remember to extract this page and send it to your canon-lawyer friend. I remind you lest the rest of this missive end in the incinerator or be torn to ribbons by your enraged and thriftless fingers. But do read on before doing anything unconsidered. This document is not being written purely for my sake but also for a purpose which must jibe with your own: it is a barrier to keep me from coming back.

You know – or perhaps you don't, so let me tell you – that between a man and a woman who are deeply involved sexually – I shy a little doubtfully at this stage from that puff-ball word 'love' – atrocious injuries can be forgiven. It is not impossible that Carlo and I, *even now*, might be reconciled. You don't believe this? You think me simple-minded? But you have not experienced the perverse pleasures of our fighting-life. I forgave him repeatedly. He forgave me – oh yes, Signora, even before my lead-pipe days, I managed to give back something of what I got – acutely embarrassing scenes in which he cut a wretched figure before friends. *Brutta figura!* Into that Achilles heel, the rotting soft spot of the vain I could always stick a claw!

It is to that same vulnerability, his fear of *brutta figura*, that this letter is addressed. By letting you, la Mammina, into our noisome secrets, it makes it harder for Carlo to forgive me. Forgive-and-forget is a package deal. But who can forget when there is a witness close to one who knows all and reminds one that she does by constant jibes? I rely on you for this. You will keep him from me and me from him – which, sadly, is what we need.

It occurred to me that if I did have to make a trip to England, Carlo would be alone in the house; he might visit the cellar and see the objects there. I was acutely embarrassed at the thought. Fantasies and their props are private: painfully so. At least they are for me. While fantasy stays in one's head, it is safe. Once it has confronted reality – like now – shame no longer attaches to it. At the intermediary stage at which mine had got stuck, while my props lay unused in the cellar, discovery can only be humiliating.

I decided to do away with the fetters. The bed was not compromising. I would pretend I had bought it as a surprise and was keeping it for Carlo's birthday or our anniversary. Indeed, as I thought about it, I became convinced that this was the truth. But the fetters with their home-sewn red velvet padding would be harder to explain. They must be got rid of. The question was how? The Volterra town council had recently been issuing plastic bags for householders' rubbish and our rubbishmen were no longer prepared to deal with the heavy old dustbins. My fetters with their bars and chains would not fit into the new little bags. I could throw them into our well but it was sometimes cleaned and they might be dragged up again in the spring. I could not bear the thought. Burying them was just as risky. The thing to do was to put them into the boot of the car, drive into the country and drop them somewhere. Unfortunately, just as I came to this con-clusion, our old Giulietta got battery trouble and had to be hauled off to the garage for a week.

It was during this week that my scenario escaped me. I had decided to scrap it and instead it began to act itself out.

Carlo got a notion that we ought to put down some wine. A friend of his had joined some club which imported French wines at cut prices. This, the friend claimed, was a once-in-a-decade year for Rhine – or Rhône? I wouldn't remember – wines. He advised Carlo to buy all he could afford and put it down. Carlo decided to inspect our cellar.

'The bulb's broken,' I told him. 'I've been meaning to get the yard man to change it. It's too high for me. I'll get him to do it in the morning.'

'I'll do it. I know where he keeps the ladder.'

'Carlo, you'll fall. Let him do it.'

This was the wrong tack. Vanity, the old weak spot, must not be injudiciously touched. Carlo gave a manly laugh, equipped himself with torch and ladder, and set off down the cellar stairs. I ran down behind him. It was wonderful, I said sarcastically into the blackness, how pathetically true to type he ran. Putting down wine indeed when we hadn't enough money to run a decent car. Was he laying it up for his children's baptism parties, assuming we ever had any?

Carlo set up his ladder. In one hand he held a fresh bulb, in the other his torch. He shone it around. Its beam caught the curlicues of the bed.

'What's that?' he asked indifferently, and began to climb the ladder. 'I'll have this bulb in in a jiffy. Switch on the light when I tell you.'

'You're not even listening!' I screamed. There was nowhere for me to hide those fetters which would be in full, disgraceful view the moment I switched on the light. 'You might discuss this with *me* before earmarking all our money for useless, snobby French wine! Damn you, Carlo, will you answer!'

Carlo removed the old bulb. He was having trouble holding the torch and keeping his balance on the ladder. 'I need three hands,' he said. 'What are you on about now?'

'Come down, Carlo, *please*! I want to talk to you. Now!' I shook the ladder.

He fell. His head banged against the iron bedpost and he lay very still. He had knocked himself out.

*

It was funny: sickly so, if you like. You see I might never have done it! I think I wouldn't have. I was so terrified of breaking his conceivably paper-thin cranium and then – my guardian angel or bad spirit did it for me. Ah well. Of course you are thinking and saying and will endlessly repeat – I can hear you as I write! – that what I should have done at this point was to ring a doctor. I had ample time now to find a temporary hiding-place for the shaming fetters and even if I had not, Carlo's health, his very life, you will say, demanded a doctor.

Well, as it turned out: they didn't. Carlo was right as rain in an hour. When he came to, lying on the bed, his feet threaded through the fetters – I had used them after all – the worst he was suffering from was a headache. In no time at all, I will admit, he was suffering from incredulity, shock, rage and sheer, unmanning bewilderment. He had no stomach for cunning that day. He failed to play the one card which would have won his release: it never occurred to him to pretend he was badly hurt.

No need to tell you about our first conversations. Carlo will describe them. I imagine I have left you matter for several years' chat – unless the subject is declared taboo. Even if it is, it will stick around: a memory responsive to hints and nudges.

Quickly then: there were rages, roars, sulks and refusals to speak. Unfairly, he looked his worst: cheeks fat with fury and black with a stubble of beard. Only on the third day did he think of reasoning with me:

'How do you think you're going to get away with this?'

'I don't expect to.'

'Then why are you doing it? What do you expect to gain?'

'Only what I've got now.'

'*What* have you got? You must want to force me to do something! *What?*'

'Nothing. I just want you like this.'

'To humiliate me?'

'You could call it that.'

'And what the hell do you think is going to happen when you release me?'

I had no answer to that one.

He was quite confident at first. He couldn't believe I'd keep it up or that someone wouldn't hear him or wonder where he was and come looking for him. He shouted a lot the first day or two, but I played the radio full-blast upstairs to show him how badly sound carried. With the basement and cellar doors shut, he couldn't hear *it*, so there was little chance of anyone's hearing *him*. Gradually he gave that up. Still, he relied on his colleagues wondering about his sudden disappearance from the office. I told him I had written a letter of resignation purporting to come from him, explaining that an opportunity to work in London was being offered him by his stepfather-in-law, that he had had to take a sudden decision, was sorry for the inconvenience caused but hoped they would understand.

'I forged your signature. I've been practising.'

'The letter's sure to be full of appalling grammar. They'll know there's something wrong.'

'No, it's all formulas. I looked through your files of old correspondence and lifted all the ready-made office jargon I could. I write better Italian than I speak. You can see the rough copy if you like.'

'They'll think it extraordinary my giving notice like that.'

'They'll be annoyed but they won't investigate. People never do.'

They didn't. Apart from one phone call which I answered saying yes, Carlo was in London, no, he didn't plan on getting back soon, we heard nothing from the office. Later in the week I went in to collect a few of his things and repeated my story to two of his colleagues. If they thought about Carlo at all, they probably thought he had been too embarrassed to show his face, envied him his influential father-in-law and forgot about him.

What followed was totally different from the scene imagined in my dream-scenario. *There* action had been fast and satisfying. I triumphed. Carlo cringed. I, like God, was in control. I spoke persuasively and Carlo saw my point. I was free. The choices were mine. Instead: I was *not* free since I was afraid to release Carlo. I disliked myself, had strong feelings of nausea, was not persuasive and, in fact, hardly spoke. My mind, as though it had been I and not Carlo who had fallen on my head, was in a state of stunned lethargy. It could cope with no more than the mechanics of the situation, the physical routine required to keep the *status quo:* answering phone calls and letters, buying food, emptying his slop bucket, et cetera. When it came to thinking of the future, thought switched off. When he reasoned with me or tried to cajole me, I shrugged. I had imagined that I would use the time I held him prisoner to explain my grudges, to make him *see* how intolerable it can be to be always on the losing side, the weak partner, the one who must submit. I think I had supposed that his own position would make this clear to him in an immediate way. Zing! Message lodges in brain. Dominant partner apprehends reality of subject partner. True dialogue based on a shared premiss can now commence.

Haha! Permit me to laugh, Signora. It is at myself. Nothing of the sort happened or – I began to see – was likely to, unless Carlo was kept chained to the bed for ten years. Chained up or free, Carlo was still Carlo – in the short run anyway – and I was still myself.

I began to understand this on the fourth day.

We had begun to settle into a routine. Carlo was letting me feed him – at first he had refused to eat. I was looking after him, necessarily, in a more intimate way than I ever had before and this aroused inappropriately motherly feelings in me. I found myself cooking his favourite food, worrying about his comfort and generally behaving more like the tender-hearted daughter of the despot in prototypal prison stories than like the implacable despot himself. *He* noticed this eventually – one thing that might be said to have been achieved was that Carlo had to start studying me and wondering how I ticked. He was learning the techniques of the underdog.

On the sixth day I came down with his lunch and found him reading a paperback I had left for him. I had not used the second pair of shackles for his arms but had looped their chain around his elbows attaching these behind his back to the bed back, then bringing the chain forward to circle his neck so that if he tried to pull his arm free the pressure would be on his own throat. His hands however were free and he could eat, drink, hold a book and manœuvre himself towards the slop bucket. The iron bar threaded through his leg-fetters was itself pierced by chains which hung down, one on the left the other on the right side of the bed, and were pad-locked together underneath. These chains were long enough to allow him to adjust his position by moving to the right or left or by bending his knees as he had done on this occasion so as to form a support for his book.

'Do you want lunch?'

'You know what I want.'

'Do you want lunch?'

'How the hell can I eat lunch? My neck is rubbed raw by this bloody chain. Every move I make it rubs. I could strangle myself in my sleep. What are you trying to do? Unman me? Why don't you castrate me and be finished? *You'll* probably be locked up in a lunatic asylum for life when they get you. Do you want *me* to have to join you there? A fine future for us. Tell me, I can't think why I never asked: is there madness in your family?'

'I'm the mad Englishwoman, you've driven me mad!'

'Christ, you are at that!'

'Do you want lunch?'

'Una, it's *you* I worry about. I keep puzzling: *what did I do?* I mean tiffs and squabbles don't normally lead to this sort of thing as far as is generally known. Or do they in England? Is there a whole, submerged, unreported section of people's lives where the primitive urges are given leeway? Incest? Mayhem? Murder perhaps?'

The ironic look on Carlo's face slipped. He had frightened himself. Murder *was*, after all, one logical way for me to get myself out of the fix I had got into.

'Una,' it was a little boy's voice. 'Una . . . I . . .'

I watched him watch me as I stood there with the cooling

lasagne. I could see doubt ooze through him.

'Give me the lunch.' He ate it silently, wiped his lips with the napkin I had brought, shot me one shifty look, then another. 'That was . . . good . . . Una?'

I took his plate and left, shutting cellar and basement doors carefully behind me. When I reached the kitchen I smashed the dirty plate hard into the sink, sat down at the table and rested my face against its scrubbed surface. So this was where we were at now! He thought I *was* mad! Was trying to humour me. Shared premiss indeed! We were communicating less than before. What a laugh! We never seemed to get our wires uncrossed.

'You don't know how to talk *to* people!' I accused him some hours later. 'You talk *at* them or get round them. You don't respect anyone enough to try and meet them half-way – certainly not your mother. Not Giovanna. Let's not mention me. It's the same with your men friends. You either tease them or defer to them. You trust nobody.'

He looked tired. 'Go on. Make yourself a good conscience. Blacken me. Do whatever it is you have to do.'

'Do? What should I have to do? You're so suspicious!'

'I'd be a moron if I weren't. Una . . . why don't you go and see a doctor? I can't get out, can I? Go and visit Dottor Pietri. You needn't tell him what you've done to me, just that you're feeling . . . depressed, nervous. Get him to give you a checkup.'

'Carlo, it's not *me!* It's *you!* Why do you think I had to do this?'

'I DON'T KNOW!' he shouted. 'TELL ME!'

'Because you never saw me. Because you treated me like an automat, a penny-in-the-slot machine. Kiss it or stick your penis in it and it goes "mmmgh!", hit it and it goes "ow", set it for the dinner-at-eight schedule and it will comply. In case of breakdown send it to Dottor Pietri.'

'You *are* mad.'

'Well that's convenient, isn't it? Much easier to assume the trouble's all in me than have to assess your own life.'

'Are you enjoying this?'

'No.'

'Then what's the point of the exercise?'

There wasn't any. I realized this now. But it was too late to stop it. My power over Carlo was purely negative. I couldn't make him think or feel differently. He's cast in your mould. Doubts are alien to him. But releasing him straightaway would be too great a risk. What happened some days later underlined that. They had been uneventful days. Carlo ate, listened to his transistor radio, sulked, tried wheedling me a bit, had a tantrum, sulked, wheedled me again. His moods went in cycles. He was getting more anxious, however, as it became clear that his office had accepted my letter and that there was no immediate prospect of anyone discovering what was going on. He had been in the cellar ten days when Giovanna rang up. You and she were off to Austria next day on your skiing holiday and she wanted to give me your address there and say good-bye. I must have been a bit constrained on the phone. Carlo, I of course told her, was out. I'd tell him she'd rung. No, no point ringing back. He'd been invited to go duck shooting with some friends and was spending the night with them. He might be away two days. They were not on the phone. Duck shooting? Yes, I said, he'd just taken it up. These friends had introduced him to it. People we'd met at a party. They had no phone. He would certainly write and tell her all about it. Giovanna said oh, well, OK, give him our love. I said enjoy yourself. She bridled. The skiing holiday is part of your get-Giovanna-well-married campaign and she knows I know this and is touchy. Also she knows that Carlo and I could do with some of the money you spend like water – but this is by the way. I only mention it to show how she came to associate the constraint in our conversation with herself and *her* concerns rather than with me and mine. 'I wish I weren't going,' she said at the end, 'but you know how la Mamma is!' She had accepted the duck-shooting story easily. I went down and told Carlo.

I suppose this made him despair. It meant I had three weeks ahead of me during which I need have no fear of discovery. It must have seemed like an eternity. He was complaining of cramps already. Now he began to complain again of the chain on his neck. His complaints distressed me. I have already mentioned that I had begun to feel motherly about him. After all: I cleaned, fed, babied him. Perhaps I felt as you do towards him? I don't know. My resentments were gone. (Who can call a baby to account?) My mind swung between terror at what he might – would – do to me if I let him loose and horror at what I was doing to him. Yes, yes, I had begun admitting to myself that eventually I would have to go and, from some safe distance, telephone someone to come and set him free. But go where? Telephone who? The world outside our house had become unreal to me. I felt bound to this nasty riveting nest of my own fabrication, could not bear to go leaving such a memory behind. My possessiveness grew with his dependence and with the odd morbid gratitude – it may just have been cunning – with which he thanked me for my efforts to make him less uncomfortable. Usually, I took care to keep out of range of his hands which were, as I told you, free. On this day too I tried to examine his neck from a safe distance, but he seemed to have gone limp from exhaustion and his lolling head concealed the area which was being rubbed by the chain. I leaned closer. Suddenly his hands sprang up and grabbed my throat. They squeezed. I tried to shout but couldn't get my breath. He squeezed again, crushing my windpipe, railing at me ('*Stronza*, turd, mad bitch! I have you now!') and his eyes were stark and crazy. He had pulled the chain tight on his own neck which was in fact rubbed raw, but he seemed now to be unaware of this. Slowly his hands relaxed and he began to cry.

'I could . . .', he sobbed, 'I could . . . Una, what have you done to us both? We're mad! We're both mad! This is degrading. It's valueless. It's against every value. Una, we were normal people, we . . . listen, Una, *ti prego*, I'll make any promise you like. But let me out. Look, I realize, I really do, that I must be to blame for some of this. As much as you. I was insensitive, I . . . But, look, this is destroying us both. Can't you see that? Can't you, Una? Una, say something.'

'You're choking me.'

'What use is there in this, Una?'

'None.'

'Listen,' his stranglehold had turned into a sort of caress, but he was still holding me tightly and his own arms were held tightly to the bed so that our movements were restricted. 'I could kill you,' he whispered. 'Don't you know that?'

'What good would that do you?'

'What good is any of this to anyone?'

His nervous excitement had found the usual outlet, he had begun trying to make love. But he was afraid to let go my neck. 'Unbutton me,' he whispered. I did. We managed to make love. I only tell you this, Signora, to show how hopelessly tangled up our emotions were: his as well as mine. We lived in a fetid bubble of dependence and rancour.

'Do you hate me?' he whispered now.

'No.'

'We must trust each other.'

'Yes.'

'Fuck,' he said, then, and then: 'you're liking it. Go on: say it. Say it! SAY IT.'

Was that strategy, Signora? I don't know, do I, any more now than I did then. I was enjoying it as I always did with Carlo. I was venting the pent humours of ten days. Slowly, his fingers uncurled so that I could move freely above him. At the end he was not restraining me at all.

'Carlo!' I wanted to weep.

'Where are the keys?'

'Upstairs.'

'Go on up', he whispered, 'and get them. Go on, Una.'

I went upstairs to the kitchen and opened the drawer where I kept the keys. My neck was hurting where he had squeezed it. I turned to look in the kitchen mirror and saw the black-berry-juice outline of his ten fingers on my throat. I closed the drawer, leaving the keys inside and did not go back to the cellar again that day. Next morning I reconsidered the risks of releasing Carlo. They did not seem to me any less than before. I went down and told him I did not intend to release him.

He didn't talk to me for thirty-six hours after that. He also refused to eat. But I did not, of course, give in. I won't say I was firm. Every moment was a flea's leap of doubt – but the effect was the same as if I had been stubbornly wedded to decision: Carlo did not get released. After the thirty-six hours, he asked for a drink. I gave him wine in which I had dissolved several sleeping pills. When he had been asleep for some time I approached him with great caution, blasted the transistor radio in his ear, poked him from a distance with a piece of wood and – lest he might be fooling – dangled a real-istic trick-shop plastic scorpion close to his face. He did not wake up. I got my keys, unlocked the padlock on the chains which held his arms and neck, unlooped them and pulled him down to a supine position. Then I got my second set of fet-ters, pulled his wrists through them, fastened them in place by pulling the bar through the lower pair of holes in each fetter, laid the entire contraption across his thighs so that his arms were parallel to his body, threaded the chains through the ends of the bar and padlocked them together under the bed as I had already done with the foot-fetters. This meant Carlo could now actually move more. He could sit up or lie down by displacing the bars whose attaching chains were fairly long, and could edge over to the side of the bed to use his slop bucket. His hands, however, were free only from the wrist. It would be harder for him to make a grab at me. While he was asleep, I brought down a basin of water and washed him all over. Then I powdered him with Roberts talcum powder. He was turning more and more into my baby: my battered baby. It humiliated me since it must him. I, who resent the body's weaknesses – remember; the source of all our trouble was my lack of muscle – had now inflicted intolerable bodily constraints on Carlo. Ironically, that very day, I found one of my own constraints had gone: my overdue period arrived. The pregnancy – *my* fetter – had either never been or had terminated itself. Who knew? One knows so little about the biological processes – and when I say 'one' I don't just mean 'I'. Doctors are as vague as any female. 'Maybe you had a little miscarriage and mistook it for a heavy period,' they'll say when questioned. 'Maybe you are just irregular?' Shrug, smile; what does it matter? Get on with it. It's the curse of Eve. *I* saw a meaning here, however. My release was a nod from Fate, old *ignis fatuus* who lurks in the madder mathematical corners of my mind making his own kind of sense. This was a *quid pro quo*. Fate helps those who help themselves. Fetter your husband, said the sign, and Fate will unfetter you. The equation comes out evenly if X is added in one place and subtracted in another. I had been approved! I have to break into my narrative here, Signora, to remind you that superstitions are only metaphors. I am no madder than you when I make my own signs and patterns – they are a filing system for otherwise unrelated perceptions – no madder, I say, than you when you accept holus-bolus the ready-made metaphor of your religion. No, don't be angry. I am really trying to get through to you, not to mock you. Let me say it another way: the arrival of my period, the abrupt flow of menstrual blood, had come too perfectly on time to be chance. Maybe something in myself had set it off: perhaps some nervous convulsion had caused the miscarriage of a real pregnancy or released the dam of a false one? Either way it had happened because of what I was doing to Carlo. The message was clear:

my interests and his were in opposition. I must cut the knot of our love/hate. I must go.

I put off going. This was the twelfth day and Carlo was still asleep. It was the thirteenth when he woke up and found the new fetters on his wrists. I think that then a sort of apathy seized him. He had tried everything, it must have seemed to him: anger, reason, threats, appeals, tears. He had refused to eat. He gave up scheming now. He had grown meek and constipated; he claimed to feel constant nausea.

'I'll give you a glycerine suppository.'

'OK.'

He let me stick it up his anus with my finger, giving no signs of shame or vindictiveness. As if I'd been a nurse. But was he apathetic or testing me in some way? I did not discover.

'Will you eat?'

'Yes.'

'I'll have to feed you.'

'OK.'

His apathy was more wearing on my nerves than his sulks or tantrums. Inaction was telling on us both but perhaps more on me since the choice dangled constantly in the corner of my brain: I *could* put an end to this. Release him. Go. But then the whole thing would have been a failure. Sometimes it seemed to be more fear of anti-climax than fear of Carlo which kept me there. I told myself I must hold out. Something might even now click in his brain. By using force on me he had invited like treatment. Since *my* use of force had resolved nothing, might he not see – glimpse, allow – that it never could or did? But *if* he saw this, would *I* believe he was seeing it? I would not. Yet craved an absolving word.

'What are you using for money?' he asked finally.

It was the fifteenth day. I was keeping notes carefully. This letter is based on them. Putting in time, I shopped, cooked, cleaned more than I ever had, wrote and rewrote drafts for

this letter, packed, tried to keep away from Carlo. I felt occasional urges to hurt him, frequent ones to harangue him. I
was sexually hungry for him. At night he filled every dream. I
was leaving, however. I had prepared a telegram summoning
you from Austria. Alternatively I might wait and send you a
letter after you got back. I wrote that, too. It must be sent, if
the telegram had not been, a few days after your return from
Austria, a month after I first tied Carlo up: my last possible
date for departure.

'What are you using for money?'

'I got some from my mother. I wrote and told her it was an
emergency. It came last week.'

'*You* can't earn any, can you?'

'No.'

'So chaining me up didn't change much, did it? You're
dependent still. *You* can't run our life.'

He had me there.

Days went by. Carlo read Gramsci's *Letters from Prison*
which he had – theatrically, I thought – asked me to buy him.
Gramsci, he told me, did gymnastic exercises every day in his
cell to keep fit. Gramsci, I pointed out, was in prison for *years*.
Gramsci, Carlo said, recommended the cultivation of a sense
of humour. Prisoners were in danger of becoming monoma-
niacs. As I was one already, that, he said, would make two of
us. Well, we were both prisoners.

On the twentieth day Carlo told me he had had a dream. He
had dreamed of his grandfather whom he had never known
but whose portrait used, he told me, to hang in your villa
at Forte dei Marmi. The grandfather, Nonno Bevilacqua, a
Bolognese with whiskers, had been angry with Carlo in the
dream for reasons which he couldn't recall and had perhaps
not understood. Carlo interpreted his dream. It meant, he
said, that he was feeling guilt for having neglected the patri-
archal virtues, let down the ideals of his ancestors, married a
foreign female and failed to keep her in line.

'*Basta!*' I shouted. 'You made that dream up. Anyway, dream-interpreting is a stupid bloody habit you could leave alone. You have enough nineteenth-century quirks without picking up the nineteen-thirtyish ones.'

'Power corrupts,' said Carlo. 'Now it's censorship. Revolt breeds tyranny, I see. I am cultivating my sense of humour.'

I started to leave the cellar.

'Turd!' he shouted up the stairs after me. 'Stupid, nit-brained female!'

'I could hurt you, you know. Badly.'

'Nit-brain! What do you think you've been doing all these weeks? Do you think my bones don't hurt? Do you think my muscles don't ache from lying in one position? And all to no end: a nit-brained, anarchic, feminine gesture. You'd better *not* let me out', Carlo yelled, 'or I'll give you the hiding of your life! I won't leave a postage-stamp worth of your skin intact! I'll cut off your clitoris. Then I'll have you committed. For the good of society! You shouldn't be loose! You're a dangerous nit-brain!'

I rushed upstairs and out of the front door, banging it behind me just in case he could hear. I hadn't been out except for quick shopping since this thing had begun. Now, I needed to get out, anywhere, to breathe. I walked with brisk aimlessness to the edge of the city walls. It was about 4 p.m. on a bleak day. It had been raining and everything shone. The massy giant blocks of stone in the Etruscan gate made the town itself look more like a prison than Carlo's cellar and I had a more oppressive sensation now than before I came out. I had trouble breathing and my breath seemed to strangle in my throat. A few schoolboys in black pinafores passed on their way home from school. They carried heavy briefcases, leaning sideways, their shoulders already half deformed by the habitual weight. It was cold and they passed smartly, not dawdling. All life was inside the houses. Flowerpots, washing-lines and bird-cages had been taken in. Doors were shut clam-tight. The whole grey, wet town, clinging to its jagged hill, was like a bereaved clam-colony whose inhabitant molluscs had migrated to richer waters. The streets were empty as river-beds. The alabaster shops which cater to summer tourists were shut. Whatever life there was was behind closed doors and, as I had no friends in Volterra, there was no door on which I could knock. I walked into a chrome-cold bar and ordered a coffee. I asked when the next bus left.

'For where?'

'Siena,' I said, 'or Florence. Livorno even.'

'*Ma* Signora, those are different directions. Where do you want to go?'

I mumbled something about connecting with a train and left. It seems I strike people now as odd. Perhaps I *am* a trifle? One wouldn't know one was oneself, would one? Carlo may well be becoming odd too. I don't like his dreaming and making threats. It reminds me of me. If only there were a memory-drug – didn't I read about such a thing somewhere sometime? In a science-fiction tale perhaps? – that would induce amnesia in Carlo, then we could wipe the slate clean, begin again. A blow on the head could induce amnesia. *Could*, yes, but how be sure it would? A blow judiciously . . . Christ, I was at it again! Fantasizing and, worse, about blows. Enough, oh yes, enough of this.

I was home by now. I went into the kitchen, made myself some coffee and wrote some more of this. Vacillation has become my rhythm. Telegram Austria now? Wait nine days more till you come back? Yes? No? Which? With all this, I had forgotten to buy food. My mind might well be slipping and if it did, even momentarily, if something happened to me, say, what would become of Carlo? Who would ever let him out? Better post the note to you in Florence. You won't get it right away but *will* get it. It will be Carlo's insurance against an accident and meanwhile I'll still have a little time to

The foregoing unfinished letter was found by Giovanna Crispi two weeks after her sister-in-law's flight to London. Whether she read it or not is unknown for she simply put it in a yellow envelope and posted it off without comment in a parcel containing a number of her sister-in-law's personal effects.

The next and last letter in this series was posted six months later in London.

Carlo,

This is to let you know that I have engaged a lawyer to start divorce proceedings. He is my mother's lawyer and his name is Mr Knulty of Penn, Knulty, Moss and Legges of Chancery Lane, London, W.C.2. He will be contacting you. He assures me that the divorce will be unembarrassing and go through rapidly.

I am afraid you will now stop reading this.

How can I hold your attention? I'll try truth: I am not writing just to tell you about Mr Knulty. He will do that himself. I want to hear from or at least *of* you. If you can't bear to write yourself, perhaps Giovanna might? Just a few bare facts: your job, your health and where you are.

I – loathsome pronoun – heard you had left Volterra and were working in Milan. Flight or promotion? If you can't bear to read this let Giovanna read it and give you its gist. It will be an improvement – any change must be – for us to communicate through third parties. Like old monarchs.

Facts about me: I have a job now. Before, I was in a clinic for a bit having what is described as a breakdown though it was actually a build-up. I gardened in the clinic – I raised tomato plants and begonias – and when I came out began designing fabrics. I regret not having learned to direct my energies before. It would have been easier on you. You can't cope with more than a fraction of a woman's attention. Perhaps no one can.

Please thank Giovanna for posting me the manuscript

which got left on the kitchen table in the skirmish at the end. I don't know whether any of you read it or whether, if you did, it explained anything. I haven't wanted to open the thing since getting it back, but I am glad Giovanna kept it from your mother. My leaving it for her was tasteless and pointless. I was . . . under strain. If Giovanna ever feels able to meet me on one of her trips to England, please tell her I would be happy – no, not that, just tell her I would be eager to see her.

It all seems long ago now, doesn't it? I do not feel apologies are relevant. What I did to you was amply compensated by what you tried to do to me when I released you. I am not talking of your physical assault. I'd expected that, which was why I managed to barricade myself in the bathroom and scream for the neighbours. I am talking about your phoning the police and trying to have me committed to an asylum.

I wonder did you realize that the police didn't believe a word of your story? The doctor didn't either. I wonder did you ever discover this or know that they took me away for my own protection and that you were the one whose sanity was in doubt? Did you know that I sent Dottor Pietri a confession? In *your* interests! That I referred him to the MS on the kitchen table for confirmation? If I hadn't, you might have had trouble of some sort on your hands. After all, remember the state in which *I* was found – no, no permanent damage. Not physical anyway. I suppose remembering all this is unpleasant. Perhaps, you won't read this far? The scandal in a place like Volterra will no doubt outlast us both. But you are in Milan. Do you remember how we longed to move there? And now you're there alone – or, anyway, not with me. Congratulations. I am truly glad for you.

As you may *not* have read the wretched MS, let me tell you one thing that was in it: I am prepared to help you to obtain an annulment of our marriage. I have old letters and a diary which can demonstrate that I entered upon it with the wrong dispositions and that, consequently, it is, in the Church's eyes, null and void as a contract. I had what they call 'a mental reservation'. Or so I shall say. To help and convenience you. In fact, Carlo, I took our marriage if anything over-seriously. I did in my own way try to make it work. I suppose you will not see this. My way was not the accepted way, it is true. I was not prepared for a lifetime of guilefully manipulating you. I was not prepared to yield time after time to the superior force of your muscle. I *had* to fight back, even if I knew I would fail. Failure is bearable. It is the inability to respond at all which dehumanizes. *You* felt this when I tied you up: outrage, indignation, disbelief that you, a twentieth-century, Western middle-class man of mind and dignity could be subjected to such treatment. But, Carlo, *I* am not different from you. Being a female doesn't make me different. 'Feminine' strategies are responses to an objective situation: lack of power. There is no 'natural' love of subservience in women.

I remember a wretched little Calabrian in a loudly striped suit and brilliantine who once pestered me for over two hours in the Milan railway station. I was between trains. The only comfortable place to wait was the station café and I couldn't move away easily because I had my suitcases with me. This caricature *papagallo* parked himself at the next table and kept up an audible stream of sub-erotic supplication. I felt trapped, publicly contaminated, and threatened to call the management. The wretched man explained that he was lonely, knew no one, craved only a little human contact and added that he had been wandering the city all day getting contempt from everyone. His final appeal was painful: '*Non sono un cane,*' he said, 'I am not a dog. I am a person. *Sono una persona.*' The shaming thing, I realized as he said it, was that for me, because of his provincial bad taste in clothes and behaviour, he *wasn't* quite a person. Obviously the Milanese felt the same. His plea was relevant. I let him sit at my table.

As I write this I realize that the analogy is imperfect. I never wanted from you the kind of charity I gave the Calabrian. I did want recognition that *I* was a person. I always knew *you* were. Putting you in the cellar was not to deny that but to shock you into seeing how precarious personality can be. But I am not trying to write an apologia. Marriage, like topiary, distorts growth. Perhaps it is always a hierarchical relationship? Obsolete? We managed to get out of it physically intact. A lot of it was worth having, perhaps worth the price. You will be hearing from Mr Knulty. *Ciao*, Carlo, and good luck,

Una

Melancholy Baby

'Ah no?'

'God help us!' Mrs Kelly sometimes greased gossip with pity. 'Aunt Adie HAS NO WOMB!'

Neighbours thrilled. 'You're not serious!'

'Had it cut out BEFORE her marriage and NEVER TOLD HER HUSBAND!'

'Go on!'

'Cross my heart!'

'And so?'

'The poor man is praying for children to this day and has herself going down making the Nine Fridays for the same Intention! And down my lady goes.'

'Gnawing the altar rails with the best!'

'It's hard to understand some people!'

'Ha! She can have the fruits of *my* womb for the asking!' Mrs Kelly slapped her protuberant belly. 'To them that have more shall be given! I do have to laugh!' She took a swig at her pint and guffawed again.

'I hear', said the postmistress, 'how she's taking her niece out of the orphanage at last.'

*

Adie lived in a run-down fishing village: a row of grey houses roofed with what might have been shards of solidified winter sea. Hope here was landlocked by the fog which rolled in to settle in the back-yard plots: mild incubators where lettuces grew greasy as seaweed, and buckets, left out to shelter rhubarb stalks, rusted red only to be resilvered by snail tracks. Round the front, owners decorated their posts with shells which had once encased flesh as sluggish as their own. She too was grey: eyes, hair and a dead pellicle of neglected pores which concealed the currents of her blood. But she had energy. When her husband's trade – he was a sign-painter – was ruined by the advent of neon, she opened a tearoom and succeeded in selling soda bread and blackberry jam to the odd Lancashire mill-worker on holiday or Christian Brother who paused on that shingly beach. At a window prettified by gingham curtains and geraniums she would sit, with her teeth in, smiling out at them as they alighted from bus or bicycle and draw their attention to the sign-painter's last effort in two-tone Celtic script: AUNT ADIE'S COUNTRY TEAS. The promissory legend followed them through their dip in the savage waters of the Irish Sea and drew them back for Teas: Plain at three bob a head or High (with fry) for seven and six. In a backward, discouraged place, she cornered or created what trade there was and soon was selling cigarettes, chocolate bars, home-made sponge-cakes and lavender pin-cushions to the charmed and hungry Britishers who began to drift in after the war. She had the toughness without the timorousness of her stock. Once, when a GI asked for a room to rest in with his fiancée, she lent him her own and, thrilled by the pound he paid her, begged him to mention her address to friends. He must have forgotten, for no other couple asked for the favour, although she inveigled a number up to look at the view.

'She's a caution!' said Mrs Kelly, Aunt Adie's char.

'Did jez hear what Aunt Adie's after doing now?'

'That one's a Godless aul' rip! If the priest were to hear of it he'd ballyrag her off the altar.'

Adie continued to knead soda bread with ardent knuckles, and her business boomed. She could do without the esteem of the draggled village women, whose heads were addled by the squalling of their litters, and she was indifferent to the opinions of the ex-sign-painter, who had settled into placid redundance. Yet her vigour, having developed the tearooms to their limits, carried her no further. She thought for a while of launching into the pastry business and even found a bakery ready to act as distributor – but she gave up the idea. ('Why work my fingers to the bone while himself sits there on his bum?') Business never became a passion with her. Church-going – another favourite filler for lonely women's lives – had no resonance in hers. Like the poised claw of a crane, her affective energies remained in suspense.

Gap-toothed, bravely lipsticked Mrs Kelly was her com-panion. 'Friend' would not be the word. Mrs Kelly's own illusions had long left her as birds leave a contaminated nest. Her husband had drunk her out of a pub, a house, and the middle class, and now – shiftless mother of five children whom she was raising on the dole, despising and despised by all around her – she took her pleasure in savage gossip. 'I do have to laugh.' It was from her that the neighbours first heard of Adie's niece, Gwennie.

'Four years', Mrs Kelly shook her head at cronies in the pub, 'in the orphanage without Adie as much as paying her a visit! She's only taking her out now because the nuns won't keep her any longer. The girl's sixteen.'

'Didn't the mother die of consumption?'

'Now you're talking. Adie's frightened silly of disease and of course the girl herself must be *prone!*' Mrs Kelly spoke with allusive refinement. 'I remember the time when a touch of it in a family was as big a bar to matrimony as madness. Still, that's no excuse for leaving her to moulder that long in an institution! What is it but a bloody sweat shop? The so-called Sisters of Charity run a laundry out of it! Plenty of unpaid labour!'

'Isn't the girl's father alive?'

'In England. Working in a pub. Sends nothing towards

the girl's keep. Or so Adie says. You couldn't believe daylight outa her!'

Adie went into town alone to meet the girl's bus which would leave her off, the nuns had written, at Aston Quay. But the green buses proclaimed only their destination – Dublin – and not their place of departure, so she began to race round in circles, bumping into the general ragtag and badgering inspectors. She wasn't even sure she would recognize the girl whom she hadn't seen since she was twelve. And why should *she*, she thought as another green bus drew in and swept to a halt forty yards down the quay, why (she puffed and ran and puffed) go pelting about like this after other people's brats? Her sister, God rest her, had married a gom from down the country, a ne'er-do-well. She panted. The girl wasn't on that bus! Adie had refused to let her sister have a share of their mother's furniture. 'Why throw good money after bad?' she had reasoned at the time. And how right she had been! Her sister's husband's brogue had been as thick in his mouth as the dirt was under his nail! A no-good country gawk! Look at her now having to take in his daughter! Who was maybe consumptive! She shuddered, wondering whether she ought to even hug the girl. She had a handkerchief soaked in disinfectant in a plastic container in her purse. 'I'll let *her* kiss me if she wants to,' she decided, 'then I'll pretend to blow my nose.'

A bus drew in and a raggedy crowd of snot-nosed urchins rushed up yelling 'porter, porter!' Adie drew away, wary of germs. A louse, she thought, might jump off one of them or a bedbug. An urchin snatched a case from a passenger and, aiming a kick at a rival, jumped clear of the bus. 'Taxi, ma'am?' he yelled at the owner of the case, a girl not much bigger than himself who plunged down the steps, planted one red claw (whose cracked flesh billowed between the joints) on his elbow and with the other landed two noisy slaps on his cheek. 'Thief!' she gasped and dragged the suitcase from him. The boy goggled. 'Hey, you. . . .' His fist clenched. Aunt Adie recognized her niece, Gwennie.

'I thought I'd die,' she told Mrs Kelly the next day. 'I was ready to sink through the ground with mortification. Oh my Godfathers! Only for the bus conductor and the inspector the boys'd have had her clothes off her back! They held them and we had to scuttle off with the suitcase and everyone sniggering at us for a pair of country gawks!'

'Ah! What could she know of the world!' Mrs Kelly sighed. 'Four years in a convent!'

'Kind father to her,' sniffed Adie who had intended telling none of this. 'We went straight to the Celtic Ice Cream Parlour. I had to sit down. I was shaking like a leaf. Do you know, I ate two Melancholy Babies and she had a Knickerbocker Glory before either of us said one word!'

These were sundaes and Aunt Adie's predominant passion. ('What's your predominant passion?' the priest had asked her once at a retreat. 'Sundaes, father!') Once a week she closed her tearooms and rode to town – twelve miles in the bus – to revel in them. They cost half a crown apiece, which was almost what she charged in her own establishment for tea with scones and a boiled egg. They were her one extravagance, a trochaic trimeter that evoked the syrupy sundae itself: Méll an Cólly Báby. It drew fizzles of saliva to her lips.

Confused by the suitcase rumpus, too outraged to even scold this atrocious niece, Adie, with no more than a 'you can leave your case with the cashier', plunged her senses in a well of marshmallow and cool cream. Goblets later, notions which had been clashing in the corners of her shattered mind ('Straight back on the next bus!' – 'Ship her to her father in England tonight!') dissolved and withdrew. She looked at the girl who would not meet her eye. Adie's descended to long lisle stockings, lumpy with darns. She recalled the price she had been required to pay for six such pairs. Further up, a belt had been dragged tightly across a discoloured gymslip in an effort to give it shape. A poplin tie was punctured by a pin which bore, impaled and bleeding, a nickel emblem of the Sacred Heart. The girl's hair was wild as overblown furze. A gawk, Adie decided and was depressed. God help us, a poor eedjit. She was not surprised. People from outside County Dublin were half-baked. Though they could be sly enough when it suited their book. Country cute. Pale between spiky lashes, the girl's eyes reminded Adie suddenly of the untarred roads to nowhere that she had taken four years before when she went down to bury her sister. The country, smothered in mildewed hedges, had stunk of rotted flax, and Gwennie's freckles struck her then as being the same colour as the little mouldering mounds. The speechless child gave her the willies. Was she a moron, Adie had wondered between shudders at the cold, the lichenous presence of failure and the hens ridden by parasites. Going through her dead sister's duds had crowned it. There was so little to note: the wedding lines, some badly taken snaps, a few cheap medals. Musty smells, clammy oilcloth, a spray of withered twigs stuck in a bottle convinced her that her sister had put up no fight at all, that the last few months must have been nothing but a spineless drift into death and out of her responsibilities. The accumulations of this foolish life got Adie down properly. There was nothing you would take as a present. The poor trumpery would have been cruel as a souvenir. She couldn't get out of the place fast enough. 'The nuns', she told the child, 'will teach you Domestic Economy. Then you can come and live with me.' But she had put off taking her from year to year.

'Well, Miss,' Adie nodded impatiently at the goblet smeared with remnants of sundae. 'Did that please you?'

'Oh ma'am,' said the girl. 'It's gorgeous! I didn't know there was annything *like* that to eat annyplace.'

Adie was moved. Contemptuous but moved. The sundaeless dreariness of convent life struck her with a precise pain which was promptly relieved by the knowledge that she, Adie, could now bring happiness to a deprived creature. It was an odd sensation, sad but agreable. Like crying at a movie. Adie was a great crier. She began to cry now and dried her eyes with the disinfectant-soaked handkerchief which stung the tender flesh of her underlids.

'Oh,' she gasped. 'Oh!'

'What is it, ma'am?' Gwennie asked.

'I was thinking of your poor mother,' Aunt Adie lied. 'Call me "Aunt Adie". Everyone does.' And she smiled bravely in spite of the sting in her eye. She leaned a cheek towards the girl: 'Kiss me,' she said recklessly.

*

'Isn't that life!'

Mrs Kelly – bulbously pregnant and terrified of twins – rocked with laughter. 'Ha! Ha! Ha!' She flung her head so far back that Adie could see the uvula glisten in the moist vaulting of her mouth. 'I do have to laugh! Sure, if I had the money to insure against them, I'd be in no need to insure! Ah well,' she told Adie, *'you've* never known the meaning of the word "trouble"! Maybe you'll learn now! *I'd* say there was more than meets the eye in the nuns wanting to get shut of Gwennie! At sixteen she was just beginning to be worth pounds and pounds to them! *Unless* there was something wrong with her health? A delicate girl. . . .'

'She's not "delicate"!' Aunt Adie shied before the word 'TB' and cantered firmly round it. 'She *was* sick. Now she's cured.'

Mrs Kelly sighed, soaked cake in her tea and spooned it between her gums. 'I suppose I'll lose another tooth with this baby! If I was you, Adie, I'd insure the girl.' Chewing, her lips, bunched in an interrupted kiss, moved across her face like a fish form on sand. 'Death is an expense! Like birth!' She paused to watch a tick eddy and descend into the grave of Adie's chin. 'But you have money. You should take out a life insurance on her.' She put an undunked piece of cake in her mouth and drank tea through it. 'I'm eating for two,' she remarked, 'three maybe! When I was a girl we were warned never to kiss consumptives. . . .' she considered her teacup, 'and never to drink from anything they . . .'

'If that's what's worrying you,' Adie snapped, 'I keep hers apart! It'd do my business no good,' she added, 'to have you blabbing all around the village. . . .'

Mrs Kelly bridled. 'Is it *me*. . . .'

Adie wasn't listening. She was remembering former plans for launching into the pastry business. She saw a van gaily painted by the sign-painter carrying AUNT ADIE'S HOMEMADE CAKES AND PASTRIES to the four corners of the county. She and, yes, Gwennie in fur coats eating Melancholy Babies in the Ice Cream Parlour. Though Gwennie's health. . . . Insurance? She'd see. The gay van blackened mournfully. Adie picked up her old tabby cat and stroked its snoring head.

'I always slept with me Mammy,' Gwennie had told her on her first night. And with horror: 'Oh, don't make me sleep alone.'

Adie imagined the anaemic pair cuddled in a cocoon of obstinacy and disease. She shoved the cat off her lap. *Sleep* with her in a germy bed indeed!

'You're not serious!' she had scolded. 'It's four years since your Mammy died. You didn't sleep with anyone in the convent, did you? Well, did you? Can't you answer me?'

The girl's closed air made Adie's voice sharpen. What was the use of having affection to give if you came up against sullenness? Gwennie looked underhand: a convent Miss. 'Well,' Adie chivvied. 'Well? *Did* you share a bed with anyone?'

Gwennie, a nerve of memory jabbed, let out a shrill giggle. 'The nuns ada creased us! One time,' she gabbled in a jet of loquacity, 'Sister Teresa-of-the-Little-Flower caught two girls in the one bed and kicked them the length of the dorm. They could hardly sit down for a week! She wore men's boots.

Mary – she was one of the two girls – said if she ever got a chance when she'd left the place, she'd come back and bust her nose in.'

Gwennie stopped as suddenly as she had begun. Her expression – practised perhaps to deceive the eyes of nuns – as moon-innocent as before.

'Oh!' said Adie and then: 'If you need anything you can call me. I'll leave my door open.'

'Okeydoke!'

Later, hearing a window bang in Gwennie's room, Adie came in and found her bundled like a hedgehog: head and all beneath a bristle of blankets. Uncovering the face, she stared a while in puzzlement and with a nagging though indefinite twinge at the vulnerably prominent eyelids: convex and blue-veined like marbles.

*

Adie put Gwennie to work in the tearoom and let her keep half the tips – generously, for she was a disastrous waitress. The nuns had discouraged baths and saved soap for the convent laundry, so now Gwennie plunged black-bordered nails in plates of white pudding and tomatoes that she plonked before customers. With a bang. And a sputter. Then pounded downstairs with the heft of a mare in foal.

'My Lord!' Mrs Kelly said.

'She'll grow out of it,' Adie excused her.

Waste energy leaped from the girl. 'Ow!' she screamed. 'Whoops! I've banged my funnybone! Drat it! Holy Smoke! Whee! Here comes the bride Forty inches wide! I'll never make it with this tray! Look out all! I'm going to slip! Oy! Ow! Saved it!' There was an imbalance about her, an air of risk as she zoomed about like an unguided motor boat. Groans and giggles preceded her as regularly as the engine's throb. But she also made faces at herself in the tearoom mirror; dodged the Goldflake ad printed across its glass, dragging a steel comb through hair which leaped, crackled and came out in handfuls of knots like rutting spiders which she saved to make a bun. She longed to put up her hair, to wear a wide swishing skirt and be grown up. Coiled inside the uncomfortable schoolgirl a woman writhed, about to burst out with the lop-sided force of leaves ripping their bud. Half shadowed by the convent still, she alternated:

> *I'd like to get you*
> *On a slow boat to China*
> *All to myself alo-o-one.*

with:

> *Come Holy Ghost send down those beams*
> *Which sweetly flow in silent streams*
> *From thy great home abo-o-ove.*

'I don't care who sends it,' Mrs Kelly observed, 'a bit of silence would be a relief allright.'

'Think of living with fifty like that!' Aunt Adie sighed. 'Those nuns must have been tough babies.'

'Brides of Christ!' said Kelly acidly. 'I'd rather have fifty like that any day and no man! Nuns have it easy!'

'Well, no one can say her health hasn't picked up', said Adie, 'since she's been with me. I brought her back from death's door!' She was sorry now that she'd taken out the life insurance. It was only a waste and after the first quarter she let the payments lapse. 'I'm more than a mother to that girl,' she told everyone. 'It's great to have a bit of youth round the house!' She bought Gwennie nylons – irregulars – for wearing in the tearoom, a plastic nail-brush and semi-heeled shoes.

Gwennie crossed her legs like a stocking advertisement.

'Jeez!' she screamed, 'if the nuns could see me now!'

'Do you miss the convent?' Adie asked.

'That dump!'

'Where would you like best to live?'

'Here. Always.'

Adie melted. 'Listen,' she said. 'We'll go to town tomorrow to the Royal. They're showing *The Girl He Left Behind Him*.'

Gwennie hugged her. The two enjoyed such outings enormously and were seen to giggle ridiculously on the bus. Gwennie was open-mouthed at the promise of her own uncommitment. She bought *The Girl's Crystal* and *Maeve's Own Weekly* with her tips and imagined that because nothing had happened to her yet anything might. Airy as a pingpong ball tossed on a jet of spray, she affected Adie with her excitement.

'More than a mother really, I feel like a *sister* to her,' Adie said, 'or a girl friend.' At one swoop she was fulfilling the roles she had mismanaged until now. The sign-painter was not included on any of these trips which began in complicity as the pair sneaked past Mrs Kelly's hovel. Adie had dropped her old companion, who was suffering from morning sickness and depressed her with complaints.

'That one would put years on you,' said she to Gwennie, 'she'd cry this year for next year.'

*

In the autumn, when tourists fell off and there was nothing for Gwennie to do in the tearoom, Adie found her a place as nursemaid with a doctor's family who lived a mile up the hill. She was to sleep in so as to be on hand in case the children needed her at night and this, as Adie told her, was to her advantage because it meant she would be spending the winter in a heated house and would have the doctor to keep an eye on her in case she had a relapse. Meanwhile better not mention the consumption. What people didn't know needn't trouble them. Gwennie was to have Sunday afternoons and two evenings a week off to spend with Adie, and the two kissed lightly when the doctor came to pick her up with her suitcase. She would be round for supper three nights later.

But she was hardly out the door before Adie began to regret her. It was four months now since the day she had gone to meet her off the bus and she could hardly remember what she had done with herself before the girl's arrival. The autumn fogs had started and clung like grey stoppers at every window. No customers came. Adie mooched round the house, considered pocketing her pride and calling on the neglected Mrs Kelly, then bit the nose off the sign-painter when he told her she was like a hen that has lost its chick.

At three on the day Gwennie was due for supper, Adie was making scones; by six she had cooked a big juicy fry and was beginning to watch the hill road. By seven all the water in the kettle had boiled away and she was in a rage. 'Ha!' said she as she filled it up again. 'All the trouble I went to! Fat thanks I get!' She put it back on the fire and stared at her waiting table. 'Selfishness of the young!' She sighed with jealousy.

Gwennie arrived at seven-thirty. 'I had to wash me hair,' she explained.

'Very dainty!' sneered her aunt. 'You never used to bother! Whom are you trying to please?'

'It'll be no time', said the sign-painter, comfortably filling his mouth with sausage, 'till she'll have a young man. She's getting to be a fine girl. She'll be walking out in no time.'

'Ha!' cried his wife. 'She'd have to be weak in the head to look crooked at a man after what she's seen around her. Little good husbands did for me or her mother or Mrs Kelly.'

'Maybe not! Aha! But ye all wanted one! And so will she! I see there's a young fellow working up at your place these nights!' He winked at Gwennie.

She told them the doctor was having a second garage built.

'That's a bricklayer,' said the sign-painter. 'Moonlighting! And it's not all bricklayer's work he's doing there either. I was passing the house the other night and seen where he put in a window and door. He could be put out of the union for that. Doing a carpenter's job. Maybe you should give him the tip to be careful.' He grinned at his niece. 'Help you get acquainted.'

'Don't either of you bother your heads,' Aunt Adie advised. 'What good did unions ever do *you?*' she asked her husband. 'We'da been in a nice pass if we'da been depending on you and unions! God help the women that rely on men! Did jez see where Mrs Kelly's hubby was taken off with a perforated ulcer? Roaring! I suppose she'll be around here begging louder than ever now. All she gets is the Outdoor Relief. She ran through the dole months ago. It doesn't do you good to think of the troubles of the world. Give us a song Gwennie.'

Gwennie sang *I love the dear silver that shines in your hair* and the rest of the evening passed off amiably.

Her next evening off, however, she was so late that when she arrived Adie and the sign-painter were sitting down to supper. She came in the door still panting.

'Oho!' the sign-painter grinned. 'I was just saying to myself, 'tis out courting with the bricklayer you were! We're no company for a young girl. His name', he informed her, 'is Mat Mullen.'

A rush of distress swept through Aunt Adie and shook her chin as she gobbled fried apple and sausage. She glanced sideways at the sign-painter with hatred.

With mild moon eyes and hanging adenoidal jaw, Gwennie explained that she had been to Mrs Kelly's with some leftover pudding that the doctor's wife had told her she might take. 'They had a big party last night and there was lashings of creamy stuff that wouldn't keep,' she told Adie. 'I knew the Kellys would be glad of it. You never saw such misery,' she went on, 'the poor kids sitting around on the floor. And it'd make your hands itch to wipe the snot off their noses.'

'How come,' said Adie, 'you didn't think to offer *me* the pudding?'

Gwennie gave her a look of surprise. 'It was only leftovers.'

'*Only* leftovers! Very uppity we are these days. Was there sherry in the trifle?'

'Honest to God, Adie, you're making a mountain . . .' begged the sign-painter.

'You shut up,' Adie told him. 'Well, was there?' She knew she sounded wrong, and was upset by this and felt that somewhere underneath she wasn't wrong at all but wronged and must dig to the truth and justify herself with it. 'Well?' she harangued.

'I dunno,' Gwennie sounded sullen.

'But you gave it to those little fairies of starving brats! Sure that will sicken them. They'll have colic all night and be raising the roof. . . .' Adie flailed about for the right words, flinging wrong ones from her with contempt. She saw Gwennie and the sign-painter exchange a glance which seared her. To think of them ganging up on her! She would have liked to embrace Gwennie but the girl's sour puss checked her. It was too late now – or too soon. 'Giving presents to strangers,' she resumed painfully. 'Lady Bountiful no less! And what about your own', she paused, 'family? That did so much for you? Brought you back from death's door when you were good for nothing but a sanatorium? Took you into this house and found you work! Is this your thanks?' The girl's sullenness enraged her now. The hangdog look called out for punishment. Gwennie's glance slid crookedly away from her own. Adie wanted to shake or slap her. Anything to get through to her so that she could take her in her arms again. Coddle, restore and love her. My own baby, she thought and groaned: 'More fool me!' She could feel spittle bubbling at the corners of her mouth. Her eyes strained, swollen in their sockets. 'I'm an ugly old woman and youth is selfish! Well, it's nothing to me. . . . Why should *I* care?' Gwennie wasn't listening. 'Are you listening?' she hissed.

The sign-painter walked across the room and closed the door

after him. That was as much disapproval as he ever showed.

'Yes, ma'am.'

At the 'ma'am' Aunt Adie's rage collapsed.

'Sure all I want is your good,' she wheedled. 'Sure aren't you more than a daughter to me? Who else have I? Who else have you? To think that the one time you had a chance to give something, you preferred. . . .' She was on the right track now. 'Not that it's the thing itself I care about but the *thought*. . . .' She paused, losing the thread. Gwennie was listening attentively now. 'Don't tell me either that that doctor's wife hasn't given you other presents that you're hiding from me. As if I'd ask you for them! Oh, I'm not the fool I may look! That Limerick lace blouse she used to wear to church – didn't she give you that? Dare you say she didn't? I haven't seen it on her this long time. Maybe you're waiting to give that to Mrs Kelly too? Or to wear it yourself for your . . . bricklayer?'

'I swear to God,' Gwennie began, 'she never. . . .'

Aunt Adie raised a hand.

'Don't perjure yourself!'

*

The next time Gwennie came she brought the blouse. Adie took it casually. 'Very nice fit,' she said, trying it on. 'It'll look snappy with my black suit. She used to have gloves to match,' she remembered. 'Why don't you ask her for them? One's no good without the other.'

'Oh I couldn't *ask* her,' Gwennie began to whimper.

Adie turned back to the mirror. 'Sure she doesn't know what she has. Spoilt rotten that kind of woman is!'

Pale hair, pale lace confronted her in the glass, cold as spray and remote as an old snap. She knew she was crumbling away Gwennie's affection. As she ruffled the flounces on her chest the glass buttons danced.

'I'll wear it to mass,' she said. 'In the bus.'

Gwennie's hand flew to her nouth. 'She'll see you!'

'So what?' said Aunt Adie. 'So what? It's mine, isn't it?'

In her blurred vision the lace thickened consistency, became a caul of lard on the sloping shoulder of a leg of lamb.

'So what?' asked the lump of grey cold meat in the mirror, 'so what?'

Gwennie wept.

*

Within a week the doctor's wife found a dozen purloined objects in Gwennie's suitcase. She questioned the girl curiously. None were of value: a few steel butter knives, some napkins, an embroidered pillowcase.

'What could you possibly want with these, Gwennie?' she wondered. 'They're hardly saleable you know!'

Gwennie got hysterical and the doctor had to give her a sedative. He agreed with his wife that the girl was a bit unstable and probably unfit to be left in charge of children. When Gwennie and the children wept over this decision they agreed, doubtfully, to give her a second chance.

'Robby and Clare adore her.' Gwennie overheard the doctor's wife say. 'I suppose that's what matters. One can't apply one's own standards to these people.'

Gwennie retailed all this to Aunt Adie who only laughed. 'You don't need them! What do you care?' she said. 'Next year we'll start the pastry business and then you'll be your own boss. You won't call the queen your cousin. We'll show them!'

She was not sorry that Gwennie should have fallen out of favour at the big house. With its wood of foreign trees imported by the doctor's grandfather, it filled her with hatred and suspicion. Its view plummeted into the bay beyond the roofs of the village. Its name was haughtily foreign: Bella Vista. Behind high walls topped with broken glass, it sprawled outlandishly and was kin only to a few neighbouring mansions: Khyber Pass, Miramare, Saint Juan les Pins, where old colonels and retired British civil servants with jaundiced skin chewed the cud of memories as snuffy, no doubt, and as alien as the smell from the eucalyptus leaves which stuck in the gutters and were floated down the hill to the village – a smell which reminded Adie of sick rooms and antiseptic. She cursed herself for ever getting Gwennie the job in that house, cursed it for making the girl independent and for giving her notions. She began to watch sourly on the nights Gwennie was not off and Mat Mullen, the foxy-haired, moonlighting bricklayer, strode up the hill with shouldered hod. He was about twenty-two, with an impudent blue eye and, Gwennie had told her, the mistress sent her out to him with cups of tea and Guinness. Had that one no sense? Or was it deliberate? Adie questioned Gwennie to know did she like him but the girl had grown sly. Ah, she said, he thought too much of himself. How did she know that? Ah, she just did. The secret burst from her:

'He asked me to a dance. In the Town Hall.'

'And you said?'

'No.'

'I should just think so! The cheek!'

'Ah,' regretfully, 'I hadn't a decent dress.'

Adie contained herself. Next day she went to see the doctor and reproached him for not keeping a sufficiently close eye on Gwennie, an innocent girl. Things improved. The garage was finished and Gwennie, more solicitous than before, bought her aunt presents with her wages and accompanied her twice a week to the movies and Ice Cream Parlour. Adie grumbled because it couldn't be more often but Gwennie said the doctor's wife was too busy with Red Cross work.

'Red Cross my big toe,' said Adie. 'That one's an ikey lass! Charity, you might tell her, begins at home. If you lie down and make a door mat of yourself you'll be trodden on. Stand up for your rights!'

'Oh,' said Gwennie, 'I couldn't.'

In February – three months after the bricklayer had asked Gwennie to the dance – Adie had occasion to go to the cinema alone. *Frankenstein* which she couldn't bear to miss was showing locally. Gwennie was not off and Adie, returning by dark from the bus stop, was pursued by monsters. Scuttling from street lamp to street lamp, she clawed at walls which, in places, yielded beneath her fingers with the suspect pliancy of moss. The stretch of road past the doctor's gate was particularly dark. Protruding stucco erections and fanciful battlements reared; ancient cedars concealed the sky. Beyond them was the sea. On the curve of road below, a line of cars, packed tight like scales on a snake, harboured lovers. Adie, hastening in the dark past the doctor's gate, heard a half smothered, wholly familiar laugh. She whipped round, plunged back. Heedless of doubt, she grabbed the woman's arm and pulled her into the lamplight. It was Gwennie. With the bricklayer. 'You . . . you!' Hysteria choked her. Gwennie wrenched her arm free and ran in. A door creaked shut. The bricklayer disappeared. Adie, who had wasted her ammunition on skirmishes, was foiled of the major battle, disarmed before the true betrayal. She turned away, groping. Below her the closed cars crouched in their ranks. 'Sluts!' she muttered at them. 'Whores!' She plunged and stumbled, almost fell down the hill, beyond the trees, to where the bay opened wide to the moonlight. 'Underhand . . .' she groaned. 'Hypocrite!' The words, not quite released, fell back in her throat with the loneliness of a sleeper's moan. 'Trailing round lanes . . . !' she spat. Down here, in gardens heavy with winter greenery, artificial pagodas and summer houses shone in a light which ignored the small village house further below, shadowed by the hill's shoulder and dank with its drainings. Leaves clattered. The sea sucked. With head hunched into her shoulders, Adie fled the empty openness of the night and at a swift lope made for the consoling limits of her own kitchen.

Alone there, later, while the sign-painter snored, she sat like Niobe and pondered. On the sly! All these months Gwennie had had nights off that she had not confessed. Red Cross indeed! Adie laughed sourly and caught a hateful glimpse of her own derision in the glass. Gulled! Gulled! That two-faced, simpering trollop had deceived her! *She* had been rationed! Two nights a week for her and how many for the bricklayer? All the sweetness to herself had been a sop thrown to stick in her gullet. To shut her up! Three for him or four? *Five* maybe? Maybe she was off every night! At the suspicion Adie went rigid with pain. What would she not have done for Gwennie! Nights blank as the bay she had just passed stretched despairingly in front of her. After such treachery whom could she ever trust? Adie, who had never smashed a possession deliberately or hardly even wept if not at the movies, sat stifling with unvented misery until, in the small hours of the morning, she dozed off in her chair.

At nine she was ringing the doctor's bell. He came to the door himself. Gwennie had taken the children to the dentist. Adie told him she wanted her niece back. She needed her in the tearooms. He said, coldly, that he thought he had gathered that the girl herself was eager to stay. Seeing his inquisitive stare, Adie tried to settle wisps of hair which she had not combed since the morning before. Her breath catching, she said, 'Gwennie is under age.'

'But she tells me', he said, 'that her father is her legal guardian.'

Adie broke down at this proof of a fresh conspiracy. 'Oh,' she sobbed. 'To think that I . . . after all, all. . . . Brought her back from death's door! Where's me handkerchief? Oh the hussy. . . . The snake! Asp in my bosom. . . . Oh!'

The doctor sat her down, gave her a glass of something, tried to soothe, talked of the understanding we must all have for the young and how Mat Mullen was a decent young man. At this Adie collected her dignity and walked out of the house.

They were all against her. There was no trust.

That morning she denounced Mat Mullen to an officer of the bricklayers' union.

*

For weeks she did not see Gwennie whose guilty conscience, no doubt of it, was keeping her embuttressed in the doctor's house up the hill. She heard from Mrs Kelly however that Mat had been given his marching orders and that, as this meant he couldn't work any more in the Republic, he was going to buy a ticket for the other side. Then news came that Gwennie too had given notice. It seemed she would wait for Mat to get a job before joining him. She had written to her father in London and had got an answer. Meanwhile, the two were observed courting on the hill roads where cedars and ilexes lent concealment even in January. By the winter twilight Adie saw them in every couple that passed up or down the road or stood at lookout points above the bay: unidentifiable match-stick figures, pausing by parapets like migrant birds. When business took her to Dun Laoghaire Harbour, she swerved towards the wooden departure pier, to scrutinize the spray-blown, pink-nosed travellers who queued, moving their bundles with intent patience. Gold-braided harbour officials ushered striding gentlemen ahead, and relatives waved despondently from behind a parapet. Gwennie's underhand countenance snuffled beneath every umbrella. Then Adie heard that Mat had indeed gone, that Gwennie had a cold, had pleurisy, had been moved to hospital with TB meningitis. The doctor came and drove Adie in, weeping all the way, in his own car.

At ten that morning, Adie sat, alone among the marble tables of the Ice Cream Parlour, and held a handkerchief to her lips. She had been there an hour when Mrs Kelly, lean and mangey after her delivery, came in to help her home.

'I couldn't face back alone,' Adie told her. 'I've been to the hospital. They wouldn't let me see her.' She sobbed. 'First her mother and now her! And those two men off in England! Her father and the other one! Leaving it all to me. Such a responsibility! Doctor Flynn says there's a new Wonder Drug they could try on her. It costs hundreds of pounds but they'd try it on her as an experiment. Free! How do I know what to say? Maybe they're using her as a guinea pig? What do doctors care for the poor? Have a sundae. No? Ah do! As we're here. I didn't know where else to go. Have a Melancholy Baby. To think she used to love coming here!' Aunt Adie sobbed again lengthily. She dabbed her face. 'I suppose I'll be alone at her funeral,' she groaned. 'Like I was at her mother's. If she dies. He wouldn't tell me what the chances were. A buttoned-up old puss-in-boots that doctor. On and on about how they do their best and the state of medical science and a lot of jawbreakers!' Aunt Adie fell silent, sighed, blew her nose and drew a corner of an envelope from her handbag. Letters protruded: P-R-U-D-E-N. . . . Seeing Mrs Kelly lean forward, she pushed it back and clamped shut, first the bag, and then her mouth as though it contained a frog which she was afraid might jump out. The frog kicked the inside of her cheeks so that they trembled, and Adie opened her mouth with a pop.

'I went in', she gasped, 'and paid up the back payments of the life insurance anyway. I'd stopped paying them for a while there when she looked so healthy.'

She turned in her chair to call the waitress and ordered a Melancholy Baby for herself and another for Mrs Kelly. The two women spooned silently into their sundaes.

'God help us but it's a queer world we live in,' Mrs Kelly said, through a spoonful of marshmallow.

'Eat up,' Aunt Adie said. 'We may as well enjoy it while we're in it.'

Oh My Monsters!

It's freakish! Appalling! I can't bear to think about it!

Thoughts forward.

To whom or what? Oh, to whom but Kiki. Yes, unknown to you, Kiki, I'm on my way. The train has pulled out of Paris-Lyon. Goodbye. Goodbye. The rural womb awaits. *Merde!* Now I've depressed myself and there's no one to cheer me. Minutes ago, a man stuck his head in the compartment door, paused, withdrew himself. Mustn't have liked what he saw. So here I'm on my own till Dijon with nary a buffer between me and me. Nothing but a litre of cognac and Nembutal in the little malachite box given me by – never mind whom. Every item I possess has a name attached, so better not start the attributing game. What will I do then? Sing? Count sheep? Make up a limerick? A lady who loved to get laid – what rhymes with that? Well, there's 'renegade': that's me, ever ready to join a new army, sew fresh colours on my faded sleeve. My armies, Kiki, are my men and – since I too have my honour – I join one at a time and keep step with the current paymaster. Yessir! I'm loyal while I last, the perfect batwoman, quick to absorb new tastes and learn to shop within the confines of almost any budget. References aplenty. *Premier prix de souplesse:* I can operate in French, British and American, upper to lower – well, better say lower-middle – class arenas. *Parfaitement*, Kiki, and don't think apologies are intended. Either now or when we meet.

Look, if I take my style and world view from my current man and he his from his current job, whose integrity is weaker? Is it better to adapt for love or money? To embrace the values of the Rand Corp., the Quai d'Orsay or the Faculté de Philo of the University of Grenoble? Or to embrace Rand etc. values through and in the person of a man?

I've no idea.

Truly. You see, Kiki, currently, I'm valueless, being manless, demobbed, out of uniform and with no reference points. The last ones turned out unreliable for the man was mad: a most disconcerting event. I wonder can you tell how disconcerting? No? Look, it was as though some executive were suddenly to learn that the corporation for which he worked did not exist, had been – say – a project cooked up by some well-funded psychologists eager to study executives' behaviour. After months – or years – of diligence on his part, they tell him 'it wasn't real', give him a golden handshake and let him go. Where does that leave him?

I wouldn't know. I've lost my criteria.

(She lost her *what*? Oh some little thing she had removed. Probably one of those feminine 'ops' so common after thirty.)

Jokes, Kiki, are getting unfunny. I'm in one, you see: the reason I never knew he was mad was that I thought he was being funny. Funny-haha, you know, but instead he was funny-peculiar. Doesn't it just kill you, Kiki. No, but it may me.

I wonder will you be glad or under strain when I turn up? I should, of course, have written – but some things are hard to get down on paper. I meant to. Really. I kept, keep, writing to you in my head.

'Dear' – goes my head-letter – 'Kiki, I do think about you. I mayn't write but I talk to you in my mind all the time. Well, "mind" is a word which makes me blush. I feel shame about using it of the place in which I spend my days and nights. It's a cerebral slum, a *louche* blue-movie house . . .'

Dear Kiki, the truth is I have no mind. That's why I can't answer your concerned and reasonable letters. You always said I hadn't. Remember? 'Anne-Marie', you said, 'is alive from her waist down. As for her head . . .' You shrugged your hump. Your hump gave you prestige. It was something the rest of us didn't have. It put you out of the running for the marriage-market and, by extension, out of our sex. Your extra protuberance made a man of you. You were, even before Jacques, Papa and Gerard died, the true *chef de famille*.

We're in open country now: bare, frozen fields. The train zips over them, quick as a fly-zipper. A nip of brandy forward. I need support.

'I hope', your last letter says, 'this marriage is not going to be another mistake. Tell me about Sam.'

Damn you, Kiki, you've made yourself my conscience. Do you know what the result has been? No, but I'll tell you. This time when we meet you're going to be told. It has meant that I've always left the job to you. Kiki has had the conscience, Anne-Marie the cunt-science. Oh weep tears of sperm and lubricant! I live in my cunt! You can't begin to imagine what it feels like, can you? Can't and wouldn't try. But this isn't a joke. Mentally I'm wound around, head between my own legs, eyes and brain swaddled in a monotonous cuntscape.

Apologia and quota of self-pity: another thing you can't imagine is what it's like to have to adjust to no longer trading on charm. At my age.

A hump-shrug here. I know. I know. Plain women have no patience with this plea, even take it for a kind of boast. You called me 'the dumb beauty' – but have you ever wondered why are dumb beauties dumb? Sister, the first reason is because they have no reason not to be and the second that the brain tuned to pleasure functions differently. Essential parts atrophy. Comes the day when it can only cope with dream. I think that's happened to mine, Kiki. When I'm woken up I panic. When I lose a man . . .

Over the last few years I've lost several. I'll tell you about one. Not Sam. A Greek who was very desirable, very grand and wanted to marry me. He changed his mind because I never emptied the ash-trays. It was a silly mistake but, you see, I wasn't tuned to the practical side of things. He was a sexually thrilling man. When we were together I could think of nothing but that and imagined that neither could he. We used to stay in bed all day, smoking; the ash from our cigarettes kept piling up and whenever a breeze blew in would sift around the room. It fell on our bed and he laughed and said we were like lovers in Pompeii and must make sure the lava would find us in the attitude of love. So we made love over and over while the curtains billowed in from the balconies like swollen sails or bridal veils and the ash circulated. It was June. We were staying at the Crillon. The weather was showery and, outside, the Place de la Concorde was all hazy and bright: a Renoir canvas. He kept telling me he loved me and wanted his mother to meet me. Then we'd ring for room-service and have food sent up with more cigarettes. When his mother did come the place was like a disaster-area: mascara on the sheets, my hair a bird's nest, pairs of tights telescoped all over the floor. The flowers he had bought me had gone rank and there were apple-cores everywhere. She stood there looking astounded and all I could do was laugh. It was really a gasp – but I had no chance to explain. Terrible memory. Forget. Suppress. She would probably not have approved of me anyway so what the hell. Mothers never do. Neither do best friends, councils of responsible kin, etc., etc. That brigade has broken more of my engagements than I care to remember. They're the Fates, the Furies. I know once they're there I'm out. Sometimes they've offered me money. Sometimes I've had to accept it. Well what do you do if you're turfed off a cruise in Crete or Reykjavik?

It's – try and understand this, Kiki – the impinging, the crash-landing of one sort of reality on another. And does this make sense to you: when really grubby moments like that engulf me, I think of you. Maybe you're my stake in the world of family-values?

That world is constantly threatening to withdraw my residence-permit. Others' mothers issue those. Matrons.

Sweet and ruthless. Marsha's the first who's ever liked me. I knew her before I did Sam. She introduced us.

'Hey Anne-Marie,' she said last week, 'I can't tell you what a kick it gives me that you're marrying Sam. I mean *we* get on so well! Now I know pleasing your mother-in-law is not the prime aim in marriage, but', endearing laugh, endearing shrug, 'if it happens it's a bonus.'

Wait, Kiki, you'll see the irony of that later.

Marsha's from New York, boozy, a hairdresser's blonde and likes a good giggle. Also she's loaded.

Vulgar Anne-Marie! *Vulgaire!* I love that word: the first strongly charged one I learned. It's so dated now! Its frank snobbery is, I suppose, vulgar in our devious days. I like your use of it: robust like the special corsets you get from your supplier in Annecy who claims his stock hasn't varied in forty years. But, darling, I'm really not vulgar, not even venal. I guy myself when I think of you but actually I'm disinterested. I'll do nothing for money. Not a thing. Oh – and maybe that's what worries you most? I imagine you worrying. You adjust your poultice, sip your gargle, spit it out and worry. Who is this man I'm marrying *now*? This Sam?

Sam? He's hard to pin down. Supply your own idea of 'attractive'. He's mine. He has that deadpan American humour which I don't always get. He'll say things like this: 'Know something, Anne-Marie? You're a double-nut! Why? Because you want to marry me and I – I'm telling you this up front – am a certified nut. Marsha had to smuggle me out of the States. They wanted to put my ass in the booby-trap. You thought I was dodging the draft, didn't you? Well what I was dodging was the nut-house. That means that for me to want to marry you is rational. A normal is an asset to a nut but the normal who marries a nut is behaving in an irrational manner, hence nuttier than the nut!'

We laughed. Christ, Kiki, I thought he was joking! More deadpan Yankee humour. Irony and all. Ha! More irony: your relief at hearing I was getting married again. I have your letter in my bag. It has grown soft as tissue from being carried there.

'I had begun to despair', it says, 'of your ever settling down to a normal life . . . wondering how responsible we might be for the way you turned out. I suppose, since you were the youngest, we did spoil you and by spoil', you elucidate, 'I mean "damage"!'

Oh Kiki, did you? How much? And how can I tell?

Several hours yet to Chambéry. Rows of poplars slide past, leafless, rasping the sky. I root in my over-night case for a Valium. The case is in sealskin, carries the creams and colours of my identikit and is known to vulgar Parisiens as a *baise-en-ville*.

I thought of phoning you – but long-distance calls upset you. I imagined you in bed – it was 6 a.m. when I got the idea – and having to grope down two flights of uncarpeted stairs to the phone in the hall. Later, you would have been watching coffee on the kitchen stove. I saw it boil over, spattering onto the white enamel as you ran to take my call. After that you would go out to feed the hens and loose the dogs, slopping through muck in Wellingtons which you would have to drag off, cursing genteel curses in the doorway then rushing to stop the phone's brash peal.

'*Crotte*,' you'd mutter, '*crotte de bique.*'

So I didn't ring. I'll just come.

'What's the matter?' you'll say. First thing. Braced, Anne-Marie means trouble, you think, has no sense, no head on her shoulders; sometimes you add 'No brains!'

This shouldn't annoy me but does. Every time. I was the only one in a family of seven sisters and one brother to pass the Baccalauréat – but somehow none of you was impressed. I am a paragraph-reader too and that counts against me. 'Skims the surface,' you say as you thumb your own laborious way down the columns of *La Croix*. When I do a long-division sum in my head, you react as though I'd done a conjuring trick: something not in the best of taste and whose reliability had better be checked. 'Remember', you say ungenerously, 'the hare and the tortoise!' Haven't you heard, Kiki, this is the jet-age? Hares have been rehabilitated. Tortoises are out! Your yardstick is obsolete – not that I'd care, if only you wouldn't beat me with it. If only you wouldn't keep on about hoping I'll settle down to a 'normal' life. God, that dictatorial word. It's going to get between us, Kiki. It's going to make it hard for me to stay. Because I'm not going to sit around wearing penitential sackcloth admitting that every last thing I ever did was aberrant and that my failure confirms the authority of your norm.

Because, darling, there are more norms in the hexagon of France than you or I could imagine. Everyone thinks theirs is best. My ex-husband, Jean-Louis, couldn't see for a minute what I found wrong with his. As a *prof de philo*, he should, one might have thought, have known about relativities and things looking different from different angles and in different temperatures. I always felt he had a band of cold air around him and his tempo was decidedly not mine. I have a high metabolism which means I do things fast. I get bored fast too, but while I'm with a man I'm totally involved. Frighteningly: I have an impulse to die when I make love. That's why I keep the Nembutal in the garage. These impulses wilt in the time it takes to get downstairs. I said this to Jean-Louis and he thought it in terrible taste. I remember him switching on the light and pulling away from me. He had a look of someone who's smelled gas and is worrying about the leak. He liked things mashed up in wordy abstractions. Then he could cope. He could cope with the most extreme notions once he'd put them into his abstract jargon, but by then I'd be bored. Besides I never did learn his vocabulary. I remember complaining – jokingly – to our local grocer that I couldn't understand my husband's philosophisms. The grocer was very quick-witted and a whizz at crosswords. He had a café in his grocery and I used to sit there when I'd finished my shopping and we'd race each other through the day's crossword. He had a dictionary of philosophical terms which he'd got for doing this and he gave it to me to help me understand my husband. 'To promote understanding in family-life,' he said. I told Jean-Louis and he was furious – said I was making a fool of him in the village, that the grocer's nephew was in his class and that now all the pupils would be laughing behind his back. I couldn't see this at all. But then I never could see things Jean-Louis's way even after I had the dictionary. We moved to Grenoble shortly after that and he began teaching at the university and bringing a brilliant female student of his home for meals. She had very little money and needed feeding, he said. While I cooked, she and he used to talk about Althusser and Husserl and *épiphénomènes* and *épistémologie and épi*-this and *épi*-that and, though I kept the dictionary in the kitchen drawer, I could never remember which was which and used to get so furious that I would find myself putting sugar in the stew and chopping my finger into the parsley. He was sleeping with her of course and when I found out and said: OK, I hoped they'd enjoy each other and I was leaving, he couldn't understand at all. It was quite normal, he said, for me to be annoyed, but it was normal for him to have been drawn to her as a fellow searcher in the same field and really the carnal thing between them had been just a moment of tenderness, a kind of seal on their friendship and no more and his long-term commitment was to me and it was not normal for me to fail to see this or to throw all up for a moment's pique. Then he used one of his *épi*-words and I saw that the whole point of the jargon was to make very ordinary thinking seem grand and to camouflage the mean caution of his commitment to life in general and to me in particular. His favourite ordinary – non-jargon – word, Kiki, was 'normal'. I've been suspicious of it since. I met him some years later in a street in Saint Tropez and we had a drink for old time's sake. He said he had almost not recognized me and I, as one does, asked had I got so old and he said no but that in the old days I used to dress in a normal way whereas now . . . I roared with laughter.

'Jean-Louis,' I said. 'Look around you. This *is* the normal way. It's what everybody's wearing.'

It was summer and I was wearing a cheesecloth caftan and sandals. He looked around and most women were indeed wearing something like it. He kept looking and then, finally, a look of relief spread over his face. 'There's a normally dressed woman,' he said, nodding at a very provincial-looking girl in a pleated tartan skirt which was the wrong length for that year, a saddle-stitched bag and imitation-Gucci moccasins: the very sort of outfit I used to wear when I lived with him. I was suddenly very moved. My throat closed up with emotion and I wanted to put my arms around old Jean-Louis. I couldn't be sure: was I feeling this way because he'd made his 'norm' out of his memory of me and would be expecting brilliant *philo* students to conform to it forever more or because I realized that if I'd stayed with him I'd have gone on being a different person to the one I am now? I don't know. Anyway, a strong nostalgia for things past seized me and I felt quite lustful towards Jean-Louis, so I got up and left. I was living with someone else at the time and, as I've said, I am quite scrupulous about keeping my polyandry serial rather than simultaneous.

As for your norm, Kiki, it upsets me to think of it. But I do. I constantly think of you and our sisters mending your gumboots with bicycle-repair kits, hair scrunched into rain-bonnets, hands, stumpy as feet, reddened and ruined from trying to raise cash by selling chicken-shit, fruit and battery-hens. I see it all through a black frame like the edge on the mourning-cards you send me with such regularity that I could paper the loo with them: 'Pray for the soul of Aunt Madeleine-Sophie who died on this day fifteen years ago. RIP.' All our older relatives are dead. The younger and more robust left years ago for Egypt, Algeria or Indo-China, moved on when those places proved inhospitable, then failed to keep in touch. You are left with your commemorative cards and a few nuns who come out of their convents on name days and holy days to eat. As monastic rules relax, they come oftener, eat more and take back scraps in bags for friends less well provided for. They never bring you anything. I see you cooking for them, making meals from scratch – no meat-cube ever entered your kitchen. Labour has no value. Jean-Luc is set to churning the old ice-cream bucket, cranking it by hand for maybe an hour, then to pick flowers for the aunts to take back to their convent altars. Jean-Luc is fourteen now: the last surviving male in a family of females, the last child in a house whose ways were set when we were all in the nursery. Only he justifies them now. Your norm, my poor Kiki, will soon be quite bizarre. Norms, you see, are shifty.

I AM NORMAL!

I once typed that out on a postcard I'd happened to find in a drawer and considered sending you. The card was one of those plump, embroidered ones with a pressed edelweiss stuck on it and I must have bought it from a beggar at some resort. You might even have liked it although it had picked up a smell of stale cosmetics from lying so long in the drawer. But when I re-read the words they looked silly. The longer I looked, the shiftier they got. In the end the type seemed to be twitching like flies getting ready to do a bunk. Would anyone normal write such a thing?

Probably, I decided, it was the baldness of the statement that undermined it. It needed context, a bit of clutter. Like my life.

Clutter is ballast. You and my other sisters know that. You weight your lives with balls and bales of string, old knives, invitations to and reject gifts from other people's weddings. Do you remember, Kiki, that you kept every scrap of plate and silver I got for mine? For my first wedding which may well – brace yourself – be my only one. Admit that it provided a good haul! The family had been marriage-shy for so long that a fund of repossessed gifts had accumulated: objects whose owners had been removed by death or a monastic vocation. They were trotted out for my benefit, gift-wrapped with some flourish, presented with relief. Who can be bothered nowadays to clean silver? Answer: Kiki can.

'You keep it,' I told you. I knew you wanted it, had seen you touch the stuff as a timid shop-lifter might: fingers poised then retreating in an empty, hankering clench.

'Keep it all!' I said.

'You're mad!' you said, 'these are your *wedding presents*!'

'But I don't want them. Really. Sell them if you like, Kiki. They're yours.'

'But that's not *normal*!'

'I think it is. It seems quite normal to me.'

'Oh *you*!' You laughed. But you kept the silver.

Darling. I'm being querulous, fighting with you already in my head – and so why then am I coming back? Because, Kiki, I'm at my lowest ebb, lost, lonely, maybe mad. Maybe. For the first time I could believe it.

'You', said Sam yesterday, 'are a double nut . . .'

It appals me to think of his saying that. I told Rosemary – the girl I stayed with last night. She's known Sam for years.

'I thought', I told her and kept crying as I tried to tell her, 'that it was a joke! You know the way Sam horses around!'

'Anne-Marie,' she said, 'he was trying to warn you. Sam's devious. Proud. He had to make a joke of it but you should have known it wasn't one. Anyone else would have! I mean – how long have you two lived together? Eight months? Well, surely then – I mean you must have wondered sometimes at his behaviour?'

'I thought he joked a lot.'

'Well he did,' said Rosemary, 'but nobody jokes all the time!'

Kiki, I'm trying to find ways to tell you – hell, there's no good way.

What about a telegram: *Engagement broken Sam gaoled. Stop. Arriving tonight. Stop. Anne-Marie.*

And stop and let me off. Sam drove through a red light yesterday shortly after telling me of his and my nuttiness. We were on our way to the country to stay with Rosemary and her husband whose name is Dirk and who was at Johns Hopkins with Sam. Sam was in a chatty mood.

'Weddings', he told me, 'are a collective celebration of blood-letting, human sacrifice and the offering of virgins – *en principe*, virgins,' here he pinched my crotch with his gear-shifting hand, 'so as to further the increase of the clan. Barbarous survivals. White veils, for God's sake! Rice! Old shoes. Will you wear a white veil, Anne-Marie, to commemorate all the white lambs sacrificed to the rite? Or a black one? Let's make our wedding recognizably monstrous. Let's invite the world's worst monsters.'

'Who are they?' I was looking out the window at a passing turnip field.

'Nixon, Ron Reagan, Shirley Temple Black.' Sam reads the *Herald Tribune* every day and his hell is entirely North American.

'Where will you get them? From the waxworks?' A Citroën raced past slick as a wet cockroach. The whole of the Route Nationale 7 was slick. I was only half listening but could tell that Sam was still sounding off in some abstract way. I turned to look at him.

He's twenty-nine and I'm thirty-five and my mind tends to get stuck in the implications of that. Worry about my shortcomings – cellulite in the thigh, morning puffiness about the eye – kept me from wondering was there anything the matter with him. You see I'm used to being the flawed one, the one on trial and this time I was supposed to be the judge – naturally, I never realized it.

'Will you get your monsters from the waxworks?' I asked him.

'I'm going to invite the originals,' he said and put his foot on the accelerator. It was a good road but we were already going too fast. 'I'm inviting Nixon and Spiro Agnew to our wedding,' he said. 'Colonel Amin and Roman Polanski. Oh and the Chilean junta.'

I was tired of the joke. Maybe because the speedometer was still climbing. 'Don't you think', I suggested, 'that they might be too busy to attend?'

Something hard and heavy landed on my mouth. It was his fist which he'd flung sideways. His ring split my lip. My neck wrenched backwards and I saw everything dark for moments with two swoops of concentric circles like luminous eyes – my own I suppose – glaring at me out of the blackness like flicked-up headlights.

'Don't contradict me!' yelled Sam.

The speedometer was at a hundred. The car wove across a miraculously empty road.

'I'm sorry,' I apologized swiftly. 'I was joking.'

'Don't you joke with me!'

'No,' I gabbled cravenly, 'no, no I won't.' There was blood in my mouth. I tested my teeth. They seemed steady. However, my tongue felt odd and my lip was swelling. I tried to think of something soothing to say. He was, it came to me in a lucid flash, a Super-Maniac. A joker in the pack, he had appeared as King of Hearts but instead was the Knave: kinkiness itself, the epitome of all male trickery. I'd known other freaks but Sam was the worst. He had given no warning. After eight months as the perfect lover, he was now, like a flipped card, showing his other face. I knew. At once. People find this odd – Dirk and Rosemary did – that I should have gone on so long having no suspicion of him then have realized at one blow. But I did. It was like that. He was, I knew then, Nemesis sent by some Dark Venus to punish me.

'We'll invite Solzhenitsyn,' Sam yelled.

'OK,' I shouted. 'As you like. Anything.'

The speedometer dropped and we made it to Dirk and Rosemary's. Thank God it was them. Half an hour after we'd sat down to drinks and chat, Sam – I can remember no provocation leading up to this – put down his vodka, walked to where I was sitting, knocked me out of my chair and began to kick me. Dirk was on him in a second. He's stronger than Sam and had him off me at once. It was all suspiciously smooth.

'You *knew*!' I challenged Rosemary in the bathroom.

She handed me cold-cream and tissues. 'What?'

'Sam's a nut-case! *Dingue!* Why did nobody tell me?' I was crying.

'It wasn't our business to tell you, but, yes, he's been committed several times. His mother . . .'

'Yes?'

'She hoped you'd cure him. He's been all right for a long while.'

'You mean nobody would have told me? At any point?'

Rosemary managed to look conniving but remote. She and Dirk are Sam's friends. After all. Fellow-Americans in France. To them *I*'m the foreigner.

'Look,' she excused, 'we supposed you'd guessed. Something . . . Besides, we weren't sure you really meant to marry him. You might have been playing along with his fantasies – joking.' Conciliatingly, she offered me a packet of Wash 'n' Dries.

Later she said, 'You'd better spend the night here.'

She went off to cook. Dirk had managed to get Sam out of the house. I'd heard the car leave. For where? I suppose I was only now feeling the shock. I sat in Rosemary's drawing-room and drank Kirs. One Kir after another, mixing them solemnly myself, pouring the clammy red drops of Cassis in various doses into glasses of cold white wine. Blood-thick at first, they dissolved in a faint blush, a memory of sweetness in the dryness. I hadn't drunk Kirs since leaving Jean-Louis. It had been our drink. In England I got onto Scotch. With Sam – oh shit and *merde*! I smashed down a glass and two pink drops jumped out of it.

'I'm sending you', you wrote last year, 'two cases of Papa's 1952 wine. His own. We found it in the lower cellar behind a vat which had got stuck and . . .'

I knew you wanted something from me. Of course.

'Poor Lucette's boy, Jean-Luc, is thirteen. He's running wild', you wrote, 'around here. I'm afraid he'll end up like poor Jacques . . .'

Poor, poor, poor. Do you say 'poor Anne-Marie'? Or not? Probably not. The injured are 'poor'. Only they. Or the dead. 'A gaggle of spinsters,' you joked, bravely facing your condition head on, 'the unwise virgins, you might call us, are hardly the people to bring up a boy. *You* . . .'

I?

More Kir. I sent you an expensive cashmere sweater and thanked you for the wine. Not wishing to feel obligated.

'I think of him', your letter had astonishingly gone on to say, 'as more your son than Lucette's. She was so briefly married, after all. Poor Gérard . . .'

'Poor' again. Think of Gérard so as not to think of Sam! Gérard married my sister, Lucette – the only one of you all who managed to have a date or get a man. Well, how could you, living up the mountains where the few middle-class males around were intent on showing the place a clean pair of heels as soon as they could pass their Bac? Lucette snatched Gérard during a six-week trip to Pau where she was taking the waters with an invalid aunt. She didn't do too badly, considering. He was reasonable-looking, a lawyer, and the fact that he would slip down a crevasse in our mountains could neither be foreseen nor held against him. I remember her triumph and the jealousy of everyone else, including our brother, Jacques, who had failed his exams that summer and thought he was stuck on the farm for life. As it happened, the Algerian war broke out and he joined the paratroopers. Another mourning card.

'I feel', you write, 'that our family has a jinx on its men.'

Have I jinxed Sam? No, he was mad before. But maybe our two jinxes flew together like magnets. Clang! What's 'mad'?

Weren't the best people 'mad', Kiki? All the risking saints and poets? Not that I want to risk. Only to be happy. Though trying too hard for that may be risky too? Like grabbing some frail, untenable flower – say a water-lily – in one's fist. Lethal. Funny: promises frighten me. I think it's because our childhood was all promise. At least that's how I remember it. I wonder: are our memories the same? Mine are parrot-bright with the sun blazing off the Alps at the end of our orchard, fruit clotting, fireflies swooping, curtains of honey being shaken from its wax in our cellars and, 'for the orphans', endless name-day and birthday parties. We were twice orphaned. First your mother died, then mine: Papa's second wife. The aunts couldn't make it up to us enough. Couldn't cosset us enough. And to me all those parties seemed an endlessly renewed celebration of some happiness to come: promises. Even the summer storms on the Alps, the red and green lightning flashes on the white peaks – can you still see them from the dining-room window? – like the flames on our birthday candles, *had* to be heralding something marvellous. Do you remember that we felt that? And how when we were getting a little older and had begun to see that all the rituals ever led up to was indigestion and a stack of smeary washing-up, one or other of us would have hysterics, throw a tantrum, weep, scream or insult the aunts? From the time I was twelve and the rest of you were in your late teens or early twenties, all the birthdays ended like that. It was expected: a kind of release. When one of us threw down her hand at bridge or her chair to rush weeping from the room, the rest felt spared. Until the next time when we would start hoping all over again. I wonder: do you remember it all differently? You may. You were hunchbacked and didn't expect to leave. When the others stopped hoping, you may have felt pleased. When *I* left you didn't mind. I was the youngest and you had plenty of company without me. Besides, it was recognized that Anne-Marie was 'flighty' and the flighty take flight. Now, oddly, you are turning your attention to me again. Old devious Kiki, leaning back on your hump in our parents' old bed and scheming away to get me to take Jean-Luc. I know why of course. Money. I got my mother's. She was much richer than yours was and when my brother, Jacques, died all her money came to me. You got the house and land. They were Papa's. But you have no cash. If I would take Jean-Luc off your hands it would help. So you are at work on me, trying to teleguide me through some layer of my own forgetfulness. I feel you tuning subliminal messages to me. Maybe that's what's bringing me back to you when maybe I should have gone looking for Sam? Mad Sam. Poor, sweet Sam.

It's not because I'm afraid of him that I didn't go to him when I left Dirk and Rosemary's. I mean I was that too but the disturbing, frightening thing was that I hadn't noticed his madness! In eight months. I kept wondering about those months as I sat in Dirk and Rosemary's drawing-room. I kept remembering jokes which had perhaps not been jokes at all but sheer lunacy: moans perhaps, sick grunts with no meaning except the purely arbitrary ones supplied by me. Where had Sam's mind been? How much was intact? When had he been sane? When not? Was sleeping with him like sleeping with a sexy Great Dane who happened to be attached to a human mistress? An unadulterated, mindless fuck? Bestiality? Oh God, I muttered and was reminded of one of Sam's jokes which was calling God and his heavenly brains' trust 'Joe & Co.' (from Jove? Jahve?).

'Joe and Co. are having themselves a ball,' he'd say when things went wrong. He imagined them up there as malign and only minimally powerful. Impish, they enjoyed sending nasty surprises of a minor sort. Right now they certainly were having themselves a ball.

'Go damn yourselves, Joe and Co.!' I screamed.

Rosemary came in. 'Something wrong?'

'No.'

She went back to the kitchen.

Kiki, I wonder about my own sanity.

You see everything that Sam said made sense to me. Sound sense, even a sort of super-sense. Even all that stuff about Joe & Co. was a sign that Sam, poor, bright, suffering Sam, *knew* – must have – about the lousy hand he'd been dealt. He knew he was a nut – which makes him that much the less of one, doesn't it? I mean he was lucid and sadly generous – he warned me, after all, though he was in love with me. I'm pretty sure of that. And all's fair when you're in love. Yet he *did* give me a fair chance to back out. As much as he dared. As much as a sane man in love would.

But why did he love me? Did he recognize some congenial folly in me?

I have known freaks before. I told you. I'm not going to go into that. Only far enough to say that I seem to attract them and now wonder why. Like calling to like?

Or *they* attract *me*? Maybe. The thing is I hate the social game, the mean commerce of it, and when I see a man refuse to play I'm attracted. Meaning? Oh nothing subtle. Just the old, sleazy double-thinks, the mild moral sag you meet every day in successful men and which successful men don't a bit mind revealing to women like me. They take off their attitudes as they might their clothes and don't suppose we'll notice contradictions. We do though. They're the very things to which we're alert. When you take your values from your men, as women do – as I find myself doing simply because my dealings with the world, society or what-have-you are usually *through* a man – then you'd like to think they're decent values and when they're not you notice. It's not, for God's sake, that I'm a prig – that would be a laugh, wouldn't it? – but, well, I do object to phoniness doing a smelly striptease under my nose and then asking me to admire its imperial vestments. But Sam, you see, was different. Unphony. Honest. Mad.

Oh I don't know. His jokes, now that I think back, weren't all that funny. He was usually smashed or stoned when he clowned. I suppose he was a bit childish. Once, for instance, he ordered ketchup in a very chichi inn outside Paris: the sort of place that has bits of saddlery on the wall and a rosette in the Michelin Guide. They'd never heard of ketchup.

'I want some,' Sam insisted. 'In a bottle. *Appellation contrôlée.*' Then he snatched up a carving knife and threatened the waiter. 'Ketchup', he told him, 'is part of my cultural heritage. Do you despise it?'

The waiter said he didn't.

Then Sam charged into the kitchen to interrogate the chef. I stayed where I was until the manageress begged me to intervene. If Sam hadn't looked so strong they would have thrown him out. But he did. The inn was in the country. No time to call the police. When I reached the kitchen, Sam was prodding the chef in the belly with the point of his knife. 'Where do you think they get the blood for Spaghetti Westerns?' he was asking him. 'Not *here.*' Another prod. 'Ketchup . . .'

Now I know the chef was right to be afraid and the thing was less funny than I thought. Oh Kiki, maybe you're right and I never did grow up!

'After all,' said Rosemary coming in to poke up the fire and justify herself, 'you are older than Sam, Anne-Marie!' She went off.

Meaning? That I was over-the-hill. Should be pleased with what I could get! A fine stud like Sam. What's a bit of wife-battery in a deal like that? Or did she just mean 'old enough to know better'? Probably.

'Where's Sam?' I asked when we were at table.

'At his mother's,' Dirk told me. 'You'll have to hide,' he advised. 'He's dangerous.'

'He attacked her once,' Rosemary told me. 'His mother. With a knife. You can't blame her for not telling you.'

She was spooning *cassoulet* into our plates and looking pleased, as conventional women often do when they get a thrill at second hand. 'I really admire Marsha,' she said excitedly. 'She's been through it with Sam.'

Oh God, I thought, don't let her tell me more. Don't let her. But already she was swallowing down her *cassoulet* and wiping her mouth, all agog. She opened it. 'He . . .' she began.

'He's been through her,' I said to shut her up. I stared angrily at her. She was fatly pregnant and smug. 'The uterus', I went on fast and loudly, 'forms a creature on the model of the object loved by the mother. This opinion was put forward by the British biologist, Harvey, some time in the sixteen-fifties. Do you suppose Sam's mother loved a circus-freak? Or a murderer or butcher perhaps?' I waved my glass, spilling some reddish drops on the cloth. I rubbed salt into them conscientiously. 'She may always have longed to be attacked with a knife, you see?'

Dirk and Rosemary looked as though they'd eaten something bad.

'I'm in love with Sam.' I began to cry.

Dirk left the table. Rosemary put the *cassoulet* back on the stove.

She put a hand on my arm. Rosemary's not a toucher. She was making an effort. 'Sam's a friend of ours, Anne-Marie,' she said gently. 'We like him. We have for years. He's OK most of the time.'

'Yes. I'm sorry. It's not you,' I accused myself. 'It's me.' I was crying into my wine. I had poured more into my glass and was now drinking a ghastly mixture of Kir, Côtes du Rhône and tears.

'Look,' said Rosemary, 'you'd better go to bed.'

She took the glass from me and led me to a small bedroom, pulled off my shoes and left me lying on a revolving bed. I suppose she went back down to call Dirk to eat the rest of his *cassoulet*.

I tried to remember what I'd said and she'd said before we had begun to argue, but I couldn't. I knew I'd mentioned you and that she'd been relieved to find I had somewhere to go.

'A trip to the country', she said approvingly, 'would be just the thing. You can't go back to Sam's place.'

Oh Kiki!

'Now', you wrote, 'that you're going to have a home again!'

You've put the evil eye on me.

Sam, Sam, Sam, Sam!

The trouble is most men don't appeal to me at all. I don't *see* them! When I find one who does I think: Maybe he's the last!

I'm drinking again. The train funnels down the diagonal from Paris to Chambéry, and as it does I find myself taking more and more little swigs. Hine. I feel its glow in my throat, chest and deep in my old, cold, ardent, widowed belly. Inner caresses, consolings, comforts. Kiki, I wish you drank. I often think of the thinness of your life and wonder do people whose pleasures are few get more and extra enjoyment from them? An intenser, richer yield? Unlikely. Inequality reigns here too.

I try to remember what pleasures you have enjoyed since growing up. Do you still go to Chambéry to eat the cakes for which it is famous? Reminding yourself that this, at least, is, though a minor pleasure, the very best of its kind?

'I know', says your fingered and furry letter, 'you have had abortions. Whatever you thought your reasons were, I feel one contributing cause was the fact that we made you into a baby for life. And how can a baby have a baby? Mind you, to have one might be the best thing for you. If you were to take Jean-Luc . . .'

'You have', you write, 'had abortions . . .'

Have you an image to put with that firmly used word? I have.

I asked Sam would he like us to have a baby.

'Ten,' he said, 'or five. I'm in favour of the decimal system. So French! Or point one of one.'

'Shut up!' I said. 'I've seen a fractured baby. Well: foetus.'

'How much of it?'

'Never mind.'

'Which parts?'

'No!'

'I'm interested.'

'For Christ's sake, Sam!'

'I'm only talking. You did it.'

'You have', I conceded, 'a point.'

'Decimal point.'

'You're sick.'

And of course he was. *Merde!* Bugger Joe & Co.! I took several Valium, not counting the number. And got to sleep.

I dreamed of an abortionist I used to know and visited twice as a client. He kept embryos in glass bottles in his garden as people keep pottery elves. It was an isolated garden and he kept some live iguanas there too in a kind of chicken run. Unlike you, Kiki, who deal with things fearlessly in the abstract, he liked to stare head-on at what he was doing. Perhaps that was where he put his pride.

'Don't you know', you said, turning up suddenly in my dream, 'that you're Jean-Luc's mother? You had a premature baby when you were sixteen and we never told you. It was smaller than these pottery elves. We were able to make you believe you had been bedridden for months with TB, then deliver you under an anaesthetic and pretend the baby was Lucette's. *She* had a husband, you see. Now if you were to take charge . . .'

'Who's the father then?'

'Ah,' you said, 'a touch of incest. Men', you said, 'are scarce around our house. Read the Bible and you'll see how they managed. It was a way of keeping patrimonies intact. Read about Lot's daughters.'

'You're mad,' I shrieked.

'It means', you said, 'that you owe us the money you took out of the family.'

'Mad!'

'Not me,' you said. 'You're the one. Disgraced the family. You gave birth to an iguana.'

'Are you all right?'

Someone was rattling my bedroom door. Dirk, my host. I'd locked it.

'Yes,' I shouted, 'a nightmare. Sorry.'

'For God's sake,' he said, 'do you always scream like that?'

He stumped off, muttering. I took some more Valium.

At breakfast he said, 'Look, I'm sorry, Anne-Marie, but Rosemary needs her sleep. She's pregnant, you know. I'm afraid *you're* in need of care. You look as though you might be having a breakdown. Haven't you got any family you can go to? Anyway you can't stay here. Sam might come looking for you.'

Later, when we were in his car driving to Paris, he asked me where I wanted to go.

I said I might go and see Marsha.

For minutes Dirk seemed to concentrate on his driving. Then: 'Look,' he said, 'I think I'd better warn you. Marsha's a bit of a bitch. She wants to get remarried, you see, and it would facilitate this if Sam were in good hands: yours. To put it brutally, she's looking for an unpaid nurse. Don't believe what she tells you. Sam's incurable. Schizoid. He can be sound as a bell for months but he always reverts. It can happen any time. I *know* this. I'm sorry, Anne-Marie,' he said. 'You've got to face it.'

'Yes.'

'Where?' he asked when we reached the city.

'My things are in Sam's flat.'

'I'll get them. You wait,' he said. He parked the car two streets away from the apartment building and took my keys. 'Read the paper,' he advised. 'I'll be as quick as I can. If I overlook some stuff, Marsha can send it on later. When you have an address.'

'Thanks.'

He was back in less than half an hour with my cases. 'No sign of Sam,' he said as he put them in the boot. 'I packed everything feminine-looking,' he explained. 'Not very tidily, I'm afraid.'

'Thanks,' I said again.

'Where now?'

'Take me to the Gare de Lyon.' I knew he wanted to be rid of me. 'I have relatives in Savoy,' I reassured him.

'Well,' he said when he dropped me off, 'if there's anything you want . . . you know.' Vaguely and looking relieved.

'That's OK.'

When he left I found a phone and rang Marsha. I wasn't sure what I was going to say but she *was* responsible for what had happened.

'Marsha, this is Anne-Marie. Do you know what happened yesterday?'

I was still hoping she'd have some explanation or antidote. 'Do you?' I asked.

Her voice rushed down the wire and I knew it was all no good. She was crying and on the booze. 'I haven't been fair to you,' she was sobbing.

'Is he curable?'

'Can you come over? Where are you, Anne-Marie?'

'Is he?'

'What, dear?'

'Curable?'

More sobs. She kept saying my name. 'Listen,' she said, 'there was a terrible scene here last night and the police came. He attacked one of them. They took him away. I don't know *where*. I have a lawyer trying to find out . . . listen, Anne-Marie, we must meet. Can't you come now?'

'You didn't answer my question.'

'I'm a mother,' Marsha sobbed. 'A mother,' she repeated. It sounded like the responses to a litany of reproach. But I hadn't reproached her. 'Can't you understand?' she asked.

'Yes,' I said. 'I can. I do.' I put down the phone.

I went to the station buffet and had a cognac.

'Marsha', Dirk had warned me, 'is as tough as old nails. Very calculating.'

I had a second cognac. Was Sam Sam, I wondered? Did the man I thought I was in love with exist and what did I owe him? I mean if he's not responsible for himself, how can I be? I've had my heart smashed up before, Kiki, like a pulverized elbow. I've found people change in my grasp like the Old Man of the Sea. I haven't the strength to go through that again. I put the glass on the counter, went to the ticket office and bought a single for Chambéry.

A one-way single to solitude. Oh Jesus! Oh Joe!

Time out for a drink. Finished the Hine. Last lovely drops still hot on my mouth. Dijon out there. Closer now to you than to Sam, Kiki.

No!

Kiki, I'm not coming back. I know. I know what you'd say but you're not going to get a chance. Besides: you don't even know I'd set out, do you? Glad I never rang now. Pre-ordained: Joe & Co. at their more short-term benevolent. Always means they've something bloody up their dodgy sleeves. Never mind. Defy the bastards! I'm going back.

I'm not normal. OK? I never thought I was. I was just too belly-crawlingly humble: persuading myself that the majority, because a majority, must be right. You belong to it, Kiki, and Jean-Louis and Rosemary and Dirk and Marsha and all the mothers and parents of all the lovers and the lovers when they stop loving and the mad when they're sane. Joe & Co. I'm not sure of. I think they're schizoid. But Sam and I are nuts and I'm the better nut because I choose nuttiness. I'll stand by mad Sam.

My own monster.

Look: you don't need me and neither does Jean-Luc. My bit of money would only buy you a dose of smothering gentility. That's all. *We* can't talk, Kiki. I've been trying to talk to you all the way from bloody Paris, all across this uptight, sour, canny, old, tired, knowing, horrible hexagon of a country where everything you can say's been said and the best things, down to the cheese and wine, are fermentings of crushed other things. I'm going off to be mad. I know it's a bit negative, a bit limited but, Kiki, I'm only me. I'd be no good looking after you – we'd brain each other – or bringing meals-on-wheels to the aged. I'm good for Sam though and he's sometimes good for me and . . . oh fuck, why try to talk?

Which brings me to a final point you might just grasp. I might xerox it on three hundred and sixty-five scraps of paper and send you one daily and then one chance day it just might – might – connect. It's this: I don't live to fuck, Kiki. I fuck to live. It's an aid, a prop. Listen: I'm not being outrageous for kicks, just trying to tell you that I'm thirty-five years old and look more. They were packed years. I'm not the girl you disapproved of at seventeen with a somewhat scuffed-up face. I'm a different person. That girl ignored your advice. She took the risks you rightly warned her against. She got burned. Right? You were right then but – watch it, Kiki, here's the surprise: that makes you wrong now. Because people who've stayed carefully out of the fire and people who've been through it are not the same. They're a different race and Sam's my race and you're not. So you can't advise me and I can't talk to you and I'm getting off this train at the next stop and getting the next one back to the *ville lumière* where I shall flame like a salamander until I go up in smoke.

And I wish to Joe & Co. I had some more lovely Hine, because I bloody need it. Wonder will the buffet be open at the next station?

Because don't think I think it's going to be easy. I'm terrified.

Pop Goes the Weasel

Tom, flat on his back, was using pain to quell his memory. His arms ached. Above him teetered a weight which he must not let slip. In his mind it was now a boulder. Of basalt. Or limestone. Not that it mattered. What did was the muscle-pain. Grittily, he savoured that. You had, he believed, to conquer yourself so as later, if need be, to tackle the world. His pupils accepted this. Most of them. Only Rafael, missing the point, had once asked if Tom was thinking of the *next* world.

Raffo could get things a tad wrong, indeed was in jail just now enforcing Tom's principles with excessive zest. He had wreaked mayhem on a pair of badasses. Fellow students said Tom shouldn't blame himself if Raffo lacked flexibility.

'He takes the American dream too much to heart!' they decided. 'Listen, he takes *karate* too much to heart.'

'And the movies!'

'It's being an immigrant.' Gary was the class intellectual. 'If you psych yourself up to adapt to a whole new culture, you'll keep looking for challenges. Raffo wanted to be like those knights in the blow-ups on our dojo walls, Tom. Dragonslayers! They must have impressed him as a kid. They'd have been some of the first things here he saw.'

Rafael had been in Tom's karate class since his family brought him to LA from Mexico at the age of ten. He'd been the first Hispanic to join and the only one to stay.

Tom, while he had nothing against Hispanics, had a test question for them. 'Ever hear of a bunch of Mexicans,' he'd ask, 'who lay claim to California, Texas and everything in between? They call it Atalanta or something like that. Do you know about them?'

No one said they did, but Tom went on putting his question. He wanted any mad Mexicans on whom he might stumble to know their cover was blown.

He didn't get to put it though to Rafael's Mom. She was a Spanish-speaker, brown as gingerbread who, one day twenty years ago, simply appeared at Tom's door with little Rafael, his baby sisters and a basketful of cakes in the colours of the Mexican flag. Raspberry, cream and pistachio! Pure cholesterol! Tinted sugar sifted from the basket; alien smells polluted the dojo and Tom couldn't have said which of his powerful personal taboos was the most acutely violated. A baby started to cry. Soothing it, the gingerbread Mom opened her blouse, thrust her cakes at Tom, and pointed to little Rafael. 'This one', she said, 'want study karate. Give me no peace. All day watch your class. From there.' Popping one tit into the baby's mouth, she pointed to an apartment balcony overlooking the dojo, then said something to the boy in Spanish, perhaps that he should show what he could do.

Tom expected shyness, but there was none.

'*Kiai!*' yelled Raffo, while performing a creditable middle-level sword-hand block in back stance. A natural! Then he did the splits. An uncle had promised to pay for his lessons.

Later, Tom wrapped up the unwholesome cakes and drove with them to a distant litter bin. He didn't want anyone's feelings hurt, but neither did he relish the smells which lingered in his dojo until he got at them with Listerine. Next day Raffo joined the class and, some years later, got his black belt. Since then, several more years had passed, and pupils from Tom's first junior karate class had now had their black belts so long that the fine Japanese silk had worn thin, and the belts were turning white. About ten old pupils still trained though, turning up three times a week – it had once been six – and Rafael had been one of the most faithful until last month when an unathletic-looking judge sentenced him harshly on the grounds that having a karate black belt was the equivalent of being armed. The guy reminded Tom of his own uncles from Salt Lake City. Stiff! Dry! Convinced of their rectitude. Years ago, two of them had come out here to LA for three days, looked down their lean Wasp noses at California, then turned and gone home. Tom got the impression that he, like the state, had been considered and found wanting. On that occasion, however, no judgement was pronounced.

'Remember, Tom,' Gary reminisced, 'how awful Rafael's accent used to be? Martin kept making fun of it until Rafael punched him in the mouth. He broke two teeth and Martin's Mom threatened to sue you.'

'I told her to go right ahead.'

'Yeah!' The class enjoyed the memory.

'Martin's Mom was quite something!'

'So was Martin!'

'Remember how we were all set to testify that he was a mean S.O.B who had it coming?'

'Martin was worse than an S.O.B. He was a small sadist. What you never saw, Tom, was what he got up to when you turned your back. Especially during sparring.'

'His Mom wouldn't let him train with us after that.'

'But when he was sixteen he came back.'

'That's right! She couldn't stop him then and he'd grown into an acceptable guy!'

'Fairly acceptable.'

'Rafael had taught him a lesson!'

Wham! Nostalgically, Tom dreamed of evils which could be simply knocked out. Flattened! Murdilized! Up-p again! Wondering if he'd heard a bone crack, he steadied the weight. His arms buckled. Effortfully, he raised them once more. As a professional chiropractor and martial artist, he knew how much too much to demand of his body.

'Push *beyond* your threshold,' was his motto.

In his fantasy the weight was a boulder which could slip, set off an earthslide and block the entrance to a cave from which fugitives had started to emerge. A girl had got out, but something had happened to the man behind her. His face was muzzled in blood, and one of his eyes, veined like a rare orchid, hung as if from a stem.

'Aa-*uuu*-wwawwagh!' Tom's anguished bellow surprised himself.

Embarrassed, he assigned it to a predator deep in the cave. Dragon? Cyclops? No, a giant earth worm. Tom had watched a video once in which a lovely, white-skinned gal changed every night into one of those. The story was by the same guy who wrote *Dracula*. Tom tried to remember his name. Gram, was it? Or Bram? Bram Something? Bellowing again, he congratulated himself on having had his dojo soundproofed. At one time he'd had forty students, and when they all yelled '*kiai*' the building shook. Neighbours complained that it sounded like the start of the big LA quake. So Tom called the sound-proofers.

Deep in the cave, something phosphorescent glowed. Tusks? Slime? Were the fugitives all safely out? 'Ninety-nine!' Tom let sink then raised his barbell one last time. 'A hundred!' Replacing it, he gave a high sign to a movie poster on the wall which showed a man hefting a rock. The man's muscles jutted. A girl, wearing the stone-age equivalent of a bikini, was creeping fearfully from a cave, and you could tell that the man would now lower the rock, corral the evil inside and join her in the sunshine. Tom's fantasies usually stopped there.

Today he held onto them, letting his mind flit through a medley in which the stone-age gal turned up in the *Star Trek* episode he'd watched last night. Slivers of reality knifed coldly in, making him shiver even as he stepped under the hot shower. Again he saw the dangling eye.

It was Jim's.

Tom, embracing numbness, turned off shower and

thought-stream, extracted a karate gi from a cottony pile smelling mildly of himself, put it on, took a quart of plain yoghurt from his office fridge and sat down to eat. The stiff sleeves creaked and he felt bolstered by routine. No point ringing the hospital yet. They'd said not to. Jim was in intensive care. Tom who hadn't cried since he was a kid felt a hardness in his throat.

The yoghurt had the clotty texture of a nose bleed, but he ate it anyway for, as health-lore changed, so did his diet. Gone were the days of steaks and pie. Like his Mormon fore-bears, he looked to the long run, but, giving up on heaven, subscribed instead to news letters on smart drugs and nutri-ents and, to keep his brain active, took challenging courses in math and the biology of ageing in which he already had a PhD. His aim was to stay healthy until researchers into our DNA cracked the code which tells us to die and reversed the message. He believed this to be imminent.

'I'd hate', he told students, 'to be the last man to go!'

Slyly timed, such remarks let him catch his breath between strenuous routines. Did the guys know, he wondered, and if so did this embarrass them? In the old days, he would have crucified anyone who said a word during training. His own Japanese sensei had run *his* dojo like a boot camp, and for years Tom, honouring the tradition, stayed inscruta-bly buttoned-up and dignified. Lately, though, he had been regarding his students as family and sharing his thoughts.

The change went back to Heppy's death. Mom's. Mrs Fuller's. Her ghostly selves gusted back if he didn't take measures – and must at some point be dealt with.

Crumpling his emptied yoghurt carton, he let one bad memory oust another. This morning, out on the boulevard, there had been a five-car pile-up. Sun-blurred after-images floated in and out of focus, hiding then brutally highlighting bone shards puncturing a cheek, Jim's fierce, extruded eye, crushed metal and a bunch of stunned faces, two of which he knew. A car had been totalled right outside this office while another, somersaulting past the centre divider, burst into flames. Tom, hearing the collision, had rushed out and there was the totalled car wrapped around a lamp post and next to it Jim's old jalopy with Jim folded into the steering wheel. In the periphery of Tom's vision, making a getaway in his BMW, was an intact but tight-lipped Martin.

Martin! Tom got the picture instantly: those assholes had meant to fake it! Holy shit! They'd planned to fake injuries and walk off with the insurance money. Martin must have talked Jim into it. Tom could imagine his spiel: 'Listen! Listen! Your old lady's busting your balls. Your car's worth zip. Just say you have a whiplash neck. We'll get Honest Tom the Chiropractor to back you up. He'll believe you and the insurers will believe *him*. We'll do it right by his office. The symptoms are a cinch to fake.'

Jim, a mild, handsome ex-lifeguard with a knee injury, was one of Nature's fall-guys. Before the knee-injury he had married a gal who kept nagging him to get off his butt and do something. But Jim didn't see what he could do and had been in here joking miserably about this. She'd made him use their savings as a deposit on a house, and he couldn't keep up the payments. He'd flunked law school and lost a job as security guard because of his limp.

Tom, hating to know about scams, averted his eyes from so much that, for a while, his disbelief in ambulance-chasers, snuff-movies and markets-in-stolen-hearts-and-kidneys had equalled that with which other people greeted his hopes of living forever. The difference was that when *they* had evidence, he bowed to it, which was more than they did to his. This amazed him whose sources included bulletins from the Centre d'Etude du Polymorphisme Humain (CEPH) in Paris where researchers had mapped the human genetic blueprint. Awesomely, human immortality had begun to look attainable and, bafflingly, his students didn't seem to care. Tom

harangued them with wonder. Just last week, Martin's pale
little eyes had blinked impassively while Tom talked right
through the limbering-up period.

Why, he marvelled, were they not ecstatic! Their generation could – Tom delicately stretched his hamstrings – be
thirty-plus forever. Didn't they grasp the privilege? Didn't
they – here he still happily, though still delicately, swung a
kick in the air – *want* immortality? Making imaginary contact,
his bare toes trembled at high noon.

'Listen, I'm in my sixties, and *I* want it!'

In the training mirror, his levitating self reminded him of a
prophet ranting in some souk! Prophet or monk. His crewcut
had acquired a tonsure. Or some white, arrowy, Japanese bird.

'Hey,' someone – Martin? – guffawed in the back row, 'if
nobody dies, the planet'll get overcrowded. They'll have to
ban sex!'

'Yeah! *You'll* have to be castrated!' Aiming humorous
assaults at each other's groins.

'It should be done now. Aids is the warning!'

'Aids! Yeah! Yah!'

'Don't touch me, man! Keep your body liquids to yourself!'

'Sex-maniacs should be interned!'

'Or at least banned from the dojo!'

Feinting and dodging, kicks snapped, punches were
pulled and white sleeves furrowed the air like paper darts.
Rowdiness was how Tom's class stopped him wasting paid-up
time in talk. Only rarely, in retaliation, did he assign them
five minutes' squat-kicking – high kicks from a low squat, like
dancing Cossacks – then, when he had them winded, return
to his topic.

Doing this had once drawn a taunt from a flagging Gary –
less fit than he liked to pretend: 'Tom! Know why immortality
appeals so much to you? It's because you don't live life! You
save it up.'

The verbal punch to the gut took the others' breath

away. How could it fail to in a dojo devoted to the values of Southern Cal? The hush, compounding unease, lasted until Gary, in a manœuvre learned from Tom who trained actors to perform it in movies, floored a phantom assailant, then whirled to demolish other lurkers – among them, surely, an unworthy self?

Tom was flummoxed. In what way did he not live? How? What could Gary mean? The attack was the more hurtful because Tom liked to be joshed. Lately, aiming to Americanize karate, he had tried to behave less like a sensei and more like a genial uncle who attended students' graduation parties and welcomed them back after their divorces – matrimony tended to interrupt training.

As a chiropractor, treating the unfit among them, he no longer nagged when their flesh proved softer than his own. Jim was one of these, a slack, needy man whom Tom should have protected. He should have warned him against Martin who last June had made some startling admissions right here in the dojo.

It was just before class. The day was hot and the door to the boulevard had been left open to cool the place down. Suddenly a collision – like a small try-out for this morning's – happened so close that the men catching the breeze had a ringside seat.

'Hey! Look!' Gary had been a rubberneck since he was ten.

'*Diosito!*' Rafael reverted to Spanish.

'Faked!' decided Martin after a quick glance. 'Half of all accidents are.' Then he told how teams of bogus victims, paramedics, lawyers and doctors – 'or', with a foxy grin at Tom, 'chiropractors' – divvied up insurance money. Later, privately, he offered to cut Tom in, as he was apparently in a position to do. There was a lot, 'And I mean a *lot*,' said Martin, to be made. 'If you don't grab it, others will.'

Tom was less shaken by the dishonesty which he knew to be rampant than by Martin's failure to see how genuinely *he*,

Tom, cared about honour. Karate, he always scrupulously taught, was as spiritual as it was physical. It was why he had chosen, decades ago, to perfect himself in an art which, at the time, few Americans understood. 'Kara' – 'empty' – referred not only to the fighting man's hand but to his need to empty his inner self of ego, leaving it as straight, clean and hollow as a green bamboo shoot. Clearly, despite years of training, this message had not reached Martin. Was the fault Tom's?

Had he, softening, let his own egotism back in? Undeniably, he had mellowed and was sometimes startled to recall a self who had favoured interning peaceniks and keeping fags and women in their place. These aims baffled him now – which did not mean that he thought right the same as wrong.

'Stop right now!' In a panic of refusal, he tried to shut Martin up. 'Stop! You mustn't say things like that around the dojo!'

'OK then! Have it your way!' Shrugging, Martin opened the door of Tom's office in which this talk had been taking place. 'Well,' he exclaimed. 'Just look who's outside!' Amused, he tilted his chin towards the car park where Gary was clearly on the watch. 'Your protector's worried, Tom! Afraid I'll stir you up and get you really mad. Give you a stroke maybe? I'm still the badass in this Castle of Virtue!'

Tom *was* mad. Stung, he warned, 'I ought to turn you in. How do you know I won't? Ten years ago I would have.'

'Ten years ago I wouldn't have told you.'

Tom turned that over in his mind. Martin had intuition: a thing you had to respect. Seeing idealism die, he had adapted and that, like it or not, was evolution. It was how humanity survived. He'd surely survive better than Gary who couldn't see beyond the tip of his own argument. Words, to Gary, were only words and films films. He and Tom battled over this and last Monday, when Tom was probing the significance of the videos he had watched over the weekend – *Batman*, which he'd seen for the tenth time, and *Bladerunner* – Gary had cut in with a 'Tom, those are films! That's all they are!'

Tom couldn't let this pass. Mindful of the jibe about his not living, he had argued with more assurance than he felt, 'No, no! Films tell you what the trends are. That's why you got to watch them. With all the brains and money that go into them, they have to reflect current thinking. Violence is going to take over. That's their message. Breakdown. It'll be every man for himself. I don't worry. I have my guns. I've always been a rugged individualist. I'll stop being a chiropractor if they bring in socialized medicine. I wouldn't work for that. I'd get another job. Adaptation is the name of the game. Individualism. Being self-sufficient.'

For Gary this was the sort of day-dreaming which had brought down Rafael.

Was it?

Wrapping an old T-shirt round a broom, Tom buffed the dojo floor while casting an occasional glance up at the dragon-and-knight images on its walls. He hadn't really looked at them in years and, now that he did, was surprised to find the dragons – robotic, feral, breathing fire – more impressive than the knights. Martin, with his fiery accidents, was a sort of dragon. Or a Merlin: a faker who even faked himself. Tom guessed that he took steroids, for his muscles were oddly swollen. Poor Rafael, though he had shown the valour of a knight errant by single-handedly giving three nasty guys their comeuppance, did not look at all like the knights in Tom's blow-ups.

These bestrode their space. Their muscles thrust past armour-plating whose scaly bristle made them too look drag-onlike. The effect was futuristic and mediaeval: a blend Tom enjoyed. It was as though the future held the best of the past in store: Paradise Two, a sequel to Eden. Later, would come the Fall.

'It's coming,' he kept telling his class. 'There were several films about it recently.' He mentioned the actresses' names.

'Great-looking gals!' As his listeners savoured this, he pulsed with their breathing pattern. Gals interested him most at a remove. 'There's a trend.'

'Tom, those are *films*!'

'No! Films', Tom had insisted, 'are real!' He corrected that. 'They anticipate reality. The thinking that goes into them does.'

Putting away his broom, he wondered who would come to class today. Not Martin, not Jim, not Rafael. Then the door was pushed open and there was Gary with a gal whom Tom recognized as Rafael's wife, Elena. Small but feisty, at one time she'd started training here, then decided she'd be better off in a women's self-defence class. Tom, not really wanting women around, had been relieved. He liked her though, and she had been very good about visiting his mother in her last months. The two, surprisingly, had grown close and Elena had spent whole days with the dying woman.

Greeting her, he asked about Rafael and was told he was bearing up.

It turned out she needed a favour. With Rafael in jail, the bank had foreclosed their mortgage and taken their house, so now they had nowhere to store their furniture. It was in a truck outside. Could she leave it here?

'Just for a bit,' she begged and explained that she hoped to rent a place soon.

'It could go upstairs,' Gary told Tom, 'in your mother's old apartment.'

Six months earlier, Heppy, Tom's mother, had died, leaving a clutter of Norman Rockwell plates, flimsy side-tables with sugar-stick legs and knickknacks so alien to Tom that, after shipping what she'd asked him to ship to cousins in Salt Lake City, he had given the rest to the Salvation Army. Only the room, where she had spent her last months, was intact. She'd had a house in Pasadena until her arthritis got bad and Tom brought her here where he could keep an eye on her during the day. She had died upstairs. Maybe it was as well to crowd out her ghost.

'Sure,' he agreed.

So instead of a karate class, there was a furniture-moving session with everyone who turned up for training pitching in. Tom relished the sociability, as neighbours dropped by, containers too big to move were broken into and objects piled on his strip of lawn. As in a garage sale, private things were incongruously displayed. A chest-expander lay between a picture of the Virgen de Guadalupe, a juicer and a bathroom scales. A long package was possibly a rifle, and a box of cakes was an offering from the girl whose misfortunes had sparked off Rafael's troubles. Elena introduced her: Juana. They were cousins. Tom, though he hadn't met her until now, knew her story from Rafael and the *L.A. Times*.

He tried not to stare. She couldn't be more than sixteen.

'Just fourteen when it happened,' Rafael had told the class. Gangsters, he explained, had kidnapped her from her village in Mexico, then smuggled her here to LA to be a sexual slave.

'Slavey?'

'Slave! She was a *slave*! They paid her nothing and kept her locked up.'

'Your having us on!'

'No.'

'What sort of gangsters?'

'Small-time ones. They own a bar in East LA where they made her work.'

The scenario seemed to belong to another place and time. Tom imagined the young Liz Taylor as Juana whose age suggested a fanciful romp with periwigs and tricorne hats. 'Yer money or yer life, yer ducats or yer wife!' Or an ad. 'Pray, take these instead,' cries the captive girl, offering brand-name chocolates to the heavies who lower their muskets, lick their lips and accept the bargain. In a darker mood, your thoughts could slide to the stolen children whose hearts and kidneys are allegedly sold to rich or desperate First World parents.

The reality was less harrowing since, by the time Rafael heard of it, Juana had been found. Her family, into which he had meanwhile married, had known who to blame – *pistoleros* who had moved to Los Angeles – so her brother, though himself a child, had set out in pursuit. Making his way across the border then, though he had neither money nor English, to the LA *barrio* where people from his part of Mexico lived, the boy had succeeded in picking up the trail of the men who, with violent thrift, were using and abusing his sister as maid-of-all-work and whore.

'So he got her home? Back to Mexico?'

'Yeah, but it took a while.'

'What a feat though! Like Samson and Goliath!'

'The newspapers helped. They made a story of it.'

'How old did you say he was?'

'About like the kid in *The Thief of Baghdad*?'

'Or *Les Misérables*.'

Without movie-world lore, the thing would have been too alien to understand. As it was, the class had to look with a new eye at their old pal, Raffo, who must, they now saw, have a Mexican border slicing through his mind: a division as hard to negotiate as a Rio Grande in flood.

*

'*Pan Mexicano?*'

Juana was offering cake. Oozing cream from a sugary slit, it looked even less salubrious than the ones with which Rafael's Mom had failed to tempt Tom twenty years ago. Juana had removed her jacket and revealed blue-veined arms. A waif. A Dickens girl. Her skin, he saw from close up, was poor. Probably ate the wrong diet and needed further salvation. In a film, the make-up people would have provided this and Tom, to his amused surprise, imagined himself transfiguring

her, as the orphaned Little Lord Fauntleroy had been transfigured, in a lace-collared velvet suit. Instead, he accepted her
cake and a coffee – Elena must have unpacked her own per-
colator, for he never drank the stuff – then walked off to find
somewhere to rid himself of both.

*

The kidnappers, Raffo had told the shocked dojo, had gone
scot free. They must have done a deal with the police though,
naturally, he didn't know details. Maybe they were stool
pigeons? Part of an undercover anti-drug-or-smuggling-
squad? Juana was sure some of the clients she'd been forced to
service were cops. By now the newspapers had lost interest –
or been warned off?

Vigorously kicking the air and, with it, the dreamed-up
faces of *pistoleros*, the class considered their society's loss
of virtue. When had the rot set in? Kick. With President
Kennedy's death? The cover-up? Kick. Water- or Irangate?
Kossovo? Kick, kick and kick again! Somewhere faith had
been lost. Mislaid. Roundhouse kick.

'Again with the other leg,' encouraged Tom. 'Add a backfist
to the face, elbow strike, upper block and back kick. Pulverize
the opposition. Yell *kiai*! Turn. Keep together! More spirit!
And again!'

Few of us, he reflected, were the straight bamboo shoots
empty of selfishness that we would have wished. The scourges
and avengers. The new brooms. Excited advice, though, was
lavished on Rafael – most of it, Tom saw with hindsight, unwise.

He tried to recall what he'd said himself, but was interrupted by Elena who wanted to be shown how to use the
barbecue. Next came a debate over who should go to the store
for refreshments and what they should buy. Beer? Mineral
water? Juice? Tom didn't join in.

There was a debt owing to that girl. 'A debt outstanding!'

Hearing the words hammer in his head, he wondered if they were his? His words to Raffo? They had a boom which reminded Tom of his father more than fifty years ago. A pillar of pin-striped darkness looming up to make him cry. Acrid-smelling. Fuming and unpredictable. 'Young man,' it scolded, 'you owe . . . owe . . .' What? To whom? 'To me,' boomed Pop and slid menacingly into focus. 'And you'll pay, young man! I'll see to that. Don't cringe! Cringing doesn't impress me. I have a duty to bring you up right, even if your mother spoils you. A duty to society!' Stiff collar. Stiff-judging mouth! Huge, terrifying fist! Slamming down, it blocked out the light as Tom fell on his back and his ears rang from the blow. Strong smells of alcohol. Once Pop dislocated Tom's shoulder. Then, somehow, he died and Tom and Mom came West. In the train, she sang a rhyme which Tom misinterpreted:

> A penny for a cotton ball,
> Tuppence for a needle!
> That's the way the money goes,
> And POP goes the weasel!

Bang! Blow Pop away! Pop-the-Weasel! Wasn't that what had happened?

Maybe the voice in Tom's head was an echo of his own? 'This city's lost its virtue!' That was his all right! He must have been remembering the lost, radiant, Pop-free LA in which he grew up: clear air, innocent leafiness, sun spraying like yellow petals and nothing to be afraid of. Even in the canyons the only danger was from coyotes which would eat a baby if its mother was an airhead and wandered off, leaving it on a rug. There had been one such case, he recalled – but things went wrong in Eden too. Eden. The jacaranda trees seemed to unravel the sky when their blossoms opened in a blaze as blue as the sea – which was there too, rippling like shaken silk. Warm and salty. Luminous, unpolluted and safe.

'We're safe,' his mother whispered, 'safe, safe, safe and we'll never go back! Never! We'll stay here together.'

So they did. She wasn't the sort of mother who'd leave him alone on a rug. Nor he her.

*

Elena, back from the store with charcoal and lighters, paused to watch Gary fix the barbecue and to tell Tom how much more culture meant to Mexicans than it did to people here. 'That's why Rafael is so impressed by your studies. He used to tell me how when you talked of the things you cared about, it went right over the heads of the class. It went over his head too but he loved listening. And he admires your beliefs. He says you are one of the last men to have principles the way the great Americans did. Ah, good! Gary's got the fire going. I'd better bring the food.'

*

Dusk found Tom sitting at the head of a table – Elena's table which had been set up in his mother's dining room – picking at take-away Mexican food. From politeness, he let *fajitas* and *chile relleno* be piled on his plate, though he remained proof against beer. *Dos Xs.* The two women were to spend some nights here. Gary had brokered the decision while Tom was ringing the hospital where Jim turned out to be less badly injured than had been feared. He was in stable condition and could have visitors soon. Tom asked about his eye but the gal at the other end of the phone was slow-witted and didn't seem to understand.

He was pleased to see Juana eat. She was not at all like the small Elizabeth Taylor, but thinnish and frail like a plant in need of a stake. Her wrists were the size of his two middle fingers and there were shadows under her eyes.

Watching him watch, Elena whispered, 'She had to leave home and come back here because of the disgrace. People were calling her the gringos' whore.' Her brothers, murmured Elena, were treated as pimps, even the one who'd rescued her. 'She needs someone older to look after her. Don't you like those *fajitas*? There's no fat on them.'

Tom said sure he did and put some chicken on his fork. Cancer, he remembered reading. They buy the good bits of cancerous chickens and cover them with chile. He hid the chicken under some onion. No way would he eat this.

'You don't eat much,' said Elena, catching him.

Tom said he'd had something earlier.

'Juana starved herself when she got home,' said Elena. 'Trying to get rid of her ass and tits from shame at being a woman. That's what the doctor said, so her mother sent her to me. It's not a convenient time to have her, but how could I say "no"? She can't go back there. There's nothing there anyway.'

'I suppose not.' Tom thought of a drive he had taken to Baja California where the First World meets the Third and green land yields to parched brown. A mile or so south of this, he'd taken a wrong turn into an encampment of derelicts sitting by a bonfire. It was dusk and the air was thick with ashes or maybe bats. Some of them stood up and closed in on his car. They waved their arms menacingly – but were bought off with the price of a few beers.

Pocketing it, they'd looked shrunken and forlorn and the thought grazed him that maybe they'd merely been directing him to the nearest hotel, a place where you could drink margaritas and listen to mariachis while the sun set over the Pacific. Where else would the gringo driver of a car like his be heading? He had no Spanish, and money, his only currency, seemed to disappoint them. Perhaps they had been hoping for news of the First World which, though inaccessible to themselves, was just up the road?

'Rafael', Elena was saying, 'sees you as his model. His father is jealous. He never liked his doing karate.'

'Why not?'

Elena looked uncomfortable.

'Does his father blame me for Rafael's trouble?'

'Sure he does, but don't let that bother you. It's how Chicano families are! The parents are fearful but the kids want to stand up for themselves. Rafael thinks of you as his North American father. Really! And your mother was a heroine for me too. Heppy! So brave when she had to defend you from *your* father! She told me how he'd get drunk and beat you senseless until she was sure he'd turn you into an idiot or maybe kill you, if she didn't kill him. And how then she had to explain this to a jury which had been turned against her by photographs of his head with the eye hanging out like a loose knob. I'm sorry, am I upsetting you? No. I know you're proud of her! She had such courage! And heart! *Corage y corazon!* She was such a small woman, no bigger than Juana, yet she told me she snatched up that statuette without thinking whether it would do the job – or of what would happen if it didn't. It was just there on a side table and could have been made of anything – ceramic, glass, but she was lucky and it was made of lead. That helped with the jury. That it wasn't premeditated. Oh I'm sure even they admired her. Anyway they found her innocent. That was great – even if she did have to leave home later. Like Juana. Juries try to be fair but gossip doesn't. Do you know that if I'm letting Juana stay with me at a time like this, it's in memory of Heppy?'

While she talked, Elena was removing plates and bringing on a 'flan'. Some sort of custard. Taken up by her reminiscences, she said no more about Tom not touching his food. He felt badly about that, recognizing a primitive violation of – what? Solidarity? Also he was hungry. Maybe that stuff about cancerous chickens wasn't true? Too late now to change his mind. Elena had scraped the plates into a garbage bag.

Pinkish refried beans mingled with tomato sauce. The business about his father's eye shocked him. Had he suppressed it? Tried to give it to Jim? 'Hanging out like a loose knob?' Yes, that was how it had been. A drooping tassel. On whom? Jim? Pop? For moments their heads fused and swam inside his own. Nacreous and messy, the eye swayed unattributably. What colour had his father's been anyway? Pop's popped eye! Now back in its socket, it lit up in Tom's memory and scanned him knowingly. It expressed pure rage and Tom was dazed with fear. Behind Pop's head, Tom's mother raised the statuette and he, despite his daze, saw – and stayed silent until his father's exploding head splashed substances which, later, had to be washed from Tom's hair. Could he have imagined this? Could he?

Blinking, he rose. 'I've got to phone about Jim,' he told the table and went down to his office.

'How about his eyes?' he insisted when he got through. 'Are they injured?'

He was told that the patient's vision did not seem impaired. Tests would be run later but as of now no injuries to the ocular region appeared to have been sustained.

Tom went into the bathroom where he rolled his own guilty eyes at the mirror and threw water on his face. His mother had clearly needed to reminisce and rid herself of her memories, and he'd never let her. Couldn't bear to be left with them himself. Oh well, too late now! Pop goes the weasel! Try and forget it all. They were both dead.

Or should he see a shrink?

He went back up to find Gary leaving along with a neighbour who had helped with the moving and stayed to eat. Elena was loading the dishwasher. She asked about Jim, then remarked that he and Martin had been trying to raise money to help pay for Rafael's appeal.

'For that and Jim's downpayment. Well, they blew it. Poor Jim!' She turned on the machine.

Its heave echoed the sensation in Tom's head.

'Are you sure?' he harried on a rising note.

'Of what?'

'That Jim and Martin . . .'

'What?'

'Never mind. Excuse me. Must talk to Gary.' He could hear him down below saying goodbye to the neighbour. A car door slammed. Tom tumbled downstairs and out to where Gary's face, gleaming in his car window, vanished, then gleamed again in the blink of a revolving sign. 'Did Jim and Martin plan to raise money for Rafael?' Tom asked.

'Tom, you don't want to know. OK?' Gary patted Tom's hand, removed it from his window pane and drove off.

Tom stumped indoors. Back in his own quarters on the ground floor, he looked glumly at his video collection. There was no way he'd get to sleep now. Why did they keep things from him? What was their opinion of him anyway? Reading the video titles like mantras, he tried to calm down. *Four Feathers, Oliver Twist, Superman Two, Silence of the Lambs* . . . Violence *was* coming all right. *Great Expectations*. Funny how much, even as a boy, he'd liked nineteenth-century English stories! That century had been a manly time for the English. Their prime. Elena had been trying to work on him. She wanted him to see her as in some way Mom's heir.

Really hungry now – he'd eaten nothing since the yoghurt – he opened his office fridge which was empty except for a can of tuna. He was starting to wolf it when there was a knock on his door. It was Elena to ask about locking up. She saw the tuna.

'Oh Tom, you're hungry! You hated those *fajitas*! I could . . .'

'Hungry? No, no. I was just tidying. Throwing this out.'

He threw it in the garbage. Rafael's family was always making him do this.

'I'll take that out, then lock the doors. You go to sleep. We've disturbed you enough.'

'No, no, please, don't bother.'

'It's no bother,' she picked up the bag.

Arguing, he followed her through the dojo. He had half a notion that he might discreetly recover that tuna since the office garbage-bag would have nothing worse in it than paper. But she evaded him playfully and seemed to be in high spirits. He remembered that she had drunk several beers.

Pausing to wave at the dragon-and-knight pictures, she said, 'Know what Rafael says, Tom? He says you're "in thrall" – that's his word – "to the dragon of memory"! That it's like in some old story about someone who's asleep and guarded by a dragon!' She nodded at a lively monster with a scarlet trim to its jaws and scales sprouting green as grass. 'This made no sense to me, so one time I asked your Mom what she made of it – and she began to cry.' Elena shook her head a few times, shrugged, then smiled, it seemed to Tom, a little sourly and added, 'Of course Rafael wants to rescue you!'

Tom didn't understand any of this and had a feeling that he didn't want to either, so he gave up on the tuna and, after saying goodnight to Elena, returned to his room.

Later, hearing her go upstairs, he put on a video, then fell asleep in front of it. Woken by hunger, he decided to go to an all-night store, only to find, on trying the outer doors, that she had taken away the keys.

*

Upstairs the rhythm of sleeping breath had changed the place; the temperature was warm and the air musky. Padding about in stocking feet, he told himself that Elena must surely have left the keys somewhere obvious. Having switched on a light in the kitchen and found no keys there, he followed its slanting gleam into the dining room which smelled of Mexican cloth – that cheesy memory of sheep – a whiff which he remembered sometimes getting from Rafael.

There was a *rebozo* on the table but no keys. Groping, his fingers alighted on flesh and someone gave a tiny scream. It was Juana who turned out to have left the bed she had been sharing with Elena, then fallen asleep in here. In explanation, she showed him the photo-romance she had been reading before turning out the light. Pointing and grimacing, she laughed at her own lack of English.

'Elena took my keys.'

'I sorry. No understand!' A breathy gabble of Spanish.

The whispers were too loud. Tom, who wanted her to look for his keys in Elena's room, led her downstairs in the hope of explaining his predicament by showing her the locked front door.

A prompt, submissive smile told him she'd got the wrong idea. Of course! The photo-romance still in her hand showed a picture of an evil seducer.

'Not that!' Waving agitated hands, he tried to shoo away her misapprehension. Poor girl! She saw men as predators!

She quailed, clearly thinking him angry, so he tried to look well-disposed but not predatory. 'It's all right, Juana. Don't worry. It's just that I need my keys. To get out. See.' Carefully avoiding eye-contact, he made a show of trying and failing to open the front door. But now her misapprehension changed. Panic clouded her. Was he putting her out? No, no. He smiled reassurance – but this too was open to misunderstanding.

'Keys?' He mimed the act of sliding one into a lock. '*Llaves?* Get it? No?' Frustrated, he flung himself onto the sofa in front of the video where Scrooge – he must have put him on earlier – was embracing Tiny Tim.

'*A!*' she cried, '*que rico!*' And, joining him, cuddled close and took his hand in hers.

He snatched it away then, as she quailed, became remorseful and led her back up to where a startled Elena awoke, rubbed her eyes and shot him an unwarrantedly knowing look.

'Elena,' he tried to keep exasperation out of his voice, 'Juana keeps getting the wrong end of the stick. Will you please tell her that I'm not putting her out, but that I don't want to sleep with her either?' The voice sounded querulous. He tried to soften it. 'Listen,' he soothed. Yes, that was better. 'Listen, you can both stay here as long as you choose. OK?'

'Oh Tom, do you mean it?'

'I . . . oh well I guess so!'

He went back down to find his TV screen curdling furiously. Turning it off, he realized that they might want to stay for months! Years even! Could he back out? He couldn't. He had, moreover, forgotten to ask for the keys. Could he go up and ask for them? No, he could not do that either. The girls would be in bed again by now. He'd embarrass them – and Juana might again get the wrong end of the stick. Yet he was hungrier than ever and his windows, since he'd had the place soundproofed, didn't open. Sitting on his couch, he could only laugh to think of Rafael in prison, Jim in hospital and himself locked in his own house and dreaming of food. Gary might say he'd always kept himself locked in and on a diet! Well, maybe so.

Upstairs was now silent, so he tiptoed back up, opened the fridge and took out Juana's last remaining cakes which were by now a little crumbly and reminded him of boyhood greeds. Bright and smeary like First Grade crayons and dripping with lipids! Thoughtfully, he chewed, then swallowed one, two, and finally four with the help of a can of *Dos Xs* beer which was in the fridge too, then went down to his bed where he dreamed recklessly that Juana was lying beside him, only to find her turning into Rafael who had the same black, brilliant eyes but was in better shape and had the grace of a healthy feline. The crumbs on Tom's lips were sweet and he imagined a prison-hungry Rafael asking if he might lick them, and himself saying 'Sure!' Rafael said, *'Hombre*, I'm weak with longing for *pan Mexicano!*' Then, somehow Tom had him in his arms. Why not, he thought and, feeling himself start to

wake up, pulled the dream back over him like a slipping com-
forter. Why not? Why not stay under here with the smell of
vanilla and strawberry and Rafael's smooth, hard body and
fresh, athlete's sweat? Because before we know it, *hombre*, pop
goes the weasel. The DNA boys aren't moving fast enough,
so we'd better be our own Merlin the Magicians – if and while
we can! Tomorrow, he thought, *mañana*, I'll visit Jim. Then
dozed again, with an eager, dreamy hunger, in Rafael's arms.

Later, in a deeper, more unruly dream, he thought he heard
himself say one day in class,

'Somebody should teach those guys! Blow them away!
Wham!'

Had he? Had he said that? To Rafael? Egged him on?
Played Lucifer? He had. He had.

Rum and Coke

I expect at any minute to hear from the nursing home where my wife is due to go into labour. They thought I was making her nervous, which is why they asked me to leave. I can't blame them. After all, what could they know of our – what? Anomalies? So now I sit by the phone, thinking of the boy – we know it's to be a boy – and of how he'll be called Frank in memory of my father: Senator Leary, whose death, to quote the obituaries, was such a sore loss to his country. Soon there will be a new Frank Leary to take his place. Symmetry and *pietas*. He'd have liked that.

He laid out his principles for me on the day, not long after my nineteenth birthday, when I took up my duties as summer barman at the Moriarty Castle Hotel. He'd got me the job. The Knights sometimes held functions there, indeed were holding one that weekend, which was why he drove me down. My mother came in her own car and stopped off for lunch. She was en route to Galway where the League to Save the Unborn Child (SUC) had organized a rally. She's one of their officers.

While she settled my father into his room I introduced myself to the head barman, who said he'd show me the ropes in the lull after lunch. Then back came my parents and my father asked me to pour him a drink: coke and rum. That surprised me because of his being a teetotaller. He grinned and so did my mother: a benedictory, parental grin. Declan's an adult now was what it decreed; then he made his speech. You could sum it up to sound like hypocrisy – until you remembered about *that* being the tribute vice pays to virtue. Anyway, his principle was simple – although its workings turn out not to be! He said he wanted me, during his stay at the castle, to do what trusted barmen around the country had been doing for years: slip a sizeable snort of rum into his Coca Cola but charge whoever was standing drinks for the coke only. Later, he would drop by and pay the difference. The common inter-est came before that of the individual. And he, a man in the public eye, must neither alienate voters nor weaken his own influence for good. What the eye didn't see didn't matter.

'But father, surely drinking wouldn't alienate many Irish people?'

'As a politician I can't afford to alienate any. For the sake of the causes I support.'

As this was one of the times when the Right-to-Lifers were making a push to stop creeping Liberalism, I guessed he meant them. 'But what', I objected, 'about your conscience?'

'That', he cut me off, 'is between me and my God.' Then he said again about the general good coming first. 'Abide by that rule and you can do what you like. Obedience', he smiled, 'makes for freedom!' And raised an eyebrow.

I laughed.

He believed in having a sense of humour. The obituaries quoted him on how disarming it could be. It was, he liked to say, a tempering mechanism. Also: that conservatives must strive to surprise and dazzle so as to steal the opposition's fire.

It's been odd reading about this clever, shifty man. To be sure, some of the reminiscences went back to his school days – and how could he have stayed the same? Ironically, though, change was a bogy of his. One writer described him as 'a man whose unwavering aim was to preserve on our island a state faithful to the more orthodox teachings of the Roman Catholic Church'. To do this, as he told me in the Moriarty Castle bar, you had to fight unethical innovation. Unchristian practices. Unseemly publications. You needed counter-seductions. Wit and paradox. Nonchalance. Panache.

No one denied he had *that*. Too much? Maybe. Maybe he ended up seducing and bamboozling himself? *I* certainly can't be trusted to judge. He was fifty-seven but looked younger, in a Cary Grant sort of way: silver wings to his hair, white teeth, big frame, flat belly. He had a good tailor and could, as the saying goes, charm the birds off the trees – or, discreetly, pull birds. I was proud of him but apprehensive as to what he expected of me – or believed in really. My eldest brother has for years been a missionary in Ecuador, and it would be a mistake to suppose this pleased my father. According to him, most missionaries nowadays were crypto-Communists. Indeed, now that the official Communists had collapsed, they *were* the last Communists. Priests – which may sound odd from a militant layman – were dangerously gullible and monks worse. He'd sent me and my two brothers to school to the Benedictines with advice to take what they taught us with a pinch of salt. He wanted us to have a grounding in religion, yes, but also to be able to take the world on at its own game. And for this, the Benedictines, he was sorry to say, were insufficiently robust. They were considered class-ier than the Jesuits, but lacked the nous to spike their coke with rum. Or their red lemonade with whiskey, which I should also be prepared to serve. Likewise tonic with vodka. Doubleness was all. I guessed that the job as barman was meant to sharpen me – and was happy about this. I had been reading Stendhal and thought of Moriarty Castle in terms of his great houses where raw young men learn amatory wit. My second brother was in Australia. As an uncle of ours put it, he and my father were too alike, and two cocks in one barnyard upset the pecking order. My sisters were married, so on whom could my father's hopes focus if not on me? I might have resented this if I had been surer of it. As it was, I was desperate to impress him.

*

I've rung the nursing home again. They're to let me know just as soon as I'm needed – and are undoubtedly being patient because of whose son I am. In this city, you are never anonymous, so may as well reap the benefits, since there are drawbacks too. It's odd: I haven't thought so much about him for months. Not since the last panegyric was read and folded away. Maybe when the new Frank Leary is hogging attention I'll forget the old one? Come to think of it, I'll *be* the 'old' Leary then. Old, worldly and not quite twenty-one! Maybe, God help me, I'll burst out in my fifties!

*

The drawbacks? Well with women for a start. Feminists. His name was a red rag to them, so I could never take things on their own terms. Every choice meant being with or against him and I always chose to be 'with'. I had – I admit – a girlish admiration for his manliness and saw women as rivals.

Away from home though – I spent three summers abroad, learning modern languages – all this changed and by my second week in Italy, when I was fifteen, I was sharing a tent with a Danish girl. The tent was a tiny thing and dyed bright orange so that hunters would not shoot in our direction. I loved that: colour of flame and folly! I was over the moon to be out from under my Irish camouflage. Our parents, of course, thought we were in a hostel, but we simply moved out and after that I swear it was the difficulty of communicating – we talked pidgin Italian to each other – which made it easy to be together. I conclude that the answer to that old conundrum as to which language Adam and Eve spoke in Paradise may be 'none'. Not being able to ask questions eliminates the tripwires of shyness, class, and wondering whether what you feel for each other is love or lust. As for the one about using 'artificial contraceptives', Vinca was on the pill and had a container with a dial which clicked forward a notch each time she took one. Streamlined

and sage, it made me glad I couldn't tell her of the preserved
foetus which my mother's colleagues toted to their lectures on
the ills the flesh is heir to. Silence was golden in our Umbrian
olive grove – and we left chatter to the crickets.

But to return to Moriarty Castle: as I wasn't yet, strictly
speaking, on the staff, my father asked if it would be all right
for me to sit down to lunch with my mother and himself.
Later, such privilege would be off limits, like the swimming
pool and the nine-hole golf course. Teasingly, he made me try
a rum and coke.

Then my mother left and, as he and I strolled back through
the lobby, he introduced me to the receptionist, a Miss Sheehy.

'This is my son, Declan,' he told her and she gave me a
funny look. I told myself that I was imagining it and took her
hand in a forthright grip. She was one of those slim, quivery
girls who shy like deer and have a curtain of dark hair for hiding behind. I guessed her to be my age or maybe a bit older.
More importantly, she was a beauty. My Stendhalian summer
partner? Why not?

Later, after the barman had shown me how to mix drinks, I
came back to the lobby. She was still on duty.

'How does it feel to be the son of a famous father?'

This annoyed me, so I countered with 'How does it feel to
be a knockout beauty?'

That got a blush. I walked off regretting the balkiness
of words. With Vinca and her summery successors I had
rejoiced in their absence. Maybe it was auricular – Christ,
there's a word! – confession which poisoned them for me?
All that talk of 'bad' thoughts. Maybe, I should become an
explorer and live in the Amazon jungle: steamy heat, warm
mud, bare-breasted Indian girls and, above all, no chat! I kept
thinking of Miss Sheehy though. That hair had a tremulous
life to it. Like seaweed. Now I'd got myself uselessly excited
and should maybe take a run around the tennis courts –
unless they were off limits too. I wondered: was Miss Sheehy?

As it happened, I had no time to find out because carloads of Knights started arriving and soon the bar was abuzz and I was kept busy. I wondered whether the castle chapel was off-limits to staff too? This seemed unlikely, so maybe I'd be able to watch them next day at their mumbo jumbo, robing and disrobing, in imitation of the Crusaders donning armour to fight the forces of darkness and fornication. I wasn't sure how close my father's connection with them was. They favour confidentiality and infiltration and he might be their man in the senate. He didn't appear in the bar.

I finished work after midnight. There was no sign of Miss Sheehy. I fell on my bed and slept.

I was awoken before daylight. My mother wanted me on the 'phone. Or rather, it turned out, she wanted my father. There was some decision to do with the rally which only he could take. Neither she nor the other Pro-Life ladies took decisions. They were there to make it look as though *women* were opposing the feminists but were puppets really. She apologized for waking me but said she'd been ringing him since last night.

'Your father's not answering his 'phone,' she told me. 'It's off the hook. I think maybe he knocked it off inadvertently and now he'll miss all his calls.'

So I pulled on some clothes, took the lift to the guests' part of the hotel, and arrived at his door just as Miss Sheehy emerged from it – or rather just as she started to emerge, for when she saw me she ducked back in. That was hard to misinterpret and froze me in my tracks. I mean if she had said 'Hello Declan' and that she had been answering a room-service call, I would have believed her. I would have accepted any plausible story because I was thinking of her in terms of my own designs, not his – but, instead, she turned tail on seeing me. For perhaps a minute, I stood transfixed. Then, as I turned to go, out she bobbed again.

'Declan, can you come here, please. Your father wants you.'

I bolted. Unthinkingly. Or rather what I was thinking was that I didn't want to know any more of his secrets.

Back in my room I started making faces at my mirror and told the clown grimacing back that I was a prize ass. Obviously he was ill and she *had* been answering a room-service call. Why, though, had she bobbed away? Clown, so as to tell him his son was outside. Clown, clown! What would they both think of me now? Worldliness, where were you? I had failed the test! Fallen at the first fence. Could my father, I even wondered, have set the thing up deliberately? I had heard of British Foreign Office candidates being tested like this on country-house weekends.

I wasn't surprised by the knock on my door. It was Miss Sheehy to say that, just as I'd guessed, he was ill. Alarmingly so. Her manner had grown agitated and she was asking for my help. 'He can't walk and we can't have the doctor finding him in my room.'

Her room? I was so flustered that we were at its door before I remembered that, just now, they had been in his. How had he got here?

She brushed away the question. 'Look, he's passed out. We should get a doctor. It could be serious! A heart attack even! But he can't be found *in my room*!' Her voice had an edge of hysteria.

She opened her door and there he was on the carpet, I saw the urgency then. Jesus, I thought. Christ! As far as I could tell, his pulse was all right. Or was it? I tried, clumsily, to compare it to my own – but it's hard to take two pulses simultaneously. Miss Sheehy became impatient.

'Take his shoulders,' she directed. 'I'll hold the door. Can you drag him to the lift? Or hoist him on your back?'

'Supposing we're seen?'

'We'll say he began to feel ill in your room. Then, when you tried to help him back to his, he fainted. I'm here because you rang the front desk.'

Good enough, I thought with relief, and gave myself to a frenzy of activity which kept my feelings in check. He was heavy but I'm strong and was able, like *pius Aeneas* fleeing the wars of Troy, to carry my father down the corridor, into the lift, then down another corridor to his room. By then, she had rung the doctor who was on his way. As I laid him on his bed, she divulged some facts. They had, she admitted, been quarrelling and her invitation to me to enter his room had been a move in the quarrel. When I left, she had rushed off, whereupon he, thinking she'd gone after me, followed her.

'He's terrified of his family finding out about us.'

'Us?' I asked stupidly.

'Him and me.'

You, I wondered dourly, and how many others? I was in a sweat of filial guilt: unfounded, to be sure, but my feelings had run amok. My father's poor, vulnerable, open eyes stared glassily and saw neither of us. Oh God, I prayed, don't let him die. Not here. Not for years! Please, God! At the same time I was furious with him. For what about my mother? Did she know – I recalled her tolerance of the rum-and-coke – that as well as trusted barmen 'up and down the country', he also had – what? What was Miss Sheehy? His heart's love or one of a team? A team of floozies? If so, how big? Basketball five? Hockey eleven? She, no doubt, imagined him to be in love with her. Might he be? I felt obscurely flouted, and confused.

The doctor, when he came, quickly changed my mood.

'It's serious,' he warned. 'He's had a stroke. I'm going to call a helicopter and fly him to Galway.'

He told us to stay in the room while he went to make arrangements. For moments we sat in silence. Miss Sheehy was as pale as paper. My father's eyes were closed now and his face was grey.

'How long have you – been with him?'

'Three years.'

'So why the quarrel now?' He would not, I was sure, have

misled her with false promises. He would never leave my mother. A Senator! A militant Catholic layman! Never in this life!

'I'm pregnant,' she blurted and began to cry.

'Don't cry!' I could have slapped her. Hysteria, I thought. Then: could he be such a fool? 'You mean you didn't use anything?' Condoning the use of artificial contraceptives led, said the League to Save the Unborn Child, to condoning abortion. Changing our legislation would open the sluice gates. I knew the arguments by heart. But what about the principle of what the eye didn't see? *Her* eyes were getting scandalously red. 'Don't cry,' I urged. 'The doctor will be back in a moment.'

'And he'll take him away. To Galway. Listen,' she clutched my arm, 'I must see him, get news of him. But he'll be in intensive care. I won't be let in. Only relatives will be. Will you help me?'

Red-eyed, feverish mistress! Outcast, beautiful Miss Sheehy. I kissed her and it was she who slapped me! Ah well, some outlet was needed. The doctor may have heard the slap for he gave us a look as he came in the door. Two paramedics were with him and in no time had my father on a stretcher. We followed them down the familiar corridors and out to the lawn where the helicopter was waiting. They loaded him on. Blades rotated; wind moulded our clothes to our bodies; then up it whirred into a misty dawn, turning silver, then grey, then fading to a speck.

I thought of 'the rapture', the bodily whisking of people up to heaven in which certain Protestants believe – ex-President Reagan for one was, I'd read in some magazine, expecting to be whisked aloft. Holus bolus, body and bones! It was an inappropriate thought. But then what was appropriate? Maybe I was in shock?

Miss Sheehy's hand was in mine. Would I help her see him, she begged, or at least keep in touch? Yes, I said, yes. I'd be leaving for the hospital as soon as I could explain things to the management here. I'd phone her this evening.

'I have this weekend off,' she told me.

Ah, I thought: they planned to spend it together. Poor father! Poor Miss Sheehy!

'What's your first name?' I asked.

She said it was Artemis. Her parents had wanted her to be a huntress, not a victim. I made no comment.

*

I've had a call from my mother. From the nursing home. No need for me, she says, to worry. First babies are often slow to arrive. She should know: a mother of five and a four-time grandmother. My sisters have been dutifully breeding. She's in her element and hasn't been in such good spirits since my father's death.

*

He never regained consciousness. When Artemis came in on the Friday evening, I disssuaded her from seeing him, arguing – truthfully – that he'd have hated to be seen with drips and needles stuck all over him.

She acquiesced, noting, with an unreadable little smile, that she was used to *not* doing things – not writing to him ever, nor ringing him up. Not at his office. Not at home. Nowhere. She always had to wait for him to make the contact. I looked appalled and she said defiantly, 'When we were together, it was pure delight. Like wartime furloughs. Utterly without ordinary moments. We met sometimes on a friend's barge on the Shannon, once on a yacht in Spain, once in a flat in Istanbul. Never for long. But he was so happy at being able to do what he never ordinarily did . . .'

Christ, I thought, he'd raised negativity to a mystique! He was a one-man cult and had brainwashed her good and proper. I suddenly realized that I disliked him deeply and had, unknown to myself, done so for years. No wonder my brothers had fled to Australia and Ecuador.

By now I had spent three days in the hospital with my mother – the stroke had happened on the Wednesday morning. There was nothing to do but wait, talk to doctors about their scans, filter their pessimism back to her, hold her hand. The staff, predictably, was assiduous, so I had a lot of help.

'Such a fine man,' I would hear them murmuring prayerfully to her in corridors and guest areas. 'What a tragedy!' Sometimes they went with her to the chapel. One of the nurses was a member of the League to Save the Unborn Child. She, she told my mother, rarely questioned the will of God but found it hard to see a clean-living teetotaller like my father struck down when the town was full of drunks whose blood-pressure seemed not to give them a moment's trouble. 'God forgive me, I'm a desperate rebel!' boasted this docile mouse, trembling under her blue, submissive veil.

These conversations, I admit, gave my mother a lot more consolation than I could provide. Communicating with her has never been my forte. She was younger than my father and totally his creature. They were what's called a fine couple. She's five feet ten, graceful, blonde-speckled-tastefully-with-grey, dutiful, cheerful, plays tennis and bridge, takes pleasure in her volunteer work for his causes and has never, in my presence, revealed a spark of even the mild brand of rebelliousness favoured by the blue-veiled nurse. None. My sisters' opinion is that she's been emotionally lobotomized. By whom?

I went from time to time to look at him. He was semi-paralysed and his face was badly askew: mouth twisted up and down in a vertical, Punch-and-Judy leer. Doubleness had finally branded him. Nobody but me, though, seemed to have had such a thought. At least nobody voiced it, and neither, to be sure, did I. My mother kept putting her hand on his brow, murmuring coaxing endearments and kissing his convulsed grey face. She hoped something might be getting through. This must have drained her emotionally for, in the evenings, she went back to her hotel and was served a meal in bed.

This left me free to dine *en ville* with Artemis Sheehy, whose weekend was, I reminded myself, available and blank. Despite my advice, she yearned to do precisely what my mother had been doing: put her long-fingered hand on my father's brow and kiss him well.

I decided – in retrospect it is impossible to disentangle my motives – to let her. From hope? Pity? As aversion-therapy? How can I say?

We had by now had a row, or rather we had had another. Our relations from the start had been edgy. Why, I queried on Friday evening, as we sat waiting for the baked Alaska – I had, since she refused to drink with me, had a bottle of claret to myself – why had she let my father cast her as Patient Griselda, while he played the Pillar of the Irish Establishment? A P.I.E., I mocked, that was what he was, a po-faced Pie! An escapee from the novels of Zola and nineteenth-century operetta! Old hat! Self-serving! A canting humbug! My jealousy revenged itself on his charm – I now thought of it as smarm – and on his unassailable advantage in the minds of my mother and Artemis: his poignantly stricken state. The new-felled Knight!

'Can you', I harried, 'deny that he is – was a hypocrite?'

What could she do, in all decency, but throw down her napkin and leave? I, waiting for the bill, had to let her go – and, anyway, knew I had her on a string. I was her only connection with him and so could let her stew. Greedy from anger – and satisfying one appetite in lieu of another – when the baked Alaska arrived with the bill, I ate her portion as well as my own. It struck me, as I walked morosely back to my hotel, that I was beginning to act like him. Ruthless and masterful. I hated myself. Still – I licked the last of the baked Alaska from my lips – it would be pointless to forgo my advantage by capitulating too soon.

Sure enough, she rang me next morning. Triumphant – but hiding it – I was sweetness itself. And contrite. She must, I begged, see how hard it was for me to hold my mother's hand by day and hers in the evening? I was painfully torn – as no doubt my father too had been. Instinctively, I was blending my image with his: an anticipation of what was to happen when obituaries appeared with photographs of his young self, looking, as was universally noted, disturbingly like me. But, to go back to my conversation with Artemis, I now made a peace-offering, which was that if she really wanted me to, I would take her to see him this evening, after my mother had left the hospital.

She accepted and, as I had tried to dissuade her, could hardly blame me for the shock. His skewed mouth dribbled. There were tubes in his nose. He looked worse than dead. He looked like an ancient, malicious changeling put together from that grey stuff with which wasps build their nests. Or ectoplasm or papier mâché made from old, pulped bibles. These conceits swarmed through my head as I watched, then, from pity, ceased to watch her.

She was devastated, disgusted, guilty: a mirror of myself. Did she also feel that hot rush of feeling which, for days now, had been distracting and perhaps healing me? The urge to fuck, which is a pro-life remedy for death-fears? People get it in wartime and, notoriously, in graveyards and during black-outs and other foreshadowings of mortality. I let her look her fill. I even left her alone lest, like my mother, she wish to kiss him. I don't know whether she did.

I waited in the hospital-green corridor, not hurrying her adieux which, whether she knew it or not, were what they were. He, the doctors had told me, would be a wreck if he lived but was unlikely to last the weekend. I hadn't told her this, but guessed she knew. Then I took her on a drive along the coast, next for a long, twilit walk along a stretch of it, and finally to a small seaside hotel, where we spent the night comforting each other and conjuring away ghosts.

My father died that night, which was just as well for all concerned, especially her. If he had lived, what would she have done? Gone to somewhere like Liverpool to have her child, then given it out for adoption? Or raised it in resentful solitude on the income he would feel frightened – if compos mentis – into coughing up? Taken an 'abortion flight' to London? Instead, once we had faced my mother with the *fait accompli* of our runaway marriage – registry office in London, followed by a conciliatory Church ceremony back home – Artemis became part of the household which, for three years, she had been forbidden to phone. Sometimes, she tells me, she used, in her loneliness, to dial the number anyway then listen, silently, to our irritably convivial voices.

'Hullo! Speak up. Who is it? Press Button B! Oh it's the heavy breather again! What do you want, Heavy Breather? If you're a burglar, we're all at home so there's no point trying to break in!'

Now she *is* in and the noses of my sisters' children – none of them Learies – are put out of joint by the glorious prospect of Frank Junior's birth. Any minute now my mother will phone with news of my new brother's entry under false colours into the Leary clan. Brother-masquerading-as-son, he will be born under the true Leary sign of duplicitous duality.

And I? Well, I'm in Law School and active in the Student Union. People ask whether I'll go into politics and my fear is that I may find myself turning into a carbon copy of my father. I am, after all, living by his principles and can't see quite how to break out. Drinking claret instead of rum in coke seems an inadequate gesture, and my support for Family Planning, Abortion and Divorce has been hailed by some of his cronies as the sort of forward-looking thinking to which he himself might well have subscribed had he lived. Times have changed, they say, and we must march to the European Community's tune if we want subsidies for our farmers. After all, providing the option to use contraception, etc., obliges nobody to avail themselves of it. And anyone who does can repent later. God is good and there's no point being simple-minded. So, they would have me think, opposing the letter of my father's laws is a way of being true to their spirit.

Maybe. It's hard to tell. Double-think is the order of the day.

Of course I rejoice in Artemis's love, though here too a shiver of doubt torments me: does she see him in me? Am I two people for her? To be sure, it's foolish to probe! We're happy and . . . there's the phone! Alleluia! Where are my car keys? Frank Junior must be on his way.

The Corbies' Communion

Liam sat, glassed-in, on a half landing crammed with photographs. It was easy to heat, which was why he came here when he couldn't sleep. Lately he had been feeling the cold.

Images of himself gleamed mockingly but could, if he twitched his head, be dissolved in light-smears or made to explode, milkily, like stars.

'Sap!' he told a young Liam. 'What was there to smirk about?' Kate had mounted bouquets of snaps in which she – why had he not noticed? – was often less than present: half-hidden under hats or bleached-out as if too easily reconciled to mortality. The solid one was himself who had seized his days with a will visible even in creased press cuttings. Cocky and convivial, the past selves could be guises donned by some mild devil to abash him. Flicking whiskey at them, he managed to exorcize the Liam who was accepting a decoration from the country's ex-president and an award from someone he could no longer place. OLD POLEMICIST HONOURED bragged a headline. GREAT MAVERICK RECONCILED AT LAST. Black-tied, white-tied, tweedy in a sequence of Herbie Johnson hats, alone, on podia and at play, the personae zoomed in and out of focus. Liam at the races. Liam on a yacht. Some wore whites as though for cricket, a game no Irishman of his stripe would have played. That ban was now obsolete. By humiliating the old masters, West Indian bowlers had freed the sport and its metaphors.

'You had a grand innings!' a recent visitor had exclaimed. 'Close to a century!' Liam, loath to be sent off to some Pavilion in the Sky, pressed an imaginary stop-button. Rewind. Replay.

But replays were nightmares and Kate featured in them all.

'Was I such a bastard to you?' he cajoled one of her half-averted faces. It was bent over a picnic basket, counting hard-boiled eggs. 'Neglectful? Selfish?' The face would not look up.

'I could kill you for dying,' he told her. His watch hands pointed to four.

He had been twice to bed, started to sleep, funked it and returned here. Catastrophe was tearing up his sky and panic circled: black as crows. Keeping it at bay, he topped up his whiskey and, from habit, hid the bottle behind a fern. Outside, the dawn-chorus made a seething churr. He was alone by choice, wanting neither minders nor commiseration.

'You were plucky,' he told a likeness of Kate, smiling in an old-time summer dress. 'But you cheated on me! Became an invalid! Querulous! If you were alive now we'd be fighting!'

Two nights ago she, contrary to what statistics had led him to expect, had died. He had counted on going first. She had always been here till now, hadn't she? Even when this spoiled his plans! The thought startled him and his crossed leg pulsed. 'Kate!' he mourned, amazed. For years he, not she, had been the adventurer.

'I know you resented that,' he told a snapshot in which a child's head bobbed past her face. 'But you were happy at first. And later wasn't so bad, surely?' He scrutinized snaps taken in restaurants and on boating holidays on the River Barrow. '*Was* it?' Helpless, he brushed a hand across dapplings from awnings and other people's menus. Cobweb grudges, forgotten tiffs. 'Damn it, Kate, did you put bad photos of yourself here to torment me? That could make me hate you!'

Spying the whiskey bottle behind its plant, he reflected that hating her would be a relief – then that she might have planned the relief.

His checked hand reached the bottle and poured more anyway. Nobody to stop him now! If she'd died twenty years ago he'd have remarried. Maybe even fifteen? Now – he was ninety. Had she planned *that*? Wryly, he raised the glass.

'To you then, old sparring partner and last witness to our golden youth!'

Losing her was radical surgery. Like losing half his brain. Like their retreat, years ago, to this manageable cottage. In the background to several snaps, their old house made a first, phantom appearance as a patch in a field, its roomy shape pegged out with string. Pacing the patch, strode Kate. Expansive, laughing, planning a future now behind them, she waved optimistic arms.

'Shit!'

He banged his head against the wall. More exploding stars! Watch it, Liam! You're not the man you were!

A civil-rights lawyer who had become a media figure in his prime, an activist who had brought cases to Strasbourg and The Hague, he had let her take over the private sector of their lives. This included religion. A mistake? Religion here was never quite private and their arrangements on that score jarred.

The requiem mass which was to have comforted her would set his teeth on edge. It was a swindle that the Faith, having brought him woe – sexual and political – when he was young, should now pay no dividends. None. He had said so to the Parish Priest, a near-friend. Running into each other on the seafront, or watching blown tulips reveal black hearts in the breezy park, the two sometimes enjoyed a bicker about the off-chance of an afterlife: a mild one since neither would change his bias. Liam was past ninety and the PP was no chicken either.

Brace up, Liam! The things to hold onto were those you'd lived by. Solidarity. The Social Contract. Pluck. Confronting a mottled mirror, he acknowledged the charge reflected back. Funerals here were manifestoes. His conduct at Kate's must, rallied the mirror, bolster those who had helped him fight the Church when it was riding roughshod over people here. You couldn't let *them* down by slinking back for its last vain comforts. How often had he heard bigots gloat that some Liberal had 'died screaming for a priest'?

They'd relish saying it of him all right! Addicts of discipline and bondage, the Holy Joes would get a buzz from seeing Liam dragged off by psychogenic demons. Toasted on funk's pitchforks! Turned on its spit! Tasty dreams! In the real world, they'd settle for seeing him back in the fold – and why gratify them? Could Kate have wanted to? She who, in the vigour of her teens, had marched at Republican funerals, singing: 'Tho' cowards mock and traitors sneer / We'll keep the red flag flying here'? Hair blowing, cheeks bright as the flag! Sweet, hopeful Kate!

On the other hand, how refuse her her Mass? Anyway how many of the old guard were left to see whether Liam stood firm? Frail now and rigid in the set of their ways! He ticked them off on his fingers: a professor emeritus, some early proponents of Family Planning, secular schools and divorce, a few journalists whose rights he had defended, his successor's successor at Civil Liberties: a barrister long retired. Who else? Half a score of widows confirmed the actuarial statistics which had played him false. Would they make it to Kate's funeral? Not long ago, he had drawn a cluster of circles which she mistook at first for a rose. It was a map showing the radius within which each of their contemporaries and near-contemporaries was now confined. Those who still drove kept to their neighbourhoods. Those who did not might venture to the end of a bus route. Not all the circles touched.

The Mass, though, would be accessible to most, being in the heart of town, in Trinity College chapel: a case of an ill wind bringing good, since the choice of venue – made when he, Kate and the twentieth century were a mutinous sixty – had lost pizzazz. Ecumenicism was now commonplace and the old Protestant stronghold had Catholic chaplains. The Holy Joes had him surrounded. For two pins he'd call off the ceremony – but how do that to Kate?

'For Christ's sake, Liam!' He raged at himself. 'There is no Kate! Hold onto your marbles! She's gone!' He poured his savourless whiskey into a fern.

*

Anger, a buffer against worse, had made him insult the PP when he came yesterday to condole. Priests, Liam had hissed, were like crows. They battened on death. Then he recited a poem which he remembered too late having recited to him before. Never mind! Rhymes kept unstable thoughts corralled.

> There were twa corbies sat in a tree,
> Willoughby, oh Willoughby.
> The tane unto the t'ither say
> 'Where shall we gang and dine this day?
> In beyond yon aul fell dyke
> I wot there lies a new-slain knight . . .'

Liam wasn't dead yet but here was the first corby come to scavenge his soul in what the priest must think was a weak moment. If he did, he thought wrong. When asked about the Mass, Liam said he might call it off. He'd see when his daughter got here. Ha, he thought, the cavalry was coming. Her generation believed in nothing. Kitty was tough – Kate's influence! The two had ganged up on him from the first, saying he was all for freedom outside the house and patriarchy within! How they'd laugh – he could just hear them! – at his seeing himself as slain when the dead one was Kate!

Ah but – the thought stunned him – the living are also dying.

> 'Naebody kens that he lies there,
> But his hawk and his hound and his lady fair.
> His hound is to the hunting gane,
> His hawk to bring the wild fowl hame,

His lady's ta'en anither mate
Sae we may mak' our dinner swate.'

Kate's remains had gone – as would his – to medical research. It felt odd not to have a corpse.

'You'll need some ritual,' said the PP. 'To say goodbye. Kate liked rituals. I used to bring her communion,' he reminded, 'after she became bedridden. Your housekeeper prepared things. You must have known.'

Liam remembered a table covered with lace. Water. Other props. Of course he'd known! He had kept away while she made her last communions just as, to please *his* wife, Jaurès, the great French Socialist, let their daughter make her first one – to the shock of comrades for whom fraternizing with clerics was a major betrayal.

A weakness?

Liam sighed and the PP echoed the sigh. Many Irish people, mused the priest, went to Mass so as not to upset their relatives. 'It was the opposite with Kate. Her religion meant a lot to her.'

'How do you know?'

'I know.' The PP made his claim calmly.

His lady's ta'en anither mate thought Liam and called the priest a carrion crow. 'The way the corbies took communion', he ranted, 'was to eat the knight's flesh. Tear him apart!'

Suddenly tired, he must have dropped off then for when he awoke the PP had let himself out. Liam felt ashamed. 'Tear him apart,' he murmured, but couldn't remember what that referred to. The word 'ritual' stayed with him though. It floated about in his head.

*

'I'm not doing it for Him!' he told his daughter, Kitty, who now arrived off a plane delayed by fog. As though her brain too were fogged she stared at him in puzzlement.

'HIM', Liam tilted his eyes aloft. 'I mean HIM.' He shook an instructive fist heavenward, only to see her gaze ambushed by a light-fixture. She – Kate could have told him who to blame – was indifferent to religion and always nagging him about the wiring in the house.

'Who's "him"?'

'God!' More fist-shaking. 'Bugger HIM. I don't believe in HIM! I'll be doing it for HER.'

'Doing what?' Living in England had made her very foreign.

'Taking', he marvelled at himself, 'communion at your mother's Requiem Mass. I'll do it for her. For Kate. She'd have done it for me.' His bombshell failed to distract Kitty from the fixture in the ceiling. Wires wavered from it like the legs of a frantic spider. He couldn't remember how it had got that way. Had someone yanked off the bulb? His temper, lately, had grown hard to control.

'I'm calling an electrician.'

Liam, on getting no argument from Kitty, started one with himself. Holy Joes aside, the prime witnesses to his planned treachery would be the betrayed: those who had dared confront a Church which controlled jobs, votes and patronage. With surprising courage, vulnerable men – rural librarians and the like – had, starting back in the bleak and hungry '40s, joined his shoe-string campaigns to challenge the collusion between dodgy oligarchs and a despotic clergy. Old now, many campaigners were probably poor and surely lonely. Not pliable enough to be popular, they were unlikely to be liked. Honesty thwarted could turn to quibbling and brave men grow sour. He wondered if they tore out light bulbs?

Startling Kitty, he whispered: 'They can put their communion up their arses.' Luxuriating in blasphemy: 'Bloody corbies! God-and-man-eating cannibals!'

*

He had grown strange. Her mother had warned her, phoning long distance with reports of his refusal to take his salt-substitute or turn off his electric blanket. 'He'll burn us down,' she'd worried. 'Or spill tea into it and electrocute himself! Stubborn,' she'd lamented. 'Touchy as a tinderbox. He's going at the top!'

Kitty reproached herself. She had not seen that these fears – transcendent, fussy, entertained for years – were justified at last. Poor mother! Poor prophetic Kate!

Sedated now, he was dreaming of her as a bride. 'Slim as a silver birch!' he praised her in his sleep. True, wondered Kitty, or borrowed from those Gaelic vision-poems where a girl's nakedness on some rough mountainside dazzles freaked-out men?

'Kate,' whimpered the sleeper. 'Kate!' His tone rang changes on that double-dealing syllable.

Saliva, bubbling on his lip, drew from a jumble in Kitty's memory the Gaelic word for snail: *seilmide*. When she was maybe four, he and she used to feed cherry blossom to snails. White and bubbly, the petals were consumed with *brio* as the surprisingly deft creatures folded them into themselves like origami artists.

Kitty wiped away Liam's spittle. Had she chosen to forget the tame snails, so as to feel free to poison the ones in her London garden, a thing she now did regularly and without qualms? She grew rucola there and basil and that heart-stopping flower, the blue morning glory, which looks like fragments of sky but shrivels in the sun. The snails got the young plants if you didn't get them first.

*

She drove him out the country to take tea in a favourite inn. Sir Walter Scott had stayed here and a letter, testifying to this, was framed in a glass case. Across from it, iridescent in a larger one, was a stuffed trout.

Liam buttered a scone and smiled at the waitress who returned his smile as women always had. 'Women', he remarked, watching as she moved off in a delicate drift of body odour, 'are the Trojan mare! *Mère.*' In his mouth the French word seethed breezily. He cocked a comical eye at Kitty and bit into the scone. 'They don't like to be outsiders, you see. That's dangerous.'

The drive had perked him up. He loved these mountains, had rambled all over them and could attach stories to places which, to Kitty, were hardly places at all. It was late September. Bracken had turned bronze. Rowan leaves were an airborne yellow and a low, pallid sun, bleaching out the car mirror, made it hard to drive. Dark, little lakes gleamed like wet iron and Liam who, in his youth, had studied Celtic poetry, listed the foods on which, according to the old poets, hermits, mad exiled kings and other Wild Men of the Woods had managed to survive.

He paused as though a thought had stung him. Could it be fear that some wild man, slipping inside his own skull, had scrambled his clever lawyer's mind?

'He's not himself,' Kate had mourned on Kitty's visits. The self Liam was losing had been such a model of clarity and grace that his undoing appalled them. He had been their light of lights and even now Kitty could not quite face the thought that he was failing. Now and again though, the process seemed so advanced as to make her wonder whether it might be less painful if speeded up? A release for him – who struggled so laboriously to slow it down.

'Yew and rowan-berries,' she heard him drone like a child unsure of his lesson – not the clever child Liam must have been but a slow-witted changeling, 'haws, was it,' he floundered, 'and hazel-nuts, mast, acorns, pignuts . . . sloes . . .'

It was an exercise of the will.

'Whortleberries . . . dillisk, salmon, badger fat, wood-sorrel, honey . . .' He faltered, '. . . eels . . . Did I say venison? Porpoise

steak . . .' His face was all focus: a knot, a noose. Its lines taut-
ened as he grasped after two receding worlds: the Celtic one
and that of the Twenties when he, and other Republicans
had gone on the run like any wild man of the woods. They'd
hardly have lived on berries though. Local sympathizers must,
she guessed, have provided potatoes and bastable bread spread
with salty butter. 'Trout?' he remembered, and his mouth
gasped with strain as if he had been hooked.

Now, though, tea and the stop in the inn had once again
revived him. The old Liam, back and brave as bunting, was
going through one of his routines. He had always been a bit
of a showman.

'In what way,' Kitty asked encouragingly, 'are women
Trojan horses?'

'Not horses,' he corrected her. 'Mares! Fillies! They conform. That's why. Anywhere and everywhere. Here, for
instance, they go to the Church and, behold, it catches them.
It gets inside *them*. It's as if Greeks inside the wooden horse
inside the walls of Troy were to breathe in drugged fumes.
They'd become Trojans, collaborate . . .'

Twinkling at her over his tea cup. The old teasing Liam.
Back for how long? As with an unreliable lover, she feared
letting down her defences. But wouldn't it be cruel not
to? Yes-and-no? Kitty was a professional interpreter. She
worked with three languages and liked to joke that her mind
was inured to plurality and that the tight trio she, Kate and
Liam had made when she was growing up had led to this.
Her mother, going further, had blamed it for the rockiness of
Kitty's marriage, an on-off arrangement which was currently
on hold.

'We were too close,' Kate used to say. 'We made you old
before your time.'

And it was true that Liam had modelled rebellious charm
for her before she was eight. How could the boys she met
later compete? Add to this that the house had been full of

young men about whom she knew too much too soon: his clients. One was a gaol bird and a bomber. Surprisingly domestic, he helped Kate in the kitchen and taught Kitty to ride a bike, running behind her, with one hand on the saddle. This, unfairly, made her suspicious later of helpful men.

'A penny for them?'

Liam's blue, amused eyes held hers. 'We', he repeated, 'send our women into the Church and *it* slips inside their heads!' She recognized an old idea, dredged from some spilled filing system in his brain.

'You sent me to school to nuns.' She had once resented this. 'Was I a Trojan filly? A hostage? Would you have lost credibility if we'd found a secular school? Or were there none in those days?'

Liam smiled helplessly.

He had lost the thread. That happened now. Poor Liam! She gripped his knee. 'Darling!' she comforted.

But he reared back with a small whinnying laugh. 'I know what you're thinking!' he accused. 'Liam, you're thinking, it's been nice knowing you. But now you're gone! Your mind's gone.'

'It's not gone. You were very sharp just now about how the Church captured me and my mother.'

'Oh, they didn't capture you the way they did her'.

'They didn't capture her either.' Kitty wanted to be fair. 'She was open to doubt. They don't like that.'

'True enough.' He seemed cheered.

'She was never a bigot.'

'So you think we should go ahead with the Mass?'

'Why not?'

*

A mash of red-raspberry faces lined the pews which were at right angles to the altar. Stick-limbed old survivors tottered

up the nave to condole with Liam and remind him of themselves. Some had fought beside him, seventy years ago, in
the Troubles or, later, in Civil Liberties. They had seen the
notices Kitty had put in national and provincial papers and
travelled, in some cases, across Ireland, to this shrunken
reunion. A straight-backed Liam stood dandified and dazed.
Ready, Kitty guessed, to fly to bits if the shell of his suit had
not held in his Humpty Dumpty self. The suit had been a
sore point with her mother.

'Riddled with tobacco burns!' had been her refrain. 'For
God's sake throw it out!'

He wouldn't though. And his tailor was dead. So Kitty's
help was enlisted. She had scoured London for the sort of
multi-buttoned, rigidly interlined suits which he recognized
as 'good' and which might well have repelled small bullets.
His sartorial tastes were based on some Edwardian image
of the British Empire which he had chosen to emulate, as
athletes will an opponent's form. Nowadays, Japanese busi-
nessman seemed in pursuit of a modern approximation of it,
for she kept running across them up and down Jermyn Street
and in Burberries and Loeb.

Liam refused to wear the new clothes. Perhaps he missed
the dirt in the old ones? Its anointing heft? Embracing him
this morning, Kitty had sensed a flinching inside the resilient
old cloth. Tired by their outing, he had regressed since into a
combative confusion.

'Kate!' he'd greeted her at breakfast and had to be reminded
that Kate was dead. He'd cried then, though his mouth
now was shut against grief. Anger, summoned to see him
through the ceremony, boiled over before it began. When
the Taoiseach's stand-in, his chest a compressed rainbow
of decorations, came to pay his respects, the mouth risked
unclenching to ask, 'Is that one of the shits we fought in '22?'

'No,' soothed Kitty, 'no, love, he's from your side.'

She wasn't sure of this. Liam, a purist, had lambasted both

sides after the Civil War and pilloried all trimming when old friends came to terms with power. Today, mindful perhaps of the Trojan horse, he was in but not of this church and, ignoring its drill, provoked disarray in the congregation as he, the chief mourner, stood attentive to some inner command which forbade him to bow his head, genuflect or in any way acknowledge the ceremony.

He softened, however, on seeing his own Parish Priest serve the mass. This had not been provided for and the PP had come off his own bat. 'For Kate,' Liam whispered to Kitty who, in her foreign ignorance, might fail to appreciate the tribute.

Suddenly, regretting his rudeness to Kate's old friend, he plopped to his knees at the wrong moment, hid his face in his hands and threw those taking their cue from him into chaos.

*

Afterwards, two Trinity chaplains came to talk to him. No doubt – the thought wavered on the edge of his mind – they expected to be slipped an envelope containing a cheque. But Kitty hadn't thought to get one ready and he no longer handled money. Its instability worried him. Just recently, he had gone to his old barber for a haircut and, as he was having his shoulders brushed, proffered a shilling. The barber laughed, said his charge was five pounds then, perhaps disarmed by Liam's amazement, accepted the offer. Liam, foxily, guessed he was getting a bargain – though, to be sure, the man might send round later for his proper payment to Kate? Perhaps the chaplains would too? No! For Kate was . . . she was . . . Liam could not confront the poisonous fact and the two young men backed off before the turmoil in his face.

*

As Kitty was leaving – she had work waiting in Strasbourg – Liam, enlivened by several goodbye whiskies, told of a rearguard skirmish with the Holy Joes. It had occurred in a nursing home where, though he had registered as an agnostic, a priest tried to browbeat him into taking the sacraments.

Liam's riposte had been to drawl: 'Well, my dear fellow, I can accommodate you if it gives you pleasure!' This, he claimed, had sent the bully scuttling like a scalded cat.

*

He rang her in Strasbourg to say he wished he was with her and Kate. Unsure what this meant, she promised a visit as soon as she was free.

'I'm hitting the bottle.'

'I'll be over soon.'

Her husband, when she rang to say she couldn't come home yet because of Liam, warned, 'You can't pay him back, you know. You'd better start resigning yourself. You can't give him life.'

*

Returning to Dublin now was like stepping into childhood. Liam, barricaded like a zoo creature in winter, had holed up in an overheated space which evoked for Kitty the hide-outs she had enjoyed making when she was five. Its fug recalled the smell of stored ground sheets, and its dust-tufts mimicked woolly toys. The housekeeper, counting on Liam's short-sightedness, had grown slack.

Interfering was tricky though. Last year, neighbours had told Kitty of seeing Liam fed porridge for dinner while good food went upstairs on a tray to the more alert Kate. The housekeeper was playing them up. Liam, when asked about this, had wept: 'Poor Kate! Running the house was her pride and now she can't.' Rather than complain and shame her, he preferred to eat the penitential porridge.

'Was I a bad husband?' he asked Kitty who supposed he must be trying to make up for this.

*

He had a woman. The fact leaked from him as all facts or fictions – the barrier between them was down – now did. 'She's nobody,' he told Kitty. 'Just someone to talk to. I have to have that. I don't even find her attractive, but, well . . .' Smiling. Faithless. Grasping at bright straws. Weaving them, hopefully, into corn dollies.

'She' – once or twice he said 'you' – 'takes me on drives which end up in churches.'

'Ah? The Trojan mare?'

'Last week we lit a candle for Kate. They were saying mass.'

'It's your soul she's after then, not your body?'

'Cruel!' His memento-mori face tried for jauntiness. 'Well, *you* can't have me to live, can you, with your fly-by-night profession! Triple-tongued fly-by-night!' he teased. 'There's no relying on you! Where are you off to next?'

'Strasbourg for the meeting of the European Parliament.'

'See!'

*

He was terrified of death. 'I want', he confided, 'to live and live.' Terrified too of relinquishing his self-esteem by 'crawling' to a God in whom he didn't believe. 'Why do people believe?' he wondered. Then: 'Ah, I know you'll say from fear: phobophobia. They want immortality.' And his face twisted because he wanted it too.

*

On her next visits, he was a man dancing with an imaginary partner. A sly mime indicated the high-backed, winged arm-chair in which, he claimed, her mother sat in judgement on him. 'Don't you start,' he warned. 'I hear it all from her!'

This, if a joke, was out of control.

'Psst!' he whispered. 'She's showing disapproval.'

Courting it, he drank but wouldn't eat, threw out his pills, felt up a woman visitor, fired his housekeeper who was cramping his style and behaved as though he hoped to rouse his wife to show herself. Like believers defying their God! Or old lags wooing a gaol-sentence to get them through a cold snap. Spilled wine drew maps on Kate's Wilton carpet and, more than once, the gas had to be turned off by neighbours whose advice he ignored. After midnight, their letters warned Kitty, he stuffed great wads of cash into his pockets and set forth on stumbling walks through slick streets infested with muggers.

'Things have changed here', cautioned the letters 'from when you were a girl! Even the churchyards are full of junkies shooting it up!'

Liam too seemed to be seeking some siren thrill as he breasted the darkness, his pockets enticingly bulging with four-and-five-hundred-pound bait.

Splotched and spidery letters from him described a shrunken – then, unexpectedly, an expanding world.

Two angels – or were they demons? – were struggling over him. An old friend and neighbour, Emir, engaged in what he snootily dismissed as 'good works', hoped to enlist his support. 'Therapeutic?' wondered one letter touchily. 'For my own good?' But Emir's causes were the very ones he had himself promoted for years. And who was the other demon/angel? The one who had taken him into churches was, it seemed, a nurse. Used to older men, she maybe liked him for himself 'though I suppose she's too young for me'. Clearly he hoped not and that it was *not* his soul which concerned her.

She was persuading him to return to the bosom of Mother Church. Any bosom, clearly, had its appeal but Emir, though more congenial, was not offering hers.

The nurse – Kitty imagined her as starched, busty and hung with the sort of fetishes to which gentlemen of Liam's vintage were susceptible – came regularly to tea. The letter stopped there. Liam had forgotten to finish it or perhaps been overcome by the impropriety of his hopes.

*

More urgent letters came from neighbours. Even in Kate's day, they revealed, Liam's mind had been wobbly. Kate had covered up but something should now be done. There had been 'incidents'. Near-scandals. No new housekeeper could be expected to cope.

Kitty dreamed she was watching a washing machine in which a foetally-folded Liam, compact as a snail, was hurtled around. She could see him through the glass window but, in her dream, could not open this. White sprays of suds or saliva foamed over his head. Did 'do something' mean have him locked up? Put in a nursing or rest 'home'? He would not go willingly. While she wondered about this, there came a call to say he had caught pneumonia, been admitted to hospital and might not live.

She was in California where it was 2 a.m. and the telephone bell, pulsing through alien warmth, jerked her from sleep. Outside, spotlights focused on orchids whose opulence might or might not be real, and night-scented blooms evoked funerals.

However, when next she saw him, Liam, though still in hospital, was out of immediate danger.

'The Corbies are conspiring,' he greeted her. 'Caw caw!' His eyes were half-closed and a brown mole, which had been repeatedly removed, had overgrown one lid. After a while, he tried to sing an old school-yard rhyme: 'Cowardy, cowardy custard, Stick your head in the mustard!'

Mustard-keen priests had, it seemed, persuaded him to be reconciled and take the sacraments. Or was it the nurse? Emir, dropping in for a visit, said that the fact had been reported in an evening paper.

'A feather in their caps!' She shrugged. 'Sure what does it matter now?'

It did to Liam who whimpered that he had perhaps betrayed . . . he couldn't say who. 'Am I – was I a shit?' His mind meandered in a frightened past. 'Cowardy Custard,' he croaked guiltily.

'Don't worry,' Emir rallied him. 'It's all right, love.' She spoke as if to a child.

Kitty couldn't. Unable to discount or count on him, she went, fleetingly, half-blind. Colours and contours melted as if she were adapting to a reversible reality in which, later this evening on reaching his house, she might find his old spry self smiling at the door.

*

It smelled of him. It was a cage within which his memory paced and strove. Trajectories of flung objects – a wall smeared with coffee, a trail of dried food – were his spoor.

*

'He wants to die,' Emir whispered next day. 'He told me so.'

The two were sitting with a somnolent Liam who had been placed in an invalid chair. Lifting his overgrown eyelid, he scratched it weakly and asked Kitty, 'Why are you blaming me? Your face is all blame. A Gorgon's!'

'No, love,' soothed Emir. 'She's worried for you. It's Kitty. Don't you know her?'

'Why can't you give me something?' he asked. 'Wouldn't it be better for me to die now – and for you too?'

You never knew what he meant.

'Kiss him,' Emir whispered. 'Say something.'

But to Kitty this wasn't Liam and she felt her face freeze. She was unresponsive and stone-stiff: a Gorgon which has seen itself.

'I'll leave you together.' Emir tiptoed out.

Liam opened an eye. 'You'll die too,' he told Kitty with malice. 'You'll succumb.'

'We all will, darling,' she tried to soothe.

'You're punishing me.' His face contracted venomously. 'The survival instinct is a torment. Why did you inflict it on us?'

She marvelled. For whom did he take her now?

He mumbled and his bald skull fell forward as though his neck could not support it. Confronting her, it was flecked with age-spots like the rot on yellow apples.

Earlier, two nurses, lifting him to the chair, had held him by the armpits and, for moments, his whole self had hung like a bag on a wire. Vulnerable. Pitiable. Limp. She couldn't bear it. Slipping an arm around his neck, she felt for the pillow. Her fingers closed on it. Would he let her help him, now they were alone? Let her snuff out that remnant of breath which tormented but hardly animated him? No. He was a struggler. Even against his interests, resistance would be fierce. Yet the old Liam would have wanted to be freed from this cruel cartoon of himself. He surely would have. Was what was left of him content to be the cartoon?

But now, touched off perhaps by her closeness, energy began seeping perceptibly through him. The bowed head jerked up showing a face suffused with relish. His chapped mouth, lizard grey on the outside, was strangely red within. As if slit with a knife, it was the colour of leeches and looked ready to bleed. 'Ah,' murmured the mouth, 'it's you. You, you,

you! I feel your magic. Give me your hand.' And greedily, it began to rush along her arm, covering it with a ripple of nipping kisses. Like its colours, its touch was alternately lizardy and leechlike. 'I betray everyone,' said the mouth, interrupting its rush. 'I *want us* both to betray them. I want to run away with you, you – who . . .' Abruptly, perhaps because of Kitty's lack of response, doubt began to seize him. Again, he managed to jerk his head upwards, his eyes narrowed and his face hardened. 'Who are you?' he challenged. You've sneaked in here. You're not who I – who's betraying who?'

'Liam, nobody's betraying. Everything's all right. I promise.'

'No, no! We're sunk in treachery. Treachechechechery! Who are you? Who? Who? Are you Kate?'

'Yes,' she told him, 'yes. But it's all *right*, Liam.' Her arm was still around his neck. Her breath mingled with his.

'So what about the other one then? You can't be in agreement. Where's she gone?' Twitching. Eyes boiling. Mouth twisting. 'Life', he told her, 'is a mess. It's a messmessmess! Where's she gone?'

'I'm her too.' Kitty held the pillow experimentally with two hands. She needed three, one to hold his head. 'I'm here,' she told him. 'And I'm Kitty as well. We all love you Liam. Nobody disapproves. Nobody.'

'A treachechecherous mess! Telling on me, all of you! Going behind my back! Trinities of women . . .'

She soothed him and he asked: 'Are you God?'

'Yes,' she said helplessly. 'I'm God.'

'You made a fine mess,' he told her. 'Life's a . . .'

'Don't worry about it now.'

'How can I not worry? *You* should know! What can we do but worry? Are we getting an afterlife, yes or no? Not that I believe in you. Are you a woman then?'

'I'm whatever you want.'

'Another bloody metaphor! Is that it? Like cricket! Like fair play!' The leech-lips protruded, red with derision, in the grey, lizardy expanse. 'Not that fair play and you have much in common!'

Kitty took her hands from the pillow. 'You always knew that,' she told Liam. 'Which was why you went your own way!'

'I did, didn't I?' He was awash with pride. 'Bugger you, I said. Man made you, not the other way round. That's why *you* never promised fair play. Not you! "The last shall be first" was your motto. Treacherous. Like me. Buried in treache-chech . . . Egh!'

His hands plucked at his dressing gown and his throat seemed to close. Was he dying?

'Liam!' She rang for the nurse. 'Liam, love, try some water. Here. Open your mouth, can you? Swallow. Please. Listen. You're not treacherous. You were never treacherous. You just loved too many people. And we all love you back. We love you, Liam. There, you're better now. That's better, isn't it? Let me give you a kiss.'

And she put her lips to the protuberant, raw, frightened mouth which was pursed and reaching for them with the naive, greedy optimism of a child.

Tomorrow she'd try with the pillow. Or a plastic bag? Would Emir help, she wondered. Might it be dangerous to ask her?

The Knight

'A drop for the inner man.'

'For the Road.'

Condon budged a heel and his spur tinkled. He knocked an elbow against the wooden partition. The snug must have been all of five feet by two. Drinks were served through a hatch. It would not have done to be seen drinking in full regalia in the public bar.

'Like sitting in your coffin,' Condon said gloomily.

'Or in a confessional.'

It was embarrassing, Condon felt. Here was Hennessy who had driven four miles to fetch him to the Meeting so that Elsie might have the car for her own use all week-end. The least she might have done was ask the man in for a drink – 'A wee wisheen,' thought Condon with Celtic graciousness – and a chat. She could have made that effort. God knew. In common courtesy. Hennessy had got him into the Knights. But no: she'd had to pick tonight to have one of her tantrums. He'd been afraid to let Hennessy as much as see her! Bitch! Angrily, he blew down his nose.

He was a choleric man with a face of a bright meaty red, rubbery as a pomegranate rind, a face which looked healthy enough on the bicycling priests who abounded in his family but on him wore a congested gleam. It had a fissile look and may have *felt* that way too, judging by Condon's habit of keeping himself hemmed in. He had certainly bound himself by a remarkable number of controls: starched collar, irksome marriage, rules of all the secular sodalities open to him – most recently the Knights – even, for a while, the

British army which must have been purgatory. He had been in it for – in his own words – 'a sorrowful decade' and, on being demobbed, married an Englishwoman in whom he detected and trounced beliefs and snobberies beneath which he had groaned during his years of service. He was currently a Franciscan tertiary, a member of two parish sodalities, of the – secretive – Opus Dei and of a blatant association of Catholic laymen recently founded in Zurich with the aim of countering creeping radicalism within the Church. Each group imposed duties on members: buttressings so welcomed by Condon that one might have supposed him intent on containing some centrifugal passion liable to blow him up like a bomb if he failed to keep it hedged. Other members looked on his zeal with a dose of suspicion. He was aware of this and made efforts at levity. He made one now.

'A bird never flew on wan wing.' The brogue, eroded in England, renascent on his return, warmed like a marching tune. 'Have the other half of that.' He nodded at Hennessy's glass.

'A small one, so.'

Condon rapped on the wood. 'Same again, Mihail,' he told the bar-curate confidentially.

'Your wife's in poor health?' Hennessy commented.

Condon sighed. 'The Change.'

'Ah,' said Hennessy with distaste.

'Shshsh.' Condon put a finger to his lips. There were voices in the public bar.

*

'Bloody Gyppos . . .' An Anglo-Irish roar. 'Regular circus. At least the Yids can fight.'

'. . . died in the frost,' cried a carrying female version of the same. 'I've started more under glass.'

'Well, here's to old Terry then. Chin-chin and *mort aux vaches*.'

'What'd you join, Terry? French Foreign Legion?'

'No, we're . . .'

'Make mine a Bloody Mary.'

Condon dug an elbow into Hennessy's side. 'Tell me,' he whispered in agitation, 'why am I whispering? Why do fellows like that roar and you and me lower our voices in public? It's our country, isn't it?'

Hennessy shrugged. 'Rowdies,' he said contemptuously.

But that wasn't it. Hennessy hadn't lived with the English the way Condon had and couldn't know. It was all arrogance: the roars, the titters. All and always. Condon knew. Wasn't he married to one? Old Hennessy was looking at him oddly. A soapy customer. Don't trust. Think, quickly now, of something soothing. Right. His knight's costume tonight in the bedroom pier-glass. Spurs, epaulets, his own patrician nose: mark of an ancient race. The image, fondly dandled, shivered and broke the way images do. Ho-old it. Patrician all right. A good jaw. Fine feathers – ah no, no. More to it than that. The *spirit* of the Order was imbuing him. Mind over matter. Condon believed in that order of things. Like the Communion wafer keeping fasting saints alive over periods of months. He was a reasoning man – trained in the law – but not narrow, acknowledged super-rational phenomena. More things, Horatio – how did it go? Membership in an ancient religious Order *must* entail an infusion of grace. Tonight was the ceremony to swear in new members. Condon being one. An important, significant moment for him, as he tried to explain to Elsie. But she was spiritually undeveloped.

'A sort of masonry then?' she'd asked when he'd told her how all the really influential Dublin businessmen . . . Certainly NOT or, anyway, not only. Why, the Order dated back nine hundred years. But the English cared only for their own pageantry: Chelsea pensioners, their bull-faced queen. Circuses! Ha! He hated their pomps, had been personally colonized but had thrown off the yoke, his character forming in recoil. Did he *know*, he wondered now as often, how thoroughly he had thrown it off? Did she? He saw himself, two hours ago, coming down the stairs, waiting, one flight up, knee arched, for her admiration. She was in the kitchen.

'Elsie.'

'What?'

'Come here.'

'Come here yourself. I'm not a dog.'

'I want to show you something.' That spoiled the surprise but she wouldn't come if he didn't beg. 'Please, Elsie.' He thought he might be getting pins and needles. Hand on the pommel of his sword, he waited.

'Huwwy then, because the oven . . .' She bustled into the hall, wiping her hands on a cloth. A lively, heavily painted woman in her forties, sagging here and there but still ten times quicker than himself in her movements. 'Ho!' she checked and roared. 'Tito Gobbi, no less! Or is it Wichard Tucker. You're not going *out* in it?'

Envy!

He walked down the stairs, minding his cloak. 'What's for dinner?'

'Steak and kidney pie.'

'My ulcer!'

'You haven't a nerve in your body. How could you have an ulcer?'

Her cooking still undermined him – the first thing he had dared notice when he'd attended those parties of hers in Scunthorpe. He'd been a filler-in then: the extra bachelor asked to balance the table. The tight velvet of her evening trousers had drawn his attention and the display of Sheffield plate. It was on his own sideboard now. ('Mr Condon likes his gwub,' she'd noted.) The 'w' she put in 'Patrick' when she began to use his name impressed him. He thought for a while it might be upper-class. ('I sweat bwicks when Patwick tells a joke!') It was a relief as well as a disappointment when she turned out to be a housekeeper who had married her ageing employer. When the old man died within a year of marriage, Condon rallied round. Mourning enhanced her attractiveness but sat lightly on her. She was quick – giddy, he thought now – and he couldn't keep up with her, seemed to get heavier when he tried. Even her things turned hostile. He remembered the day her electric lawn-mower ran off with him. Weeping with rage, he had struggled to hold it as it plunged down the area slope and crashed through the kitchen window – with himself skidding behind: Handy Andy, Paddy-the-Irishman! The servants were in stitches. He didn't dare ask her not to mention it, could still hear her tell the story – how many times? – to neighbours over summer drinks on the wretched lawn: 'And away it wan with pooah Patwick!' They had neighed, hawhawed, choked themselves. He hated them. Buggers to a man. Bloody snobs in their blazers with heraldic thingamybobs on the pockets. Always telling him off. ('In England, people don't say "bloody"!' '"Bugger" is rather a strong term over here, old man!' So well it might be!) What he'd put up with! And if you *didn't* put up with it you had no sense of humour. Well, their day was done. India, Ghana, Cyprus, even Rhodesia . . . Little Ireland had shown the way. Let England quake! The West's awake! The West, the East – which of them cared for England now?

'Ah Jesus, that stuff's out of date,' Patrick's cousin told him when he came back to live in Ireland. 'Our economy is linked to England's. Let the dead bury the dead! And isn't your wife English?'

Her! He looked at her scraping out the remnants of pastry from the dish. Greedy! But she kept her figure. People admired her. 'A damn fine woman,' they told Patrick who was half pleased and half not. He had never forgiven her evasion of his embrace in the car coming from the church ceremony and the way she had lingered in the hotel bar before making for their bedroom. He had lingered too but, damn it, that was understandable. *He* was chaste, whereas she – decadent product of a decadent country. Bloomy and scented like a hot-house flower warmed by the trade winds of the Empire.

'Why are you looking at me like that?'

'I was thinking', Patrick said, 'we Irish are a spiritual people! All that about the Celt having one foot in the grave, you know? Well, the older I get, the truer I know it to be.'

She hooted.

'I suppose you don't want pudding?'

'What?'

'Apple charlotte.'

He held out his plate. 'No cream?'

'Oh Patwick! Your waist bulge!'

'I *want* cream.'

He scattered sugar on the brown cliffs of his charlotte. Brown, crumbly hills and crags such as the Knights must have defended against Turks and Saracens. The Irish branch to which Patrick belonged, lacking aristocratic quarterings, had a merely subsidiary connection, but Patrick managed to forget this and anyway *she* would never know. He took and ate the last brown bastion of charlotte from his plate.

She was fidgeting with hers. Afraid of carbohydrates. Her contaminated beauty excited him and sometimes, when she was asleep beside him, he would lean over and, between the ball and finger and thumb, fold the wrinkles into uglier grooves. Smoothing them, he could almost restore her to her peak, a time when men used to look after her and draw, with final cocks of the head in his direction, interrogation marks in the air: how, their wonder grilled him, had *she* come to marry *him*? How? Mmpp! Small mystery there when you came down to brass tacks. Widow's nerves. She wanted a man. Anything – he lambasted himself – in trousers. *Much* more to the point was the question: why had *he* married her? He was a man given to self-query. Pious practices – meditation, examination of conscience – imposed by the various rules he had embraced had revealed to Condon the riches of his own mind. It was theatre to him who had rarely been to a theatre if not to see a panto at Christmas. The first plushy swish of the curtain – he kept his thoughts sealed off in social moments lest one surface and reveal itself – the first dip into that accurately spotlit darkness, when he had a spell of privacy, was as stimulating as sex. How, today's Mind demanded of yesterday's, had it made itself up? Why? What if it had it to do over again? Any regrets? Any guidelines for the future? Doppel-ganging Condons stalked his own mental boards. *Why had he married* was a favoured theme to ponder on drives down the arteries of Ireland – frequent since Elsie, despite his work being in Dublin, had insisted on buying a 'gentleman's residence' in County Meath. 'Why?' he would ask himself, as the tyres slipped and spun through wintery silt or swerved from a panicky rabbit. 'Why? Why? – Ah, sure I suppose I was a bit of a fool! Yes.' Marriage had looked like a ladder up. It had proved a snake. 'A bit of a fool in those days, God help us.' Better to marry than to burn – but what if you burned within marriage?

Condon still awoke sweating from nightmare re-enactments of that First Night. 'Saint Joseph,' he still muttered, as he fought off the dream, 'Patron of Happy Families, let me not lose respect for her!' ('Patwick', she used to say, 'is a tewwible old Puwitan! Of course that makes things such fun for him! It's being Iwish!') He had gone to complain and confess to an English priest who reassured him. It was all natural, an image of Divine Love. Condon knew better, but let himself be swayed. Hours after she had said good night he, stiffened by a half-bottle of port from her former husband's stock, would mount the stairs, stumble briefly about in the bathroom and, in a gurgle of receding water, in darkness and with a great devastation of springs, land on the bed of his legal paramour. ('Patwick! You make me feel like Euwo-o-opa!') So let her. Who'd turned whom into an animal? If this is natural, natural let it be! Her cries were smothered, her protests unheeded.

The swine revenged themselves on Circe: multiplied, enormous, he snuffled, dug, burrowed, and skewered ('Patwick, you might *shave!*') flattening, tearing, crushing, mauling, then rolling away to the other end of the bed to remark, 'I see the hedge needs clipping. Have to see to it. Sloppy!' For his spirit refused to follow where his flesh engaged. He felt embarrassed afterwards, preferred not to breakfast with her and took to slipping out to a hotel where he was able, as a bonus, to eat all he wanted without hearing remarks about calories.

Tonight he would be taking a vow of Conjugal Chastity, promising 'to possess his vessel in sanctification and honour'. (Ha! Put a stop to *her* gallop!) Formerly, Knights' wives had been required to join in the oath – imagine Elsie: a heretic – but that practice had been abolished. Fully professed Knights took vows of celibacy.

Condon had long concluded that Elsie's appeal for himself had lain in her Protestantism. Bred to think it perilous, he had invested her and it with a risky phosphorescence. Which had waned. Naturally enough. Marooned, the buoyant Medusa clogs to the consistency of gelatine, and what had Protestantism turned out to be but a set of rules and checks? More etiquette than religion. Elsie got the two mixed up. He doubted that she saw a qualitative difference between adultery and failure to stand up when a woman came into the room.

'A bahbawwian,' she'd start in, the minute some poor decent slob like Hennessy was well out the door. 'The man's a bahbawwian! You've buwwied me among the beastly Hottentots!'

His people.

'No, Patwick! They are *not* fwiendly! It's all a fwaud! They're cold and sniggewing and smug! Bahbawwians!'

Well, there was no arguing with prejudice. And he knew right well what it was she missed in Ireland: smut and men making passes at her. What she'd have liked would be to hobnob with the Ascendancy. Hadn't she wanted to follow the hunt tomorrow?

'The foliage will be glowious! Amanda's keeping two places in her jeep. I'd have thought you'd have wanted to *see* the countwy. You *talk* enough about Ireland.'

He didn't. He hated land untamed by pavements, had a feeling it was cannibalic and out to get him. Explicable: his ancestors had been evicted *off* it after toiling and starving *on* it. He'd got his flinty profile from men pared down by a constant blast of misfortune.

'Please, Patwick. I told the Master we'd follow.'

'No.'

The word 'Master' embarrassed him. He hated hunts: the discomfort of Amanda Shand's jeep rattling his bones over frozen fields and withered heaps of ragweed. Booted and furred, the women would squeal and exchange dirty jokes as they followed the redcoats ('Pink, Patwick! Please!') on their bloody pursuit down lanes like river-beds where brass bedsteads served as slatternly gates, and untrimmed brambles clawed.

'I'm spending the night at the club. I can't make it.'

She pouted.

He shrugged.

She made little enough effort with *his* friends, so why should *he* put up with Miss Amanda Shand of Shand House, a trollopy piece, louse-poor but with the Ascendancy style to her still: vowels, pedigree dogs. The dogs she raised for a living, and was reputed to have given up her own bed to an Afghan bitch and litter. But, until the roof fell in on them, those people kept up the pretence. Elsie could have helped consolidate his position – he'd hoped for this – if she'd been the hostess here that she'd been in Scunthorpe. He needed friends. He was a briefless barrister and had been too long abroad. She could have increased his support so easily if she'd turned her charm on his clerical relatives. But no. *They* didn't stand up when she came into a room.

'A priest in this country takes precedence over a woman, Elsie.'

'You've buwwied me among the beastly Hottentots!'

And tears. And accusations. Why did he leave her to moulder here? She'd given him the best years of her life. Why shouldn't she come to his meeting tonight? Even Masons had a women's night.

Masons!

'The military monks, to whose Order I have the honour to belong, were celibate. There is no place for women in our ceremonies.'

More tears. He stayed on guard. In a long war, victory can be short-lived and tears a feint. When she said:

'Don't you care for me any more?' he answered,

'I love nobody but Jesus.'

'Oh!' Her mouth fell open unguardedly and showed her fillings. 'Jesus!' she repeated. 'Jesus!' She used a little scream and ran out of the room.

In the old days, she used to flatten him with humour. But then, on her own ground, she'd had a gallery. Without one, Jesus became invincible.

Patrick, beginning to feel sorry for her, was pouring her a drink, when the doorbell rang. Hennessy. Patrick put down the glass and ran to head him off. He mustn't come in. A guest would resurrect Elsie who could make him her sounding-board, stooge, straight man and microphone to funnel God knew what bad language and hysteria to the clubs and pubs of half Dublin.

Condon bundled Hennessy down the stairs and back into his car.

'Right you are,' Hennessy kept acquiescing. 'Right, right, Condon. We'll have a drink in the local. I love pubs. Nice and relaxed. Fine, don't give it a thought.'

*

Voices from the public bar:

'Remember that time the UN took a contingent of Paddies to the Congo? No, dear, *not* the Irish Guards, the Free State Army. All dressed in bullswool. *That's* what they call it, cross my heart. No, of course *I* don't know is it from bulls, but it *is* as thick as asbestos and thorny as a fairy rath. And off they went dressed up to their necks in it to the Congo. Left, right, left, right, or whatever *that* is in Erse.'

'To the tropics.'

'Must have been cooked to an Irish stew.'

'Ready for the cannibals.'

'Which reminds me, Amanda, where are we dining?'

'Not with me, dears, I haven't a scrap in the place.'

*

So Amanda Shand was there. Patrick drank morosely. Hennessy stood up and said he had to go where no one could go for him. Patrick reflected that Hennessy was a bit vulgar sometimes all right. A bit of a Hottentot.

*

'. . . hear the one about the two old Dublin biddies discussing the Congo. One says a neighbour's son has been "caught by the Balloobas" "By the Balloobas, dija say, Mrs?" says her crony. "Oh *that* musta been terrible painful!"'

Laughter.

'And the one about . . .'

Patrick closed his ears. Hear no, see no, think no evil. Difficult. It wormed its way everywhere, sapped the most doughty resistances.

He thought of a visit he had made that morning to a clerical cousin confined in a home for mad priests – a disagreeable duty but Patrick had felt obliged. Blood was thicker than water and he had promised his aunt he'd go. He'd come away feeling pained. Weakness flowed like a contagion from Father Fahy. A mild fellow, shut up because of his embarrassing delusions, he thought himself the father of twelve children with a wife expecting a thirteenth.

'I don't mind the number,' he had confided to Condon, 'I'm not superstitious about such matters. As a priest . . .' The smile flicked off and on. It was not impressive, for his teeth fitted badly and there were no funds to get inmates new ones. As long as he stayed shut up here, ecclesiastical authority saw little point in throwing good money after bad. 'Poor Anna is worn out, tense, you know, frayed. She worries about our eldest, Brendan, who's up in the College of Surgeons and . . .' The priest had names and occupations for every member of his imagined brood. 'You know yourself, Patrick, women . . .'

Fahy confided doubts about the Holy Father's policy with regard to birth-control. 'Poor Anna is a literal believer,' he groaned, 'a simple woman.' He must have been a bad priest, a shirker. Wasn't he trying to shift anxieties, which had sifted through the confessional grating, on to Patrick himself, the confessor's confessor? Distasteful that a priest should imagine a wife for himself with such domestic clarity! How far, one tried to wonder, *did* the imaginings go? Bad times. Our Blessed Lady had foretold as much in 1917 to the children at Fatima. 'My Son', she had said, 'has drawn back His hand to smite the world. I am holding it back but my arm grows tired.' It must be numb by now. Well, Patrick was doing his bit, joining the Knights: a warrior against the forces of darkness. War. The language of the Church was heady with it but practice dampeningly meek. St George had been struck off the register of saints.

'No, no and no, I won't be beaten down!' Amanda Shand's voice rose in a flirtatious shriek. 'The doggies are my bread and butter! Damn it all, Terry, I'm a single girl and . . .'

*

Girl, thought Condon. Forty if she was a day. Selling one of her hounds. That sort lived by myth: distressed lady, *morya*. Couldn't take a *real* job because if she worked from nine to five as a secretary, she would *be* a secretary. Dabbling in dog-breeding she could live off the smell of an oil rag and be a lady still. He doubted she saw meat more than once a week. Patrick had no patience with the like. Where was Hennessy? Bit of prostatic trouble there. What were we but future worm-food?

*

'Seriously . . .' Terry's voice now. 'It's the youth. I hope I'm no old fogy. I'm thirty-nine and like my bit of fun. I don't mind long hair or free love or any of that, but I think they've lost sight of some jolly important matters, what with all this fraternizing with nigs and . . .'

'*Who's* going out to fight for nig-nogs, Terry? Bet you don't even know which side you'll be on!'

'Right! You're absolutely right. I don't give a damn which side I'm on. They're all black to me, haha. No, but I do have a purpose. I think the next great war will be with the coloureds. Don't laugh! I mean *they'll* be attacking us. Look at South Africa, Rhodesia, the US. They've got the message. It's easy for us to sit on our bums in Southern Ireland – the last country where a gentleman is recognized as such, by the way, which is why I like it here – to sit here on our bums and disapprove of the white supremacists. Much too easy. It may be less so in the future. Look at China. Count them up. They want what we've got, right? Right. I don't say I blame the poor buggers but every man's got to fight his own corner. And there isn't enough to go round, right? Besides, a lot of decent things would go down the drain if the West went under. . . . Well, the long and the short of it is I'm going out to fight *for* the nigs in order to train myself to fight *against* them.'

'And for the lolly.'

'And for the lolly.'

'Upon this battle depends the survival of Christian civ., what?'

'Right.'

'. . . all that we have known and cared for will sink . . .'

Someone, not Terry, began to deliver in tones wavering between drunken parody and drunken sentiment, a speech which slipped through Condon's defences. With astonishment, he realized that he and the rowdies in the bar had something in common. There was that fellow, in his literal, simple way, heeding the call of the times and assuming the military part of the knightly mission at the very moment when Condon himself was shouldering its spiritual side. They complemented each other. Well and why not? Hadn't Protestant volunteers fought the Turk with Catholic knights at the siege of Malta? Patrick stood up. He was thinking of going into the bar when he heard Amanda say:

'Hey, what about giving Elsie a tinkle?'

'Elsie who?'

'Elsie Condom or Condon or whatever. She's got a soft spot for old Terry here and she's sure to produce sandwiches. Her lord and master's almost certain to be off the premises. Bet she'd like to light your fire, Terry, on your last night.'

'Got her number?'

'In the book. Listen, it'd be doing a good deed in a naughty world to poke old Elsie. Seriously. She doesn't get much and. . . .'

'What about yourself, Amanda . . .'

'Oh *well*, if . . .'

Patrick collided with Hennessy who was finally returning and pushed him, for the second time that evening, backwards out the door and into his own car. A yellow Austin Healey with a GB on its rump was drawn up beside it. Patrick resisted an impulse to give it a passing kick. His mind jumbled thoughts, like a washing-machine throwing about soiled linen and, above it, he managed to chat about how time-was-getting-on-sorry-Hennessy-but-better-be-hitting-the-road-slippery-as-well-be-off-betimes. The man must think he was mad.

Patrick felt a thrust of humiliation knife him. He felt almost tearful. An unskinned part of himself had been reached. He had thought he and Elsie had something, a . . . union . . . a solidarity which . . . In his own head he groped sadly, reaching an unexplored place. Hennessy's voice came to him but he couldn't distinguish the words. He felt exposed, mutilated. Hennessy's Volkswagen funnelled down the hedgy roads. Briars scraped the windows and squeaked.

'There should be a quorum,' Hennessy was saying. 'We should hold out for that.'

'Yes,' managed Condon.

'And what's your position on the other matter?'

What matter? Which? Had Hennessy *heard*?

'I . . . what?'

'Are you feeling all right?'

'No. I had a dizzy spell. I'm afraid I missed . . .'

'Oh well, it doesn't matter.' Hennessy sounded miffed.

But Condon had to know. 'No, no *tell* me.'

'I've *been* telling you! Corcoran wants selection of the ambulance corps to be left up to him and his henchmen. A matter of getting the strings into his own hands and . . .'

'Ah.'

Condon's mind drifted again. Didn't she *care* for him at all then, if she . . . Oh, and that was what *she* had asked him! He groaned.

'Are you in pain?'

'No, no, slight twinge. My ulcer. . . . Nothing serious.'

He *must*, would, pull himself together. Mind over matter. Yes.

The Knights' ceremony was being held in a Dublin hotel. An entire floor had been taken over, but members spilled into corridors and stairs and lobby where, cloaked and armed, they drew the eye, impressing the serf-grey citizenry with their spiritual and temporal pelf. A drunken poet got into the lift with Condon and Hennessy. Pink and pendulous, his nose (Condon reproved himself for thinking) resembled a skinned male organ. The poet fixed the Knights with his tight, urine-yellow goat's eyes and grinned. A notorious lecher, he was not the sort of man with whom either would choose to associate, but they were, as always in Dublin, on nodding terms with him.

'How are things, Ian?'

'A wet old night.'

'Ha,' roared the poet in a peasant brogue, assumed, as all Dubliners know, to make them feel effete, urban and far from the loamy roots of things. 'How are our Knights T-T-Templars? Still as r-r-rand-d-dy and roistering as when they were burnt at the stake by Philipe le Bel? Burnt,' he hissed, 'b-b-burrrrntt and their goods confiscated, ha! Not that *that's* likely to happen again. There's a rising tide of p-p-permiss-ssiveness, as they call it now. Still secret, still underground but about to oo-ooz-z-z-ze up and submerge us all in a f-f-f-foam of s-s-sperm! The age of Eros is upon us. I've just c-come back from the cu-cu-cunty counthrrry where they've been enjoying a spell of warm weather, and yez'd never credit the goings on I witnessed under hedges and d-d-ditches.'

'I'm sure we wouldn't,' Hennessy told him. 'This is our door.' He stepped out with a gelid nod. 'Be seeing you.' But the poet followed them.

'Maids and matrons,' he roared. 'Wedded wives f-f-fu-fuck-ck-cking in the f-f-fields. Cuckoo eggs in every nest. Maybe your own spouses are . . .'

Condon hit him. Before he knew it his fist had shot out and caught the pink, wettish – he felt it wet on his knuckles – nose. Or was the wetness blood? It was. His knuckles were stained with it. The poet had been put on a couch and his collar loosened.

'He's OK. Just a nose-bleed.'

'Head back, Ian, hold your head back.'

'No, better not. The blood makes you sick. Indigestible. Spit it out. Get us a glass. Thanks. Mind the carpet now.'

'Hold his nose over the glass. In, man, in. Poke it in.'

'Get him to a bathroom.'

'Good thing it happened on this floor. No scandal. How did he get in?'

'Gate-crasher.'

A Knight walked up to Condon. 'Come and wash your hands too. He's all right, drunk, deserved what he got. Do him a world of good.'

Other voices joined in.

'What was it he said about . . . Condon's wife?'

'Shush!' And loudly: 'Someone should have done it long ago. A foul-mouthed fellow, a gurrier.'

'A fine lesson for him. A low type. You're a hard man, Condon. A true Knight, haha!'

Surrounded by his fellows, Condon felt his agitation abate into a lapping tide of excitement. Someone must have given him a brandy because, as the ceremony began, a manservant in cotton gloves, tapped him on the arm to recover the empty glass. He gave it to the man and himself to rituals he had been studying for some weeks. This was to be a brief and worldly affair because of the hour and place. Mass would be celebrated in the Order's chapel next morning. Would he stay? He had intended to but now was not so sure. The panoply of the differing ranks of Knights and monks confused him. All wore crosses recalling the crusades on which knights had gone leaving wives locked in chastity belts. Or was that myth? Had the first Knights been celibate? And had such contraptions been widely used? Very unsanitary, if so. He had seen one once in a museum. Was it the Cluny museum in Paris? He wasn't sure, reproached himself for not achieving a prayerful mood. *Oh my God, I am heartily sorry for having offended*

thee, and I detest my sins above every other evil . . . Did he? He
did not! He was glad he had pucked that obscene fellow on
the gob. Watch what's happening. You'll miss your cue. The
oath of conjugal chastity brought back figures crouching in
a corner of his brain: Terry-the-nig-killer and Elsie. Niggers
for that sort began at Liverpool. No holds barred with wives
of nigs or Papists. No holds barred with any wives in profli-
gate England. Adultery winked at. Since Henry the Eighth.
Ruin seize thee, ruthless king, Confusion on thy banners
wait . . . That was some other . . . *Would* she? NO. Ah no,
she was forty-four – still dirty-minded, though, had violated
his privacy in talk with Amanda Shand. Don't trust, you can't
trust her. Ah God, his knightly honour was a joke, besmirched
in advance. Maybe, at this very . . .

He made to leap up but a hand pulled him back, recalling
him to the time and place. 'Not yet,' whispered Hennessy,
thinking Condon had mistaken the cues printed on the slips
of paper which had been handed out. 'Not till after the hymn.'

Nigs. Knicks. Patrick sank back on his knees. To think she
should spoil a moment of such spiritual significance, dragging his soul down to the level of her own. A stain on one
Knight's honour must affect the Order as a whole. Every
man responsible for his woman. He had read in the *National
Geographic* about adulteresses somewhere in Africa being
impaled per vaginam. Punished whereby they had – but the
idea was repugnant. Better punish the lover like in *The Cask
of Amontillado*. Brick him up. By God if he came home this
night and found them at it! Jesus, let them not, because if
they . . . Please, Jesus. He'd have no choice. But. Universally
recognized. *Crime passionnel.* Juries let off the husband. And
the heavenly jury? *Veni creator spiritus* . . . The hymn ended and
the Knights rose creakily. Not one was under fifty. Patrick's
head reeled and and whirled. Pounded.

'Well now, let's toast our new Knight of Honour and
Devotion.' Hennessy led him off.

There was no slipping away. They drank fast and gar-
rulously. At one point Condon was sick. He threw up with
decorum, in the lavatory, unknown to any. He ate a pepper-
mint to sweeten his breath. Coming back, he brought the
conversation round to Parnell and Kitty O'Shea.

'The woman was an adulteress.'

'But was it fair to punish her lover and the millions who
depended on him? The course of Irish history might . . .'

'You're forgetting the scandal! The scandal to the souls of
those same millions! How could the Church . . .'

Rounds of drinks waited, marshalled like skittles. Four
brandies had been bought for Patrick. The bar was closing
but every man wanted to stand his round. Honour obliged.

Suddenly, Condon said he needed to get home. Urgently.
His wife was unwell, subject to giddy spells, and might not
hear the phone.

'Can I borrow your car?' he asked Hennessy. 'I'll get it back
to you tomorrow.'

Hennessy gave him the keys.

Patrick took them and rushed out of the hotel, started the
car without warming the engine and raced hell-for-leather
out of Dublin and into the hedgy embrace of country roads.
Here he was forced by an attack of nausea to pull in and found
himself, out of the car, weeping in a ditch and embracing
a thorn tree. 'Elsie,' he groaned, to his own astonishment,
'Elsie!' He began to roar and bellow like a bull, filling and
emptying his lungs with desolate twanging air. After some
minutes he got back into the car, feeling wet and so par-
alytic with cold he could hardly touch his fingers around
the stick-shift. He put on the heater and drove in shivering
sobriety back across the mountains, concentrating on the
road and reciting prayers to calm his nerves. '. . . disease of
desire,' he whispered mechanically, 'to possess his vessel in
sanctification and honour, not in the disease of desire as do
the Gentiles who know not God . . .'

As he turned into his own winding drive, darkly flanked by rhododendrons, he got a glimpse of Elsie's lighted window and her silhouette, heavier than he had remembered it, closing the curtains. He rounded the last curve and came on the battered yellow Austin Healey which had been parked earlier in the public-house yard. Standing by its nose – he must have been looking at the motor, for the bonnet was raised – like a moth in the glare of Patrick's headlights, was a man in a check sports coat: Terry. Patrick drove straight for him, as though following a traffic signal in the man's gullet. He could see into the pulsing throat and even the flap on the uvula glistening against the dark interior. There was a thump. Patrick's head hit the headrest behind him. The man fell forward on to the Volkswagen then, on the rebound, into the unbonneted engine of his own car. Heels up, arms flopping, he was carried backwards as the two cars pursued their course into a tree. The Austin Healey buckled, the man's limbs crunched within the integument of his clothes. Patrick – although he was to prove to be suffering from minor concussion – felt nothing.

Moments later, Elsie found his cloaked figure, bending over the wreckage, howling in the elated, almost musical accents of dogs on a moonlit night. 'I *did* it. Jesus, I did it.'

*

That version never got out.

Connections rallied. Witnesses testified that the Englishman had been drinking heavily in the pub. They surmised he must have lost his way and strayed up Condon's driveway in search of the cross-roads. In all likelihood, he would have neglected to turn on his lights. That Condon should round the bend of his own driveway at an incautious speed was understandable at so late an hour in a gentleman tired after a long drive and eager to get home to his bed. A regrettable accident.

*

Terry's friends waked him jovially, pleased with the excuse for a little extra drinking. 'After all', said Amanda Shand, 'he was only a bird of passage.' The Condons, she has heard, were getting on together as never before. He had taken her for a change of scene to Malta and *she* had sent Amanda a card saying she was 'having a whale of a time'.

The Religious Wars of 1944

At dusk, Mr Lacy, the keeper, eager for his tea, rang a bell to chase dawdlers home. They were hard to flush out, because the park was dotted with gazebos – 'follies' built in the Famine days to provide work – and if you hid in one you could always get out later by climbing the tall iron gates. There were places too, where footholes had been gouged in the perimeter wall.

'I'll have yez summonsed!' Mr Lacy's peaked cap sliced through the dimness. Authority shone from his brass-buttons. 'I'll tell yeer Mammies.' There was a by-law – but what was a by-law? – forbidding anyone to linger in the locked, possibly perilous park.

Mysterious goings-on had been reported. A girl from Teresa Dunne's school had fainted when a man did some momentous thing, appearing to her out of a bush. The *gardai* had come, but then the matter was hushed up and the girl cowed into discretion.

'I'll tell you what she saw,' Mrs Malahide offered Teresa. 'If you like.' They were in the Malahides' drawing room, and Teresa, whose mother had sent her over with a cake, was waiting to be given back the plate. You couldn't trust Mrs Malahide to return it later. She was a bit scatty, a Protestant, and, according to some, 'a gentlewoman, though no lady'. She would say anything and was, intermittently and dangerously, Teresa's mother's friend.

'Well?'

Teresa was torn. She was reluctant to learn secrets from Mrs Malahide, who would rob them of their versatile glee. Not knowing kept open a shiver of possibilities – but

Mrs Malahide was a belittler. She could shrink the Wars of Troy. 'Men fighting over a bitch,' was how she once described those.

'Don't mind her,' people advised. 'She's that way because of her lip.'

She had a harelip, without which she would have been a beauty – would have stayed in England and married her own sort rather than poor, decent Jack Malahide. Instead, here she was in an Irish village, cut off by the war and living, said gossips, on 'the smell of an oil rag'. Teresa herself had seen the grey, scummy broth of sheep's lung which Mrs Malahide left on the stove for her children's meal when she and her husband took off for the pub. He, a parson's son, had served in the colonial service and now made simple toys which people bought because the Emergency had cut off supplies of better ones. Bright and two-dimensional, his hobbyhorses bounded up the village street between the legs of four- and five-year-olds whose sisters held skipping ropes by the snug, beechwood handles he had painstakingly turned on his lathe. He had a marvelling smile and worshipped Mrs Malahide.

'Poor Jack,' sighed his cronies. Yet they liked her for her spirit and because, when not blasting the sour grapes of life, she was, said Teresa's mother, 'great value'. Mrs Dunne, while deploring her friend's morals, hailed in her that fine contempt for convention which titillates the Irish.

'She's great company,' she acknowledged, 'and hasn't a pick of human respect.'

That was what worried Teresa. For how reconcile the ideals of her school nuns with tolerance of Mrs Malahide, who must be the most brazen thing alive? Lipstick ran up the crack of her harelip, and contamination oozed from her. She had a moustache yellow from chainsmoking, and today – Sunday – her feet lazed in cinders which had spilled past the confines of her fenderless hearth. Drifts of turf-ash had possibly settled in her hair, which was like the plumage of an old hen. Both hair and ash had orange streaks, like fossil memories of fire.

Scattered on the floor were the *Sunday Pictorial* and *News of the World*, banned English papers which had been smuggled past the Customs inside copies of *The Catholic Herald*. Teresa read the headlines with an affronted eye: SCOUTMASTER FOUND TROUSERLESS . . . A fold concealed where DECEIVED MISTRESS CHOPS OFF LOVER'S . . .

To quell the riot in her mind, she told herself that perhaps no more had been chopped off than the lover's tie. But no: not in that paper, or Bunty Malahide wouldn't trouble to smuggle it in. Dirt was what she liked. Scandal. *Her* mind was beyond description.

'Impure,' the nuns would have said, but the word fell short. Failing to anticipate Mrs Malahide, they had sent Teresa forth into the world, unfit to cope and were perhaps no fitter themselves. Tender rituals absorbed them, and most of last term had been spent planning the Feast of the Immaculate Conception, for which every girl had been required to buy a ten-shilling lily. Those whose families found this a strain might, the nuns conceded, substitute a chrysanthemum. But the concession was reluctant. Each donor was to say 'O Mary I give thee the lily of my heart! Be thou its guardian forever,' then present a bloom securely tipped with waterproof paper, lest sap stain her white uniform skirt.

'You could hardly', the nuns' smile was rueful, 'say "I give thee the chrysanthemum of my heart."'

'It was Lacy.' Mrs Malahide had grown impatient. 'He exposed himself to her. I don't know why your mothers don't tell you the facts of life. Poor bugger's been sacked. I suppose his family will starve. Do you' – she drew greedily on a cigarette – 'take my meaning? We're not talking about the exposition of the Sacrament!' On her lips the words sizzled into blasphemy.

Teresa gasped. Outrage released a babyish prickle of tears. Turning to hide this, she was once again assaulted by the headline CHOPS OFF . . . What? *That!* What else did they keep harping on Sunday after Sunday in the *News of the World?*

'Why will Mr Lacy's family starve?' She made fast for the periphery of the story.

'You tell me!'

In exasperation, Mrs Malahide drew on her cigarette, then emptied her lungs: *pfff!* Smoke coiled, and her hare-lip was very visible. 'It was his penis,' she told Teresa. 'He showed it to her. Can you tell me why that would make a girl of her age – nearly your age – faint? How old are you now? Twelve? Thirteen? Haven't you ever seen your father without his clothes? Or your brother? Well then? It's a necessary part of nature as you'll soon discover. I blame those nuns for poisoning your minds. Sick sisters. Why hide things – unless they're being hypocritical, which I have no doubt they are!' And Bunty Malahide began to tell how Father Creedon – a man crippled with arthritis – was enjoying the sexual favours of all the nuns in the local convent. Like a cock in a barnyard or a victorious stag. Exciting herself, and possibly forgetting to whom she was talking, she worked up conviction. She always downed a glass or two of Tullamore Dew while reading the Sunday papers.

Teresa was fired by battle-frenzy. The abuse of adult privilege outraged her, and the maligning of the nuns called for punishment. 'Bear witness to your religion,' she had been taught two years ago, in confirmation class, but the occasion had not arisen until now. Avenge, O Lord, those slaughtered saints whose bones . . . The spirit of old wars curdled her blood. She could feel this happen: clots blocking the flow as they did in anatomy charts. Evil was incarnate before her. Her eyes felt squinty, and the air glowed red.

The funny side would strike her later: for Mrs Malahide's flights of fancy would have been brought down to earth by a single look at Mother Dolours' dowager's hump, or at pale little Mother Crescentia who flew into such passions about 'men keeping women from the altar'. Quite suddenly, while putting a theorem on the blackboard, this meek nun would swing around, stab the air with chalk, and launch a polemic so ahead of its time that, years later, when the issue became a live one, few of the girls she had harangued would recall her yearning to be a priest. At first, the idea was too odd to shock, and by the time it did Mother Crescentia's bones would be mouldering in the very graveyard whose soil, if you believed Bunty Malahide, was white with those of strangled babies sired by Father Creedon.

'Why else', Bunty wanted to know, 'would nuns wear those bulky clothes? It's to hide their pregnancies! Holy Mothers forsooth! You don't think he goes there to hear confessions?'

'She needs a gag!' Teresa told her mother later. She would have cheerfully watched Mrs Malahide burn at the stake. At the very least, the Englishwoman should be forced to eat her own unwholesome words. Instead, magnified by laughter, they mocked Teresa when she rushed off, feeling every bit as assaulted as the girl in the park must have done when confronted by Mr Lacy.

For weeks the memory rampaged on. She had not tried to argue. What would have been the point? Bunty Malahide loved a fight and the one way to hush her would have been to agree with her. Teresa couldn't. That would have been a betrayal of sweet-cheeked Mother Fidelia, who had made her pupils promise to profess their faith without false diffidence and arm themselves against ridicule. Mother F., an ardent and pretty nun, inflamed her pupils, and for a whole term Teresa had day-dreamed about her, imagining shared heroics and intimacies so private that when the dentist pulled one of her teeth she went without gas lest she babble them out under its influence. For a while, even thinking of Mother F. made her skin tingle.

What could have possessed Mr Lacy? Had he perhaps been taken short and having a pee?

The story of his fall must be true, though, for he was now doing odd jobs in the Dunnes' garden, where he looked old and bald without his uniform peaked cap. And maybe it was also true that his family was hungry, for one night when Teresa looked out her window, she saw him by moonlight stealing cauliflowers and putting them into a sack. Poor Lacy! She remembered his old threat, 'I'll have yez summonsed,' and it struck her that she could do just that to him. Not that she would! The precariousness of self – he had lost some of his – was too upsetting. Earlier, she had seen him shelter from the rain under the empty sack, and his head had looked no bigger than a fist. Falling asleep, she dreamed that someone had exposed Mother Fidelia's poor, cropped head. Nuns gave up their crowning glory when they took the veil.

*

Her mother had had a row with Bunty Malahide over what she'd said to Teresa, and then made it up.

'How could you?' reproached Teresa.

But Mrs Dunne said you had to make allowances. Bunty's life had not gone well. That was why she lived here. The Irish were good-hearted, unlike her own sort, who despised her for marrying down. 'She's good-hearted herself,' argued Mrs Dunne. 'Look how kind she is to Greta.'

Greta was German and in need of kindness, now that Germany was losing the war. The map pins with which Teresa's father marked Allied and Axis movements had reversed direction, and the march round and round the sofa, with which he and her brother Pat hailed the theme music before the BBC news, had acquired new swagger. '*Léro léro lillubuléro*,' crowed Pat, lifting high his small, fat knees. Sometimes he banged two spoons together. He was six. '*Lillubuléro bullenalà!*' The tune was Irish, and a lot of our men were fighting with the Allies, so, although we were neutral, and miffed by Mr Churchill's threatening to seize our ports, we wanted his side to win. Pat planned to kill Hitler when he grew up.

You tried to hide such thoughts from Greta, though, and even Bunty, who hung out the Union Jack when Englishness welled up in her, refrained from trampling too brutally on Greta's sore feelings. With victory in sight, she managed – most of the time – to be forbearing.

'Well, she trampled on *mine!*' Teresa blushed. The word 'feelings' reminded her of Mother F., and her anger at Bunty Malahide mingled with shame over a treason of her own. Queerly, at the height of her crush on the nun, she had felt impelled to write a mocking verse about her and to circulate it among her friends. The risk had excited her, as if she half hoped to be caught. Childishly, the jingle began with the words 'The dark witch of Loreto', and, as it went from desk to desk, someone changed 'witch' to 'bitch'. That brought Teresa to her senses, and she snatched back her rhyme. She could be expelled. Girls *had* been for less – for trespassing in the nuns' part of the convent or spying on the pool where they took sea baths in long, cotton dresses. Disrespect for the 'brides of Christ' was a sacrilege, and she spent nervous days wondering if a copy of her jingle had escaped her.

The reality of her fear freed her. She now felt only pity for Mother Fidelia, stuck in her make-believe – which, it occurred to Teresa, was not unlike the games she and her classmates had played when they were small. Using penny-leaves for currency, they had sold field daisies for eggs and brown dockleaf blossoms for tea. Grass became string and rhubarb leaves wrapping paper. What difference was there between that and offering the Virgin the lily of your heart? The 'brides of Christ' didn't even eat in public. If you gave one of them a sweet, she kept it for later. Everything was for later. They did nothing now, which was why it was so unfair of Mrs Malahide to pretend they did.

'If I were you,' said Teresa's mother, 'I'd talk less about

feelings! Remember how you hurt Greta's at Christmas?'

How forget? It had been the talk of the village, after a dirndl-skirted Greta, her queenly braids done up in a crown, had given a children's party. As if Christmas were something on which Germans had a special claim, she had invited all the small local children to celebrate it, and, in the end, most parents had decided to let them go. After all, the woman was not thought to be a Nazi, and she and her non-German husband were desperate to have babies but couldn't. Let her have ours for an afternoon, said the villagers magnanimously. Jack Malahide supplied a bran tub to be groped in for prizes, and Mrs Dunne sent Teresa to help and to keep an eye on Pat, who was a bit of a handful.

He was also the child whom Greta knew best, so she asked him to start things off by inviting a little girl to dance: a mistake. Pat, when shy, sat on the ground. Plonk. Backside down. There was no budging him.

Greta didn't understand this. Hunkering down to coax him, she brought the fun to a standstill, and shushed the other children, who became bored. There was – people said afterwards – a German stubbornness to this, and a barren woman's pedantry. She kept on and on at Pat, while the others fidgeted and pinched each other and a boy grabbed the baby Jesus from the tasteful German crib. It was when someone pulled the plug on the fairy lights and several children began to cry that Teresa lost her head. 'Pat,' she cajoled, 'ask Annie to dance. You'll never grow up and kill Hitler if you're afraid of a small girl.'

At first she didn't notice her gaffe, much less connect it with what happened next, which was that Greta gave a small scream, rushed to the telephone, and told the village operator that she wanted everyone to leave. Yes. Now. At once! Parents were to fetch their children. The party was over. 'Take them away! I know now what you tell them behind my back! Oh you Irish are false! Tell the parents. Their children steal Baby Jesus and wish to kill Hitler. You hate me secretly.'

Helplessly, Teresa tried to restore order while Greta sobbed, Pat still sat on the floor, and the more enterprising small boys pocketed the marzipan crib animals, which had been cooked with sugar-rations contributed by their mothers. Then someone put *Heilige Nacht* on the gramophone. It was Jack Malahide, who had borrowed the rector's car – those who had petrol during the big Emergency were expected to help with minor ones – and was now piling children into it to deliver them home. Meanwhile, his wife calmed Greta down and comforted her with whiskey.

It was only when Teresa heard Bunty say to Greta that Teresa hadn't *meant* to upset her that she knew she had. Greta, her flaxen plaits askew, was weeping over the ruins of her crib. Where, she wanted to know, was Baby Jesus? And the marzipan donkey? She looked like a wronged maiden in a tale by the Brothers Grimm.

*

Peace was made. But Greta was not the same. Like poor Lacy, she had lost her plumpness and her trust.

It wasn't all Teresa's fault. The Church of Ireland – Protestant, despite the name – let Greta down, depriving her of spiritual comfort, since she, who was also a Protestant, had nowhere else to go. But how attend its services? Its small, embattled, but adamant congregation prayed hard against Germany, called God to its colours, and sang in unwavering chorus 'Thou who made us mighty, make us mightier yet.' Since 'us' meant Britain, this annoyed the native Irish as much as it did Greta. Patriots marvelled at the old oppressor calling itself 'Mother of the Free', and from time to time on a Friday night broke into the church to pee ritually on its floor.

Friday was payday, when even poor Lacy, defying the confines of his life, was to be heard smashing his own possessions, driving his wife to despair, and chanting in the spirited abandon of drink, 'Twas there that you whispered tenderly that you loved me, would always be Lily of the Lamplight, my ow-w-w-wn Lily Marlene.'

This cut Greta to the quick. 'Even our songs they steal!' she wailed to her false friends, Mrs Malahide and Mrs Dunne, who consoled her with soft words and hard liquor.

*

January was snowy, and Colonel Williams' pond froze, which gave people a rare chance to bring out their skates. The Colonel offered to supply a barbecue. No invitations were sent, since all were understood to be welcome – all, that is to say, except Greta. Williams, an ex-British officer, would not fraternize with the enemy.

'Will she have the nous to stay away?' worried Mrs Dunne. 'I've dropped hints, but Greta's not one to take them.' Mrs Dunne sighed. Neutrality was tricky.

Teresa had her own troubles. She had, after some hesitation, suspended her feud with Mrs Malahide so as to borrow her toboggan. It was the only one in the village. Everyone else used old sheets of corrugated iron.

The Malahide attic was a trove of odd tackle: snow shoes, pith helmets, motoring veils and other aids for facing intemperate conditions. These, like the scaly tail which is kept hidden in the story of the mermaid who marries a fisherman, testified to their owners' alien nature. The Malahides had lived in places whose foreignness clung to them. Jack Malahide, for instance, had a parasite in his blood which, according to local gossip, could only be caught on the rare occasions when it emerged to walk across his eyeball.

While rummaging up there for skates for her mother, Teresa had had a shock.

'I found a poem of yours,' said Bunty Malahide, coming up behind her so suddenly that Teresa nearly let a trunk-lid fall on her own neck. 'It slipped from your pocket. About a nun. It's quite funny,' she congratulated. 'I must say you're a dark horse!' And she proceeded, teasingly, to recite it. 'I added a verse.'

This was of course crude. All about nuns with buns in the oven. Father Creedon's name figured in it *and* Mother F.'s! Teresa felt sick – the more so because of something which had recently happened in school. 'I'm disappointed in you!' the nun had told her hurtfully. 'You've let me down. You're as silly and lightminded as the rest. '

What had sparked the thing off was a discussion of the Seniors' Christmas play. This was about a pagan who got converted on his wedding day, then found himself in a moral dilemma when fellow-Christians wanted him to be a martyr while his bride claimed that he owed himself to her. It was resolved – predictably if you knew convent plays – by the bride's own conversion. The thing was in hexameters. Deadly in more ways than one. A kind of trap, Teresa sensed, for girls like herself whom the nuns hoped might have a vocation. To elude this, she asked Mother Fidelia whether the converted bridegroom wasn't a bit prone to spiritual pride? What about his telling his Christian mentor, who was deploring his reluctance to get himself killed, that the mentor didn't know what it was like to have a wife? This, as Teresa remarked reasonably, was only a day after his wedding. How much could he know about having a wife himself? After one night?

Mother F. blushed. Unprecedentedly. And the class dissolved in glee. Teresa, though usually quicker than the rest, was the last to see why. Sex, to be sure! The topic had, she saw with shock, invaded not only the sanctuary of school but the mind of Mother Fidelia. Indignantly, Teresa, too, blushed, and when accused by the nun of letting her down, felt that the shoe was on the other foot. Like it or not, the lily of her heart was festering and likely, as Shakespeare warned, to smell far worse than weeds!

And now here was Bunty M., source of slime and vulgarity, gleefully reciting Teresa's embarrassing jingle. Why had she ever written it? To check her own feelings for Mother F.? But there was no time to ponder this. *Imagine* if Bunty – you couldn't put anything past her! – were to show it to other people?

'Give it back to me,' begged Teresa. But Bunty said the poem was now half hers and she wanted to copy it out.

'I'll give it to you at the pond, this afternoon,' she promised worryingly.

Teresa didn't dare argue.

*

Colonel Williams did things in style. Two small boys with brooms were keeping the ice clear of slush, and Mike Lacy had been set to mind the barbecue. Carefully pricked wartime sausages, made mostly of bread-crumbs and lard, squirted siz-zles of grease into the charcoal. Anglo-Irish ladies sailed by on skates bought on foreign holidays before the war. This, noted Mrs Dunne, had been one of the villages of the Pale. Even the Lacies were of English stock, having come over, generations back, to serve in a mansion which had now dis-appeared. Colonel Williams lived in its dower house, which would no doubt be torn down one day too. His sort and their habitats were doomed.

'The big-house people had their good side.' Mrs Dunne surveyed the pretty scene. 'Liked to make a show. "Showing the flag," they called it. But at home' – she lowered her voice – 'they'd live on the smell of a sausage. We had a maid who'd worked for them, and she was as thin as a lath. They starved her and themselves. Half an egg they'd give her for Sunday breakfast! Imagine.'

She spoke briskly while fastening her borrowed skates. Greta, Mrs Dunne was relieved to see, hadn't come. Neither had Bunty Malahide, for whom Teresa was anxiously looking out, refusing to be distracted until Colonel Williams begged her to help with the sausages. There was hot wine as well, which was to be kept from the younger fry. Teresa surreptitiously drank the better part of a glass before deciding she didn't like it.

Her mother skated towards her, showing signs of agitation. 'Greta's just come and gone,' she whispered. 'The Colonel cut her dead. I tried to talk to her, but she rushed off in a state. There was something bad, too – for Germany – on the one-o'clock news. Somebody should be with her. Help me off with my skates. No. Better go ask Father Creedon to look after her. I saw him coming up the field. Quick! Take the toboggan and head him off. Ask him to hold the fort until I come.'

So off whizzed Teresa to intercept the priest and, having sent him on his errand of mercy, trudged back up the slope to the barbecue, where the Colonel was discussing the incident with Bunty Malahide. What could one do, he shrugged, but set an example? War was war, and it was a damn shame the Irish hadn't joined this one. They were natural fighters. A crying shame! Still, better not spoil today's merriment. He lowered his voice, and Teresa heard no more. He was a straight-backed man who, when walking around his property, carried a long, swooping, metal-tipped tool for rooting up weeds. You had, he told Bunty, to take a stand. Stick to your guns! What? Bunty kept nodding her head.

'Yes,' she sighed. 'Yes.'

Teresa, who was keeping an eye on her, saw with surprise that Bunty's sardonic look was gone. She and the Colonel stood in a small bubble of intimacy. Of course, they were two of a kind and maybe lonely. Maybe they found us as alien as we did them? The thought was unwelcome. She had to admit, though, that Bunty looked pinker and younger than usual. Her eyes sparkled, and Teresa remembered people saying that Bunty would have been a beauty, but for her lip. For a moment she even had a look of Mother Fidelia.

Behind Bunty, Mrs Dunne now moved into Teresa's field of vision as she cut across the field, slipping in the soft snow. She was trying to catch up with Father Creedon and Greta, who had taken the path.

'Can't run with the hare and hunt with the hounds!' said Colonel Williams who was obviously upset.

'Just look at that!' Bunty waved towards the dip in the field where Father Creedon was trying to hold up the stumbling Greta. His black suit glowed against the snow and, as they watched, she lurched and he caught her in his arms.

Bunty shaded her eyes with her hand. 'He's getting a feel in! Well, good for Greta. Better her than the nuns! She'd *like* a bun in her oven! A gift from Holy Ireland to take home to Germany when the war ends! That reminds me, I've got your poem here,' she called to Teresa. 'I've added another bit. Do you want to hear?'

'No!'

'It's quite racy! Listen . . .'

But she got no further, for Teresa – or was it Mike Lacy, who had been at the wine? – now shook the barbecue, so that the sausages fell onto the coals and the sudden fatty blaze had to be dealt with by the Colonel. When things were restored, Teresa dusted off the salvageable sausages and threaded them on a spit while Mike laid out a ring of fresh ones.

The way he was standing, they looked like penises sprouting at belly level from his old black suit. Or the spokes of a monstrance. 'Exposition,' thought Teresa, and was shocked at the effect Bunty Malahide had on her thoughts. Might this be irreversable? A lasting contamination? And could it have leaked from her mind to Mother Fidelia's? Removing a split sausage from her spit, she saw that a piece of smouldering coal had got stuck inside it. Giddily, she became aware of Bunty's voice rabbiting on in her head and, mingling with it, like wireless interference, a line from a prayer: 'Cleanse my lips, O Lord, with a live coal.'

'Here. Have a sausage.' She pinched the fatty meat tight over the coal, handed it to Bunty, and watched with a thrill of horror as the harelip closed jauntily on the burning mouthful.

Under the Rose

Dan said – to be sure, there was only his word for this; but who would invent such a thing? – that, in their teens, his brother and he had ravaged their sister on the parsonage kitchen table. Their father was a parson, and when the rape took place the household was at Evensong. Dan described a fume of dust motes sliced by thin, surgical light, a gleam of pinkish copper pans and, under his nose, the pith of the deal table. Outside the door, his sister's dog had howled. But the truth was, said Dan, that she herself did not resist much. She'd been fifteen, and the unapologetic Dan was now twenty. It had, he claimed, been a liberation for all three.

'The Bible's full of it,' he'd wind up. 'Incest!'

The story was for married women only. Dan specialized in unhappy wives. *Mal mariées*. He sang a song about them in French, easing open the tight, alien vowels and letting the slur of his voice widen their scope: *ma-uhl mah-urrr-ee-yeh*. It was a Limerick voice, and those who resisted its charm said that the further Dan Lydon got from Limerick the broader his accent grew. The resistant tended to be men; women always liked Dan. To hear him lilt, 'My lo-hove is lo-ike a r-red, r-red r-ro-ose' was, as respected matrons would tell you, like listening to grand opera. His vibrancy fired them. It kindled and dazzled like those beams you saw in paintings of the Holy Ghost, and his breath had a pulse to it, even when all he was ordering was the same again, please, and a packet of fags. Words, moving in his mouth like oysters, put town-dwellers in mind of rural forebears and of the damp, reticent lure of the countryside.

The parsonage of Dan's youth lay in grasslands watered by the River Shannon, flat country shadowed by those cloud formations known as mackerel backs and mares' tails – arrangements as chameleon as himself. He was a bright-haired, smiling boy, who first reached Dublin in 1943, a time when the Japanese minister rode with a local hunt and the German one did not always get the cold shoulder. Dan's allegiance was to the noble Soviets, but he was alive too to sexual raciness blown in like pollen from the war-zones. Change fizzed; neutrality opened fields of choice, and values had rarely been shiftier.

'So where is your sister now?'

Mrs Connors did and did not believe his story. 'Tea?' she offered. Tea was his hour. Husbands tended to be at work. Mr Connors was a civil servant.

Dan took his tea. 'She had to be married off,' he admitted. 'She has a sweet little boy.'

Mrs Connors dared: 'Yours?'

'Or my brother's? I'd like there to be one I *knew* was mine.' His eyes held hers. Putting down the cup, he turned her wrist over, slid back the sleeve, and traced the artery with a finger. 'The blue-veined child!' he murmured. 'Don't you think children conceived in passion are special? Fruits of wilfulness! Surely they become poets? Or Napoleons?'

Phyllis Connors was sure Napoleon's family had been legitimate. On her honeymoon, before the war, she had visited Corsica. 'Their mother was addressed as Madame Mère.'

'Was that the model Connors held up to you? "Madame Mère"!' Dan teased. 'On your honeymoon! What a clever cuss!'

The teasing could seem brotherly; but Dan's brotherliness was alarming. Indeed, Phyllis's offer to be a sister to him had touched off the nonsense – what else could it be? – about incest.

Nonsense or not, it unsettled her.

He was predatory. A known idler. Wolfed her sandwiches as though he had had no lunch – and maybe he hadn't? The parson had washed his hands of him. But Dan had a new spiritual father in a poet who had stopped the university kicking him out. Dan's enthusiasm for poetry – he was, he said, writing it full-time – so captivated the poet that he had persuaded the provost to waive mundane requirements and ensure that the boy's scholarship (paid by a fund for sons of needy parsons) be renewed. Surely, urged Dan's advocate, the alma mater of Burke and Sam Beckett could be flexible with men of stellar promise? Talents did not mature at the speed of seed-potatoes, and Ireland's best known export was fractious writers. Let's try to keep this one at home.

The poet, who ran a magazine, needed someone to do the legwork and, when need be, plug gaps with pieces entitled *Where the Red Flag Flies*, *A Future for Cottage Industries?* or *Folk Memories of West Clare*. Dan could knock these off at speed and the connection gave him prestige with the under-graduates at whose verse-readings he starred.

It was at one of these that Phyllis Connors had first heard him recite. The verse had not been his. That, he explained, must stay sub rosa. Did she know that Jack Yeats, the painter, kept a rose on his easel when painting his mad, marvellous pictures of horse-dealers, fiddlers and fairs? Art in progress was safest under the rose.

After tea, Dan talked of procreation and of how men in tropical lands like Ecuador thought sex incomplete with-out it. That was the earth's wisdom speaking through them. RCs – look at their Madonnas – had the same instincts. Dan, the parson's son, defended the Pope whose church had inher-ited the carnal wit of the ancients. 'The sower went out to sow his seed. . . .'

Talk like this unnerved Phyllis, who was childless and unsure what was being offered. What farmer, asked Dan, would scatter with an empty hand? 'Your women are your fields,' he quoted, from the Koran. 'Go freely into your fields!' Then he extolled the beauty of pregnant women – bloomy as June meadows – and recited a poem about changelings: 'Come away, O human child . . .'

Phyllis, thinking him a child himself, might have surrendered to the giddiest request. But Dan made none. Instead he went home to his lodgings, leaving her to gorge her needs on the last of the sandwiches.

He came back, though, for her house was near the poet's, and after drudging with galleys would drop by to cup hands, sculpt air, praise her hips, and eat healthy amounts of whatever was for tea. Refreshed, he liked to intone poems about forest gods and fairyfolk. 'And if any gaze on our rushing band', he chanted, 'We come between him and the deed of his hand, We come between him and the hope of his heart.'

Why did he not come after what he implied was the hope of his own heart? Wondering made her think of him more than she might otherwise have done, and so did seeing him in The Singing Kettle, eating doughnuts with the poet's wife. Peering through trickles in a steamy window, she thought she saw the word 'love' on his lips. Or was it 'dove'? His motto, 'Let the doves settle!' meant 'Take things as they come.'

Phyllis decided that some doves needed to be snared.

*

Soon she was pregnant, and when she went into the Hatch Street Nursing Home to give birth, Dan brought her a reproduction of Piero della Francesca's Madonna del Parto, with the pale slash where the Virgin, easing her gown off her round belly, shows underlinen more intimate than skin. His finger on Phyllis's stomach sketched an identical white curve. He teased the nurses, relished the fertility all about, and was happy as a mouse in cheese.

It turned out that the poet's wife was here, too, and for the same reason. Her room was on another floor, so Dan yoyoed up and down. Sometimes he brought gifts which had to be divided: fruit, for instance, from the poet, who still used Dan to run errands. Or books, review copies from the magazine. When a nurse let drop that the poet's wife had the same Piero Madonna on her side table, Phyllis wrapped hers in a nappy and put it in the trash. If there had been a fireplace, she would have burned it, as she had been trained to do with unwanted religious objects.

Her baby received her husband's first name, and the poet's baby the poet's. Dan – though neither couple asked him to be godfather – presented both infants with christening mugs. One had been his and the other his brother's, and both were made of antique Dublin silver. Early Georgian. The official godfathers, fearing odious comparisons, returned their purchases to Weirs Jewellers and bought cutlery. Phyllis wondered if Dan's brother knew what had happened to his mug. Though the war was now over, he was still overseas with the British Army.

'He'll not be back,' Dan assured her, and revealed that the parsonage had been a dour and penurious place. Its congregation had dwindled since the RC natives took over the country in '21, and attendance some Sundays amounted to less than six. Pride had throttled Dan's widowed father, who did menial work behind the scenes and made his children collect firewood, polish silver, and dine on boiled offal.

'He wouldn't want the mug,' said Dan. 'Too many bad memories!' The brothers had left as soon as they could, and getting their sister pregnant had been a parting gift. 'If we hadn't, she'd still be Daddy's slave.'

*

Some years went by, and Dan was a student still, of a type known to Dubliners as 'chronic', one of a ragged brigade who, recoiling from a jobless job market, harked back to the tribally condoned wandering scholars of long ago. This connection was often all that raised the chronics above tramps or paupers, and the lifeline was frail.

But out of the blue, opportunity came Dan's way. The poet, who had to go into hospital, asked him to bring out an issue of the magazine bearing on its masthead the words 'Guest Editor: Daniel Lydon'. Here was challenge! Dan toyed excitedly with the notion of publishing his secret poetry, which he yearned, yet feared, to display. These urges warred in him until, having read and reread it, he saw that it had gone dead, leaking virtue like batteries kept too long in a drawer. Stewing over this, he fell behind with the magazine and had to ghostwrite several pieces to pad the thing out. As part of this process, he decided to publish photographs of A Changing Ireland. Hydrofoils, reapers-and-binders, ball-point pens and other such innovations were shown next to Neolithic barrows. The Knights of Columbanus in full fig appeared cheek by jowl with an electric band. Portraits of 'the last Gaelic storyteller' and some 'future Irishmen' rounded out the theme. The future Irishmen, three small boys with their heads arranged like the leaves of a shamrock, were recognizably his nephew and the recipients of his christening mugs – and what leaped to the eye was their resemblance to himself. The caption 'Changelings' drove the scandal home.

The poet, convalescing in his hospital bed after an operation for a gentleman's complaint, told his wife, in an insufficiently discreet hiss, that he had paid Dan to do his leg work, not to get his leg over. Reference was made to 'cuckoo's eggs', and it was not long before echoes of this reached the ear of Mr Connors, the proverbial quiet man whom it is dangerous to arouse. Connors, who had done a bit of hacking in his bachelor days, had a riding crop. Taking this to the student lodgings where Dan lived, he used it to tap smartly on his door.

When Dan opened this, Connors raised the crop. Dan

yelled, and his neighbour, a fellow-Communist, who was on the Varsity boxing team, came hurtling to the rescue. Assuming the row to be political and Connors a member of the Blue Shirts only reinforced his zeal. Shoving ensued; Connors fell downstairs; gawkers gathered, and the upshot was that an ambulance was called and the opinion bandied that the victim had broken his back. Some genuine Blue Shirts were meanwhile rustled up. Men whose finest hours had been spent fighting for Franco, singing hymns to *Cristo Re* and beating the sin out of Reds, they were spoiling for a scrap, and if it had not been for Dan's friend spiriting him out the back they might have sent him to join Mr Connors – who, as it would turn out, had not been injured, after all, and was fit as a fiddle in a couple of weeks. Dan, however, had by then prudently boarded the ferry to Holyhead, taking with him, like a subsidiary passport, the issue of the magazine bearing his name as 'guest editor'. It got him work with the BBC, which, in those days of live programming, needed men with a gift of the gab and was friendly to Celts. Louis MacNeice and Dylan Thomas were role-models, liquid stimulants in high favour, and Dan was recruited straight off the boat.

*

So ran reports reaching Dublin. Pithy myths, these acquired an envious tinge as Dan's success was magnified, along with the sums he was earning for doing what he had formerly done for free: talking, singing and gargling verse. Others too were soon dreaming of jobs in a London whose airwaves vapoured with gold. Hadn't Dubliners a known talent for transubstantiating eloquence into currency? And couldn't every one of us talk at least as well as Dan Lydon?

Declan Connors doubted it. Despite himself, he'd caught snatches of what nobody had the indecency to quote quite to his face: a saga featuring Dan as dispenser of sweet anointings

to women. These, Connors understood, had needed prepa-
ration. Persuasion had been required, and Dan's boldness
at it had grown legendary, as an athlete's prowess does with
fans. The gossips relished Dan's gall, the airy way he could
woo without promise or commitment – arguing, say, that in a
war's wake more kids were needed and that his companion's
quickened pulse was nature urging her to increase the supply.
Nature! What a let-out! Any man who could sell a line like
that in Holy Ireland could sell heaters in hell.

'He's a one-man social service!' A wag raised his pint.
'Offers himself up. "Partake ye of my body." He'd rather be
consumed than consume!'

The wag drained his glass. His preferences ran the other
way. So did those of the man next to him, whose tongue wres-
tled pinkly with ham frilling from a sandwich. All around,
males guzzled: women, in this prosperous pub, were outnum-
bered ten to one. Connors, sipping his whiskey, thought, No
wonder Lydon made out. We left him an open field!

He could no longer regret this, for after ten barren years of
marriage, Phyllis had had three children in quick succession.
It was as if something in her had been unlocked. He supposed
there were jokes about this, too, but he didn't care. His master passion had turned out to be paternal, and Declan Junior
was the apple of his eye. The younger two were girls and, as
Phyllis spoiled them, he had to make things up to the boy.

For a while after the scandal, the couple had felt shy with
each other, but had no thoughts of divorce. You couldn't in
Ireland, and it wasn't what they wanted. They were fond of
each other – and, besides, there was Declan, of whom it was
said behind Mr Connors' shrugging back that he used his
blood father's charm to wind his nominal one around his little
finger. A seducer *ab ovo*.

Small-mindedness! Envy! Anyway, time heals, and when the
boy was picked, surprisingly early, for his elementary-school
soccer team, and later won ribbons for show jumping,

Connors – a sportsman – knew him for his spiritual son. Even if the kid was a Lydon, he was a better one than Dan – whose brother, Connors recalled, had been decorated for gallantry in the war. Skimming the entry on Mendel in the encyclopaedia, he learned that hereditary character was transmitted chancily and, remembering the poltroonish Dan draped over arm-chairs and cowering during their fight, decided that Declan Junior had nothing of his natural father's but his looks.

Connors still took an interest, though, in the news trick-ling back from London, where Dan's free-lance was said to be cutting a swath: he had apparently acquired a new patron, a literary pundit who, though married, was partial to a hand-some young man. And now Connors noted an odd thing: admiration was ousting envy and Dan's stature in the saga growing. Needless to say, his news was slow to reach Connors, since nobody who remembered their connection would wish to re-open old wounds. It came in scraps and, by the time he got them, these were as spare and smooth as broken glass licked by recurring tides.

As Connors heard it, then: Dan's new benefactor's mar-riage, though possibly unconsummated, was harmonious, for his wife had money. The couple were fashionable hosts, and Dan was soon glowing in their orbit – singing ballads, referring to his secret *oeuvre*, and enlivening their soirées with tales of Irish mores. The pundit's wife, the story went, was a handsome, angry woman who had hated her father, but having agreed to inherit his money, would make no further concession to men, and slept only with those she could pity or control. As her husband didn't fit the bill, she had lovers. Dan was soon servicing both her and the husband who, being both jealous and smitten, was in the dark about this.

Here the story fractures. In one version, she 'gets preggers', which so shatters the husband that his violence leads to a mis-carriage and Dan's subsequent flight to Paris. But there was an implausible symmetry to this, as though running dye from the Dublin episode had coloured it; a likelier account has no pregnancy and the jealousy provoked by someone's indiscretion. Deliberate? Careless? Either way, Connors learned, Dan left England, the marriage collapsed and the husband, previously a rather nerveless knight of the pen – who had, in his own words, 'failed to grapple with his subjectivity' – finally did so in a book which raised him several rungs on the literary ladder. This was before the Wolfenden Report; homosexuality was still a painful subject, and the grappling was judged brave. Dan, as midwife to his lover's best writing, could be said to have done him a good turn.

Meanwhile, Declan Junior was in his teens, and his mother – noting that if you cut the heart from his name you'd be left with 'Dan' – feared leaving him alone with his sisters. An idle fear: girls bored him, and so did poetry, to her relief. Not that Dan himself had yet published a line, but the appelation '*Poète Irlandais*' clung to him, who had now – wonder of wonders! – married and settled in Paris. The word was that an old Spanish Civil War hero, whose memoirs Dan had been ghost-writing while sleeping with his daughter, had, on catching the pair in flagrante, sat on Dan's chest and said, 'Marry her.' A bad day's work for the girl, tittered those Dubliners who still remembered Dan. One or two had looked him up on trips abroad and reported that he was doing something nowadays for films. Script-doctoring, was it? And his wife had published poems before their marriage, but none since. Maybe she didn't want to shame him? Closer friends said the marriage was a good one, and that no forcing had been needed.

Why should it have been? Marisol was bright, young, had a river of dark hair, and gave Dan the tribal connection he had always coveted. His ravenous charm came from his childhood in that bleak parsonage. Marginal. Clanless. Left behind by the tide. Catholics – whose clan had dispersed his – did not appeal, but the Left did. The Spanish Civil War had

been Dan's boyhood war, and the more romantic for having
been lost. Dan loved a negative. What, he would argue, was
there to say about success? The surprise was that the Anglo-
Saxon ruling classes could still talk and didn't just beat their
smug chests like chimps. If it weren't for their homosexu-
als, he claimed, they'd have no art. Art was for those whose
reality needed suborning. It burrowed and queried; it . . . et
cetera! Dan could still chatter like a covey of starlings, and
the Limerick accent went down a treat in French, being, as
people would soon start to say, *médiatique*.

Along came the Sixties. The Youth Cult blossomed just as
Dan – in his Forties – began losing his hair. Juvenescence
glowed in him, though, as in a golden autumn tree. His fresh-
ness was a triumph of essence over accident, and he became
an acknowledged Youth Expert when he made a film about
the graffiti of May '68. Graffiti, being, like pub-talk, insolent,
jubilant, and an end in itself, was right up his street, and he
was soon in Hollywood working on a second film. It came
to nothing, which confirmed the purity of his response to
the ephemeral, and he continued to fly between Paris and
California, dressed in light, summery suits, and engaged in
optimistic projects, some of which did throw his name onto a
screen for a fleeting shimmer.

One evening in Paris, he came face to face with Connors
and Phyllis in a *brasserie*. They were at different tables, and
could have ignored each other. As their last encounter had led
to Connors' departure from the scene in an ambulance and
Dan's from Ireland, this might have seemed wise. Sportingly,
however, Dan came over. Shiny and aglow, his forehead –
higher than it used to be – damp with sweat. It was a hot
night. Hand outstretched. A little self-deprecating. He had
heard their news, as they had his, and congratulated Connors
on a recent promotion. Family all well? Grand! Great! He
was with *his*. Nodding at a tableful of Spaniards. Laughing
at their noise. Then, ruefully, as two of his wrestling children

knocked over a sauceboat, he said he'd better go and cope.

Soon the waiter brought the Connors two glasses of very old cognac with his compliments. They accepted, toasted him and, watching his gipsy table, remembered hearing that 'the poor bastard' had saddled himself with a family of idlers whom he had to work overtime to support. Dan's father-in-law, it seemed, had emphysema. Marisol's brother yearned to be a pop star, and she herself kept producing children. How many had they? Phyllis counted three, who were dark like their mother and did not look at all like Declan Junior. As she and Connors left, they thanked Dan for the cognac.

Afterwards, they discussed the encounter half sharply, half shyly. Looking out for each other's dignity. Not mentioning Declan Junior whom Phyllis, her husband guessed, thought of as having two fathers. Blame could thus be moved about or dissolved in the whirligig of her brain. And she could play peekaboo, too, with romance. He suspected this because – the evening had brought it home to him – he, too, had an imaginative connection with Dan and had not liked what he saw in the *brasserie*. It had depressed him. Spilled gravy and domesticity cut Dan down to size, and a life-sized Dan was a reproach, as the saga figure hadn't been at all. The connection to *that* Dan had, somehow, aureoled Connor's life and added a dimension to his fantasies. For a while, it had even made Phyllis more attractive to him. An adulterous wife was exciting – and he had often wondered whether it could have been that extra zest which had led to his begetting the two girls.

Water under the bridge, to be sure! The Dan Saga had not stimulated his sex-life for years. What it did do was make him feel more benign than might have been expected of the sober civil servant he was. Broader, and even passionate. It was as if he himself had had a part in Dan's adventurings. That, of course, made no sense, or rather the sense it made was private and – why not? – poetic. Dan, the unproductive poet, had, like Oscar Wilde, put his genius into his life: a fevering contagion.

Or so Connors must have been feeling, unknown to himself. How else explain the gloom provoked by the sighting in the *brasserie*? Phyllis didn't seem to feel it. But then women saw what they wanted to see. Connors guessed that for her Dan Lydon was still a figure of romance.

*

It was around this time that Declan Junior began to disappoint his parents. A gifted athlete who handled his academic work with ease, he had come through university with flying colours and Connors, convinced that the boy could star in any firmament, had looked forward to seeing him join the diplomatic corps or go in for politics or journalism. Something with scope. Instead, what should their affable, graceful boy do on graduating but take a humdrum job in a bank and announce that he was getting married! Yes. Now. There was no talking him out of it, and it was not a shotgun wedding, either. Indeed, Declan Junior was rather stuffy when asked about this. And when you met the girl you saw that it was unlikely. She was limp-haired, steady and – well, dull. Here was their cuckoo, thought Connors, turning out too tame rather than too wild. If there was a Lydon gene at work, the resemblance was more to the family man he and Phyllis had glimpsed in Paris than to the satyr whose heredity they had feared. Had they worked too hard at stamping out the demon spark?

That, they learned, was still riskily smouldering in the vicinity of Lydon himself. Connors heard the latest bulletin by a fluke, for he had grown reclusive since Declan's wedding and more so after the christening, which came an impeccable ten months later. He was, to tell the truth, a touch down in the mouth. Brooding. Had Phyllis, he wondered, been cold with the boy when he was small? Could guilt have made her be? And might there be something, after all, to Freudian guff? Till now Connors had dismissed it, but there was Declan married to a surrogate Mum. *Born* to be a Mum: she was pregnant again, and had tied her limp hair in a bun. Cartoonish, in orthopedic shoes, she wore a frilly apron and loved to make pastry. Declan was putting on weight! Ah well.

The latest about Lydon was that, hungry for money, he had agreed to be a beard.

A what?

'You may well ask,' said Connors' source, a man called Breen, who swore him to secrecy. Breen was on leave from the Irish Embassy in Rome, which, said he, was in a turmoil over the thing.

'But what *is* a . . .?'

Breen looked over his shoulder; they'd met in the St Stephen's Green Club. 'I can't tell you here.'

So Connors brought him home and settled him down with a whiskey, to tell his story before Phyllis came in. She was babysitting Declan III, known as Dickybird, who was at the crawling stage and tiring. His mother needed a rest.

Breen's hot spurts of shock revived Connors' spirits. The Dan Saga thrilled him in an odd, outraged way, much as the whiskey was warming and biting at his mouth. Recklessness, he thought welcomingly, a touch of folly tempered the norms and rules.

Lydon, said Breen, had been acting as cover for one of the candidates in the upcoming United States election, a married man who was having it off with an actress. Needing to seem above reproach – 'You know American voters!' – the candidate had engaged Dan to pretend to be the woman's lover.

'He was what's called a beard – travelled with her, took her to parties, et cetera, then left the scene when the candidate had a free moment.' The beard's function was to draw suspicion. For the real lover to seem innocent, the beard must suggest the rut. And Dan did. Though he was now fifty, an aura of youth and potency clung to him.

'It's all in the mind!' said Breen shrugging.

Outside the window, someone had turned on a revolving lawn-sprinkler and the family Labrador, a puppy called Muff, was leaping at its spray. That meant that Phyllis and the child were back from their walk.

Breen said that what Lydon's wife thought of his job nobody knew. The money must have been good. Or maybe she hadn't known – until she was kidnapped. Kidnapped? Yes. Hadn't he said? By mistake. At the Venice Film Festival. By Sardinian kidnappers who got wind of the story but took the wrong woman. 'The candidate's rich, and they'd hoped for a big ransom.' This had happened just three weeks ago.

Connors was stunned. A changeling, he thought, and felt a breath of shame. Play had turned dangerous, and he felt angry with himself for having relished Lydon's tomfoolery.

'The Yanks came to us,' Breen told him, 'asking us to handle the thing with discretion – after they'd got the actress back to the US. You could say we're *their* beard!' He grew grave, for there was a danger that the kidnappers could panic. 'Sardinians feed their victims to their pigs, you know. Destroys the evidence. They're primaeval and inbred! Islanders! No, *not* like us. More basic! Crude! Their life-way was easy to commercialize just because it *was* so crude. With them vengeance required blood as real as you'd put in blood sausage. Quantifiable! Material! We, by contrast, are casuists and symbol-jugglers. Closers of eyes . . .'

A flick of embarrassment in Breen's own eye signalled a sudden recognition that this could seem to refer to the story – had he only now remembered it? – of Connors and Dan: a case of eyes closed to lost honour. With professional blandness, he tried to cover his gaffe with an account of the Embassy's dilemma: on the one hand the papers must not learn of the thing. On the other, the kidnappers must be made to see that there was no money to be had. Breen castigated Lydon, whose sins were catching up with him. His poor wife though . . .

Connors tried to remember her face in the Paris *brasserie*, but could not.

'That louser Lydon!' Breen, intending perhaps to express solidarity with Connors, threw out words like 'parasite' and 'sociopath!' When you thought about it, a man like that was worse than the kidnappers. 'He breaks down the barriers between us and them. He lets in anarchy. He sells the pass.'

Connors tried to demur, but Breen, warming to his theme, blamed society's tolerance, for which it – 'we' – must now pay. 'Bastards like that trade on it.' Someone, he implied, should have dealt with Lydon long ago.

Connors ignored the reproach. Off on a different tack, his mind was cutting through a tangle of shy, willed confusions. He recognized that what he felt for Dan was love or something closer. Far from being his enemy, Dan was a part of himself. Luminous alter ego? Partner in father- and grand-fatherhood? Closing his ears to his companion's sermon, he looked out to where Phyllis and Dickybird had caught up with the golden Lab, on whose back the child kept trying to climb. Shaken off, he tried again: a rubbery *putto*, bouncing back like foam. The wild Lydon heritage had skipped a generation and here it was again.

Excited by the whirling spray, the puppy scampered through its prism while the infant held onto its tail. The child's hair was as blond as the dog's, and in the rainbow embrace the two gleamed like fountain statuary. They were Arcadian, anarchic, playful – and propelled by pooled energy.

'It's a terrible thing to happen,' Connors conceded. 'But I wouldn't blame Lydon. Blame the American candidate or the Italian state. Hypocrisy. Puritanism. Pretence. Lydon's innocent of all that. Blaming him is like, I don't know, blaming that dog out there.' And he waved his glass of whiskey at the golden scene outside.

We Might See Sights!

Under a furze bush one day – they were taking a pee – Madge broke with Rosie Fennel. She was ashamed – which was why she chose such a moment.

'Look, Rose,' she said, 'I'm afraid I can't play with you any more. I might *catch* something from you. It's not your fault and I like you still, but . . . it's the way your family lives. You see that, don't you?'

'Yeah,' said Rosie.

They both crawled from under the bush and stood up. Rosie had blonde, naturally curly hair, abundant as an aureole and alive with lice. She had a mouthful of bossy teeth and a foamy laugh. Madge had been her friend for three years – since they were ten. Rosie was good gas to play with: game, a tease, a liar. She went bare-legged in winter, to bed, swimming or to the movies at whatever hour she chose, and was free from the rules that plagued Madge who stood before her now, feeling ridiculous in her gym slip, woolly bloomers that – she had just noticed – snapped pink welts on her stomach, and childish-looking pigtails.

Rosie laughed. 'Well!'

'Well, good-bye, Rosie.'

'Cheero.'

Madge ran down the hill, her laced boys' shoes clattering like hooves. ('Like a horse!' said the nuns in school. 'Hoyden!' 'Lice!' they had said. 'Aren't you ashamed? A doctor's daughter! You should have your head shaved!')

Madge ran in her own gate, down the path, up the stairs and burrowed under the bed where she gibbered to herself in the dark for maybe half an hour, scrawling the springs above with her nails, gabbling that she had been awful. Awful! A filthy stinker! She hated herself! And the worst of all was that Rosie hadn't seemed to mind. But she could never look her in the eye again. Never.

She kept away from the village all day, but next morning her mother sent her up to the pub for cigarettes and there was Rosie outside the lounge door, watching the men play pitch-and-toss. (Rosie laughed at their cheek, knew how to give back as good as she got.) She waved at Madge:

'Howaya doin'?'

'Fine,' said Madge and fled. She had to pass Rosie's house where three younger sisters sat scrabbling in the dust – there was no real floor, just earth – and Joe, the father, neither drunk nor sober, hands on knees, stared before him with eyes like wet pebbles. He called something but Madge pretended not to hear.

She rushed down the street for fear of being hailed and maybe questioned about what she had said to Rosie by one of 'the village'. ('The village' were people who lived in houses like Rosie's; others were what Madge's mother called 'people like ourselves'.) They would think her stuck up. 'I'm not really stuck-up at all,' thought Madge. 'Not really. Not inside.' But felt branded.

She moped for weeks after that; read a school book in the bus for fear someone might talk to her and, in the end, struck up with Bernie O'Toole whose father owned the village pub and who, like herself, attended the private convent school in the nearest town. They were the only two kids from round about who did. ('Kids' was Rosie's word who liked Americanese. '*You*', the class nun told Madge when she heard her use it, 'may like to fancy yourself as related to goats! *We* prefer to believe our charges are at least human!')

Bernie was a bit of a stick. She was from the country and shy, but there was a free flow of raspberryade from the pub to the

O'Toole kitchen so Madge took to doing her homework there.

The O'Tooles weren't quite 'people like ourselves' either. They didn't visit Madge's parents or their friends. ('Though they could buy and sell us,' said Madge's mother.) Mrs O'Toole flapped about her dark kitchen like a downcast bird in flow-ered aprons, made cakes and chatted endlessly with her skivvy – none other than Rosie's elder sister, Bridie, whom Madge, of course, knew well. She and Madge eyed each other and talked over-politely for a week after Madge had started coming to the O'Tooles', then one evening Bridie – she had been handing Madge a glass of lemonade – bounded back-wards and shouted in a very grand voice:

'Eugh! *Deugh* excuse me! I wouldn't want you to *catch* anything!'

Madge went red – she could feel herself – to the tips of her ears. After that it was war to the knife between her and Bridie. Which was more comfortable really. You knew where you were.

'Here's Miss Madge,' Bridie would yell when Madge arrived. 'Her ladyship has come!'

'Bridie's got a tootsie,' said Bernie slyly, being on Madge's side, and giggled till her pale eyes watered. They were like raw eggs at the best of times. Wettish. Slightly loose. 'The milkman's her fella!'

'A tootsie! A tootsie! Hee, hee, hee!' The little girls giggled while Bridie banged saucepans about. Bernie's brother, Pat, giggled too and clattered his spoon on the tray of his high chair. He was strapped into it though he was too big and his thighs bulged against the sides. 'Gloughgh!' he howled, and slobber fell on his bib. 'Gluggle!' He had a pale, plump face so peppered with freckles that they formed a small saddle on the bridge of his round-nostrilled nose. His eyes were slanted and he had a puffy look like a stuffed cloth doll. He might have been eight or nine.

'What is it, Pat? Now what set him off?' Mrs O'Toole ran

in to wipe off the slobber. 'Tell Mummy, pet! Gluggle,' she said too for she claimed to be able to make out what the child said, and talked back to it with the same noises. 'Pat's my boy,' said she and wiped off his saliva.

'Can she really make out what he says?' Madge asked Bernie when her mother had gone.

'Seems.'

'Listen, what's he like – the tootsie?'

'Hee, hee,' said Bernie. 'You jealous?'

'Silly galoot! What I mean is: what do they do anyway?'

Bernie shrugged. 'Go for walks on the beach. Ma saw them go into the cave.'

'Jeez, that's dangerous. Did you know that was an old copper mine? My Daddy says they had to stop working it because of earth slides. There are passages going right under our hill and . . .'

'Well *they* don't explore any passages you may be sure!' Bernie was contemptuous. 'They just neck!'

And then – being unavowably inquisitive – the girls said no more.

Bridie was a fattish girl with an enormous bosom that shook like clotted milk inside her overall. She wore no bra and, from standing over the O'Tooles' cooking stove, gave off a stew of heavy odours. There was, Madge remembered, only a yard tap for her and Rosie to wash at.

''S a wonder she hasn't creepiecrawlies!'

'She *had*! Ma combed them out with a finecomb!'

'Phew!' said Madge. Then – for hadn't she caught them herself from Rosie? – 'Poor thing!'

'That Bob Cronin didn't mind!' Bernie sniggered. 'Nor the milkman. Ma says she's man-mad!'

'Seven o'clock! Jeepers, I've got to fly!'

'See you tomorrow.'

'Bye.'

Rump uppermost in the O'Toole yard, Bridie was washing

clothes in a bucket. Her thick thighs and glossy pink knickers struck Madge as offensive.

'I'm off,' she told the rump.

'Eugh, Madam Madge! *Good*-bye!' came from the bucket.

A group of ratty-looking youths held up the pub wall, sharing a cigarette butt and staring, it seemed to Madge, with foolish insolence before them. She sprayed them all with her imaginary water-pistol, containing, she decided, sour milk. But felt unassuaged. Like a volley of spittle from her mouth, the one word 'BOYS!' crackled with sudden ringing scorn.

They gaped and the next thing she was racing down the macadam, ears burning, eyes blurred with shame.

'Cretin!' she scolded herself. 'Half-wit! Dope!' Inside her own gate, she flopped against the post. 'Jeez,' she gasped. 'You're a real loony! They'll have to tie you up, Madge Heron!'

*

Saturday was Bridie's half-day and Mrs O'Toole said the girls would have to take Pat for a walk. *She* had things to do. Madge was fed up the minute she saw him. He was pinned into an enormous scarf, snotty as per usual and looking like – well like what he was. By now, however, she'd accepted too much O'Toole raspberryade to protest. Still she promised herself, they could at least avoid the main roads. She wasn't going to let anyone she knew see her walking out with *that*!

'What about going to the beach?' she proposed to Bernie.

'Bet Bridie's there with her heart-throb! We might see sights!'

'You've a dirty mind, Bernie O'Toole!'

'Go on! Pretend that wasn't what you were thinking of yourself!'

Madge scrabbled at the loose plaster in the O'Toole yard

wall. A colony of albino insects raced. 'That's right,' she said. 'It wasn't.'

Flies patrolled the veil Mrs O'Toole had thrown on her meatsafe. Who else used outdoor meatsafes any more? The O'Tooles were that stolid! Bernie had the same round nostrils as her brother: punctures in a boneless nose. 'Her whole face is like his,' Madge noticed, 'all puffs!' In school the nuns never had a thing on her. Slyboots! 'If she giggles now,' Madge thought, 'I'll hit her.'

'I'm fed up with double-meaning talk!' she told Bernie.

'Oh yeah?'

'*Yeah!* What's it to us if Bridie smooches or runs after fellows? If you want to know why we're going to the beach, it's' – Madge, on impulse, dredged up a half-shelved dream – 'to explore that cave! No boys have done it. Nobody. How many kids our age have a chance like that? All those passages. Empty for years! Centuries maybe. Anything could be hidden there. We'll need', she recalled, 'a bicycle lamp and candles to test the oxygen.'

'What about Pat?'

'He can wait outside.'

'I'm going into no dirty old cave,' said Bernie. 'You know as well as I do that trippers use it for a lav!'

'*You* can wait outside if you want. That way if I get into some scrape you can give the alert.'

This echo from the *Girls' Crystal* began to work on Bernie.

'I don't mind cadging lamps and stuff,' she wavered. 'Though if anything happens to *you* I'll be the one to be blemt!'

'Pooh! They'll all know it couldn'ta been *your* idea!'

All the way downhill they discussed the cave, astonished suddenly that they had never tackled it before. Madge said she wouldn't be surprised if the Germans – who were known to have landed money and radio equipment along this coast – hadn't hidden stuff there during the war. Most had been caught the minute they landed but you never knew.

'There might be unexploded dynamite,' said Bernie.

*

The cave, hidden by a curve in the cliff, had to be reached by scrambling past rocks and rock-pools where slime and algae covered dormant crabs. The girls took turns carrying Pat and were puffed by the time they reached the great cleft itself. It was fringed by a growth of greyish marine vegetation and its base was moist with rivulets of reddish ooze.

'I'm going no further!' Bernie, an image of country caution, plonked herself on a rock.

'You can *look* in, can't you? Jeez, you might come to the *opening*!'

'That's the stinky part!'

'Not now it isn't! The tides wash right in at this time of year!'

Placing their feet on dry spots among the issuing scum, the two approached.

'Pat,' his sister told him, 'you stay where you are!'

He had settled on an apron of dry pebbles between two rocks. Crooning to himself, his blunt, starfish fingers clutched, dropped and again clutched at smooth pastel stones. Sandy-haired, freckled and pale, he was almost invisible among the mica glints of the brownish-whitish rock: a dappled animal returned to its own habitat.

The girls stepped some way into the cave. Its upper vaulting was lost in darkness; the black gullet, piercing the interior of the hill they had just descended, presented no contour. Under the beam of Madge's lamp, a stretch of inner wall sweated a red liquid which gathered in darker trickles.

'Blood!' Bernie whispered.

'Copper!' Madge reminded her. 'It's a *copper* mine!'

Growing used to the dark, they were able to make out boulders and, in the far end, a slit of richer, velvety black.

'The passage!'

'Shshsh! There's someone there!'

To one side of the passage were two shapes. On a spread macintosh, a man and a woman lay with their heads tilted towards the interior of the cave. Madge was astonished that she should have missed them before for they were pitching and surging in a repetitious undulation, disagreably similar to the agony of grounded fish. The woman lay uppermost and her skirt, rucked up to her waist, showed a patch of shiny pink.

Madge felt a rush of nausea. 'Let's get out of here.'

'What do you bet it's Bridie and the milkman! The dirty things! I'm telling Ma!'

'Come out, willya!' Madge began to back away.

Bernie caught her arm. 'Half a mo'! Look at Pat!' she whispered. 'Jeepers *look* at him! Pat!' she whispered urgently. 'Come here!'

The child had crept in behind and around them. Now he was half-way across the cave, making for the still jouncing couple.

'Blawchlee!' he gurgled happily. 'Blawdee!'

'Leave him,' Madge whispered. 'They'll have fits if they think *we* saw them! Bridie's fond of him,' she reassured Bernie when they were outside. 'We'll pretend we didn't see him mooching off.'

'We could call him!'

'OK!'

'Pa-a-at!'

'Now give them time to send him out.'

The girls sat on a rock. 'Pa-a-at!' Bernie yelled again.

Madge found a linty twist of paper in her pocket with a bull's-eye and acid drop welded together. She tried to prise them apart but they fell, bounced off the rock and rolled into a scummy pool. 'Hell' she cried. 'Everything's the same today! Spoilt! Everything!' Biting her nails, she stared into the water where a sea anemone waved delicate fretted tendrils, enfolding its flower-like heart against the danger. 'Stupid slow thing!' said Madge. 'If those sweets had been something dangerous it would be dead by now!'

'Don't they shoot poison?' Bernie wondered. 'Pat!' she began to call again. 'Pa-a-at!'

With a yelp and a scutter of pebbles, Pat appeared at the mouth of the cave; he stumbled on the scum, picked himself up, collected his clumsy body for a last rush and threw himself on Bernie, hugging her knees and gobbling.

She stroked his large, cropped head. 'Whatsa matter, Pat? It's OK now. It's all OK!'

There was a man behind him. Madge stared at him and he stopped to stare back. He had a muddled aghast look. His mouth was like a hole burnt in cloth: unformed, struggling as she had often seen Pat's. Indeed he had a look of Pat: clumsy, bulbous-faced and as if, when he made a noise, it too might be a meaningless gobble. One hand held up his trousers while the other groped inside them to tuck in the tail of his shirt. He was making a poor fist of it and was not, it occurred to Madge to notice, the milkman. At last he managed to bring out some words: 'Tan his arse for him!' he shouted in an English accent. A tripper. 'Little Peeping Tom. . . .' But he looked uncertainly around.

'He's afraid', Madge guessed, 'that we've got grown-ups with us!' She was enraged by the man's language and appearance. Her throat was knotted with anger and it was some seconds before she managed to yell: 'Mister, you leave that kid alone! He's not right! He gets fits!'

'Shsh! Madge!' Bernie begged.

'I'll say he's not right!' the man muttered. 'My God!' He began to button his pants and glanced at Pat whose face was buried in Bernie's lap. 'You don't know what he was doing . . .'

'And what were *you* doing, Mister? We could get the guards after you!'

'Dickie!' a woman's voice called from the cave. Another

English voice. Not Bridie's. 'They're only kids. No need to get your dander up.'

'Oh hell!' The man turned back. 'Delights of Nature!' He was muttering as he went into the cave. 'Have to run into the blooming village idiot. . . .'

'Dickie!' the woman's voice called.

'The guards!' Madge yelled after him. 'Cheek!' She was boiling with disgust and fury. 'Chasing Pat like that! Who does he think . . .'

'Shut up, will you!' Bernie whispered. '*I'm* going! Come on, Pat, I'll give you a piggyback!'

Madge followed them. Half-way up the hill she took Pat from Bernie. He was heavy. 'Gee,' she gasped. 'That fellow was worried!'

Bernie pondered. 'I wonder what Pat saw? Sights I'll bet! The English are terrible dirty!'

When they reached the end of the grassy slope, Madge eased Pat off her back and flopped down between two bushes. 'Got to rest!' she groaned. 'I'm puffed!' She found another bull's-eye and gave it to Pat. He sat sucking it, his round face further distent by its bulge, his eyes inflamed. The girls looked at him with interest. The afternoon had been a wash-out. They felt cheated.

'Think he saw *everything*?'

'Must have!'

'Well, there's no getting it out of *him*!' Madge spoke with a mixture of relief and regret.

Bernie began to giggle. 'I dunno about that! He might *do* it for us!'

Madge stood up. '*Now* you're talking!' She began to unbuckle Pat's belt. 'Pat,' she soothed, 'show the game the man was play-ing! Show us, Pat!' She gurgled encouragingly. 'Let's play, Pat!' She peeled down the stiff, stained short trousers until she was confronted by his little boy's body: yellowish, smelling of pee, with bits of fluff tucked under the loose skin.

'*Madge!* He'll tell! My Ma understands him! Madge!'

Madge ignored her. 'Whose idea was it anyway? Spoilsport!' She whispered to Pat: 'Come on! Show us! What were they doing? Show!'

Bernie smirked. 'OK then. *I'*ll show you something!' She began tickling the loose flesh between the little boy's legs.

The child let out a wail, pushed her violently from him and began to shiver again.

'OK,' his sister told him. 'OK! So you don't want to today! Hold your hair on!'

But Pat was down on his back now kicking with frenzy. Bernie stared at him with wet eye orbs. 'Oh Madge! He's having a fit!' She began to cry. 'He'll tell, Madge!' she moaned. 'My Ma understands what he says and my Da'll crease me! It's all your fault. It's a mortal sin.'

Madge was indignant. 'It's *not* my fault!'

'It is so!'

'Oh for Pete's sake! There's a *pair* of you!' Madge tried to seize Pat who was writhing. Maybe it *was* a fit? His face was crab-red and there was spittle on his lips. 'Pat,' she begged. 'Can't you *do* anything?' she shouted to Bernie. 'At least shut up crying yourself! You're only encouraging him!'

But Bernie just wept. 'He'll go off his head for good!' she sobbed. 'The doctor told Ma. If he's excited. And it'll be your fault, Madge Heron! All your fault! And what'll me mother do? Uuughhuu!' She joined her high shrill wail to Pat's.

'SHUT UP!' Madge was distracted. 'Both of you! Pat!' His mouth was more than ever like a black hole burnt in his face. He was slobbering but had stopped howling. She picked him up. 'Quiet,' she told him. He peed on her. He must have felt it happening for he began to wail once more. She put him down. 'Oh God, the filthy thing. . . .' She felt like crying herself. 'WILL YOU AT LEAST QUIT CRYING!' she roared. 'If anyone comes they'll think we're killing the little beast! STOP!' He wouldn't. She smacked his face. For a moment he did stop and stared at her, wall-eyed, too much white showing. Then he began to yell worse than ever. She picked up his belt – a proper man's leather one cut down – and gave him a lash across the legs with it. 'Now will you stop? Will you, will you?' She was staring in horror at the pink welt on his poor pale idiot's body before Bernie got to her. 'What a beast I am,' she thought. 'All beasts!' Bernie was upon her.

'You stop that, Madge Heron, you . . .'

She gave Bernie a shove with her knee that caught her in the stomach and sent her rolling. 'Beast,' she thought, 'but I won't stop for her! I am a beast, I . . .' and again she raised the belt but the child had crawled away and Bernie was on her again.

'You're out of your mind, Madge Heron!' She tore the belt from Madge's hand and, pulling one of Madge's feet from under her, sent her flat on her face on the grass. Madge lay where she had fallen, not listening to Bernie's shouting, not listening to the child who was now quieted and snuffling gently to itself a few yards off. 'I can't,' she thought but couldn't think what it was she couldn't do. 'Grass,' she thought and buried her face in it. 'Blot it out. Grow over it, let me forget it. Grass, nothing but grass. . . .'

The Widow's Boy

When her husband was reported missing on the Russian front, Nino's mother bore up and went to work to keep shoes on Nino's feet and bread in his mouth: two things which his father must have needed sorely at the end. Cardboard boots, if you could believe what you heard now, were what had been issued to Italian troops. Boots of smartly blackened cardboard or, at best, stiffened felt which melted to nothing in the snow. Thin coats. Inadequate rations. Nino imagined his dying father losing his toes and gnawing thirstily at an icicle. The gnawing face was the one in the photo-portrait on his mother's dressing table because, without it, Nino could not be absolutely sure of how his father used to look.

For a while he had confused him with Jesus who, in his portrait, was suffering from severe blood-loss. Nino's grandmother begged Jesus to bring Nino's father home, but Nino reasoned that a man so afflicted could not be of much assistance – and was proven right when a letter came confirming his father's death.

His mother cried then, and so did Nino, though his father was by now a mere smudge in his mind, fading along with Jesus who, said Gianni the cobbler, had been promoted by priests and Fascists to make us toe their line. "'Blessed are the poor in spirit,'" sneered Gianni and added bits of mock-Latin, "'for theirs is the Kingdom of Heaven!'" Thanks Lord, but we'd sooner have the Kingdom of Here. *Gratias agamus tibi!* Maybe it was real Latin? Gianni had been to school to priests, though he was now a Communist and had heard Russian comrades confirm the story of the cardboard boots.

The sign swinging over his shop was a golden boot and that too seemed like a confirmation. Nino ran messages for him, picking up worn shoes and delivering mended ones to customers who sometimes gave him a tip. Being a widow's boy had rewards.

It had drawbacks too though, and Nino wondered how their life might have been if his mother, instead of losing a husband, had lost a leg or been disfigured just enough for there to be no need to worry about her honour. As it was, she was the prettiest widow around – which was not the advantage you might think. Widows were fair game. Jokes about them made fellows dig each other dreamily in the ribs while lurking in the school bog, taking deep drags at forbidden cigarettes. Girls, it seemed, were different. They were shy and if you went too far with one you had to marry her. But widows wanted it – whatever 'it' was. Sad addicts, they longed for what they'd once enjoyed, and when Nino's father was freezing his arse in the Russian snows, his young wife had surely been suffering the fiery frustrations of passion in her lonely bed.

When the other kids talked this way their words had such a zing that Nino was ready to join in their secretive snigger and let himself dream of sinking into soft, embracing snow. Glittering, he thought. Gaudy. Like rainbows on ice. Then he remembered his mother looking tired in her cotton pinny and grew confused. He looked at the shoes which she had polished for him last night, after working a ten-hour day. Snow and fire were hazardous, and so, it seemed, was the 'it' that everyone wanted. Well, let them find it in some other family, decided Nino, who should have put a stop to all this before.

'Alone, all alone in her mournful bed!' repeated his best mate, Pippo, who lived in the same *palazzo* and walked to and from school with him every day. 'That's if it *was* lonely and not occupied by some randy draft-dodger.'

And though he knew that Nino's mother lived a hard and blameless life, Pippo let blue cigarette smoke snake insinuatingly from his nostrils. He loved romancing, and his older brothers had given him a taste for smut.

'Shut your face, moron!' Nino had to say then, though he knew Pippo would enjoy giving him a bloody nose which, sure enough, he did, for he was big for his age and his brothers had trained him to box. The worst of it was that, from then on, Nino's friends grinned whenever the word 'widow' was pronounced. Sometimes it was only the ghost of a grin – or maybe, as they claimed, Nino was imagining things, having grown suspicious and nervy like a scalded cat? What was undeniable was that the word 'widow' cropped up everywhere. In church the priest talked of the widow's mite, and at night in the piazza there was a drunk who sometimes started yelling that Italy had been widowed by the death of Mussolini and whose friends had regularly to make him pipe down. Then a poster for an operetta called *The Merry Widow* was put up all over town, and it was months before the last copies were overlaid by electoral notices – 'Vote for La Pirra and De Gasperi!' – and by ads for films featuring Fabrizio, Toto and the alluring but worn-looking Anna Magnani. Maybe the reason she was so popular in those years was that she looked as if, like so many others, she had seen bad days but managed, pluckily, to survive. *She* looked like someone's widow – oh, why did he have to keep thinking of widows?

And why did he have to have a widowed mother? She was a good one in every other way: neat, sensible and not too strict, and her pasta was never mushy or underdone. Somehow, though, her niceness, like her prettiness, could be turned against her – *them*. As if it were bait.

'A nice Mamma you've got there!'

You could sift that for smutty meanings and, even if you didn't, the words twisted in your mind. 'Nice' how? In what way?

The most embarrassing thing happened in, of all places, the English-language class which the school had introduced because the British Institute was lending it a teacher with a prepaid salary. He was Mr Williams, a lanky, long-haired man who read English poems aloud from a book. One was about a boy who worried about his mother. Mr Williams threw back his long hair and recited slowly so that the boys could study his accent.

> 'James James
> Morrison Morrison
> Weatherby George Dupree
> Took great care of his Mother,
> Though he was only three.'

The class fidgeted. The poem struck them as odd. Or silly? No: odd.

> 'James James
> Said to his Mother . . .'

Finding that his audience wasn't with him, Mr Williams switched to a funny, fluting voice:

> '"Mother," he said, said he;
> "You must never go down to the end of the town . . .'"

Baffled, the class heard him out as he explained about the English sense of humour. 'Come on,' he pleaded jovially. 'Laugh, chaps! This is a funny poem.' And read:

> 'James James
> Morrison's Mother
> Put on a golden gown,
> James James . . .'

As it dawned on them that the joke was about concern for a mother's good name, the boys grew indignant. Good names were a sore subject and had been so ever since the Fascists said we had tarnished ours by betraying our German allies – only to be told that Fascism was what had tarnished it. Either way, hard feelings were hard to shake off, and of all people the English – who had egged on the betrayal – should be treating us with kid gloves. Instead, here was Mr Williams trampling on sacred values like motherhood and committing *oltraggio alia patria*. An insult to the nation, a major offence! The class looked ready to riot.

Then Pippo created a diversion. He explained why, for us, the poem wasn't funny. 'Here,' he told the Englishman, 'if there's no father, the son takes his place and if the boy is a widow's son like Nino here, then . . .'

Pippo meant no harm. Intent on enlightening Mr Williams, he forgot his earlier teasing of Nino – who, however, did not. The poem had caught him on the raw and Pippo's words pricked and prodded at his mortification.

'If Nino's mother brought men to the house,' elaborated Pippo, 'or if she wore a golden gown and went . . .'

It was pedagogic. Pippo was enjoying teaching the teacher and Mr Williams enjoying being taught. He smiled encouragingly at Pippo whose response – a raised eyebrow, the ghost of a grin? – caught the tormented Nino's eye and precipitated his attack. Hurling himself at his friend, Nino hammered his face with his fists. Pippo, after a stunned pause, drew back his own large fist and punched Nino – who was spindly with match-stick legs and wrists – so hard that he fell backwards into a desk. Pippo then leaped on him, blacked one of his eyes and began pulling the noose of his tie so tight that he might have strangled him if Mr Williams had not pulled him off.

'You see,' Pippo taunted instructively. 'Widows' sons end up crazy. They have the worst of all bargains. They're like cuckolds who don't even enjoy what's on offer themselves!'

Again the maddened Nino lunged, and again Pippo punched him. The *bidello* or school porter, a big, muscular fellow, had meanwhile been attracted by the noise and in two ticks cleared the room. Pippo was sent to the headmaster and, while the rest of the class went home, Mr Williams loosened Nino's tie, took him to the bathroom, washed his face and examined him to make sure he wasn't badly injured. Then he gave him a lift in his car to the nearest chemist's shop where the chemist, a friendly man, was just pulling down his shutters. He drew the two in, patched Nino up and produced brandy, which Nino took for medicinal reasons and Mr Williams from good fellowship, and the upshot was that the two men took Nino home to his mother who, in gratitude for their concern, invited them to join herself and Nino for a plate of pasta.

Afterwards Nino, packed off to bed and muzzy from the brandy, heard them singing as the chemist picked out a tune on Nino's father's old squeeze-box. Both he and Mr Williams liked opera and were soon talking of coming back on another evening with a guitar. Nino groaned from fear of scandal and of what the neighbours must think. Here was the widow entertaining not one man but two, while her guardian and chaperone – himself – was out of commission. This no one must ever know.

English class, after this, became a purgatory. Mr Williams' marked friendliness towards himself was, Nino felt, compromising, but an outright coldness between them could, on the other hand, arouse worse gossip, since it was known – everything was – that Mr Williams and the chemist had been back twice to the house, and that the two had taken Nino and his mother rowing on the Arno, followed by dinner at a trattoria.

He tried talking to his mother about the dubious propriety of this but she laughed, saying that there was safety in numbers and that the two men were lonely, living as they did in noisy boarding houses where they enjoyed no privacy and were fobbed off with coffee made from toasted barley and sauce made from offal. It was only Christian, she insisted, to make them welcome in her large, pleasant flat in these tough times. Besides, they kicked in something to pay for the food. Then she pinched Nino's ear playfully and kissed the top of his head. She didn't take him – or life – seriously at all.

Some time after this she started travelling around Tuscany, selling cosmetics and doing demonstrations in small towns where ladies came to learn how to apply and remove make-up and to have massages and facials. She did this in *profumerie* and in the sort of small chemist's establishment which sold cosmetics as well as drugs. Maybe her friend the chemist had helped her get the job? She would, she explained, sometimes have to be away overnight and so Nino was going to have to stay with his grandmother. Yes, Nino, no arguments please. This was a promotion and we needed the money.

'I don't want to hear any more of your nonsense and I sincerely hope you'll give up fighting and settle down to your studies.'

Nino's grandmother lived a train-ride outside the city and it would have cost too much for him to travel back and forth to his old school, but luckily it was now the summer vacation and who knew what the autumn would bring? His mother hoped to get a job back in town before long.

Being with his grandmother wasn't all bad. It got him away from the treacherous Pippo, into whom he would otherwise have bumped every day in the lift and on their shared stairway. He spent the first weeks of his holiday reading, and his mother came by every Sunday.

Then he and his grandmother had a tiff. She was stricter than his mother – more old-fashioned – and wouldn't let him go to the race track with some boys he had met. Nino decided to ask his mother for permission and, as his grandmother had no telephone, went out to ring from a café. There was no

answer at first, but as it was still very early in the morning –
he had got up specially – and his mother might still be asleep,
he let the phone ring and ring. Finally someone picked it up.
A man's voice spoke. It was Mr Williams'. 'Hullo,' it said,
'hullo. *Pronto.*'

Nino hung up and left the café. Without thinking, he
headed for the station, took the first train which was full of
commuters, dodged the ticket collector, and reached the city
just about the time his mother usually left for work. When he
reached her flat, though, his key didn't work. Someone inside
had drawn the bolt and when he knocked they didn't open.

Walking like a sleep-walker – there was, he knew, no sense to
what he was doing but he did it anyway as if he was a wind-up
toy which someone had set in motion – he went downstairs
and round to the back of the house, where he began to shin
up the drainpipe which, three floors above, ran past the balcony of their flat. It was a mad thing to do. Useless. What
did he want? A scandal? Or to show her that he couldn't be
fooled? Just to show her. Just . . . No, it was crazy. Foolish! He
was on the point of giving up when someone hailed him from
the second-floor balcony. It was Pippo.

'Hullo. What are you doing?'

'I forgot my key,' Nino lied.

It was months since their fight and Nino found that he
wasn't angry with Pippo any more. He was angry with *her*!
Let Pippo see her, he thought furiously. Let everyone! Maybe
that would teach her!

'I thought you were a burglar.'

'No.'

'Come in the front door,' invited Pippo. 'I'll let you in and
you can climb up from here. We have a stepladder.'

Nino, not knowing what to say, let himself drop into the
yard, then, reluctantly, went round to the front and slowly
up the stairs to Pippo's flat. This, he told himself, was a bad
mistake. Maybe everyone in the *palazzo* knew already, and

if they didn't, what was the point of his letting them know? Pippo must know. Maybe he, Nino, was peculiarly half-witted and lacking in common sense? Maybe he should turn around and take the train back to his grandmother's? By the time he reached Pippo's door he was crying and had smeared dirt from the drainpipe all over his face, though he didn't know this until Pippo commented on it.

'Your mother's not in,' said Pippo. 'The couple is, though. I think she lets them have the flat when she's away.'

'What . . .' But he couldn't bring himself to ask. What couple? Who?

'Don't feel bad about it,' said Pippo unexpectedly. 'I think it's just from friendship. Not for money or anything. I don't think that. Nobody does. Your Mamma's just lonely. She likes the bit of music and their company.'

By now he had pushed Nino out onto the balcony and up the stepladder, so that he could see in the window to his own sitting room where Mr Williams and the chemist were naked as truth itself and lying in each other's arms.

Will You Please Go Now

Lost among the demonstrators was a rain-sodden dog. Up and down it ran, rubbing against anonymous trousers and collecting the odd kick. It was a well-fed animal with a leather collar but was quickly taking on the characteristics of the stray: that festive cringe and the way such dogs hoop their spines in panic while they wag their shabby tails.

'Here boy! Come – ugh, he's all muddy. Down, sir, get away! Scram! Tss!'

People threw chocolate wrappers and potato-crisp packets which the dog acknowledged from an old habit of optimism while knowing the things were no good. It was tired and its teeth showed in a dampish pant as though it were laughing at its own dilemma.

Jenny Middleton, a mother of two, recognized the crowd's mood from children's parties.

'Don't tease him,' she said sharply to a dark-skinned young man who had taken the animal's forepaws in his hands and was forcing it to dance. The dog's dazed gash of teeth was like a reflection of the man's laugh. 'Here,' she said, more gently, 'let me see his tag. There's a loudspeaker system. It shouldn't be hard to find his owner.'

'I'll take him,' said the man at once, as though, like the dog, he had been obedience-trained and only awaited direction. 'I will ask them to announce that he has been found.' Off he hared on his errand, like a boy-scout eager for merit. One hand on the dog's collar, he sliced through the crowd behind a nimbly raised shoulder. 'I'll be back,' he called to Jenny, turning to impress this on her with a sharp glance from yellowish, slightly bloodshot eyes.

He was the sort of man whom she would have avoided in an empty street – and, to be sure, she might have been wrong. He was friendly. Everyone at the rally was. Strangers cracked jokes and a group carrying an embroidered trade-union banner kept up a confident, comic patter. The one thing she wasn't sure she liked were the radical tunes which a bald old man was playing on his accordion. They seemed to her divisive, having nothing to do with the rally's purpose. When the musician's mate brought round the hat, she refused to contribute. 'Sorry,' she told him when he shook it in front of her. 'I've no change.' Turning, she was caught by the ambush of the dusky young man's grin. He was back, breathing hard and shaking rain from his hair.

'The dog will be OK,' he assured her. 'The authorities are in control.'

This confidence in hierarchy amused her. The next thing he said showed that it was selective.

'They', he nodded furtively at the musicians, 'come to all rallies. I am thinking maybe they are the police? Musicians, buskers: a good disguise?' He had a shrill, excited giggle.

'There are plenty of ordinary police here,' she remarked, wondering whether he was making fun of her. She felt shy at having come here alone in her Burberry hat and mac. The hat was to protect her hair from torch drippings and was sensible gear for a torch-light procession. But then, might not sense be a middle-class trait and mark her out?

'Bobbies', he said, 'are not the danger. I am speaking of the undercover police. The Special Branch. They have hidden cameras.'

'Oh.'

She eased her attention off him and began to read the graffiti on the struts of the bridge beneath which their section of the procession was sheltering. It was raining and there was a delay up front. Rumours or joke-rumours had provided explanations for this. The levity was so sustained as to suggest that many marchers were embarrassed at having taken to the streets. Old jokes scratched in concrete went back to her schooldays: *My mother made me a homosexual*, she read. *Did she?* goes the answer, conventionally written in a different hand. *If I get her some wool will she make me one too?* There was the usual Persian – or was it Arabic – slogan which she had been told meant *Stop killings in Iraq!* The man beside her could be an Arab. No. More likely an Indian.

'I know them,' he was saying of the secret police. 'We know each other. You see I myself come to all rallies. Every one in London.'

'Are you a journalist?'

'No. I come because I am lonely. Only at rallies are people speaking to me.'

Snap! She saw the trap-click of his strategy close in on her: his victim for the occasion. It was her hat, she thought and watched his eyes coax and flinch. It had singled her out. Damn! A soft-hearted woman, she had learned, reluctantly, that you disappointed people less if you could avoid raising their hopes. Something about him suggested that a rejection would fill him with triumph. He did not want handouts, conversational or otherwise, but must solicit them if he was to savour a refusal.

A graffito on the wall behind him said: *I thought Wanking was a town in China until I discovered Smirnov.* Don't *laugh*, she warned herself – yet, if she *could* think of a joke to tell him, mightn't it get her off his hook? Would Chinese laugh at the Smirnov joke, she wondered. Probably they wouldn't, nor Indians either. Wankers might. They were solitary and the solitary use jokes to keep people at bay.

'You see,' he was saying, 'I am a factory worker but also an intellectual. In my own country I was working for a newspaper but here in the factory I meet nobody to whom I can talk. Intellectuals in London are not inviting working men to their homes. I am starved for exchange of stimulating ideas.' His eye nailed a magazine she was carrying. 'You, I see, are an intellectual?'

'Goodness, no.' But the denial was a matter of style, almost a game which it was cruel to play with someone like him. She had never known an English person who would admit to being an intellectual. In India – Pakistan? – wherever he came from it would be a category which deserved honour and imposed duties. Denying membership must strike him as an effort to shirk such duties towards a fellow member in distress.

Her attempts to keep seeing things his way were making her nervous and she had twisted her sheaf of flyers and pamphlets into a wad. Am I worrying about *him*, she wondered, or myself? Perhaps even asking herself such a question was narcissistic? Objectivity too might be a middle-class luxury. How could a man like this afford it? He was a refugee, he was telling her now, a Marxist whose comrades back home were in prison, tortured or dead. Perhaps his party, would take power again soon. Then he would go home and have a position in the new government. *Then* English intellectuals could meet him as an equal. He said this with what must have been intended as a teasing grin. She hadn't caught the name of his country and was embarrassed to ask lest it turn out to be unfamiliar. It would have to be a quite small nation, she reasoned, if he was hoping to be in its government. Or had *that* been a joke?

'We're moving.' She was relieved at the diversion.

The trade-union group started roaring the Red Flag with comic gusto and the procession ambled off. He was holding her elbow. Well, that, she supposed, must be solidarity. The rally was connected with an issue she cared about. She did not normally take to the streets and the etiquette of the occasion was foreign to her.

'*Let cowards mock*', came the jovial Greater London bellow from up front, '*And traitors sneer . . .*'

'I'm as foreign here as he is,' she decided and bore with the downward tug at her elbow. He was small: a shrivelled man with a face like a tan shoe which hasn't seen polish in years. Dusky, dusty, a bit scuffed, he could be any age between thirty and forty-five. His fingers, clutching at her elbow bone, made the torch she had bought tilt and shed hot grease on their shoulders. She put up her left hand to steady it.

'You're married.' He nodded at her ring. 'Children?'

'Yes: two. Melanie and Robin. Melanie's twelve.'

The embankment was glazed and oozy. Outlines were smudged by a cheesy bloom of mist, and reflections from street-lights smeary in the mud, for it was December and grew dark about four. Across the river, the South Bank complex was visible still. He remarked that you could sit all day in its cafeteria if you wanted and not be expected to buy anything. His room, out in the suburbs, depressed him so much that on Sundays he journeyed in just to be among the gallery- and theatre-goers, although he never visited such places himself.

'But galleries are cheap on Sundays,' she remonstrated. 'Maybe even free?'

He shrugged. Art – bourgeois art – didn't interest him. It was – he smiled in shame at the confession – the opulence of the cafeteria which he craved. 'Op*u*lence,' he said, stressing the wrong syllable so that she guessed that he had never heard the word pronounced. 'It is warm there,' he explained. 'Soft seats. Nice view of the river. Some of the women are wearing scent.'

On impulse and because it was two weeks to Christmas, she invited him to join her family for lunch on the 25th.

*

When the day came, she almost forgot him and had to tell Melanie to lay an extra place just before he was due to arrive.

His name – he had phoned to test the firmness of her invitation – was Mr Rao. He called her Mrs Middleton and she found the formality odd after the mateyness of the rally when he had surely called her Jenny? Their procession, headed for Downing Street, had been turned back to circle through darkening streets. Mounted police, came the word, had charged people in front. Several had been trampled. Maimed perhaps? No, that was rumour: a load of old rubbish. Just some Trots trying to provoke an incident. Keep calm. Then someone heard an ambulance. An old working man gibbered with four-letter fury but the banner-bearers were unfazed.

'Can't believe all you hear, Dad,' they told him.

Mr Rao tugged at Jenny's arm as though he had taken her into custody: the custody of the Revolution. 'You see,' he hissed, 'it is the system you must attack, root and branch, not just one anomaly. There are no anomalies. All are symptoms.' He was galvanized. Coils of rusty hair reared like antennae off his forehead. 'Social Democrats', he shouted, 'sell the pass. They are running dogs of Capitalism. I could tell you things I have seen . . .' Fury restored him and she guessed that he came to rallies to revive a flame in himself which risked being doused by the grind of his working existence. He laughed and his eyes flicked whitely in the glow from the torches as he twitted the young men with the trade-union banner in their split allegiance. A Labour Government was loosing its police on the workers. 'Aha!' he hooted at their discomfiture. 'Do you see? Do you?' His laughter flew high and quavered like an exotic birdcall through the moist London night.

*

'You remember that demo I went to?' she reminded Melanie. 'Well, I met him there. He's a refugee and lonely at Christmas. A political refugee.'

'Sinister?' inquired her husband who'd come into the kitchen to get ice cubes, 'with a guerrillero grin and a bandit's moustache? Did he flirt with you?'

This sort of banter was irritating when one was trying to degrease a hot roasting pan to make sauce. She'd just remembered too that her mother-in-law, who was staying with them, was on a salt-free diet. Special vegetables should have been prepared. 'Did you lay the place for him?' she asked Melanie.

The girl nodded and rolled back her sleeve to admire the bracelet she'd got for Christmas. Posing, she considered her parents with amusement.

Jenny's husband was looking for something in the deep freeze. 'He did, didn't he?' he crowed. 'He flirted with you?'

She should have primed him, she realized. James was sensitive enough when things were pointed out to him but slow to imagine that other people might feel differently to the way he did. Mr Rao would be hoping for a serious exchange of ideas between men. Stress serious. He had been impressed when she told him that James, a senior civil servant, was chairman of a national committee on education. But now here was James wearing his sky-blue jogging suit with the greyhound on its chest – a Christmas present – all set to be festive and familial. He was a nimble, boyish man who prided himself on his youthfulness.

'Will Mr Rao disapprove of us?' he asked puckishly and tossed his lock of grey-blond hair off his forehead.

'Listen, he's a poor thing.' Jenny was peeved at being made to say this. 'Be careful with him, James. Can anyone see the soy sauce? I've burnt my hand. Thanks.' She spread it on the burn then went back to her roasting pan. Melanie, darling, could you do some quick, unsalted carrots for your grandmother? Please.'

'Better do plenty,' James warned. '*He* may be a vegetarian. Lots of Indians are.'

'God, do you think so? At Christmas.'

'Why not at Christmas? You'd think we celebrated it by drinking the blood of the Lamb.'

'People do,' said Melanie. 'Communion. There's the doorbell.'

'I'll go. Keep an eye on my pan.'

In the hall Jenny just missed putting her foot on a model engine which James had bought for five-year-old Robin and himself. An entire Southern Region of bright rails, switches, turntables and sidings was laid out and there was no sign of Robin. Did James dream of being an engine-driver, an aerial bomber or God? Or was it some sexual thing like everything else? Through the Art Nouveau glass of the door, she deduced that the blob in Mr Rao's purple hand must be daffodils, and wished that there was time to hide her own floral display which must minimize his gift.

*

'You were mean, horrible, appalling.'

'*He* is appalling.'

'Shsh! Listen, please, James, be nice. Try. Look, go back now, will you? They'll know we're whispering.'

'I'm not whispering.'

'Well you should be. He'll hear.'

'Jenny, you invited him. Try and control him. He has a chip a mile high on his . . .'

'Well, allow for it.'

'Why should I?'

'You're his host.'

'He's my guest.'

'God! Look, get the plum pud alight and take it in. I'll get the brandy butter.'

'If he suggests Robin eat this with his fingers, I'll . . .'

'Shush, will you? He doesn't understand children.'

'What does he understand? How to cadge money?'

'He didn't mean it that way.'

'He bloody did. Thinks the world owes him a living.'

'Well, doesn't it? Owe everyone I mean.'

'My dear Jenny . . .'

'Oh, all *right*. Here.'

She put a match to the brandy-soaked pudding so that blue flames sprang over its globe making it look like a scorched, transfigured human head. 'Go *on*. Take it while it's alight.' She pushed her husband in the direction of the dining-room and stood for a moment pulling faces at the impassive blankness of the kitchen fridge. Then she followed with the brandy butter.

Later, she came back to the kitchen to clean up. Vengefully, she let the men and her mother-in-law cope with each other over the coffee which their guest had at least not refused. He *had* refused sherry, also wine, also the pudding because it had brandy on it and had seemed to feel that it was his duty to explain why he did so and to point out the relativity of cultural values at the very moment when Robin's grandmother was telling the child how to eat game politely.

'Only *two* fingers, Robin,' she'd been demonstrating daintily, 'never your whole hand and only pick up a *neat* bone.'

'We', Mr Rao scooped up mashed chestnuts with a piece of bread, 'eat everything with our hands.' He laughed. 'There are millions of us.'

The anarchy of this so undermined Robin's sense of what might and might not be done on such an extraordinary day as Christmas that he threw mashed chestnuts at his grandmother and had to be exiled from the table. The older Mrs Middleton was unamused. Mr Rao bared his humourless, raking teeth.

'You are strict with your children', he said, 'in imparting your class rituals. This is because as a people you still have confidence and prize cohesion. Maybe now you must relax?'

Nobody chose to discuss this. Doggedly, the family had helped each other to sauce and stuffing and Mr Rao began to use his knife and fork like everyone else. A diffidence in him plucked at Jenny who saw that the incident with Robin had been meant as a joke: a humorous overture to the member of the family whom he had judged least likely to reject him. But Robin himself had been rejected, exiled to his room, and disapproval of Mr Rao hung unvoiced and irrefutable in the air. Seen by daylight, he was younger than she had supposed at the rally. His was a hurt, young face, puffy and unformed with bloodshot eyes and a soft, bluish, twitching mouth. He wanted to plead for Robin but could only talk in his magazine jargon. Perhaps he never spoke to people and knew no ordinary English at all? She imagined him sitting endlessly in the South Bank cafeteria reading political magazines and staring at the river.

'Pedagogical theory, you see . . .' he started and James, to deviate him – Robin's exile had to last at least ten minutes to placate his grandmother, interrupted with some remark about a scheme for facilitating adult education with which he was concerned.

'It's designed for people who didn't get a chance to go to university in the first instance,' said James. 'We give scholarships to deserving . . .'

'Could you give me one?' Mr Rao leaned across the table. 'Please. Could you? I am needing time to think and that factory work is destroying my brain. Have you worked ever on an assembly line?'

'You may certainly apply,' James told him. 'It's open to all applicants.'

'No.' Mr Rao spoke excitedly and a small particle of mashed chestnut flew from his mouth and landed on James's jogging suit. His words, spattering after it, seemed almost as tangible. 'No, no,' he denied, nervous with hope. 'You see I apply before for such things and never get them. Inferior candidates pass me by. Here in England, there is a mode, a ritual, you see. It is like the way you educate your son.' Mr Rao's mouth twisted like a spider on a pin. 'You teach him to give signals,' he accused. 'To eat the chicken *so* – and then his own kind will recognize and reward him. I give the wrong signals so I am always rejected.' He laughed sadly. 'Merit is not noted. In intellectual matters this is even more true. Examiners will take a working-class man only if they think he can be absorbed into their class. I cannot.'

'Then perhaps', said James, 'you are an unsuitable applicant?'

'But the university', pleaded Mr Rao, 'is not a caste system? Not tribal surely? You cannot afford to exclude people with other ways of being than your own. Even capitalism must innoculate itself with a little of the virus it fears. Intellectual life' – Mr Rao swung his fork like a pendulum – 'is a dialectical process. You must violate your rules,' he begged. 'Isn't that how change comes? Even in English law? First someone breaks a bad old law; then a judge condones the breaking and creates a precedent. I have read this. Now *you*', Mr Rao pointed his fork at James, 'must break your bureaucratic rule. Give me a scholarship. Be brave,' he pleaded. The fork fell with a clatter but Mr Rao was too absorbed to care. 'Give,' he repeated, fixing James with feverish eyes as if he hoped to mesmerize him. The eyes, thought Jenny, looked molten and scorched like lumps of caramel when you burned a pudding. The fork was again swinging to and fro and it struck her that Mr Rao might not be above using hypnotism to try and make James acquiesce to his will.

She leaned over and took the fork from his fingers. He let it go. His energies were focused on James. The eyes were leeches now: animate, obscene. Melanie and her grandmother were collecting plates. They were outside the electric connection between the two men. Murmuring together, they seemed unaware of it. James's mouth tightened. Mr Rao, Jenny saw, was in for a rocket. But the man was conscious only of his own need. It was naked now. He was frightened, visibly sweating, his nails scratched at the tablecloth. He wiped his face with a napkin.

'Men in lower positions must obey rules,' he told James. '*They* will not let me through. Only you can make an exception. Is not the spirit of your scheme to let the alienated back into society? I am such a man,' he said with dramatic intonation. 'I', he said proudly, 'am needy, alienated, hard-working and well read. Do you not believe I am intelligent? I could get references, but my referees', he laughed his unhappy laugh, 'are tending to be in gaol: a minister of my country, the rector of my university. Oh, we had an establishment once.'

'Then perhaps', said James, 'you understand about the need to eliminate personal appeals? Nepotism: the approach which corrupts a system. Did you', asked James with contempt, 'pick my wife up at that rally because you knew who she was? Wait!' He held Jenny's hand to stop her talking. 'I'm quite well known. A number of people there could have recognized and pointed her out to you. A man like you is ruthless, isn't he? For a higher aim, to be sure.' James spoke with derision. 'No doubt you feel you matter more than other people?'

The stuffing had gone out of Mr Rao. His head sank. His mouth, a puffy wound mobile in his face, never settled on an emotion with confidence. Even now there was a twitch of humour in its gloom. 'Oh,' he said listlessly, 'many, many personal appeals are granted in this country. But it's like I said: I don't know the signals. I am an outsider here.' He stood up.

'Please!' Jenny wrenched her wrist from her husband's grip. 'Mr Rao! You're not going yet, are you?

But he had only stood up to welcome Robin who, released from his room by his grandmother, was returning in a haze of smiles and sulks.

*

The dishwasher was on. Its noise drowned his approach and added urgency to the hand she felt landing on her arm.

'Jenny!' Mr Rao's shrewd, nervous face peered into hers. 'I go now. I am thanking you and . . .' Words, having betrayed him all day, seemed to be abandoning him utterly. 'Sorry,' he said as perfunctorily as Robin might have done. 'It is not true what your husband said.'

'Of course not. I'm sorry too – but I'm glad you came.' She smiled with a guilty mixture of sorrow and relief. After all, what more could she do? She gave him her hand.

He didn't take it. 'I appreciated this,' he said too eagerly. 'Being in a family. You know? Mine is a people who care a lot about family life. I miss it. That was why meeting little Robin, I . . .'

She thought he was apologizing. 'It's not important.'

'No, no. I know that with children things are always going wrong and being mended quickly. That is the joy of dealing with them. I miss children so much. Children and women – will you invite me again?'

She was astonished. Unaccountably, she felt a stab of long-ing to help him, to visit the unmapped regions where he lived: eager, vulnerable and alone, with no sense of what was pos-sible any more than Robin had, or maybe great, mad saints. But how could she? The dishwasher had finished a cycle and begun another. It was so loud now that she could hardly hear what he was saying. He seemed to be repeating his question.

'We're going away for a while in January,' she began eva-sively. 'Skiing . . .' But evasion wouldn't do for this man. She looked him in the eye. 'I can't invite you,' she said. 'James and you didn't hit it off. You must realize that.'

'Will you meet me in town? I'll give you my number.'

'No.'

'Please.'

'Mr Rao . . .'

The wound of his mouth was going through a silent-movie routine: pleading, deriding, angry, all at once. 'The poor have no dignity,' he said, shocking her by this abrupt irruption of sound. 'They must beg for what others take.'

Suddenly, he had his arms around her and was slobbering, beseeching and hurting her in the hard grip of his hands. The sounds coming from him were animal: but like those of an animal which could both laugh and weep. One hand had got inside her blouse. 'A woman,' he seemed to be repeating, 'a family . . . woman . . .' Then a different cry got through to her: 'Mummy!'

Melanie, looking horrified, stood next to them. The dishwasher, now emptying itself with a loud gurgle, made it impossible to hear whether she had said anything else. Behind her stunned face bobbed her grandmother's which was merely puzzled. The older Mrs Middleton was a timorous lady, slow to grasp situations but constantly fearful of their not being as she would like.

'Mother!' yelled Melanie a second time.

Mr Rao, deafened by lust, loneliness or the noise of the dishwasher, was still clinging to Jenny and muttering incomprehensible, maybe foreign, sounds. She heaved him off and spoke with harsh clarity to his blind, intoxicated face.

'I'm sorry,' she said. 'I'm sorry. But will you please go now. Just leave.'

Afterword

Rereading the early stories in my first collection (1968) is, I find, like making a trip to a now defunct Ireland. It was the country of TB, earthen floors and lice; and the poverty lurking behind the efforts at jollity kept revealing itself. Hand-me-down clothing and bad dentistry were only half the story.

Yet it wasn't all depression, even if some of my stories and titles suggest that it was. When I wonder about the futures of my characters, the word that comes to mind most insistently is resilience. Variety too. Irish people, like Italians, often cherish both. Some of the stories in this collection – though I doubt if many readers would guess which – are entirely invented; others are not. But all of them, I hope, are gutsy and likely to survive the challenges they face.

When I imagine myself returning to the places where my characters and situations were conceived – most were urban, apart from those set near or in Killiney Village – I think of taking a balloon trip in their wake. Would they like each other? Maybe not. Would they like me? What, my X-ray eyes? Why should they? Some people get angry at being put into a story. Others quite enjoy it. But why worry about this now, especially as most of them are dead?

In her Introduction to *The Faber Book of Modern Stories* (1937), Elizabeth Bowen claims that 'The Short Story is a young art. As we now know it, it is the child of this century.' I soon discovered that this was both true and misleading. Stories, after all, appear in the Bible. Fantasies, folk tales, ghost stories, excerpts from Homer and *The Thousand and One Nights* all go back a long way. Hunter-gatherers, whose cave paintings offer such vivid images of their interests and activities, may well have delighted in stories too. Bowen's conception of the modern short story really refers to the subtle and allusively suggestive short narratives that her generation of writers found and admired in the Russians, Turgenev and Chekhov, and Maupassant in France.

Miss Bowen also insists that stories should never seem contrived. 'Execution must be voluntary and careful,' she adds, 'but conception should have been involuntary . . . the sought-about for subject gives the story a dead kernel.'

If contrivance also touches on the matter of rewriting, then her point is a debatable one for those of us whose revisions are often a search for simplicity. But I cede the debate to others. Before leaving Bowen, however, I want to quote her again: 'The story', she argues, 'should have the valid central emotion and inner spontaneity of the lyric.' Indeed, she claims, 'poetic tautness and clarity are so essential to it that it may be said to stand at the edge of prose'.

Tautness can be the result of hard work, and this reminds me of my father's – Sean O'Faolain's – astonished report of how on one occasion, when staying at Bowen's Court, he came on Elizabeth rising from her writing table and noticed that her face was dripping with perspiration. He should not have been so astonished, for he too worked long and hard on his stories, and his close friend, Frank O'Connor, would sometimes rewrite work which had already been published. This was too much for Sean. He described it as self-plagiarism and refused to do it.

There is of course the question of how the impulse to start a story begins. Looking back, I am reminded of the jokes and chaff around my parents' lunch and tea tables in South County Dublin after the War, and of how at some point a guest might remark, 'There's the germ of a story there.' Whereupon whoever had supplied the gossip might raise a hand and playfully claim, 'Copyright.' Surprisingly, some stories thought up in this casual way actually got written, and still more surprisingly, people who were not themselves writers would sometimes give an anecdote to a writer friend. I am here reaching back to the 1950s, in the course of which I left Ireland, and so don't know if such activity went on later. But what I do know is that after I left, I missed the offers of collaboration. The subtle gossip whose input can be vital in connecting life, love, and other disturbances is, I would argue, an asset to almost any drawing room.

*

The short story, some critics insist, should be short, as implied by Miss Bowen. And the bad feeling generated between the late American short-story writer, Raymond Carver and his editor at Knopf, Gordon Lish, shows how toxic disagreements about this could be. Lish seems to have been deft and ruthless when cutting Carver's stories, while Carver in turn felt sharp resentment as he wondered about how fellow writers would react on learning of his surrender to his editor's demands. A letter from him to Lish, written in 1980, reveals how painful such submission could be. It begs Lish's forgiveness, but insists that he 'stop production' of Carver's forthcoming collection of stories, which Carver's friends had read in earlier, uncut versions. Lish's cuts had been savage. Two stories had reportedly been slashed by nearly seventy per cent, and many others by almost half. Digressions and descriptions had been eliminated, and endings changed or cut, leaving their author unnerved to the point of desperation. A recovering alcoholic who had been described as 'a fragile spirit', Carver confessed in his letter that he was 'confused, tired, paranoid and afraid'.

When I consider discussions about length in the short story, I see that the subject raises a false problem. My own stories range in length from three to forty-two pages. Equally to the point, a short story may grow into a novella. The question then arises, when is a novella a novel? I will only add that limiting length in short stories – and this can be arbitrary – is most likely to be done by the fiction editors of magazines, such as *The New Yorker*, which published my first story. This also means that when writers submit stories to a magazine, they do so with the magazine's expectations in mind.

*

My parents' generation liked telling mine of the tough times suffered by theirs. One image which sticks with me is the description by Sean and Frank O'Connor of how they, as boys, used to come out of their noisy houses to find peace to read after dark by the light of street lamps. This made me wonder about how different the stories I was hoping to write would be from Sean's. They had to be different because Ireland had changed while I was growing up and, unlike my parents, I had not spent my summer vacations learning Irish from native speakers. Instead, I had shuttled between long stays with French families and spells at Italian language schools. In spare moments, I also learned to recognize rude French words, such as *con* and *conne*, whose English equivalents would not enter my vocabulary for years. The daughters of the French families I stayed with didn't use them, nor did I, but local men sang them lustily at us whenever we got on or off their bus.

Oral stories still lingered in the wilds of West Cork in my parents' youth, and it has been observed that the freakish events which occurred in them had a purpose, which was to hold the attention of a semi-literate audience that did not enjoy the convenience of being able to check on the details of a story if the listeners became distracted and lost the thread. With luck, however, the freakish event would have imprinted itself on their memories, as must have happened to many readers of Flannery O'Connor's story, *Good Country People*, which is about a bible salesman who makes off with a young woman's prosthetic leg, and more recently to readers of equally shocking fictions by Mary Gaitskill and A. M. Homes.

Celtic wonder tales can be as odd and unpredictable as those found in Homer, but they can also be grotesque. Here is a snippet to show what I mean. I draw it from one of my mother's retellings of stories, which she assured me went back 'a couple of thousand years'. They tended to start more or less like this:

'It happened that at this time Ireland was frequently raided by savage bands of sea-robbers called the Fomorions, who swept down from their lands in the northern mists . . . Their King was Balor of the Evil Eye, and this single eye could cause an enemy to drop dead, as if struck by a thunderbolt. But as Balor grew old, the great flappy eyelid drooped over the deadly eye, and had to be hoisted up by pulleys and ropes, and the eye directed by his men on the one he wished to destroy.'

There is a touch of Monty Python here and indeed a flavour of Myles na Gopaleen. Something cartoonish also pervades the image of poor Balor. It reminds me of the English comics which my parents disapproved of and which I used to beg to be allowed to look at, when I saw other children in our bus folding them into their school bags.

My story *Man in the Cellar* may be said to have freakish traces. Cast in the form of a letter from a young English woman to her Italian mother-in-law, telling her how badly her marriage was going, it was written in the 1970s, when Italian feminism peaked, and rumours were rife about how certain brave young women had broken a doctor's legs as punishment for his refusal to help one of their friends get an abortion, although this procedure had been recently legalized. The rumour was possibly false and only devised to scare recalcitrant doctors into being more helpful in the future.

Cruelty and argument can enliven a story, and there was

a good deal of cruelty in the civil-war stories of my parents' generation.

Looking at my own early stories, which often take place among children, I can see that some may have been altered re-enactments of the tales that we were all told in childhood. My early stories focus on the trip wires of class and cruelty, as seen through a child's eyes in our local village. Topic is everything, it seems! Because when I travelled, lived abroad, and wrote about that, the stories grew kinder – not, however, as kind as my father's. He was fond of his characters, whereas I was often impatient with mine and more detached. The fact that he often forgave their foolishness showed that he was fond of Ireland itself, where he lived for most of his life. I, instead, left it and found that I was happier elsewhere.

Has the Irish imagination grown more gentle? I would like to think so, and to think too that small angers took the place of Balor's killing eye, just as the libel action seems in some respects to have replaced older forms of violence, such as duels and ambushes. Could cruel pranks have come in as substitutes for murders? Who can tell? Children – I find with some shock – in one of my own earliest stories can entertain fierce fantasies. I have just reread one about a thirteen-year-old girl attacking a small, retarded boy. This is pure fantasy. I never knew of such a thing happening in our village, and certainly did not participate in one. But – is this worse? – I allowed it to happen in my head.

In our junior convent school, the nuns used to warn us that women, if given a chance, could become much more wicked than men. This shocked but also flattered us, even though we were unable to imagine any great wickedness. But it led us to wonder about the nuns. Had they locked themselves into convents, we asked each other, from the fear of unleashing fierce impulses? Such thoughts made school, and indeed life, a lot more interesting.

Acknowledgements

'Dies Irae', 'Her Trademark', 'Melancholy Baby' and 'We Might See Sights!' from *We Might See Sights!* (Volume) © Julia O'Faolain, 1968. First published in Great Britain in 1968 by Faber & Faber.

'It's a Long Way to Tipperary' from *The London Magazine*, 4, 1969 © Julia O'Faolain, 1969. Published in Great Britain in *Man in the Cellar* (Volume) in 1974 by Faber & Faber.

'Man in the Cellar' and 'The Knight' from *Man in the Cellar* (Volume) © Julia O'Faolain, 1974. First published in Great Britain in 1974 by Faber & Faber.

'Oh My Monsters!' from *New Review*, 1976 © Julia O'Faolain, 1976. Published in Great Britain in *Daughters of Passion* (Volume) in 1982 by Penguin.

'Daughters of Passion' from *Hudson Review*, 1980 © Julia O'Faolain, 1980. Published in Great Britain in *Daughters of Passion* (Volume) in 1982 by Penguin.

'Rum and Coke' from *Scripsi*, Vol. 1, 1981 © Julia O'Faolain, 1981. Published in Great Britain in *Best Short Stories 1994*, edited by Giles Gordon and David Hughes, by Heinemann.

'Will You Please Go Now' from *Company*, 1981 © Julia O'Faolain, 1981. Published in Great Britain in *Daughters of Passion* (Volume) in 1982 by Penguin.